A Walk in a City of Shadows

Urban Legends

An Alien Sun Press Book

A Walk in a City of Shadows

An Anthology of Urban Legends

Published 2023 by Alien Sun Press

Edited by Gordon B. White, Sarah Walker, Phil Breach, Nora B. Peevy, & Jill Hand

Cover Art by Dan Sauer

Interior Art by Alan Sessler, Sarah Walker, & Russell Smeaton

Interior Layout by Michael Adams

Mrs. Saltonstall's Dybbuk by Adam Bolivar was originally published 2021 by Jackanapes prress

Special thanks to:

Peter Weigel, creator of

Boecklins Universe

&

Ryoichi Tsunekawa, creator of

Great Victorian

custom fonts used in this volume

Project Coordinated by Sarah Walker

ISBN:13: 9798374142990

All contents © 2023 the original authors

Table of Contents

Foreword by Sarah Walker with Jill Hand 9

Already Weeds are Writing... by Jayaprakash Satyamurthy 17

Accident Black Spot by Phil Breach 21

The Other End of the Line by Gordon B. White 25

Do Not Read This by Sarah Walker 43

Market Price by Can Wiggins 57

School's Out by Jill Hand 81

Case#7: The Babes in the Woods by Nora B. Peevy 101

Undercity by Tom Sewel 113

The Office on The Seventh Floor By Malcolm Carvalho 119

The Bandage Man's Way by Wendy Wagner 131

Bloody, Meaty Ends by Maxwell J. Gold 143

Satanic Panic by Chelsea Arrington 145

Bridge of Lies by Hayley Arrington 147

Blucifer By Carolyn Kay 151

Along a Rural Highway by D. L. Myers 161

Face the Music By Duane Pesice 165

Half-Sick of Shadows By R.W. Moffat 169

Table of Contents

Mother Will Be Displeased by David Barker 187

Fish Story by Scott J. Couturier 199

Beware the Slenderman by Manuel Arenas 217

Third Eye Delight by Jennifer Caress 219

Mrs. Saltonstall's Dybbuk by Adam Bolivar 233

Invoking a Playmate by Laura Davey 247

Spring-Heeled Jack by Ashley Dioses 251

Midnight Train from Tokyo by John H. Howard 253

The Yellow Man by Shayne K. Keen 275

Coulrophilia by K.A. Opperman 293

The Legend of Johnny Nepkin: A Home-Grown Bogeyman by A.P Sessler 297

Necker by Grant Bright 311

Figures of Shadow by Frank Coffman 321

The Visitors Michael S. Walker 325

Danse De L'Amour by Ivan Zorich 331

The Snakes of Errington or The Legend of Specky Eggy by Russell Smeaton 339

You Will Know Not the Hour by Sean M. Thompson 355

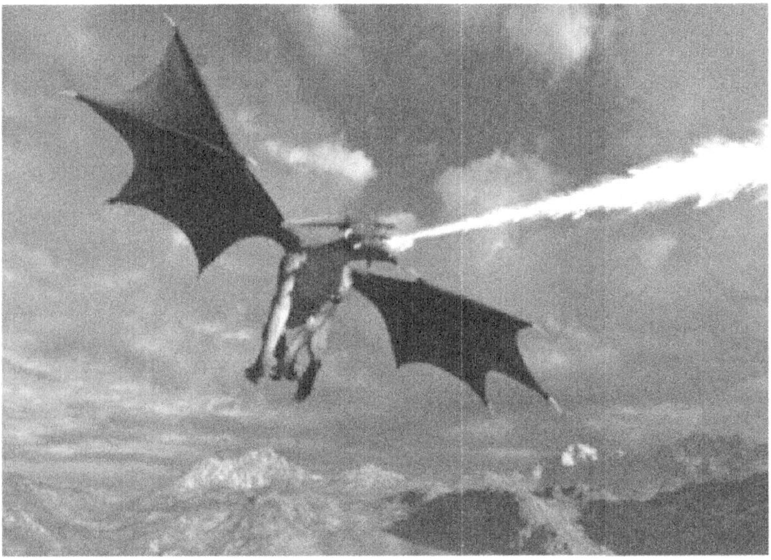

Foreword
by Sarah Walker
with Jill Hand

How does one define real and unreal? How about the truth and a lie? As you read this foreword, you might be thinking "well that's a dumb question! I know what is real and what isn't." But before you say that, why don't we try a little exercise. Imagine it is the end of society. You can imagine whatever disaster scenario you like: a nuclear war, a volcano, a massive earthquake, or maybe zombies have decided it is time to crawl out of their graves to come to find living folks to eat.

Now imagine you don't have any food in your fridge, so you decide to go looking for sustenance. You begin to walk through your town, but as you wander looking for a candy bar, a sandwich, anything to stop your growling stomach, you discover what you should have known. All the stores are closed, either looted or shut. As you pass by one you think perhaps the owner has died, probably via zombie. You shudder.

Upset, and growing ever hungrier, you turn a corner and stop in surprise. Right in front of you an open briefcase full of hundred-dollar bills sits half open! It lays in the street, unclaimed.

Finders' keepers! You think giddily and shout "hurray!" You lean down to grab a pile of that sweet cash out of the briefcase…and stop.

Why? Yes, finding the briefcase seems like a dream come true, but it is not under your current circumstances. You look around at the rapidly darkening town as the sun sets on Armageddon. None of the businesses that used to sell food are open. There are no grocery stores. no 7-11's, no restaurants, no Chinese food, no Taco Kings. There aren't even corner

Foreword

stores or bodegas anymore.

Your stomach gurgles again.

Maybe you could try to eat the money itself? You take one of the hundreds and shove it in your mouth. You almost gag yourself spitting it back out. It is clearly not meant for sustenance as it tastes terrible! Then in a sudden and terrible epiphany, you finally understand.

The bills are now useless, worthless without the society that created them there to back it up.

Now back to urban legends and what this foreword is about. If you were to look up the folklore definition of urban legend you'd probably get something like this, *"a popular term for a narrative concerning some aspect of modern life that is believed by its teller to be true, but is actually untrue"* (Ellis 2008:1) or *"a humorous or horrific story or piece of information circulated as though true, especially one purporting to involve someone vaguely related or known to the teller"* (Ellis 2008:2) or how about Merriam Webster's dictionary and their definition which says, *"an often lurid or anecdote that is based on hearsay and widely circulated as true."*

Using these definitions, we could say then that urban legends are stories that can be fantastical, gory, and crazy, but mostly they are stories with the main defining characteristic of being claimed to be *true* by the teller. And though often the veracity of these legends is dependent upon a flimsy and anecdotal kind of "it happened to my cousin's friend" supportive evidence, the stories still disturb and fascinate partly because they are called REAL. Somewhere deep in our minds that is the thing that clinches it. That is what can frighten us the most.

Now we get to the point in my writing this foreword. Myth and belief are both deeply intertwined with the experience of being human, as is the act of creating culture. Through our culture, we gain our worldview and our general perception of the environment around us. What this means is if our culture tells us something is real or true, we agree as we are basically primed from the start of our lives to learn our culture from the people around us. Any anthropologist will tell you sociality and teaching are how humans survive- we show each other what the world is, what food is good to eat, what people to trust. It even goes as far as to tell us what is beautiful, what is ugly, and even what is *good* or what is *bad*. You see, much of the time the reality of something is determined only by our cultural belief in it. Ghosts, gods, monsters, zombies. Humans are the ones who decide when something is real, or unreal, and your culture is the one who helps you decide that.

We create value.

And this is the way we make the unreal real in culture.

For instance, think about the legend of dragons. On the first page of this foreward is a wonderful one made by my good friend Russell Smeaton.

As you can see, this dragon is what you are probably thinking of when you are told to visualize a typical European "fantasy" dragon. In the European tradition, these dragons spit fire, hoard gold, and like to eat townspeople. Occasionally they kidnap maidens. Daenerys Targaryen rode one in *Game of Thrones*.

According to Jill Hand, who helped me in writing this foreword, legend has it that St. George, England's patron saint, killed a dragon in order to rescue a captive princess. The encounter is said to have happened in a province of the Roman Empire in what is now central eastern Turkey. The Crusaders brought the story back home with them, where it became woven into the knightly medieval code of chivalry.

So here is the question, did St. George really kill a winged, fire

Foreword

breathing dragon? Or was the beast something else, a large snake, perhaps, or maybe some sort of crocodile? We may never know. Up to now there has been no to evidence to either prove or disprove the story, but it hasn't stopped people from imagining these creatures as real.

Here's where it gets interesting. Dragons are not just in European myths. In fact, Jill did some digging and found that they appear in almost every culture's mythos, as far back as 2100 BCE, when the

Mesopotamians described a scaly creature with the hind legs of an eagle and the forelegs of a lion. Its body was long and thin, and it had a horned head and a snakelike tongue.

It's an impossible animal, and yet the ancients left testimony carved in stone that it, or something close to it, *was real.*

Ancient China even had dragons that were said to have the ability to control the wind and the rain. These were long scaly creatures, similar to our idea of sea serpents. Unlike the European version, these dragons were benevolent, bestowing good luck and wisdom on deserving humans.

The Aztec and Mayan cultures as well as the ancient Egyptians had dragons that were sometimes revered as gods. Up in North America, the Algonquins and a few other North American Indigenous people saw creatures similar to dragons called Thunderbirds that were huge, flying creatures. The flapping of their enormous wings was like the sound of thunder, or so the legends say.

There is even evidence of a sort for some of this. Two murals that were said to have been painted on limestone bluffs above the Mississippi River in Alton, Illinois, long before the arrival of Europeans to the area.

These pictures depicted a pair of frightening winged creatures called Piasa Birds. These creatures are definitely *not* birds and though the original paintings have long since disappeared, modern recreations show something that looks very much like the "dragons" described by the Mesopotamians.

So, the question is: why did all these different cultures, separated by time and distance, insist that dragons were real? Could it be that at some point, far back in ancient history, there really were dragons? Or are they just a myth, a spooky campfire tale about a monster?

Or maybe humans created them.

Now that you know that these concepts like money, monsters, gods, and more are often the creation of a culture, what do you think we might be creating with these following urban legend tales? Could there be a 'real life' Slenderman? Or how about a dybbuk with terrible intentions of its own? Or how about a convenience store in the middle of nowhere that has more in common with an anglerfish than your local Circle K? I ask you to think about the stories we whisper to one another under our sheets late at night. Are these tales of phantoms actually the beginnings of a new belief system reaching up from some unknown depth in our human culture's unconsciousness? Perhaps they are the shoots of a living and very real creation of our own.

Perhaps this is how God, and even the devil was born.

What follows is an anthology of stories about the shadowed world we humans have been sculpting for a very long time. Within us those memories of sitting around campfires keeping the night at bay still survive and even thrive despite our new digital age. Why else would we still be afraid of the dark even in a house in the middle of a city?

These memories are part of us, imprinted on our DNA, and these memories have power.

What follows is a tome dedicated to that place that we humans have grown over our 300,000-year existence as *Homo sapiens*. It is a place of dark creatures, and even darker imaginings, within which we are busy creating new realities, realities inhabited by new gods… and new demons

Foreword

made by our own design.
Sarah Walker
and
Jill Hand
Fall 2022.

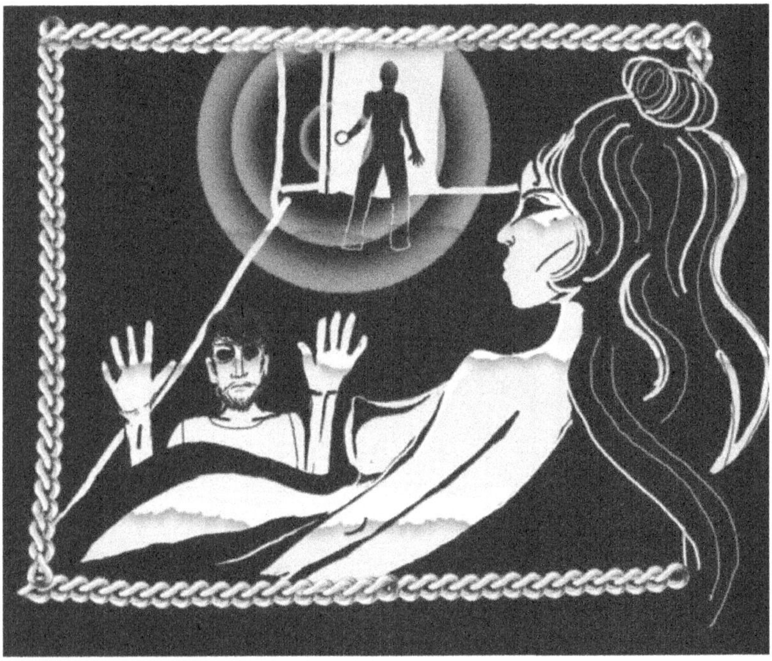

Already Weeds are Writing...
by Jayaprakash Satyamurthy

There's a palace outside the city. It hides behind towering walls and overgrown greenery. The gates are rusted shut, the grilles too closely spaced, the spikes on top too sharp and high for potential intruders.

There's a sign on the gate, and it's always clean and fresh: Do Not Enter - Guard Dogs Patrol the Premises.

They say the last inhabitant was a mad old princess and her dogs. Once she died, childless, the staff stole everything that wasn't bolted down, and fled. Others say that the old royal family decided to turn their back on the modern world. They secured their title to the property in perpetuity, turned the grounds over to feral dogs, or to a coolly murderous security agency, and hid away in the rambling old palace. Periodically, young people from the nearby villages disappear, and that's how the increasingly feral descendants of the family keep their bloodline going and restock their larder.

The up-to-date, no-nonsense types say it's all nonsense, this is just a rotting old palace tied up in decades upon decades of red tape and litigation. Any day now, the gates will be broken open, the wilderness cleared away and the palace turned into a luxury hotel or broken down to make room for a gated community or a tech park, whatever pays the most.

Me, I say truth is often multiple-choice. And sometimes the correct choice is one you didn't know existed. So, follow me into this palace of mystery. We'll see what there is to see. Follow my bend of thought - yes just like that - and we'll walk through the walls. Beautiful. Down the path, just discernible in the overgrown lawn, past the lolling, broken statuary, the dry fountain, the ornamental pond turned into a cesspool of mosses and insects, we reach the slumbering palace, up the stairs, across the portico through the enormous twin doors.

Already Weeds are Writing...

Here is a world of art. I'll wager you never expected that. Here, in the foyer, and along the corridors, paintings by Svetoslav, son of Nikolai. For he was the last owner, not some mad princess or race of feral royals. These paintings are not unlike his father's art, but slicker, the colors more garish. Some portrayals of dusky women, like the dancer he moved to this country to be with, and these almost approach the condition of kitsch. But I am being unkind - I can see much of this art is eloquent and that it speaks to you.

Now, into the grand parlor. The heart of this old palace. Glowing with old Nikolai's canvases, hung here, masterpieces unknown to the rest of the world. Visionary scenes - monks, ascetics, Jesus, the Buddha. But most of all, those soaring, transcendental mountainscapes that so mesmerized a gent from Providence. I suppose you've heard of him - you have the weedy, rapt look of a fan or a chronic masturbater. If there is a difference.

Anyway, those disappearances, from the neighboring areas. How to explain them if there are no security guards, no hounds on the prowl, no feral homophagous scions?

Here, through this narrow passage, pick that book off of the shelf - A Treatise on Realism by RP Upton - step back as the shelf slides away. Don't mind the odor. You'll get used to it in a moment. Throw up if you must, but out here in the passage, I must insist. Feeling better now? Let's go inside.

When Svetoslav travelled in the United States, he met another visionary painter, quite the equal of Nikolai, but whose genius was of the abyss. A Bostonian named Patrick. He followed Patrick into the abyss, saw what that daring pioneer saw, and like many others, fled in horror, returning to the safety of empyrean visions. Celestial balm for a soul seared by a glimpse of the ghoul-realm, the under-world, the basement hell.

Unlike others, Svetoslav always kept in touch with Patrick. When the American had to leave his country, Svetoslav welcomed him to his own home, set him up with living quarters and a studio in this corner of the palace. For Svetoslav knew - the thesis needs its antithesis, the ideal its opposite. The greatest wisdom is balance.

But where is that balance now, you ask me? Come, come, balance, like wisdom is fragile. Neither Svetoslav nor Patrick was to blame if the fine balance these two men had achieved with their divergent, complementary artistic quests, came to be broken at last. It is a ghoulish realm, my friend, a voracious universe.

These paintings horrify you? How could anyone conceive, and execute such things? Look closer. These are not just paintings. They are portals. Yes, move closer, really look. Press your face right up to the canvas, the membrane. Feel the hot, dank gust from the depths.

Step closer, step inside. Feel context slide, as it does in the face of a true masterpiece. Can you truly tell me anymore which is the inside of this painting, and which the outside? Do you understand more about appetite now, and what fulfils it?

Do you remember when I told you old Nikolai's paintings were the heart of this palace? These, my poor friend, are its maw and gut. This palace will stand. It will outlast cities, empires, cobwebs, and weeds. You, in your own humble way, will be part of its eternal life. I know, I know, this is agony. Just bear with it - the rest is eternity.

If only the balance had been different. Then perhaps you would be tunnelling through joy to eternities of enlightenment. Well, think of this as the same, only inverted. Perspective, as all three gentlemen whose canvases hang in this palace would agree, is everything.

And now, as the weeds write their testament in the dust, I bid you goodbye. Goodbye and good night.

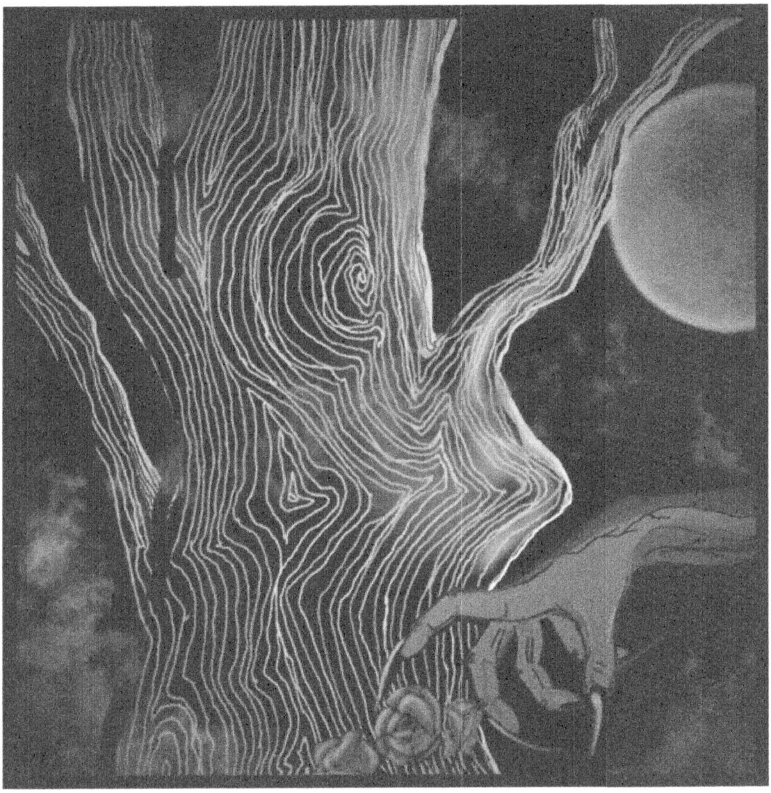

Accident Black Spot
by Phil Breach

Great, scarred oak that looms at town's north edge;
ancient, twisted, 'pon the outer bend
of road where divers hapless drivers died.
About its girth, sad notes and posies tied.
This curvature, that served their shattered end,
was once a mere; dark, still, and girt with sedge.

That pool, fed by a deep, eternal spring,
was lair to Her since oak was acorn seed.
Since oak that birthed that seed was seed in turn,
and on, back through the ages' yearly churn.
A deity, She was, akin in breed
to Grendel's dam. A hag. A primal thing.

The road was once a mere and muddy track,
a sacred path that humankind would take,
since long and hoary yore, 'pon Winter's eve.
At the pool's edge, trussed and daubed they'd leave
their offering: a child, for to slake
Her hunger, flesh to savor, bones to crack.

Accident Black Spot

With blood-scent in Her long and twitching nose,
waiting for Her squirming sacrifice;
ogre-tall, with rusted iron claws,
with flint-keen fangs that crowded in Her jaws.
Black Annis, She, as cold as cracking ice
(Although Her pool was blessed and never froze).

Her power swelled, and as it did the ground
about Her flourished. Hunters' game ran rife.
When they settled down to farm, the soil
yielded riches; fecund, without toil.
All dearly bought with pink and bawling life,
snatched up and rent apart before it drowned.

First Copper Age, then Bronze Age waxed and waned.
Time's wheel revolved, 'til iron shod the plough.
The legions came; no fools, they left Her be,
dared not approach Her mighty, awful tree,
with infant skulls festooning every bough,
and bark, with gore of sacrifice, bestained.

Then came the brutal cultists of the Cross.
Before or since no horde have been so cruel.
They brought their nailed god unto the village.
They brought their lies and rapes and hymns and pillage.
They brought unholy poisons to Her pool,
polluted it, and rendered it to dross.

Phil Breach

Defiled, bereft, She fled within Her oak,
and fell to leaden slumber limned with grief.
The mourning spring-head turned its course around,
descended to a delve too deep to sound.
Then, when a year had passed for every leaf,
within Her ancient bole the hag awoke.

Dried up now, a curling knot of thirst,
now rooted 'pon that vicious hairpin bend.
So, if to drive that stretch of road, it calls you,
be not surprised if accident befalls you.
She works Her will to bring you to your end.
The local folk all know that place is cursed

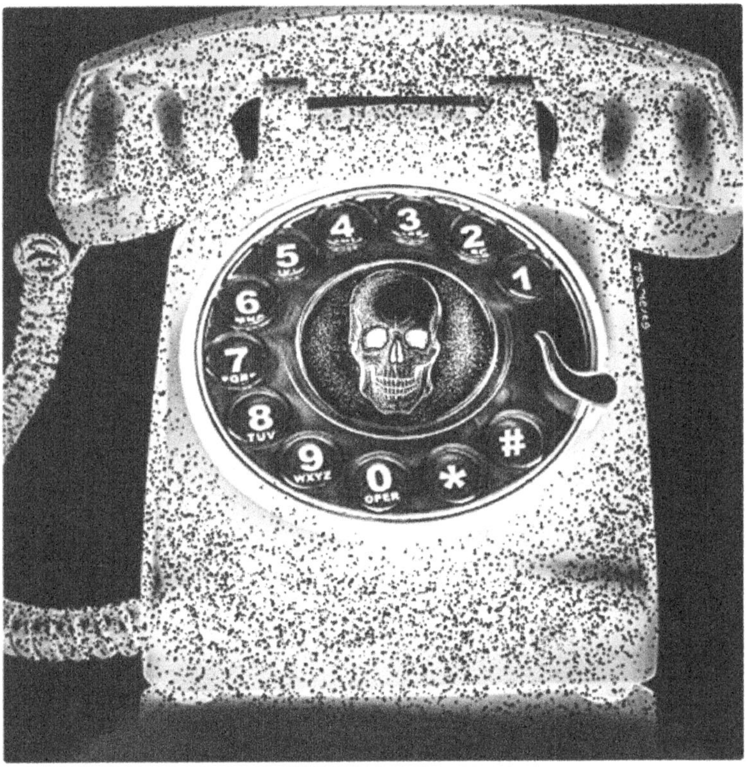
TUV
WXYZ
OPER

The Other End of the Line
by Gordon B. White

I can't say for sure that I've ever seen a ghost, so this story isn't completely mine. My childhood friend, Perry Harris, gave it to me—I think—shortly after my father died and I was back home in North Carolina for the memorial service after his cremation. I hadn't seen Perry since we were maybe fifteen, so it had been over twenty years, but I placed him quickly enough when he came through the family's receiving line.

"Gordon," he shook my hand and held it. "I'm so sorry for your loss."

"Thank you," I said. "It was good of you to come."

For most of the well-wishers, which was enough. They'd smile sadly or tell me, "I sure will miss your daddy," or "He was a fine man," and then shuffle down the line, on to my brother to repeat the process. There was a uniformity to it, of course, but there was also a comfortably overwhelming sincerity that left no room in the moment for anything but the ritual. Perry, though, didn't move on.

"Well," I cleared my throat as the rest of the line began to back up behind him. "I'm sure Dad would have really appreciated your being here. He always talked about those times we camped out in the backyard as kids." I was babbling. "Or the birthday parties. Or—"

"The time we went ghost hunting?" Perry said. His eyes lit up, but the older gentleman behind him gave a pained look. Perry was still holding my hand, his palm clammy and now starting to sweat. He'd lingered long enough that the smell of stale cigarette smoke from his jacket was mixing with the cloying scent of the funeral bouquets around us and I began to feel lightheaded in the heat.

The Other End of the Line

"Exactly," I said, forcing a smile. I hadn't thought of that ghost-hunting trip in years, but the whole event came back at the mention. A night in a so-called haunted house, some friend of my dad's old family home out in Tennessee. It had been spooky as kids, sure, and a lark to think back on later, but why should Perry mention that unprompted? I could also see the older relatives nearby weren't exactly pleased to overhear talk of ghosts with my father's cold ashes just in the other room.

"Tell you what," I said to Perry. "If you come by the reception afterwards, I'd love to catch up. It'll be a better time and place for it, okay?"

It seemed to dawn on him that the receiving line had stopped, and his face turned bright red. He quickly nodded and shook my hand again—having not once let it go—and then pulled away, on to my brother, the next in line. The sweaty palm he had left cooled quickly, and as I wiped it discretely on my pants leg, I wondered why that particular ghost hunting trip was so important to Perry. Of course, those thoughts were immediately pushed to the side as Uncle Edwin grabbed my hand and began to tell me what a fine man my father was.

⌘

It was an hour or so later, at the reception at my dad and his wife's house—well, her house, then—when Perry found me again. I had finally extricated myself from an increasingly tipsy group of aunts, loosened my tie against the early summer evening's humidity, and was in one of the borrowed folding chairs with a warm beer sweating in my hand, when Perry sat down next to me. He nodded and I forced a smile, no attempt to hide my weariness, but he offered me cheers with the can of Coke he was drinking, so I returned the gesture. The smell of fresh tobacco on him rekindled that desire for a smoke that even years without a cigarette hasn't fully cured me of. A longing that goes well with melancholy, it seems.

"Hey, thanks again for coming," I told Perry. "Dad would ask after you every once in a while, so I'm sure he'd be glad to see you're doing well."

Perry thanked me and we made small talk for a moment. The usual: where we live, what we're up to, all appropriately vague. Then we fell into an awkward silence. Perry shifted uncomfortably, and I did, too, the uneasiness seeming to spread.

I felt the need to say something, since being the son of the deceased made me something between a host and a guest of honor, both of which seemed to bear the burden of guiding conversation. I decided to bring up something inconsequential; what, I can't remember, but I began. "So —"

"My dad's dead, too," Perry blurted out.

"Jesus, man, I'm sorry." Caught off-guard, I was scrambling to offer condolences. "I had no idea. Are you okay?"

"Oh, no," Perry said. "I mean, yeah. I am now. It was a few years back; you'd already moved away."

An image of Perry's father, Randy Harris, came to my mind. He'd been a mechanic by trade, but I remembered the sleepovers we had as kids at his little house out in the unincorporated county. Those were lawless nights, or at least as lawless as we could be in middle school. Up all night, bonfires out in the wide-open yard, R-rated movies. I could still see Randy in his recliner behind us boys as we watched TV, his feet up as he rolled cigarettes by hand over a bamboo lap tray. That smell of cut tobacco, not yet burnt, lingered in my nostrils even now, and I was craving a smoke again.

"Well," I said, "I'm still sorry for your loss. It seems so sudden."

Perry nodded. "Heart attack."

"Ah," I replied. Mine had been cancer—not from smoking, though. We sat for another awkward moment, and then Perry broke the silence this time.

"So, do you remember when we were kids, and your dad took us ghost hunting?" Perry asked. It was this again.

The Other End of the Line

"I do," I said, but warily. I wasn't sure if he wanted to reminisce or had some other motive for bringing it up, but I was over anything to do with ghosts or spirits or the afterlife. In those days I was still numb from the realization that I would never see my father again—not tomorrow; not in ten years; not after I died, either. I didn't want to entertain any false hopes, but just get through my stages of grief with as little bullshit as possible. Ghost hunting wasn't a discussion I wanted to have, but Perry seemed to sense this and shook his head.

"I don't want to talk about that," he said. "It was so long ago, but I just bring that up because it always stuck with me how your dad was open to the possibility of," he squinted, searching for the words, "strange things?"

"Sure." I nodded. My father had his spooky side. He had a lifelong interest in spirits and superstitions left over from the rural tobacco fields of his youth, which neither time nor schooling nor being a father nor even cancer had ever fully diminished. However, since his passing, I was realizing just how little I really knew him. What memories were left of him were all slowly turning into myth, and I'd never be able to ask him how much of it all— the tall tales, the haunted houses, the ghosts—he'd actually believed. I'd never know for sure how much of it he had only pretended to believe in order to entertain us as kids, or maybe how much he wanted to believe, even if he knew it couldn't really be true. But sure, Perry's assessment of my father as open to "strange things" fit.

"He always kept an open mind," I agreed.

Perry looked relieved, but I could tell he wasn't happy. He looked as if a weight had lifted from his shoulders, but only a small one.

"Okay, great," Perry said. "So, in that spirit, I hope you'll keep an open mind, too. Because I want to tell you a story about something that happened after my father died."

⌘

Perry's father, Randy, had died quick, which is its own kind of blessing and its own special hell. A massive coronary just killed him dead one night, right on that same recliner I remember. Luckily, he was found by friends the next day, so he wasn't alone too long.

The service was nice, Perry said. The extended family came out, including down from Virginia and over in Tennessee, and they saw Randy off in fine style. Sparing the particulars, there was music and drinking on into the night, both before and after the service. Although Perry took it hard, Randy went in light and love to rest in peace, or so it seemed.

Despite having two children, Randy had never married and was unattached at his passing, so it fell to Perry as the oldest child and only son to get Randy's effects in order so that the little house in the unincorporated county could be put back on the rental market. It was fine, though. Perry's sister Charlene—"Charlie," to fit in—had to head back to her home in the mountains, and perhaps there are some things a son is better equipped to deal with than a daughter, particularly when one's bachelor father exits unexpectedly. And so, it was on the same day Charlie said goodbye and pointed her old blue Volvo station wagon westbound on the highway that Perry went out to the house with a fresh roll of Hefty yard waste bags and a couple of repurposed cardboard boxes from the warehouse at work. He figured it'd be a day, maybe the weekend, tops.

It was slower going than expected. He started in the living room, clearing up the trash and emptying the little sooty mountain in the ashtray. He put the books in boxes, the magazines, and papers in the trash bags. All the while, that threadbare recliner sat watching, its bruised cushions still holding Randy's space. Little by little, though, the familiarity of the room diminished as the comforting clutter of a life was taken away. Eventually, only the chair remained, and so Perry moved on.

The bedroom, however, was more than he was ready for. It felt like a violation, Perry said, to go through his father's dirty clothes pile. His underwear and sock drawer. His bedside stack of well-thumbed Popular Mechanics and Hustler magazines. But go through them Perry did,

The Other End of the Line

taking the salvageable clothes and stripping the bed sheets to wash and donate to Goodwill, boxing up a few other items to add, like the clock radio and the table lamp. It was the closet, though, where Perry found the black telephone.

The black telephone was an old model—heavy, with a rotary dial and coiled black cord connecting the handset to the body. Perry said that when he picked it up, he could feel as much as he could hear the actual ringer inside tremble. There was no cord to plug it into a jack, but even as he hefted it up, Perry could envision it on the shelf next to the fireplace in his own apartment.

It wasn't a particularly odd find, as far as the things that Randy had accumulated over the course of his life. He'd always fancied himself an outsider artist, and so it was easy to imagine he'd picked the old telephone up and held onto it with the intent of cannibalizing it for pieces in a collage project down the line. Or maybe it had simply provided some singular aesthetic draw that compelled him to keep it intact. So many objects like that had ended up in Randy's closet: a sharkskin jacket, even though the only formal clothes Randy had owned was the suit they buried him in; a flint arrowhead the size of Perry's open hand; a collection of warped vinyl records of 1940s operas, but without a turntable in the house.

But the black telephone had its own peculiar gravity. A weight more than just the thick ebony block of Bakelite and the big staring eye of the rotary dial might on their own provide. When Perry picked it up from the shelf, the hidden mechanisms inside vibrated such that he could feel the warmth of ringing bells travel up the bones in his arm and into his skull. He felt something like a moment of peace. So, he set the telephone aside, spared from the garbage bags or the "Donations" box.

At the end of the weekend, with the little house empty of everything except for the furniture which movers were scheduled to pick up, Perry took the black telephone back to his apartment on the outskirts of Raleigh. He put it on the shelf beside the fireplace in his living room, letting it sit there like an urn. It seemed to him, Perry said, like a conversation piece for something he might never be able to talk about. Of course, that was until the black telephone started ringing.

Not during the day, of course. It wasn't plugged in. It didn't make any sound while you were awake, Perry told me. While the sun was out, it was absolutely silent. In your dreams, though?

It wasn't the first night, not even the first week, but maybe eight or nine days after it first came in the house. Perry said he "almost knew" he was in a dream when he first heard the heavy brass trill from the other room. It wasn't so much that he rose from bed and walked down the hall to the living room, but that in the inhalation of silence between one burst of ringing and the next, he found himself there beside the empty fireplace, staring at the heavy black telephone. He described it as feeling like he knew that where he was wasn't the real world, but that he hadn't yet come to acknowledge that truth.

The phone rang again. Perry picked up the handset and slowly brought it up. "Hello?"

There was a muffled sob on the other end. "Oh, Perry," the man's voice said, and Perry's heart stopped. "Son."

The waiting quiet on the other end of the line echoed through the cold plastic in Perry's hand, mixing with reverberation of his own blood in his ears, bouncing through and back out of the earpiece until his head was filled with the rush of static. It couldn't be.

"Dad?" he whispered.

"Oh, thank God!" The voice on the other end was hazy, distant, but it sounded like Randy Harris. Coming through a bad connection, sure, but that slight drawl, the hint of phlegmy rasp left over from his hand rolled smokes? Those were unmistakable.

"Dad?" Perry said again, although he knew it was. "Where are you?"

"Oh, son," his father said. "I'm so glad I reached you. It's so lonely here."

Perry's scalp crawled. He looked towards the living room's window on the far end to get some bearings, some connection to the world beyond. His living room was arranged so that his front door was one side, while the opposite wall had a full-sized window that looked out into the

The Other End of the Line

woods beside his building. With no neighbors over there, Perry often left the blinds up, and even at night the soft glow of the streetlamps from the complex's parking lot just around the building's corner afforded a slight but restorative view of the trees beyond. In this dream, though, the world outside was a solid, inky black, the color of the bottom of the sea. It was the same glossy darkness as the black telephone itself.

"Don't worry," Perry's father said. "Charlie is here with me, I think."

He jumped at his sister's name. "Charlie? What do you mean?"

"I don't think she saw the truck. But it's been so lonely, son," his father said. "I'm just glad to have the company here." Behind his voice, somewhere in the distance, was a sound that might have been a woman crying. Maybe.

"No, Dad!" Perry shouted into the line. "Wait!"

But the line clicked dead. Total silence. Then Perry woke up in bed.

Well, Perry asked me then, do you know how crazy you would sound if you texted your sister half a dozen times at 3:27 am and then called her cell until she woke up just to make sure she was alive, all because you dreamed your dead father called you on a disconnected antique phone? The answer according to Perry is "pretty crazy." The relief at hearing her voice, however, even if it was cussing him out, was apparently worth it.

Perry didn't actually go into the whole "dead father on the phone" explanation, but he did tell Charlie he'd had a bad dream and was worried about her. He told her it might be some kind of premonition—something about a truck and looking out. She called him a few more names but calmed down enough to hear him out. There must have been a seriousness in Perry's voice which convinced her that at least he believed it, because she finally said, "Okay, okay. I'll be careful on the road. I promise."

"Okay," Perry said. "And hey, I love you."

Charlie just groaned. "Uh huh. Don't call me again." And she hung up.

Perry went back to bed. He woke up groggy the next morning, still with a mild hangover of dread, but more fully flushed with embarrassment. He had to check his cell phone, but yep. There was the proof. He really had roused his sister out of bed in the dead of night because of a stupid dream. The mortification stuck to him through his morning shower. The stupid sentimentality of his words still coating his tongue despite three cups of black coffee. This was going to gnaw at him all day, he knew it.

And then his cell phone rang: "CHARLIE."

"I'm sorry about last night," Perry said, even before 'Hello.' "I just—" But the sound of near-hysterical crying stopped him short.

"Hello?" He tried not to panic. "Charlie?"

"Oh my god," she managed to choke out between sobs. "You were, you were right."

The Volvo was totaled but Charlie, by some grace, was fine. She'd been backing out of a service station after filling up on her way to work and the pickup coming down the road never even slowed down. It was a miracle, she told Perry, because she hadn't even seen it coming. If Perry's call hadn't still been echoing somewhere in the back of her mind, if she hadn't decided, for whatever reason, to humor her brother in absentia and pause right there to double-check her blind spots, the truck would have killed her. She was still in shock now, sitting on the curb waiting for the cops and the paramedics, but she couldn't not call Perry immediately to let him know he saved her.

"I don't know how you knew," she said. "But thank you. Thank you. Thank you."

Perry didn't know what to say. The only thing he knew was that he wasn't going to mention their dead father at a time like this.

As for the black telephone, it stayed there in the living room by the fireplace. Perry picked up the receiver, but of course there was no sound on the other end. Not even an echo in the handset, just a wall of nothing. He turned the rotary dial and felt the vibrations of the motors, but nothing more. What else had he expected? Did he think he was going to start getting nightly calls from his dead father?

The Other End of the Line

Well, it turns out it wasn't quite "nightly."

Three nights later, the night after the moving men had come to clean out the recliner and other final remnants of furniture from Randy Harris's little house, Perry found himself again standing in that same sunken living room dream with the same pitch-black window and the black telephone ringing. Like walking through water, he crossed to the shelf next to the yawning mouth of the empty fireplace. He picked up the handset.

"Hello?" Perry said.

"My son," came the reply. It was the same voice—his father's voice—although it sounded perhaps a little clearer. There was less of an echo, almost as if he were moving closer.

"Dad, I miss you so much." Perry was surprised at how the words came out. He hadn't planned on saying them, but there in the middle of the dream, with his father's voice on the other end of the black telephone's line, he couldn't stop himself. "I can't stop thinking about how much the world sucks now. It seems like everything is just rotten without you."

"Shhhhh, shhhhh," his father whispered. "It's all right."

Perry fought to hold back a sob, as he said, "No, it isn't. I don't know how I can go on." He got to the "isn't" part before breaking down and slobbering out the rest.

"Perry," his father said. "Hush. Don't cry. Look, do you want to see me? Would that make you feel better?"

The tears in Perry's eyes froze; mid-sniffle, he turned into a statue. Even in the dream world of the black telephone, there was something about the offer that struck him wrong.

"I ... I," Perry stuttered. "I'm not—"

"Go to the door and look outside," his father said.

Perry didn't answer.

"Perry, I've come a long way." His father sighed and the exhalation stretched and stretched into a long wailing wind that blurred into static, as empty as the space between the stars or the darkness outside the living room window, but then—once everything went silent and the vacuum across the line seemed to pull on Perry's eardrum through the receiver—he heard the beginning of the inhalation, and slowly the world congealed back around him and into his father's voice. "Just go look. I'm out by the parking lot."

Holding the handset in one hand, Perry picked up the phone in his other and walked slowly to the front door as the darkness watched from the window on the opposite wall. His apartment was on the ground level, and from his front door the lawn and concrete walkway sloped gently down to the complex's parking lot below. Approaching the peephole, he half-expected to put his eye to glass and see only the solid black that still blanketed the world outside the window on the living room's far side, but no. The glow of the orange streetlamps was dimly shining back inside through peephole's lens, even before Perry looked through.

"Are you coming?" his father asked on the other end of the line.

Perry put one eye up to the glass and closed the other. "I'm here," he said.

"Do you see me?" his father asked.

Through the fisheye lens, the parking lot was bowed and distended. The orange lamps made everything pumpkin-colored and failed to fill in the shadows enough for Perry to see much beyond the blocky silhouettes of the cars scattered across the asphalt.

"No," Perry said. "Where are you?"

"I'm waving," his father said. "Can you see me know?"

Perry squinted, straining to detect anything out there in the dim light and heavy shadow. Nothing seemed to be moving; it was all as still and flat as photograph. He peered deeper, though, willing himself to see something, anything. There, in the corner, next to that white Camry? Or maybe the blue Ram?

"Where are you?" Perry whispered.

But there was no answer.

The Other End of the Line

"Hello?" he asked into the phone. "Hello?"

But the only sound that came back was a distant muted grumbling, as if his father had left his end of the line lying on a beach with the low tide rolling out in the distance. The dream faded away into nothing.

As Perry got ready for work the next morning, he decided that his misery might be having a merry time playing tricks on him, but enough was enough. His father was dead and that was that. The calls were just some part of his bruised psyche stuck in the bargaining phase of grief, pretending that if Randy Harris were gone, some deal could be struck that allowed Perry to still speak with him. But Perry knew it wasn't healthy. The fluke about Charlie aside—and really, Charlie was such a reckless driver and their dad had always been on her about it so much that it was really nothing more than a lucky guess—the only thing these calls were doing was making Perry feel worse. The distant voice; the loneliness. And the offer to see his father? Perry shivered just thinking about it, even as he walked out of his apartment into the warm sunlight and head down towards the parking lot.

See his dead father? No, thank you. He was just glad that his dreams hadn't gotten too far. That he hadn't—

Perry stopped at the end of the walkway, just at the curb. On the ground was a little twist of white paper, burned at the end. Without even realizing it, he was already bending down. Please be a joint, he whispered to himself, please just be a roach left by a neighbor. But he could already tell from the odor. It was a smell almost too strong to rise from something so small, but which was buoyed up by familiarity. Reinforced, dare he admit it, by hope?

It was a hand-rolled cigarette. He recognized his father's tobacco.

Was it sensible? No. Perry knew that, but he also couldn't deny that now it felt like something big was about to happen. Everywhere he went that day and the next, it was as though his father might pull up outside the warehouse at lunch or maybe just come around the corner of an aisle at the grocery store. Hell, Perry's cell phone seemed to crouch in anticipation, always just on the verge of flashing "DAD." It was like being a kid on Christmas Eve, he said, but never knowing when the night might end or what exactly might come down the chimney.

Perry thought about sleeping with the phone beside his pillow, but ultimately decided against it. That's the thing about magic, isn't it? If you don't know exactly how it works, you don't know what you can safely change and so you just sort of freeze everything as it is. You don't dare move a hair out of place, lest you ruin the spell.

Yet night after night, nothing. No more ringing, no more dreams. It got to the point where Perry was so anxious about not dreaming that he couldn't fall asleep. He would lie there in the darkness staring at the ceiling, trying not to worry too much about worrying too much, spinning himself into tighter and tighter coils like the black telephone's cord.

Would it ever happen again? It took seven more nights, but then, yes.

As with all the dreams, Perry found himself in the living room again, with the phone ringing. This time, though, the sensation was different. Rather than the metallic clang echoing off of empty walls and into the hollowness beyond, the room felt denser. The air within it had a different sense of weight. It was enough to change the timbre of the bell into something almost meaty, but as soon as the second ring began, Perry leapt for the black telephone.

"Hello? Dad?" he practically yelled into the receiver. "Are you here?"

"My son," his father said, the voice clearer now than ever before. "I'm almost there. I've been so lonely."

The voice was so close, so immediate, that Perry flinched, swearing that he could almost feel the hot breath on his ear. It was enough that he looked around the living room to see if anyone was there, but no. As he looked towards the dark window on the far end, though, he thought he caught a glimpse of movement. A slight tremble in the darkness, as if one single shadow was moving among other shadows.

"Is that you, Dad?" Perry asked, taking a small step towards the window.

"I'm almost there, Perry," his father said.

Perry squinted at the sheet of almost solid darkness outside the

The Other End of the Line

window. Yes, there was definitely some small, almost cramped movement just beyond the glass.

"Are you at the window?" he whispered.

A knock at the front door at the other side of the house shattered the stillness and Perry screamed into the phone.

"Let me in Perry," his father said across the phone. The hollow rap at the door behind him repeated. "Open the door and let daddy in."

Still standing by the shelf, Perry turned his attention from the dark window at the far end of the living room to the front door on the opposite side. The gentle cigarette-sized glow coming in through the peephole went dark as something beyond obstructed the outside light.

"Is that you at the door?" Perry asked. "But, but then who's at the window?"

"Please let me in, son," his father moaned over the line even as the front door handle rattled. "I've come a long way to see you. Just open the door and let me see you."

Perry's palms were sweating, the heavy black plastic handset slipping in his grip. He leaned towards the front door, still tethered by the coiled black cord to the body of the telephone on the shelf and unsure of what to do. Then he heard another, fainter sound: a tapping on the glass at the living room window.

On one side of Perry, the door handle jiggled; on the other, a faint but insistent movement just beyond the glass begged for his attention.

"I don't know," Perry said. "I'm not sure what's going on."

The voice on the phone sighed. "Please, Perry. Don't leave me alone again. If you just let me in, I can leave this place behind. I just need to see that you're okay and then I can move on. Okay?"

Perry held his breath. The words he knew he needed to say burned in his mouth, but he couldn't keep them back any longer. "How do I," he hesitated, "how do I know it's really you?"

And then the room burst into illumination as a great blinding light from the woods outside the living room window poured in. It was cold and brilliant, and Perry flinched from the beam, but even as he did, he could now see a shape pressed against the glass, backlit and casting its shadow into the room

"What's that?" the voice on the phone snarled and a new wave of insistent rapping from the front door tried to tug Perry's attention away from the window. "Don't look at that," the voice said. "Open the door!"

Squinting against the harsh white light, at first Perry couldn't make out what it was he saw. A thing in the window; no, not a thing. A person. Someone lit from behind like an actor before a spotlight, pointed directly in through Perry's window. Still holding the telephone receiver to his ear, he shielded his eyes with his free hand and tried to make out who it was standing just outside the window of the dream house.

It took a moment to adjust to the glare, but then he could see the details and it ripped his stomach out. It was his father. His real father.

There was Randy Harris, staring in at the window. His arms were stiff by his side, with one wrist bent up, the knuckles tapping on the glass. Randy was wearing his suit, too—his only suit, the one they had buried him in—but his eyes were wide open, pinned directly on Perry. Perry had never seen such a look of pure terror and he was so riveted by it, that it took him a second to register what was wrong with his father's mouth.

At first, it looked as though his father had grown his mustache back —thick and dark—but then Perry realized it was a trick of the light. It was his father's mouth opening wider, wider, in a silent scream of warning. It stretched past where his jaw should stop, the yawning hole spreading down his neck, his chest.

Then the light cut out and Perry was standing in the dark living room again, the black phone still clutched to his ear.

"Are you there?" The voice that no longer sounded quite as much like his father's as it perhaps had just a moment ago asked. "Son? I'm sorry for getting angry, boy. Just let me in, okay?"

And then Perry realized that what he was talking to wasn't his father. It never had been.

"Who is this?" he asked. "Who are you?"

The Other End of the Line

"Ittt'ssss your faaaather," the voice stretched and cracked as it spoke. "Meee." It began to cackle, the noise deteriorating into a throaty laugh.

"Your daaaaaddy."

The front door handle shook violently, rocking the door in its frame.

"Let meeeee innnnn!"

In his dream, Perry slammed the receiver down and the jolt of it hitting the cradle woke him. He sat straight up in bed, every hair on end and tears streaming down his face. Outside a truck pulled into the parking lot and the beam of its headlights through the curtain passed over Perry once like God's own searchlight, then left him in the darkness. He sat there alone with the sound of nothing but his own blood ringing in his ears.

That, Perry said, was the end of the black telephone. He waited until full daylight—9 am—then put the phone in a Hefty sack, double-bagged it, and drove it down to the dumpster in the parking lot of the Methodist Church across town.

Even with it gone, however, Perry still had trouble sleeping. Lying in the dark, alone, the rush of blood and tinnitus in his ears always seemed to be rising like a wave, ever on the verge of cresting into the ring of a bell. He couldn't help but think that whatever had been on the other end of the line was waiting just out of sight for a momentary lapse in Perry's vigilance so that it could reach back out and touch him. Without the telephone to channel it, though, how would he know when it was coming?

⌘⌘⌘

"Jesus," I said to Perry when he was done. "Why'd you tell me that?" My skin crawled there in the echo of his story. I could almost hear the cracking voice on the other end of the line, the sick wet laughs, and the rattling door. I shivered, even though the room was sweltering under the crowded press of the now more-than-slightly tipsy aunts and cousins, the well-wishers turned into toast-makers and glad-handers.

"I told you that because you're going to miss him, Gordon. You're going to miss him real bad, and not just now when the pain is fresh, but when the ache of it settles in. You're going to wish you could talk to him.

You're going to think, as you lay there in bed at night with the whole dull absence of it on you, that you would do anything just to hear his voice."

Perry stood up to leave. He reached out again as if to shake my hand, but I didn't respond, the thought of his clammy palm suddenly repulsive. He shrugged, and a small grin surfaced as he lowered his hand.

"And one night," he said, "you're going to dream about a black telephone, just ringing and ringing. And I want you to remember something before you answer it." "What?" I asked.

"That there's always someone—something—so lonely and desperate to get in, so hungry for company, that they'll use any trick in the book." Perry's grin grew into smile, wider and wider, his mouth stretching further and further, until I had to look away.

"Goodnight," he said, and then he turned away and faded back into the boisterous crowd, chuckling as he did. As he disappeared into the merry bodies, the sound of his laughter was swallowed up in the greater noise, until soon I was left alone with nothing but a distant ringing in my ears.

END

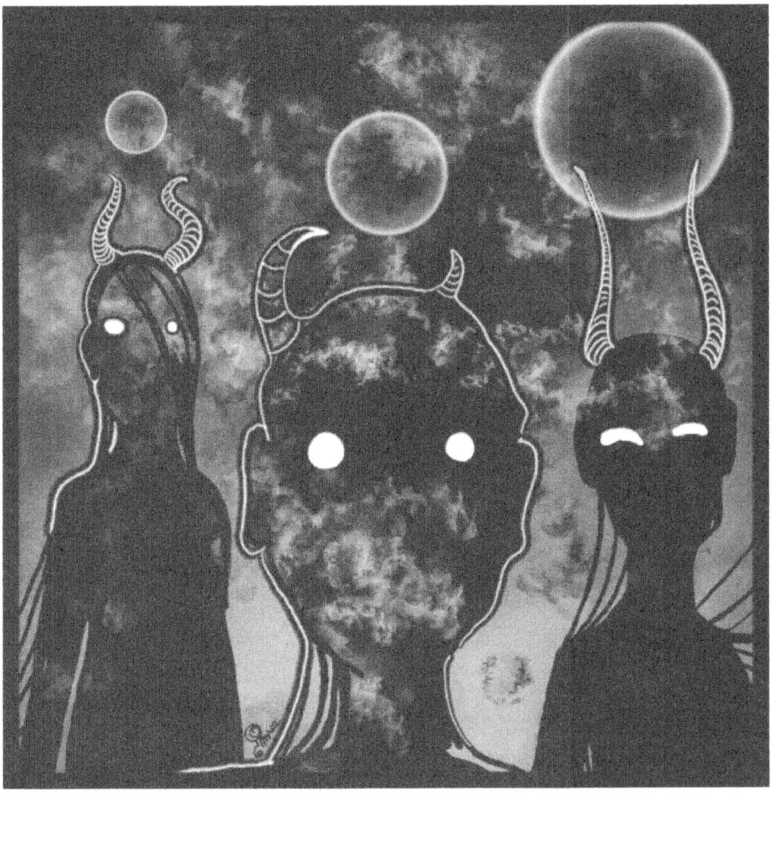

Do Not Read This
by Sarah Walker

Do not read this.

I mean it.

I really mean it.

Go on…just go ahead and skip to the next story in whatever book this is in.

Or scroll along to the next webpage if you're reading this on your phone or computer.

Point is, do yourself a favor and just move along.

….

But wait….

Are you still here?

You are, aren't you?

You're still here. Even after I warned you. Even after I told you not to read this, you're still reading.

I know you are.

Do you want to know how I know you are still here?

Because I would be. I know what I would do when offered a bit of prohibited knowledge. Like Eve, I would take a bite of that forbidden and terrible bitter fruit. I would do it even knowing that in biting it I would be changing my fate forever.

Even knowing I would be damning millions.

No, I wouldn't stop reading. I would have to know. It is a bit funny you know. Even now, even after everything that has happened, and is continuing to happen, I would still have to know. I wouldn't change wanting to know, even after the way the ending turned out. I would still write this story.

Do Not Read This

And I would still betray you.

That is the sickest part of this whole mess.

That is probably why they chose me.

My apartment is dark, except for the glow of my desk lamp. Joe, my husband, is sleeping. I envy him his peaceful rest, oblivious to what I can see on the wall beside me. I can see their black cutout shapes.

No, I am being silly. Probably that is just my lamp casting a shadow on the white plaster wall… But didn't it just move? Shift?

I need to write faster so I can get this out before it is too late.

I do not know where they came from. I only know that a few months ago they began to appear in my dreams. At first they were simply observers on the edge of perception. I have vague memories of waking up feeling uneasy, disturbed by an unremembered event in a dream. The details were fuzzy, as they often are in dreams, but I know one of them was watching me from the sidelines. Watching with ravenous intent.

The watching didn't last, though.

Soon they were active agents in my dreams. I would find myself walking through a surreal landscape resembling a Salvador Dali painting, when a sudden inexplicable fright would come over me. Turning, I would see the black shadow smoothly striding along next to me, its lithe form a sinuous river of black smoke. Though I could not see its mouth, I knew it was trying to tell me something. I could hear it murmuring.

It made a thrumming sound, like that of a motor running in a deep metallic coffin. That sound, and the sense that whatever was making it was close by, close enough to reach out and grab me, if it wanted to, would jolt me awake. I'd lie there in a full-blown terror, my heart thumping so loudly my ears would be ringing.

Thinking about those dreams, I am starting to sweat even now.

Describing fear is much harder than one would imagine. It's easy to write that a dream was so terrifying that it seemed entirely possible, as I woke up, gasping and sweating, that my heart would stop beating, just seize up and quit. You, the one who is reading this, are probably thinking, big deal, it was a nightmare, so what?

Fear is subjective. What scares one person is nothing to another. But believe me when I tell you these dreams were some of the most horrific I have ever had. It wasn't like anything happened in the sense of my being violently attacked. No. Instead, the terror was more a quiet inferno. It was a fear of something existing that should not exist. Though my conscious mind would try and sneak some logic into the madness of unconscious dreaming and whisper that the terror was just a product of REM, deep inside I knew it was something else.

But like all things, including intense fear, it would fade. Soon after waking my heartrate would go back to normal and I would begin to doubt the reality of the experience. It is strange how there is always an undertone of electrical buzzing in my head now. It came that first time I dreamt of them, and you know what? That sound is never completely gone. Maybe they are tuning me in somehow, like a living occult radio.

I started to hate sleep. At first, I tried everything to get rid of the dreams. I got prescribed antidepressants. But those had no effect except to make my eyes sting and give me a headache. Next, I tried sleeping pills. They made me gain eight pounds. The only other thing they did was make it so I could no longer force myself awake without feeling drunk and heavy limbed. On top of this, even after pulling myself from that thick and viscous swamp of being doped, I would ultimately fall right back asleep, stumbling into the same nightmare, tangled in a sticky web that I could not see or avoid, the sleeping pill refusing to let me escape its grasp.

And do you know what else?

I discovered quickly that trying to stop the dreams only made them worse.

Soon I was staying up until one, two, three, four in the morning to avoid sleep. I would then force myself awake around 6 a.m. to try to stop that late-sleep dream state before it happened. The problem with doing that is your mind really needs that deep REM sleep phase. That is when your brain washes away toxic proteins and waste, so that you can think

Do Not Read This

and function the next day. And if you don't sleep, if you stay up for days on days, you're going to start to get a little strange. You'll even start seeing things if you are sleep deprived enough.

In fact, if you go without sleep long enough, you'll die.

But those dreams were so horrible, I think I would have done anything to stop them, no matter how extreme it was.

I guess that's what I'm doing right now.

Anyway, one of the ways I would keep myself awake all night was by watching late-night TV. Mostly I would tune into horror films. I am a horror writer after all. Horror lovers will get this, while others might not, but watching horror movies helps me relax. For me, seeing the monster contained in the television, seeing it located in the geographical space of fantasy, made it so I could manage the strange dreams. Finally, I would pass out and get a few hours of dreamless sleep before the shadow people would arrive again and haunt me, sitting on my chest, pinning me down, staring into my eyes with their deep unsettling hollowness. This would startle me awake in terror.

One night after I'd been living like this for a few weeks, I was up again and watching that old Boris Karloff film *The Mummy*. I have seen it multiple times. It is one of my favorites. I can repeat dialogue from it. As I was watching I started to drift off when something scurried in the background.

I was instantly wide awake. Had I just discovered a fluke in one of the most famous horror films of all time? I dragged my finger on my phone and reversed the scene. Yes, there it was, but now it was not something small, scurrying in the scenery. No, now it looked like a man's silhouetted shape in the background of a scene where Boris Karloff is talking to Ardith, a woman who he believes is his reincarnated lover from his past life. I have seen this scene many times but had never before noticed the shadowy shape in the corner.

I brought the phone closer to my face to try to see if I was mistaken somehow. At first my mind tried to make sense of it. I thought it had to be Karloff, casting a shadow on the ground, admittedly at a weird angle.

I reasoned that I was only noticing it now because I was watching the film on a smaller screen.

But then it moved, turning towards me, and revealing itself to be far too thick to be a shadow, too darkly pregnant. And most importantly, it was anthropomorphic. It jumped towards the camera, fully obscuring the rest of the actors, and making the entire screen go black. I tried to shout in fear, I couldn't help it, but I could not move. It was like every single one of the muscles in my body had been dripped in freezing mercury. I couldn't even throw the phone away from me.

Luckily, right then, Joe walked in. When I looked back at the screen, the film was back to normal. Confused, I scanned the screen while Joe asked me why I'd just shouted.

I hadn't thought I had managed to yell, but clearly, I had. Still, I didn't want to tell him about the dream. I feared that even thinking about those shadow people would call them back. I felt that as long as I denied their existence, they couldn't have power over me. I knew somewhere deep within my mind that believing in them would give them energy off of which they would feed and become stronger. Then they would be able to do more than frighten me; they would be able to hurt me. So, I lied and told Joe I'd had a bad dream about losing my job.

Maybe he knew I was lying because he looked at me oddly, but he said nothing more. He is good like that. He understands that when you truly love someone, some things are best left unsaid. After we'd gotten into bed together, and he'd turned off the lights and began snoring, only then did I start to think about what was happening to me.

A black tsunami of dread swept over me. This was not the last time this sort of thing would happen. In fact, it was probably going to increase in frequency. Something told me the experiences were leading up to something. I knew that whatever it was, it was trying to break through whatever line was drawn between us, dividing our two worlds. Deep down I knew it was going to succeed. It was as if a hungry lion was fixated on me, preparing to pounce.

I was its prey.

Do Not Read This

I was powerless.

I was terrified.

I pushed the fear away as soon as sun hit my face. Life went on. No one tells you that in the midst of a war, life keeps going on, but it does. You eat, you have good days and bad. Soon I was back to looking at it from an observer's point of view, able to distance myself from the exquisite terror of these beings.

I even tried to find a realistic reason for the occurrences. A nonparanormal reason. I looked up sleep paralysis and decided finally, when all other possibilities were shown to be unlikely, that this disorder had to be what I was experiencing. Certainly, shadow people didn't actually exist, living in an alternate dimension and feeding on fear. *Of course, they don't really exist,* I would tell myself, no matter how much my mind was screaming they did.

Obviously, I'd lucid dreamed while watching *The Mummy* and when it changed into a nightmare, I'd experienced sleep paralysis. I was more stressed than usual at work, worried about the pandemic, and about my writing career. All those things were the reason for the dream, not that there are entities existing at the edge of our perception, creatures that feed on us like we are cattle.

That is the funny thing about paranormal happenings. People constantly argue that if ghosts and magic and demons existed then we would experience them all the time. There would be videos and photos, real ones, not the kind that are staged or photoshopped. There would be verifiable accounts in scientific journals about people who died, or nearly died, from contact with a malevolent paranormal entity.

But has it ever occurred to you that such evidence exists? Go to YouTube or Google- and then type in "shadow people." Go ahead. I will wait.

Notice how many videos there were? Hundreds.

Thousands.

Tens of thousands even. Could all of those videos be fake? I mean, think about it. Statistically, how likely is it that all the videos about shadow people are faked? And then realize that even if just one percent of the videos of supposed shadow people sightings are real, then shadow people do exist.

Even if only one of the videos is real. Consider the implications of that.

Maybe they are beings from an alternate dimension. Maybe they are ghosts or demons. But whatever they are, they are not harmless. Don't ever think that they can't hurt you, because I promise you that they most certainly can harm you. Perhaps that is their whole point.

Maybe they are feeding off us.

I have found video after video, article after article, about people being terrorized by these shadow creatures. It happens all over the world. From Asia to Africa to Europe, these figures are always described the same way. Some of the people who experienced them even ended up dying. Recently a man who claims to suffer from them made a movie about people's experiences with them. He asserts that some people really do die as a result of being what I'll call *visited*.

How? Most often it is from suffocation, though sometimes there is no clear cause of death. In the cases where the person 'suffocated' medical examiners will say the person simply stopped breathing while they were asleep. The lack of oxygen then brought on a fatal heart attack or a stroke.

The question that came to me was why? Why won't people accept that the unseen exists? I mean, take infrared light. Just because we can't see it, does that mean it doesn't exist? Or radiation. Or viruses. Just because you can't see these things with the naked eye does not mean they don't exist.

So once again, why don't people admit these things might be real and might be a very real danger?

I will tell you why. People tend to disregard anything that interferes with their version of reality. They simply won't allow it to exist, even if it is screaming two inches from their face with a bloody skull and black holes for eyes, even if it is sucking their souls dry each night when they

Do Not Read This

sleep.

It is a case of cognitive dissonance. We are trained to believe reality is a certain way. Ghosts and monsters don't exist. What dies stays dead. Then, if you are presented with evidence to the contrary, if you have an experience that is utterly inexplicable according to all the laws of nature as you've come to accept them, you will simply disregard it. You will go back to hiding your head in the sand.

You're probably wondering what happened to me.

I grew used to the shadow things plaguing my nightmares. I adapted to sleeping only a few hours each night. Occasionally I would see one of them in a film or photograph, but I managed to tell myself it was a hallucination, a product of my overwrought imagination.

And maybe that would have continued if I weren't married. Maybe I would have just gone along with these night terrors. Maybe they would have slowly fed on me, and I would have simply faded away and died if Joe hadn't been there to see it too.

But he was.

One night a few days ago, I awoke to Joe standing over me, shaking me awake.

"Turn off your damned computer," he said. He sounded groggy and his eyes were bloodshot. And no wonder; it was the middle of the night.

Confused, I looked around the bed to see if I had fallen asleep playing a walking simulator again. I do it all the time. But my computer wasn't there. I remembered then I hadn't been playing a videogame. I had been so tired I had simply laid down and out I had gone.

"I went straight to bed, Joe. I didn't play a videogame tonight." I yawned, "Jesus, why'd you have to wake me up?" His concerned expression suddenly shifted, a hard edge taking over. Years of literally doing nothing but living on a motorcycle have made him a bit hypervigilant. He walked over to the side of the bed and grabbed the baseball bat we keep there in case someone breaks in.

"No one is in here. If there was someone in the house, don't you think the dogs would have growled? Please let me go back to sleep, Joe." I groaned, exhausted by the chronic sleeplessness and nightmares.

"I heard someone talking. I know I did." Clutching the bat, he walked around the room, turning the lights on. He flipped the bedspread up, and looked beneath the bed, his left hand gripping the bat tight.

"You heard someone speaking? It was probably me."

"Sarah, I am not joking. I heard you, yes, but I heard someone else in here."

"What do you mean?" I yawned.

"I heard a man's voice."

Confused and more than a little creeped out, I sat up.

"There's nobody here but us. I must have been talking in my sleep."

"And doing impersonations of a man? I know you used to act in plays, but Sarah, this was definitely a man's voice. No matter how hard you tried you could not fake that voice."

Though the room was warm, and I was wrapped in blankets, I was suddenly cold. I watched him pace, holding onto the baseball bat, and my anxiety rose. Joe rounded the room one more time, opening the closet and pushing aside clothing on hangers, but there was nobody there. He walked out of the bedroom. I could hear him as he walked through the whole house, finally coming back after he was satisfied no one had gotten in.

He got into bed with an odd look on his face. I was scared, but I didn't want him to know the strange stuff that had been happening to me, so I tried to sound interested instead of frightened.

"You were probably dreaming." I touched his back and felt him flinch a little.

"Listen Sarah, I was not asleep. I was in the living room watching TV and the dogs started to growl at the bedroom door. I got up and as I went into the bedroom. I heard him. I know I heard a man whispering." He rubbed his eyes.

I thought of the shadow people I had started seeing in my dreams and even in films when I know I was awake.

Do Not Read This

"Did you hear what was being said?" I asked. Joe pushed himself up on one elbow and looked out the window into the backyard. Seeing no one out there, he laid down again.

"Only a little, but that's why I woke up."

"Okay, what was he saying?"

He didn't respond. Growing irritated I prodded his back.

"What did he say?"

Joe rolled over halfway and looked at me with haunted eyes.

"He said that if you don't kill yourself soon, they are going to start taking everyone you care about, one by one."

⌘⌘⌘

After that, I could not sleep. I would lie in bed, thinking, night after night. But finally, the toll on my body became too great and last night, I fell asleep.

This dream was different. I was in some place that was like an ocean of static. I could feel the electricity around me, buzzing over my skin. It was like swimming in hot carbonated water. As I moved through this weird medium, I realized I could hear someone pacing me, just out of sight. When I moved, they would move. I didn't yet know I was dreaming; the sleep was too deep. I was confused, but not yet frightened.

Then they appeared. Like a flickering black wind, they swam in and out of focus. Each time they faded they would be closer when they came back. I tried to move, to run somewhere in this weird place, but the more I tried to get away, the heavier my limbs became and the harder it was to breathe. Suddenly I fell and the electrical field vanished. Now I was floating in black ether.

I could hear something sniffing. It was moving around me and growling, a deep subbase noise that set my teeth on edge and made my hair stand on end. I tried to sit up but could not. I tried to scream but could not.

Then I felt it. A heavy cold weight crawling up my body, its sharp nails poking into my flesh. I still couldn't see it. I couldn't move my head to position it so that I could.

I screamed in my head that it was a dream, and I needed to wake up, but I couldn't. Nothing I did would bring me out of the unconscious state.

I felt the weight as it settled on my chest. I looked up and I could see two eyes the color of hot coals spat from a roaring fire. It looked at me and I knew that it knew I could see it. It spoke. You know what we want…

The voice was a deep man's voice, just the way Joe had described it.

I tried to shake my head no.

I wouldn't kill myself for these creatures. I had been down that self-destructive road before and there was no way I was going to be tricked again by my own subconscious.

Finally, I managed to shout "No" at the thing on my chest.

And suddenly I knew, I understood. This thing could not be killed. This thing had been around for millennia. It was the thing born of fire when we were made from clay. And now that it had locked onto me, it would not leave until it got its fill.

Unless….

You know…. you know….

And I realized I did.

It slowly crawled off of me and I found myself lying in bed, a thin gray morning light washing in. I sat up and ran over to my computer.

Joe was still asleep; I could hear him snoring. I thought of my mother, my siblings, my friends.

I thought of what I would do to protect them.

These things, these shadow people wanted to be fed. And to feed they needed people to believe in them. How best might I get people to do that very thing?

Do Not Read This

I began to write.

I told you at the beginning, didn't I? I told you not to read this.

I warned you.

But still you read.

And I knew you would. Maybe that makes me a terrible person. But I know I am safe now. And they won't bother me anymore if I just do this one thing and share their existence with the world.

A bit of advice: When they come tonight, don't resist.

Just let them take a little. You have so very much life in you. You can share a bit, can't you?

It's better for us all.

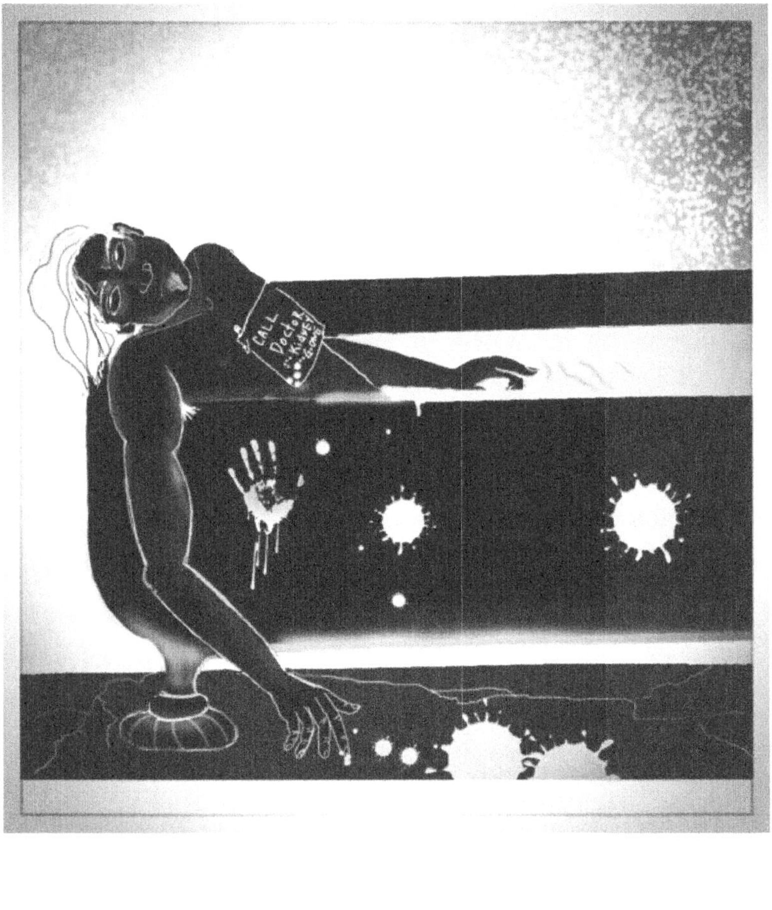
CALL
Doctor Kidney

Market Price
by Can Wiggins

"To market, to market, to buy a fat pig, home again, home again, jiggety jig ..."

19th c. nursery rhyme

Damn. The smell. The smell's what set me off. It's what always sets me off and I end up embarrassing my partner Lawrence, myself, and probably the corpse we've run up on during whatever investigation we're in the middle of by puking wherever I am.

I held back once and liquified lunch came out of my nose – which I don't want to talk about. Even Lawrence gave a heave when he saw that.

"Never seen anything like it," he told me later. "I thought your head had exploded."

When our then-police captain Pat McCurdy came on the scene, he made no bones about being unhappy that the evidence would end up close to useless.

But that story aside, there's nothing like opening a storage unit in the middle of a Georgia summer and finding four bodies in various states of decomposition.

Trust me. Nothing.

⌘⌘⌘

"I dreamed Kip McDonald went missing." Grace rattled her morning paper like a tambourine, despite claiming she had a hangover. She drank her coffee black that Saturday rather than her usual cream and sugar blend. She downed some aspirin and refused breakfast. She said she didn't trust her stomach yet, but Grace doesn't eat a hell of a lot any given day.

Market Price

Still, she does better than me. When I have a hangover, I can't even hold a newspaper, let alone do anything as advanced as read it. Not as bad as it could have been, considering the shindig we'd crashed the night before.

I guzzled an ice water then tossed in my two cents.

"Well, Kip McDonald is not missing," I said, "not even in your dreams. He does what he always does, Gracie. He saw a pretty face and took off. I admit it's rude, even for Kip – especially at a party he's cohosting – but I'll bet fifty to a hundred he's holed up somewhere with his new flavor of the weekend. It's not like he's never done this. He takes off all the time and leaves the heavy lifting to others."

"Is that our Kip McDonald you're talking about?" Carter asked. He had ducked into the dining room to nab a fresh cup of joe, catching the end of our conversation.

"Yes, honey. James Hamilton McDonald the Third. Or is it the Fourth?" Grace asked.

"I can't keep up with what or who passes for high society," I said.

Carter grinned. "Well, it sure as hell ain't Kip McDonald, forget how much money his daddy's got. Remember, we've known that bird since grade school," he said, nodding towards Grace.

"And what a little shit he has remained," she added.

Carter Jones knows everybody who's anybody from Myrtle Beach to the mighty Mississippi. His syndicated columns along with his Modern South articles in regional publications see to that. His family of doctors and lawyers opened doors for him, but he thumbed his nose at medicine and law, preferring journalism and social hobnobbery, fueled by liquor and gossip.

"I thought you and Kip were pals," I said.

"If you count blowjobs part of being pals, we were the best of friends in college."

"Kip tried everything at least once and kept *on* trying it if he wasn't sure how he felt," Grace said.

"What're you working on now?" Carter sidled over to me, looking at the files spread out on the table. "Affair du jour?"

I turned the photographs over. Carter's the type of person who stops at the scene of an accident to find out if it's someone he knows.

"Oh, come on," he said. "I need a new job if you need a new sidekick."

I laughed. Carter's always working, his byline courted like an old-time Southern belle.

"Carter, you'd lose your mind if you saw what I see."

"Yeah? Well, you're going to go bugshit crazy one day from all that carnage." He kissed the tops of our heads, then left to start his day, a long lean hound of a man, his auburn hair cut close.

"Besides which," Grace said, "Lawrence Henry would kick anybody's ass if he thought they were trying to muscle in."

"You just want us together because we make a good-looking couple," I said. She snickered and rattled her paper again, looking for what she called nuggets.

Lawrence and I have a PI business near downtown Atlanta. We have little to do with the cops and vice versa. It's not like TV or the movies where everybody is hand in glove solving cases together in a couple of hours because someone caught a lucky break. That's strictly fiction – until it isn't.

However, if there's a weirdness about a case, something off-center, that's the one we get calls about – from the client and sometimes from the police. Go figure.

Not that I'm complaining. We've made Kallas & Henry work for the three years we've been gone from the force. Nothing's perfect but being manhandled by perps plus an occasional fellow officer soured me on the uniform, as did the disparity and other soul-sucking events that stacked up on the wrong side of the scales of justice.

Then, something happened, something nobody talks about much even now, and it came close to breaking a few officers in the department.

𝕸arket Price

When that case wrapped up, Lawrence and I had a couple of bourbons and agreed to fold our tents and silently steal away, like an old poem says.

So, a new beginning. Lawrence called it a reset, like the geek he is. We'd hold on to each other, keep our loyalty and partnership. We'd remain professional above and beyond and grow the agency together.

While we also had – okay, I'll admit it – *fraternized*, that had to go the way of all flesh too.

"I hate giving that one up," he laughed.

"Same here, pal. But we can't muddy the water we're drinking."

⌘ ⌘ ⌘

Let me say right now that I should pay more attention to what Grace Allgood reads on the weekends. She's smart as hell but she scours tabloids and weeklies for bottom of the barrel laughs and what she says give her ideas for the books she writes for a near-rabid fanbase.

Some of these rags spout celebrity gossip or advise eating peaches to destroy cellulite on your ass, plus there's the occasional sighting of Sasquatch in the "Around Town" columns.

In other words, fact is printed beside fiction, lending a layer of respectability for an easily led reader. CDC reports are alongside pieces about JFK's still-functioning brain, hidden somewhere in a lab or cave or on a "hidden Nazi moon base." United Way articles are beside astrologers' doomsday predictions. A photo of the face of Christ on a piece of toast is nestled next to a police report, a report which is the real deal or someone's getting sued.

So, when I heard Grace talking about harvested organs, I thought she had started jawing about – well, I didn't know what about except it happened to be Grace running her mouth. I thought she was sounding out another scare fest for her readers.

Little did I know …

Lawrence stopped by for the files plus one of Mattie's buttered biscuits. Nobody minded, least of all Mattie.

"I swear I might as well be your mama," she said. He grinned and popped half a biscuit in his mouth. He's probably the son she wanted instead of the one she got, but that's a nest of vipers we don't talk about.

"Lawrence, have you heard about organ harvesting?"

Lawrence swiveled around and gave Grace his full attention. "No. Wait ... what?"

"Organ harvesting."

"Gracie, if you're talking about what I think you are, it's nothing but a story."

She told him in no uncertain terms what she meant.

"I'm talking about men picking up beautiful babes in a bar, then waking up naked in a tub of ice with a note telling 'em to get to the hospital if they want to live, because – 'hey, thanks for the kidney, *duuuude.*'"

Mattie's laugh shook the house, and she wiped tears from her blue eyes. "Gracie, people're gonna think you're cracked."

"And they've got stitches!" Grace hollered over Mattie's guffaws.

Lawrence shook his head. "No, no. That's an urban legend. It's a terrible story and used to be even worse. It started with the honey trap being an Asian woman, all hot babe mama-san," he hesitated a moment. "Sorry. I'm telling it like I heard it the first time. It used to be racist as hell.

"Anyway, it's the same story, more or less. She's his wildest wet dream come true. He gets drinks for her and himself to unwind, and then? They go to his suite which he doesn't remember because he's already drugged. He gets sliced and diced and she lifts an internal organ – usually a kidney – to sell on the illegal market. And he wakes up, like you said, in a tub full of ice with a note telling him to get to the hospital if he wants to live.

"But it's a bullshit story, Gracie."

"Well, I'm reading about this bullshit story more and more,

Lawrence," she said. "I wonder if somebody's started setting it up, making it real."

I got a kick out of Gracie winding up for who knew what kind of pitch.

"Sounds more like it's going through another spin cycle," Lawrence said.

"See, that's what I want to find out. That's what I want to know because that would be a great chiller to write about. I could make her a monster," Grace said.

"Monsters are always humans," Lawrence said.

I butted in. "Man, I gotta hand it to you, Grace. You write some scary shit, but you jump outta your skin quicker than anyone I know."

"One kidney goes for seventy-five large. Just saying." She winked, then went back to her papers and coffee.

⌘⌘⌘

The weather changed later that day, and a low-hanging cloud sat on Atlanta while much-needed rain got dumped. Good for clearing the air and good for watering the gardens but, like everything else in Atlanta, it didn't last long enough.

The week had been quiet, but we'd cleared out a couple of cases that didn't seem to be going anywhere. Then, they took off and were over and done. They weren't huge windfalls, but we were happy with the bonuses we got.

My phone went off. I recognized the number immediately. Lawrence. And he got straight to the point.

"We got a call, Jo."

"A client? Wait. Are you still at the office?" "Yeah. Got our name from a Mr. Carter Jones." "Carter? That's interesting," I said.

"Wait'll you hear who it is."

"You sound like my mother. Tell me now."

Can Wiggins

"Abigail McDonald. Jim McDonald's old lady." "Wait a minute. James Hamilton McDonald the *Third?*" "Or Second or Fourth," he laughed.

"I'll be right there," I said. And I almost made it, too.

I peeled out of the driveway, wondering why one of the richest people in the state wanted to talk to a two-person operation. If Abigail McDonald had called us for a consultation, there could be only one explanation.

Something *had* happened to Kip. Grace would never let me live it down. And she'd never shut up about her dream being a sign.

⌘⌘⌘

I parked my car behind the building that houses our office. I practically ran up the stairs. It's nice enough where I work. It's seen better days but what hasn't. The paint's fresh, the linoleum clean. Our furniture's old school, the colors deep greens and blues and there's a plush couch a person can sink into but still have back support. Believe it or not, people want that. So, we give it to them along with the real goods we offer.

We want people to feel comfortable and comforted. We want them to talk, tell us what's really going on, things they won't tell other people – not their loved ones, not their ministers or rabbis, not their lawyers.

People have secrets, even good people. And the fear of those secrets getting out can turn a good person into a fucking monster.

We see people when they're often at their worst or most frantic. We do everything to make their visit as quick and painless as possible. And we make good money, whether they use us or not.

I found Lawrence at his desk, a few well-placed papers before him. He likes looking busy, sending a message that we're on the case, that we're successful, we can get the job done. Telling people to "take a number, have a seat, we'll be right with you" still works. But we rarely

Market Price

schedule people back-to-back.

It's not privacy as much as secrecy. Nobody wants to be seen at a P.I.'s office. Stupid but true. They assume people assume the worst.

And they're often right.

⌘⌘⌘

Abigail McDonald entered our office and stood stock-still for a moment as if drinking us in or, more likely, allowing us to drink her in. Good-looking in her heyday, she cultivated a look and demeanor on its way out before she was born. Her hair was perfect, coiffed in a style that could only be described as Stage and Screen, and so icy white it almost blinded me. Her outfit had probably cost more than I had earned in a month. Her left hand bore a thick gold band with a diamond that would have choked a pig.

Since she was old school South, there were polite introductions and a brief mention of Carter Jones's recommendation, then she sat down, cranked up, and took off.

"My son is missing. Kip. Well, that's his nickname. James Hamilton McDonald the Third." She handed us a recent photo of the subject. "He's been gone 24 hours. I know that doesn't seem like a long time but it's unusual for him."

"Why do you think he's missing?" Lawrence leaned forward; his amber eyes fixed on her powder-perfect face. I thought of a snake charming a bird.

"I don't think," she said. "I know."

"Were you supposed to meet? I want to be sure I understand you. Start from the beginning," Lawrence said.

She settled back into the couch, a melodramatic sigh escaping her Cadillac Red mouth.

"I know what Kip's like. What his life is like – I know his proclivities, there's no way not to know," she said. She kept her eyes down, playing embarrassed for all it was worth. "No way to hide everything from your mother, especially when she keeps tabs on you. There. I've said it. I know where he is almost all the time, who he's with." "You have him followed," I said.

She nodded slowly, then looked down at her hands as she twisted that obscenely large ring. I knew this might be a confession of a different sort and I caught Lawrence's eye and raised a brow. He followed suit. Abigail McDonald didn't notice. She threw all her energy into her act, which meant she had more invested in her performance than paying attention to us.

She had a good reason for being nervous which she told us right off the bat. "Kip calls me every morning at nine o'clock sharp. He calls me every night before I retire for the night. Again, nine o'clock sharp. He's always been good about that. But after his dad's illness, he hasn't missed calling me once."

"Until now."

She nodded. "Kip isn't what I'd call a bad person. He's gotten into his fair share of scrapes here and there. He's smart – so smart, he's never seemed happy or satisfied with anything he chose or wanted or even had when he worked for and got it."

"Does Kip have enemies?"

She looked startled. "Enemies? I don't think so. Not real enemies."

"Mrs. McDonald, what do you think a real enemy is?" I asked. I knew of at least two payoffs involving minors, which never hit the news. I knew about three drunk and disorderly charges that disappeared and one drunk tank episode where somebody other than Kip was on the receiving end of a beatdown.

"I don't know of anyone who would want to kill him. That's what I mean."

"Okay," I said. "Well, let's take that off the table. Would they want to blackmail him? Extort him? Does he owe anyone any money? And again, I mean real money like I mean a real enemy."

She shook her head vigorously. "There's no way. Kip's careful about money and, of course, he has plenty. We saw to that, his father and me. We didn't want anyone to take advantage of him and we didn't want him to be stupid with what – or who – surrounded him."

"Plenty of people around him now," Lawrence said.

"Yes. My social butterfly. He's a people person. Plus, a little over a year ago, his father had a stroke. Mild, but we kept it very quiet. We had to. Corporations are like pools – only they're full of sharks instead of people. We feared Jim would be taken out of the game if you know what I mean. Off the board and out of his own company," she seethed. I couldn't blame her for that.

"So, Kip has his hands on the wheel now. It's all behind the scenes. For all intents and purposes, Jim's still running things. But Kip has been the one shoring everything up."

I nodded. The good son. Par for the course.

"Any old girlfriends, maybe?" Lawrence piped up. "Somebody looking to get back at Kip over a broken engagement or other arrangement?"

"He would've told me if a woman – or a man, for that matter – was causing trouble." She lifted her chin in what she probably thought was a show of defiance. "And yes, I'm well aware of my son's after-dark escapades."

"Then I guess you're aware that people who really know and spend time with Kip call his house *Chez* Whore of Babylon," I said.

I saw by her expression she hadn't been aware of that at all. I plowed ahead.

"Ma'am, I don't move in the same circles as your son but word on the street is, he gives parties that are pretty goddam wild. And he has friends – or acquaintances, let's say – that also move in different circles. The type of circles that occasionally get brought in for questioning."

"He was never the same once he went to Europe." She shook her head. "Who knows what influences a young person and why?" I lifted my own chin. I wasn't buying her blame game.

"Mrs. McDonald, if Kip really is missing – and Mr. Henry and I have no doubt that you believe he is – it would help us immensely if you know of anyone you think we could speak with."

"Someone who might know his private comings and goings," Lawrence said.

"I assure you I have told you what I know." I can't swear to it, but it looked like she fluttered her eyelashes at my partner. I decided to broadside her.

"Because, Ms. McDonald, you say you keep tabs on your son. But if he's involved in something not on the up and up, something important, don't you think someone else is doing the same thing?"

⌘⌘⌘

She paid us our retainer in cash with the promise of a huge bonus if we found him in 24 hours. "I don't want the police involved unless it becomes absolutely necessary. I don't want a paper trail. I'm sure you understand."

"We'll do what we can within the law, of course."

"Discretion is our mantra," she said. "It's the better part of valor, you know."

We closed the door behind her and heard her walk away. Her high heels sounded like gunshots.

"I doubt Kip understands either of those concepts she just mentioned," I said.

"Mommy dearest," said Lawrence.

⌘⌘⌘

Sunday morning found Lawrence and me making plans to go to The Down and Dirty, a little-known Greek café. "You know all the best places," he said.

Market Price

But a call came in that took us to a very different place in more ways than one. Pops Gillespie reached out to me, which is how we ended up in Decatur.

I've known Pops most of my life. I recognized his voice and picked up, placing him on the speaker.

He'd been chummy with my dad, on and off the grift since they'd been in the Air Force. That checkered history, filled with all kinds of folks, might be why I started out as a cop, and I think it's why I ended up a P.I.

He had a problem out at his business. Somebody had called him with a complaint, and he checked it out and something bad might've happened.

"Could you come out here, Jo, to the storage units? Meet me at the office and advise me what needs doing?"

Lawrence asked Pops why he didn't just call the police.

Pops said, "I feel safer calling anyone besides the police, especially since I got a record."

I horned in. "We'll be there within the hour, Pops. Hang tight." I broke the connection and gave Lawrence the side-eye.

"Just because Pops is an *old* Black man doesn't mean he's not worried something will happen to him if cops show up. Which it very well could, depending on the cops and depending on what he's calling about. And don't worry, he'll pay us for our time."

"I'm not – I'm not worried. I dropped the ball," Lawrence said, his face the reddest I'd ever seen. "I didn't think, Jo. I apologize, I didn't mean any disrespect to Mr. Gillespie. I didn't know."

"I know you didn't."

I talked him into going to Decatur with me, dangling the promise of paying for his brunch or lunch or dinner. Agreed, because I know the best places.

Also agreed because it was the right thing to do.

So, we hightailed it to Decatur. While that might sound like no big

Can Wiggins

deal, traffic is always problematic now, coming or going, even on weekends. What were once 'tried and true' shortcuts don't always work now. But we were lucky, making it in 20 minutes.

We zipped down Clairmont, turned on to East Ponce, and floorboarded it to Decatur's back side towards our target. It didn't take long but it's easy to miss, which I did when I turned too late and had to backtrack.

Pulling in at U-Do-It Storage, I tapped the horn a couple of times. Pops had worked the job for several years and Regional let him make his own hours. He'd stayed on the straight and narrow for years, usually closing the office all day Sundays.

The fact that he skipped church to get us on the premises told me plenty.

Pops came outside, one hand raised as he shambled down the steps. He moved slowly and deliberately, like his feet hurt. And, sure enough, I saw he wore house slippers.

I hopped out of the Ford, happy to see him. "Hey, Pops!" He grinned when I hugged him. Business aside, when he had needed help, Pops had called someone he knew and trusted.

"Mr. Gillespie," Lawrence called. Pops let go of me and shook hands with my partner.

"Pleasure to meet you."

"The pleasure is mine, sir."

Pops gave Lawrence the onceover. "Say, ain't you Tut Henry's boy?"

Lawrence widened his eyes. "Yes sir. Did you know my father?"

"I sure did. A good man. Sorry to read about his passing."

"I appreciate that," Lawrence said. Tut Henry had been a hard-ass. Decent enough from all accounts but no bending, no bargaining, no looking the other way. It had been a smart move from Pops, mentioning the father to the son who still adored the man.

No hard feelings, right? Right. Moving on.

We talked a minute about times gone by, then hit the office.

Market Price

Temperature-controlled is always good in Georgia, especially in summer. Pops always set his radio to jazz and Horace Silver's "Lonely Woman" played in the background. He stepped behind the counter and retrieved a set of keys from a drawer.

"Tell me about this unit that's giving you problems," I said.

"Sure. Well, I had a lady come in and rent the unit a couple months back. High-class lady," Pops said. "Came in with a man, white. I'm pretty sure she's white."

"What do you mean?" Lawrence asked.

"She had herself all wrapped up. Wasn't hot then, so it probably wasn't uncomfortable. She wore shades so I couldn't see her eyes, and like I said, she looked white but ..." he shrugged. "She wore a hat, had long hair. Straight as a damn board and shiny – I mean *shiny* black. Could 'a been a wig but it looked like the real thing to me."

"Okay, anything else that made her stand out?"

"She dressed high-end. Good stuff. Brand names. Carried herself like she was used to the good life if you know what I mean. We usually don't get high on the hog types renting here, to be honest."

He continued his description of the encounter as we left the office. We took our time, walking in between the buildings to get to the one that counted.

"The man with her was muscle. She did all the talking. When she finished, she just turned around and walked off. He paid in cash. Six months, up front. It ain't that big a wad of cash but plenty big enough.

And it all seemed off. Something felt off to me."

"Okay," Lawrence said. "Did you see a car or --?" "I did. A white SUV. I might have 'em on surveillance." "Tell me why you called. What happened?" I asked.

"Jo, I got a call this morning at my house from a friend renting a unit here. Church member. Said they went into the building where their unit is, and they liked to've been sick 'cause of a smell." "Uh-oh," Lawrence said.

"Well, they weren't fooling. I went in there before I called you and I didn't open it all the way because --." He shook his head, then sighed.

"Jo, I've been in a war, and I've been in a prison. I know what dead smells like."

Lawrence and I both stopped in our tracks. I braced myself as I watched Lawrence's rosy cheeks disappear behind a sudden pallor. This sounded more and more like a horror show waiting for us.

And, like I said at the start, a few minutes later I was bent over from the smell Pops warned us about. Lawrence pinched his nose while Pops held a bandanna over his.

"She's always done this," Lawrence announced, like that made it okay.

"Don't I know it," Pops said. "I can't figure out how the hell she ever worked for the police."

"Man." I straightened up and placed a forearm over my nose, looking at them with still-watering eyes. "We're going to *have* to call if it's a body."

"I'd like to know what it is if it ain't one."

Lawrence – wanting an up-close and personal experience for some ungodly reason – knelt and stuck his head under the door Pops partially rolled up for us.

"Fuck!" He jumped up. "Mr. Gillespie, call the police, get 'em out here right now."

His words sent a chill over me. I already knew. Hell, we all knew.

His eyes glittered, an anguished expression on his face as he turned to me. I stepped towards him, ready but not ready for what he said. "Jo. There are at least three bodies in there."

⌘⌘⌘

It didn't take long for a literal quiet-as-a-tomb storage unit to transform into a hub of activity. Cops were there in less than five minutes, locking down the area after seeing the gruesome spectacle in Building B. The usual ensued -- flashing lights, a blocked street, crime scene tape. Folks showed up, rubbernecking, shouting, screaming, trying to take photos on iPhones.

By that time, Lawrence and I had masked up and Pops had been walked to his office, a uniform outside the door. "Don't say anything to anybody," I told him.

The medical examiner, a no-holds-barred woman named Jeanne Cohen, arrived with her bag of tricks. We exchanged hellos and she stepped into the unit proper. We gave her plenty of room and stayed out of her way, teetering on the threshold. Four bodies were laid out in formation, a macabre welcoming committee. Blood – old and new -- spackled the unit's floor and walls.

"Oh dear," she sighed.

"Right?"

"This reminds me of a horror movie I saw once," she said.

"Once is enough when it's like this," Lawrence cracked.

We hung around because everyone, including Jeanne, said we needed to be available. "We're going to get grilled," Lawrence murmured.

A solid baritone suddenly echoed through the hall. "Every time I think I've gotten rid of you two birds, you swoop back down and shit on everything."

I knew that voice. I turned and saw Pat McCurdy staring at me and – nearby – the last bit of sick I'd brought up.

"Jo, I see you're up to your usual tricks," he said. He clapped me on the nearest shoulder, then extended the courtesy of a handshake to Lawrence.

He breezed past us and the detail. No big deal, right. Then he got inside the unit.

"Jesus," he muttered. He smeared Vicks across his upper lip to cut the worst of the stink. "How long, Jeannie?"

"Hard to say, but this one?" She pointed to the freshest in the gruesome quartet. "Maybe two days. I'll know more when I get 'em downtown. Sooner the better."

"A serial killer. Just what we need," Pat said.

"Don't jump to conclusions, McCurdy." Jeanne's tone held a slight scold. "Might be a spree," she said, and then she shook her head, her dreadlocks swinging. "But I doubt it."

"So, what've we got right now?" Pat asked.

Lawrence and I put our heads together while Pat and Jeanne yammered. Before long, people would show up, people with credentials – real and alleged – wanting the scoop for the next day's headlines. Lawrence said the situation could be the worst since the Atlanta child murders. I agreed.

"No identification found. All four seemed in good shape before shuffling off their mortal coils. Literally." Jeanne looked over at a body being painstakingly maneuvered into a body bag. Slippage starts sooner than folks think.

"All four are Caucasian males," she said. "In their thirties, early forties. They have all their teeth or at least very good dental work. They should be easy to find if they're in the system and I figure they are somewhere if not here. No tattoos. No tracks." She straightened up, finished for now. "These were probably upper-middle or middle-class guys. Manicures on two of them. Tans. One was manscaped. These boys took care of themselves."

"Think they knew each other?" Pat asked.

Jeanne shrugged. "Maybe. They didn't die at the same time. Let's get 'em downtown. And McCurdy? Something else." Pat moved closer.

"Yeah?" he asked.

Lawrence motioned me over with a subtle nod. While I didn't want to get any closer than I already had, I had seen worse, I'm a professional, plus my partner needed me.

"Does it look like this guy maybe had surgery recently?" Lawrence whispered as we heard Jeanne say, "surgical wound."

Market Price

I leaned in. This earned a scowl from one of Jeanne's assistants, which I ignored.

Nobody touched the body, of course. But I easily spotted a purpled bumpy ridge trailing around his side, from abdomen to flank, just under his ribcage, along with --.

"Stitches," I whispered.

Lawrence nodded. "Stitches," he murmured. "*Grace.*"

I widened my eyes at him as he wiggled his brows. We stood there for a second as everything sunk in. But following a grump from Pat McCurdy, we vacated the unit while the bodies were taken care of by the real professionals. We walked closely behind our ex-captain, Lawrence asking if we could view the recording Pops had mentioned to us and, we guessed, the police.

He agreed immediately. We still had a good relationship with McCurdy and had helped him more than once with information. Plus, it didn't hurt that we had been one of his better teams and maintained that good relationship with him, blustering aside.

We viewed what turned out to be a near-useless, static-heavy recording of the car and the couple Pops identified as the ones renting the unit. We stepped outside with McCurdy, who maintained his composure. The sun hung low in the sky and all we had were four bodies in various states of death.

More bad news? The paperwork the woman had filled out for Pops proved bogus. Of course.

Lawrence and I hoped to see our respective homes before dark. Since we didn't work for the city, we got out earlier than her finest. I didn't hear any complaints.

We knew there was the possibility we'd get another call from McCurdy to tie up any loose ends. We weren't worried about it, but I checked on Pops, who seemed fine. We wouldn't have left otherwise.

⌘⌘⌘

Later at the house, Lawrence downed what remained of his after dinner drink. No brunch but we had picked up dinner from The Family Jewels. That restaurant is choice and Lawrence deserved it.

"Jesus. This is going to be a PR nightmare, sorry to sound like McCurdy. Everybody and his brother will go apeshit," Lawrence said.

"It's the full moon tomorrow. Wonder how many cases we'll get outta people riding the fumes from this one?"

"Jeannie called it. Those guys were in good shape."

"Weird," I said. "And that surgical scar? That gave me the creeps. It's like somebody nabbed the guy when he left the hospital."

"No dregs of society, so to speak. Not addicts, I bet."

"Yeah? I'll still bet on drugs being in their system," I said. "I can't see anyone sitting still while they get carved up and who knows what else."

"Who knows what else," Lawrence whispered. "Why do we get all the crazies?"

"Oh buddy. Everybody's getting all the crazies now."

We talked to Grace who knows plenty about weird things, weird people, weird habits, and places. She has to know for her writing, her fans, her own interests. She's simply wired that way. We thought we might get another perspective – a very different one, at that – on why someone would do this.

She didn't disappoint.

"I took a deep dive into why this legend is popping up again. People are unsure who the enemy is now, so everyone is the enemy. Women have always been the enemy so it's okay to bash or beat them, rape them, kill them and now they're supposedly going after men, taking them apart and selling them off piece by piece for money. Sounds nuts, but that's another twist on this.

"Aaand, it's a foreign country doing this because? USA, USA, USA!" she chanted, deepening her voice to sound like the mostly male crowds at protests and sports events we'd been seeing. "Home team, in other words.

Market Price

They're coming after us. If we're not careful, they'll beat us."

"What else?" Lawrence asked. "We don't know if they all were cut on but that one we saw sure was. And recently."

"Yeah," she nodded. "And it could be somebody doing this just to throw people off the real game."

I leaned forward, puzzled. "What's the real game?"

"They're really after one particular person but need to make it look like something else." She shrugged. "They don't care who they grind up as long as they get their target."

"Jesus."

"That's why this week's paper has a neat little name for the killer: 'The Organ Grinder.'"

The door opened and Carter blew in. Dressed in his usual pristine white Oxford and jeans, he still looked rumpled. That came across because he was upset, hungry, and – he admitted – tired.

"Kip McDonald isn't missing anymore," he said. "He's been found."

"Is he okay?"

"Sort of."

Lawrence stood up, and I could tell he felt as jittery as I did. We all stood, staring at Carter. We must have looked like we were in a war room to Mattie.

"What ... are we celebrating? Should I pour everyone a drink?" she asked.

"What do you mean, sort of?" I said.

"They dumped him outside Grady Hospital."

"Jesus."

"Yeah. He had a note on him." He shook his head, gritting his teeth.

"And I mean on him. His collarbone. Someone pinned it to his flesh." "Holy shit."

Carter shook his head, an explosive sigh escaping him. "Sorry. It's just --. I'm going over there now."

Grace sank back down on the couch.

"Abigail wants an investigation," he said. "A private one. She doesn't trust the cops. Her words. I gotta go, guys. She's waiting on me in Carter's room."

"We'll follow you."

⌘⌘⌘

Kip's exclusive private room was deeply, profoundly quiet. He talked dreamily to his mother as the morphine kept him from screaming his guts out. She held his hand, smiling at her one and only baby. I remembered Carter had said Abigail McDonald's given name had been hellcat. She didn't look like a hellcat now.

"I met her at the party," he croaked. His pale eyes darted around the room and rested on the three of us standing beside the bed. "The birthday party for Carter. She was – beyond beautiful."

I nodded. Abigail McDonald held his hand. I had to hand it to her. She was tough enough to be tender which is what he needed. He needed his mom. He needed to think things would be okay, that things were under control again now that Mom was here. Everybody needs that sometimes, I guess.

"She had someone with her. They wanted a threesome and – sorry, Ma." He attempted a smile, a brave face for the woman who didn't have enough money in the world to help him any more than she already had.

"So, I went with them. We drove over to the Four Seasons. Sat in the bar for a quick drink. Negotiate."

"When did you know you were in trouble, Kip?" I asked. No need to really grill him but dammit, I wanted to know. I wanted these bastards caught.

"When I woke up." He made a noise like he was attempting a laugh, but it sounded more like a hit dog. He would have a rough time of it and sooner than he realized.

"There was a note," Abigail said.

"Anyone have that note?" Lawrence murmured.

"The police," Abigail said. "The doctors took it off him and I read it. The police thought I might recognize the handwriting, but I didn't." She placed her free hand on her son's arm, as the other rested lightly on his clenched fist.

Tears filled her eyes, but Abigail McDonald managed to keep them from spilling down her face, a face free of makeup. No worries over ruining her mascara. No concerns over her lipstick smearing. She kept up what composure she had for the wreck that laid before her on a pristine bed.

"A hospital can't really help but go ahead and make the call." She turned to face me. I saw her ageing each second as her son's countdown took him closer to the edge.

"That's what was in the note," she said.

Kip moved, suddenly restless. "She took a kidney, right, Ma? The Organ Grinder took a kidney."

Abigail McDonald leaned forward and kissed him as his eyes closed and his breathing slowed.

"No, darling," she whispered. "She took both."

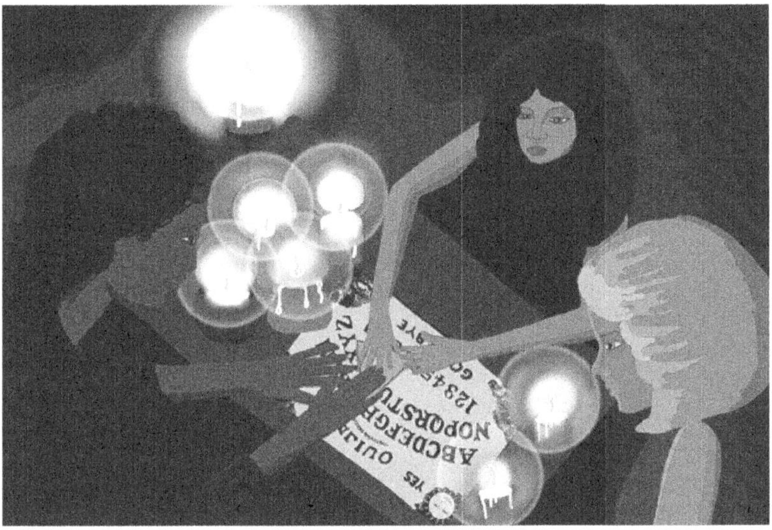
YES
ABCDEFGH
NOPQRSTU

School's Out
by Jill Hand

After the tragedy everyone agreed it was a bad idea to build a school on top of a graveyard. Accusing fingers were pointed and blame was placed, as it always is when something terrible happens which in hindsight could have been prevented. If the Titanic had only had enough lifeboats! If Andrew Carnegie and his wealthy pals had maintained the dam at their private hunting and fishing club before it collapsed, flooding Johnstown, Pennsylvania and killing 2,200 people! If the intelligence community had paid more attention to the threat posed by Al-Qaeda before September 11, 2001! If. If. If.

Hindsight is full of ifs.

No one intended for the above-mentioned calamities to happen. Certainly, no one intended to leave bodies behind in the Van Brunt family graveyard. When the last of the Van Brunts – a looney old lady named Cornelia Van Brunt - died in 1901, bringing an end to a line whose members had once been numerous and influential, the town bought the property at auction. It tore down the 200-year-old old Dutch Colonial house, with its small-paned windows and rounded gambrel roof. Then it leased the land to farmers, reserving three acres on which to build a school.

The school was intended to provide for the education of the town's children in kindergarten through twelfth grade. Its outer walls were made of red bricks, in the ponderous Richardsonian Romanesque style that was popular at the time, all pointed windows and recessed doorways and arches supported by clusters of squat columns. It had a dizzying number of gables shaped like inverted capital-letter Vs.

As the pièce de résistance there was a bell tower, equipped with a bronze bell weighing 2,050 pounds, thirty pounds less than the Liberty Bell. The bell was dubbed Zeke, in honor of Ezekiel Steuben, a general

School's Out

in the Continental Army and the town's founder. It rang at the opening and close of each school day.

The people of Steuben, New Jersey, were proud of their new school (those who didn't complain about the increase in the school tax.) Attendees at the ribbon-cutting ceremony took note of its central heating and electric lights and indoor plumbing and separate rooms for each grade level, as well as separate entrances for boys and girls. That last item was intended to discourage tomfoolery and flirtation.

In short, Steuben School had the latest in up-to-date pedagogical accoutrements as they were reckoned in the early years of the twentieth century. The townspeople felt the fine new school made them superior to the residents of neighboring communities, who had to make do with one-room schoolhouses lit by oil lamps and warmed by potbelly woodburning stoves.

Alas, what was once the height of architectural fashion began to seem dated and even hideous as the decades passed. By 1970, when I attended Steuben School, it had come to resemble something from a Hammer horror film.

The once-bright red bricks had become stained and dirty, the result of withstanding almost seven decades of harsh Northeastern winters. The slate roof tiles were streaked with blue-black algae, while the bell tower had become sullied with the guano of crows and bats. The bell itself – old Zeke - no longer rang. The last time someone tried to ring it, to mark V-E Day, it gave a single, hollow clang before the wooden cradle holding it in place split in half.

Zeke, free for the first time since 1903, rolled down the steps of the tower and out the door at the bottom, narrowly missing the school's custodian, Joe Siciliano. Joe had taken it upon himself to ring the bell in celebration of the defeat of Hitler and his goose-stepping minions.

Joe leaped out of the way, narrowly avoiding being flattened by the runaway bell. Heart pounding, he uttered a blistering curse at it in Italian. Thrusting his thumb between the first two fingers of his right hand and wiggling it, he shouted, "Kiss my ass, you lousy piece-a junk!"

The bell came to rest at the foot of a tall pine tree, where it stayed until it was taken away and melted down for scrap. The bell tower remained empty, except for birds and bats. By 1970, when this story begins, Steuben School was a sad husk of its former self. The sight of the semi-abandoned building, its many gables, pointed like witches' hats, rearing into a flaming orange October sunset as bats flew around the tower, was enough to make shivers run up the spines of even the bravest teenage boys.

I use the term "semi-abandoned" because by then, the top two floors were no longer in use. With the completion of a consolidated high school in nearby Bradbury in 1955, Steuben students in grades nine through twelve were bused the four miles to Bradbury Township Regional High. That left the top floor of Steuben School empty, its scuffed wooden floorboards gathering dust as spiders spun webs in the corners of the high-ceilinged rooms.

Despite Joe Siciliano scattering poison pellets, a flourishing population of rats and mice moved in where once girls in poodle skirts and bobby socks and boys in neatly pressed chinos and Oxford shirts, the collars turned up to show they were cool, learned about civics and algebra and what Herman Melville was getting at in *Moby-Dick*.

Around the same time as the high schoolers started being bused to Bradbury Regional, a middle school opened in Steuben. Students in grades six through eight, who previously would have had their classrooms on the second floor now went there instead.

That left the ground floor the only part of Steuben School still in use. That and the basement. The basement was where the dead kids were.

Aunt Rose, my mom's older sister, was the one who told me about the dead kids. She casually mentioned that she used to attend Girl Scout meetings in the school's basement, where the rifle range was.

Surprised, I asked. "There was a rifle range in the basement?"

"Oh yeah," she said nonchalantly, as if there was nothing unusual about that. "That's where we practiced for our marksmanship badge."

"The Girl Scouts had a marksmanship badge?"

School's Out

"Well, sure," she said. "You mean they don't now?"

I was a Girl Scout. As far as I knew we didn't have a marksmanship badge. I told her so.

Aunt Rose shook her head. "Kids today are soft. How do you expect to defend yourself against an invasion if you don't know how to fire a rifle?"

I shrugged. I hadn't thought about that. "Did you guys think you were going to be invaded?"

Aunt Rose lit a Virginia Slim and blew a cloud of smoke. We were sitting on my front porch when this conversation took place. Smoking wasn't allowed in the house. Mom's orders.

"We were fairly certain of it. There was a war going on. German U-boats were sighted off the coast. One surfaced near a beach in Long Island and some German saboteurs got out," she said.

"Gee," I said. "What did they do?"

"Nothing. They were caught right away. They intended to blow up bridges and power plants and department stores owned by Jewish people and who knows what else. We had to be prepared, in case any Germans showed up in Steuben. That's why the Girl Scouts learned how to shoot rifles."

I could easily imagine Aunt Rose firing a rifle at ranks of advancing Nazis. She was a tough cookie. A shop steward with the United Auto Workers union, she worked on an assembly line, building tractors and other agricultural equipment. I thought any Nazi who tangled with Aunt Rose would regret it.

"That's kind of cool," I said. All we did in Girl Scouts was sing stupid songs like "The Bear Went Over the Mountain," and make useless crafts, such as a thing made out of yarn and popsicle sticks called an *Ojo de Dios*. "Thanks to Girl Scouts, I can field-strip a rifle, clean it, and put it back together in under five minutes," Aunt Rose said proudly.

"What happened to the rifle range?" I asked. It was gone by the time I started kindergarten. All that was in the cavernous basement was a cafeteria that smelled of grease and sour milk, and two restrooms, one for girls and one for boys. Joe Siciliano, the custodian, had a little cubby hole office down there, too. It was where he hung out, when he wasn't poisoning rodents or cleaning graffiti off desks or sweeping up puddles of puke with a push-broom, using pink stuff that came out of a big metal drum and looked and smelled like ground-up pencil erasers.

You might be surprised by how often kids vomit in school. Nerves over test-taking and having to eat horrible school lunches like Salisbury steak and green beans that aren't green but a sickly, dingy gray, tended to cause the old digestive track to rebel and hit the eject button. Kids, especially little kids, specialize in peeing their pants and puking.

Aunt Rose threw her cigarette butt into the bucket filled with sand on the bottom step of the porch. My mother had placed it there for use by her big sister and any other visitors who had the nicotine habit. "They closed the firing range after Sylvia Dorfman blew a hole in the wall with a machine gun and dead bodies fell out," she said.

"What?" My eyes must have been as big as saucers because she grinned.

"You never heard about this before?" she asked.

"Are you talking about Ms. Dorfman, the librarian?" I tried to picture prim Ms. Dorfman, with her permanent wave and handknit sweaters, her glasses hanging on a chain around her neck, firing a machine gun. I couldn't do it.

"The very same. Back then, Sylvia was a little hellion. She used to give our troop leader, Mrs. Carlisle, conniption fits," Aunt Rose said.

"Where did she get a machine gun?" I was only ten, but I knew machine guns weren't something that could be easily acquired.

"Mrs. Carlisle's brother-in-law, Bradley, brought it. He was a state trooper. He got it out of the evidence locker at the state police barracks. He thought we'd be interested in seeing it because we were learning about firearms. It wasn't a smart thing to do, but then Brad Carlisle wasn't the sharpest quill on the porcupine," she said.

"What happened?" I asked. "Did he let the girls shoot it?"

"He did not," Aunt Rose said. "He put it together, set it on a tripod,

85

loaded it with an ammunition belt filled with pointy cartridges, and showed us where the trigger was. He explained that it was very dangerous, and we weren't to touch it. He said we should just look at it.

Then he excused himself and went to use the restroom." "And that's when Ms. Dorfman fired it?" I asked.

"Not at first. At first, we only looked at it. Mrs. Carlisle was sitting off to the side, writing a letter. Every so often she'd look up, tell us to be careful, then go back to writing. We got bored waiting for Trooper Carlisle to come back so somebody, I forget who, dared Sylvia to touch the trigger. She did, but she didn't just touch it; she pulled it all the way back. She said later that she didn't think it would go off." "Holy cow!" I said.

"Holy cow is right," said Aunt Rose. "There was a clattering roar as it sprang into life. The girls, Sylvia included, screamed, and ran for the basement stairs. Mrs. Carlisle dove to the floor. Trooper Carlisle ran in from Joe Siciliano's little office where he'd been talking to Joe, swearing a blue streak. By then, the machine gun had fallen over and was lying on its side, still fastened to the tripod. It fired all the bullets on the belt. They went straight through the brick wall, blowing a big hole in it, and cutting through another brick wall, this one a lot older, blowing a hole in that.

"When it got quiet, we crept back inside. There was a sharp tang of gunpowder in the air and something else, something nasty and rotten. Brad Carlisle stood there, frozen, in a haze of smoke, looking like he didn't know whether to shit or wind his watch. He was staring down at a pile of broken bricks, and a heap of dirt and dead bodies that were mostly bones."

"Holy cow!" I said again. "Did he get in trouble?"

"If he did, I never heard about it," Aunt Rose said. "He was still a state trooper when he was killed about five years later, chasing a stolen car on Route 46 one winter night. His trooper car skidded on a patch of ice and rolled over."

"He wasn't wearing a seatbelt?" I always wore a seatbelt. Mom insisted on it.

Aunt Rose lit another Virginia Slim. "He should have been, that way he might still be alive, collecting a pension, but like I said, Brad Carlisle didn't have much going for him, brain-wise. He failed to buckle up. When they pried him out, using hydraulic rescue tools, he was dead."

Aunt Rose said the bodies that fell out of the wall belonged to children. They had been buried in a common grave. There was no grave marker. There was nothing to identify them; they were just five kids thrown into a brick-walled hole in the ground.

When the school went up, the builders weren't as careful as they should have been to make sure all the bodies were removed from the old Van Brunt family cemetery. There are laws about that now. The Family and Private Burial Grounds Preservation Act of 2012 stipulates that no new construction or excavation can be done within fifteen feet of a private burial ground unless approval is given, in writing, by a descendant of each person interred there.

With the last of the Van Brunts having died in 1901, there was nobody left to ask for permission. From what I read later in the records of the Steuben Historical Society, the graveyard at the Van Brunt homestead was duly dug up and the occupants of the graves relocated to Valley View Cemetery. Except, as it turned out, for the bodies of the five children in the common grave. The construction workers who dug the school's basement must have overlooked those. Maybe by accident.

Maybe on purpose, if time was running out before the school had to be finished.

The children could have been Van Brunts, or they could have been servants, or slaves. There used to be slavery in New Jersey. It wasn't abolished here until 1804. A lot of people don't know that, but it's true.

According to Aunt Rose, the medical examiner said the bodies belonged to children between the ages of ten and fourteen, three girls and two boys. He judged the cause of death to have been smallpox. It struck the New York-New Jersey area in 1792, and again in 1894. By the condition of the bones, he thought the children were victims of the 1792 outbreak.

School's Out

"They were down there a long time," I said. Aunt Rose nodded somberly. *Down there, in the dark*, I thought, and felt goosebumps pop up on my arms. I thought about how it must have been for them, slung into a hasty grave, no coffins, no stuffed animals, or favorite toys tucked in with them, not even a gravestone with their names on it to mark their final resting place.

I was ten years old, and easily shocked. I was soon to learn that worse things happen, such as what happened when I had a séance to try and contact the dead kids.

Aunt Rose gave me the idea. She had no children of her own. I believe that she loved me, considering me to be the next best thing to a daughter, but she also liked screwing with me. She thought my parents coddled me, which they did. I was an only child and was thoroughly spoiled, given just about every new toy Mattel produced. My bedroom closet and dresser held enough clothes and accessories to outfit three girls.

If I wanted something all I had to do was ask and it would appear. To Aunt Rose's way of thinking, I needed to be frightened every now and then, for my own good, to toughen me up. Otherwise, I was in danger of becoming what she called a "namby-pamby," a wimp, in other words. "You know what would be fun," she said, taking a drag from her Virginia Slim. "You could have a séance in the school basement. Try and contact those dead kids."

I knew what a séance was, from movies and TV. My friends and I had tried having one once, at a sleepover at Sherri Nelson's house, using her Ouija board.

The Ouija board didn't work. The planchette refused to move, failing to put us in touch with President Kennedy or Marilyn Monroe or even with a dead person who wasn't famous, like Sherri's grandmother.

"You could borrow your mom's keys and let yourself into the school some night. Take a few of your friends. Bring candles and have a séance," Aunt Rose suggested.

"I don't think Mom would let me borrow her keys," I said. My mom ran the school cafeteria. She had a key to the front door. It was a massive bronze thing, like a key to a castle. On the same keyring was another, smaller key. It unlocked a door in the rear, next to a loading platform, where pallets of school supplies and ingredients for school lunches were delivered.

Aunt Rose raised her eyebrows. "I didn't say 'ask,' I said 'borrow.' Take the keys out of your mom's purse and go have a séance. It'll be fun. Your friends will think you're a hot shot," she said.

Séances, ones that work, aren't fun. They're terrifying. I didn't know that then. What I wanted was what most kids want: the approval of my peers. If sneaking into the school at night and having a séance would make me popular, I was all for it. My thoughts instantly went to how I was going to pull it off.

I asked, "What do I need candles for?"

"Atmosphere," Aunt Rose replied. "Ghosts only come out when it's dark. Also, you don't want to turn on the overhead lights. Somebody might notice they're on when they shouldn't be and call the police."

I was young, but I wasn't stupid. Given Aunt Rose's history of screwing with me, I needed to confirm that her story about the bodies wasn't made up. The next day in school, I raised my hand and asked to be excused to use the restroom. I went downstairs to the basement. I'd been down there hundreds of times, but I'd never really looked at the walls before. Sure enough, there was a big section of bricks that were a slightly different color than the rest.

"What are you doing?"

It was Joe Siciliano, the custodian. White-haired, stooped over, Joe had pushed a broom and cleaned toilets at Steuben School for most of his life, giving him a proprietary interest in the old building. If a kid was staring at a wall, mesmerized, he wanted to know why.

"Is this where the rifle range used to be?" I asked.

"Yeah, during the war."

Joe was of an age when "the war" meant the Second World War, not the one in Korea or the war we were having then, the one in Vietnam.

School's Out

"Is it true the Girl Scouts blew a hole in the wall with a machine gun, and dead bodies fell out?"

I thought he'd laugh and ask me where I'd heard that. Instead, he said, "It was Brad Carlisle's fault. What a moron, letting little girls play with a machine gun." So, it was true.

Now I'll tell you something interesting. You know the saying, "Knowledge is power?" I'll amend that to "Knowledge *has* power."

The right sort of knowledge (or the wrong sort, depending on how you view it) can be powerful indeed. My newfound knowledge about the dead kids buried in a common grave behind the basement wall, coupled with something I didn't know, because my parents didn't tell me, made me every bit as dangerous as the machine gun Trooper Carlisle brought to show the Girl Scouts. More dangerous, in fact, because nobody died as the result of the trooper's poor judgement.

It turned out I had the ability to contact the dead. It was a talent I inherited from my mom's grandmother, Carmilla Waldeck. She'd been famous in her day for making furniture dance in midair. Under her control, tables gave off raps in answer to questions put to the dead. It was said that she'd been able to make ghosts materialize and drift through the séance room.

Harry Houdini, the famous escape artist, was a dedicated debunker of phony mediums. He investigated her. Afterwards he refused to comment. Not a single word. And Houdini usually had plenty to say to the press when he unmasked a fake medium. The fact that he said nothing makes me wonder whether he thought she was the real deal.

Eventually, something happened at one of her séances that put an end to her career. One of the four sitters – that's what they call people who go to a séance - clawed her own eyes out. Another jumped through a closed window, cutting himself to ribbons. A third dropped dead of a heart attack. The fourth had a stroke and died the next day. As for Carmilla, she spent the rest of her life in a mental hospital.

What happened at my great-grandmother's last seance?

Her daughter, my Grandma Enid, never spoke about it, except to say once, "People said something must have got in that shouldn't have." She refused to say any more, not about what got in, or where it went after everyone in the room either died or went insane.

I learned all that later. All I knew then was that my mom had "feelings" that allowed her to do things like guess the correct number of dried beans in the jar at the county fair. One of those feelings told her to pull over abruptly when we were driving home one time. I was in the passenger seat, seatbelt buckled, the way Mom insisted. We were rolling along, chatting about this and that.

Far up ahead, a drunk driver was in the wrong lane, barreling straight toward us. Mom couldn't have seen him, but she *knew*. She broke off what she was saying and hauled the steering wheel hard to the right, the tires bumping as she drove off the road and into a field. Moments later the drunk driver whizzed past, missing us, and hitting the car behind us, totaling it, and seriously injuring the driver.

The sound of the crash was still echoing in my ears as Mom pulled back onto the road, on her way to find a pay phone and call an ambulance. "I had a feeling something was wrong," she said.

Aunt Rose didn't have feelings, not that kind, anyway. Neither did her mom, my Grandma Enid. Grandma Enid didn't know who was on the phone without picking up the receiver, in those days before Caller ID. But Mom knew. "Don't answer," she'd say. "It's your friend Vera Ecker. You know how she is; once she starts gabbing, she never shuts up."

Grandma Enid would answer anyway. Sure enough, it was always who my mother said it was.

Mom's "feelings" were a diminished version of my great grandmother's abilities, a gentle woodland stream compared to the mighty Niagara Falls of power that enabled Carmilla to make furniture dance and ghosts materialize. Charles Fort, the writer, and researcher of anomalous phenomena, called such abilities wild talents. Carmilla's wild talent came roaring down the bloodline to me, exploding in full force at my first and last séance, the one that began in the school basement.

Nick Westover rode up on his bicycle as I stood in his driveway,

School's Out

talking to his sister Barbara. Due to a fluke in the school calendar, both Nick and Barbara were in my grade, even though their birthdays were almost a year apart.

Nick's bike was a wondrous sight to behold. It had ape-hanger handlebars and a banana seat and was plastered all over with stickers made by Wacky Packages, a division of Topps, the chewing gum and baseball card people. The stickers advertised joke products like Weakies, Breakfast of Chumps, and Dampers disposable diapers. Wacky Packs, as we called them, represented the absolute pinnacle of adolescent humor.

Nick had further customized his ride by attaching a transistor radio to the handlebars. As he peddled up, Jan and Dean were singing about Surf City, where there were two girls for every boy.

Nick skidded to a stop, the front tire of his bike coming within inches of the toes of my Keds.

"Hey, losers," he said to Barbara and me.

"If you'd run into me, I would have punched you in the nose," I told him.

"I'd like to see you try," he replied.

Those pleasantries out of the way, he got off his bike, turned off the radio, and sat down cross-legged in the grass. "What're you losers up to? Having a meeting of the Ugly Club?"

"I'm having a séance in the school basement. It's going to be at night. People are sneaking out to go to it," I said.

Nick's eyes lit up. Sneaking out of the house at night was something teenagers did. We younger kids aspired to do it, but so far there hadn't been anywhere to sneak out to. We were too young to hitch a ride into the city to go to a rock concert, or to hang out in the woods, drinking beer and smoking. An offer to sneak out to a séance was about as good as it was going to get, and Nick wanted in.

"That doesn't sound as stupid as most of your ideas. I'll go," he said.

"I didn't invite you," I said.

"I'm going or else Barbara doesn't go. Case closed."

"You can't stop me from going," Barbara told him indignantly.

He smiled sweetly. "Mom can stop you, if I tell her."

Barbara informed him that tattletales should go to jail and stick their heads in a garbage pail. Then she relented. "Okay, you can go." "Smart move. I'm bringing Ricky Baumer," he said.

Ricky Baumer was the star of the fifth grade. Smart, athletic, good looking in a junior Beach Boys sort of way, he was the most popular boy in our class. If Ricky Baumer was going to my séance, it meant that some of his popularity would rub off on me.

Like a society hostess, I'd made up a guest list of people I owed favors to, as well as those who would bring me the most cachet by accepting my invitation. Sherri Nelson was going because I'd gone to her sleepover party. Barbara was going because she was my best friend. Cathy Mitchell was going because her parents had a Shore house where I'd stayed one weekend.

With Nick and Ricky, the guest list was complete. It would be a small but select gathering. Besides me, there would be two boys and three girls, just like the dead kids whose grave was disturbed. Two boys and three girls. And me, the unsuspecting conduit.

Sneaking out proved to be easy. On Sunday night, I waited for my parents to go to their room. As soon as I heard the theme music for *The David Susskind Show* start from the portable TV on Dad's dresser, I crept downstairs and out the back door, flashlight in hand.

It was shortly after 11 p.m.

The school was three blocks away. I'd walked there dozens of times, but never at night before, by myself. It was spooky seeing the huge old building, its windows dark, silhouetted in the moonlight. *Looming*, I thought uneasily. *It's looming.*

There was a scuffling sound behind me. Then something struck me between the shoulder blades. I whirled around.

"Ha-ha gotcha!" said Nick. He'd crept up and thrown a piece of gravel. Ricky Baumer was with him, and Barbara.

School's Out

"I brought candles," said Barbara. She held up her lunchbox, on which Barnabas Collins from *Dark Shadows* leered and bared his fangs.

"I brought matches," said Ricky, tossing his head to shake his hair out of his eyes.

We stood there, looking at the darkened building. I felt in my jacket pocket for the keys I'd swiped from Mom's purse. Suddenly I didn't want to go inside. Something about going inside felt wrong, but that was silly. It was only our school. Nothing bad could happen in our school. We'd have some spooky fun and go home. Nothing to it.

The next day would be Monday, a school day. We would boast to our classmates about what we'd done and bask in the glow of their envy.

That was the plan, anyway.

We waited by the loading dock at the rear of the building for Sherri and Cathy to arrive. Looking out over the darkened playground, Nick pointed to the swings. He asked Ricky, "What would you do if those started swinging by themselves?"

"Man, I'd run away so fast I'd leave a cloud of dust behind, like the Road Runner. Meep-meep!" said Ricky, and we all laughed.

Just then Sherri appeared from around the corner of the building, accompanied by Cathy. "I brought the Ouija board," Sherri said, holding out the box with the mystical board inside.

Cathy giggled. "I can't believe we're doing this; this is so cool." I unlocked the door, and we went in.

It was dark in the basement, the only illumination a thin, yellow light filtering through the windows from the sodium vapor lamps on poles outside, no doubt put there to deter vandals. Barbara arranged four candles in glass holders on one of the lunchroom tables. Ricky took out a book of matches and lit them.

"Got 'em all with one match," he said, blowing the flame out with a flourish.

"What do we do?" Nick asked. "Are we supposed to ask the ghosts to come out?" He called, "Hey, ghosts! Come on out!"

We waited. Nothing happened. It was eerily quiet.

"You have to use the Ouija," Sherri said, taking it out of its box. "We all put one finger on this thing, here, and ask questions. The spirits make it move around the board, spelling out messages."

We did as she instructed, each of us placing a finger on the planchette. Sherri asked, "What is your name?"

Slowly, creepily, the planchette began to inch forward, spelling C-A-S…

We watched in breathless fascination, as it slowly slid across the board.

"Oh my god," Cathy whispered.

There was a pause and then it moved again. P-E-R.

Casper.

Nick burst out laughing. Barbara elbowed him in the ribs. "You jerk; you were moving it."

"You should have seen yourselves." Nick made an idiotic face of stunned, babyish amazement, mouth hanging open, eyes goggling.

"Let's try again. Be serious, this time," Sherri said.

We tried again. Nothing happened. The planchette refused to move.

"Maybe it's broken," Ricky said.

"It didn't work the last time, when we tried to contact your grandmother," I reminded Sherri.

We considered what to do next.

"You know," Ricky said slowly, "it could be that the ghosts aren't down here. Kip told me that the reason why they closed the third floor wasn't to save money, like they said. It was because it was haunted. That was the real reason why the high schoolers have to go to Bradbury Regional. Kip said there were faces looking in the windows from outside, dead faces."

He looked around at us, as we pictured dead faces looking through the windows. He went on, "That's not all. None of the kids wanted to use the bathrooms up there because they heard voices coming out of the plumbing. One girl fainted, that's how scary it was."

Kip was Ricky's older brother. He was a senior in high school. As such, his word carried considerable weight with us lowly fifth graders. If Kip said the third floor was haunted then it must be.

"What about the second floor? They closed that, too, when they built the middle school," Cathy said.

"Also haunted," Ricky said crisply. "Not as bad as the third floor, but it's haunted, all right. Kip said so."

We looked at each other. None of us were keen on climbing the squeaky wooden stairs to the abandoned top floor, but nobody wanted to back down and be accused of being chicken.

Finally, Sherri broke the silence. "Let's go up," she said.

We went up. Ricky in the lead, carrying a flashlight, followed by Nick, Sherri, Cathy, Barbara, then me, carrying another flashlight. The flashlight beams sent shadows wobbling and bobbing as we went upstairs, past the familiar, cozy first floor where our classrooms were, bright with bulletin boards and posters advertising bake sales and club activities, past the deserted second floor, where classroom doors and lockers stood open, nothing inside but darkness.

We peered through the glass panel in the door on the landing at empty trophy cases. The floor had accumulated a layer of dust, a single set of footprints showing where Joe Siciliano had made his janitorial journeys. It was as silent as the catacombs of Rome.

We kept going up, to the third floor.

"Third floor, ladies' lingerie, sporting goods, and hair salon," Nick quipped, mimicking an elevator operator. He pushed open the door and we followed him through.

It smelled bad up there, stuffy, and dusty, like Grandma Enid's attic. The rat poison Joe Siciliano scattered must have done its work because there was a dead rat in front of the door to what had been the Home Economics room. Something fluttered past, and we flinched. A bat. One of the bats that made their home in the empty bell tower. At the end of the hallway the door to the tower stood open. Joe must have left it like that, or else the wind blew it open.

"I don't like this," Barbara whispered.

"I do," Nick said. "I like it here, a lot. I think I'll move in."

I looked at the illuminated dial on my watch. The hands stood straight up. Midnight.

"If we're going to have a séance we'd better get started," I said.

Sherri took out the Ouija board and we knelt on the floor around it, our fingers on the planchette. Ricky lit the candles and we started again. "Is anyone there?" Sherri asked. "If anyone's there, speak to us. Give us a sign."

Nothing.

I didn't feel well. The back of my neck ached, and my eyes throbbed. I felt queasy, the way I did when I'd been in the sun too long. I wanted this to be over. I wanted to be home, curled up safe in bed, but I also wanted whatever was up there to come out. I was *hungry* for it to come out. I was certain something was there, watching us. I could feel it watching. I dreaded seeing it, but at the same time I needed to see it. "Come out," I shouted. "Stop hiding and come out." The door to the tower slammed shut.

We leaped to our feet.

The planchette began racing madly around the Ouija board. Without anyone touching it, it zipped from letter to letter, lightning fast, too quick for us to make out what it was saying, if it was saying anything. Then it lifted off the board and slammed into the wall. The Ouija board slid along the floor, toward the door of the tower, which was furiously opening and shutting, the noise booming and echoing in the empty corridor.

Cathy shrieked and ran for the door to the stairs, the rest of us following.

It refused to open.

Nick shoved Cathy aside and tried pulling it, instead of pushing, although we knew perfectly well that wasn't how it opened. You had to push on it to make it open. There was no lock. No way to keep it closed, but it wouldn't open.

Our backs to the door, we looked toward the door of the tower. Footsteps were coming down the stairs, dragging, limping footsteps. The candles in their glass holders flickered and went out, one by one.

"Okay, okay. I've had enough. I'm through with this shit. I'm outta here," panted Ricky. He moved toward the Home Economics room, where the dead rat lay in the doorway.

"Where are you going?" Sherri yelled. "We shouldn't split up, it's when you split up that the monsters get you."

"Fire escape," Ricky wheezed, barely managing to get the words out.

There was a fire escape outside one of the windows in the Home Ec room. If we could get the window open and climb down, we'd escape this nightmare, because nightmare it was. It had to be. It couldn't be really happening. There couldn't be shadowy forms emerging from the door of the abandoned tower. They were shriveled and decayed and were about as tall as we were. They were the five dead kids from the common grave.

"No! Go back! Go away!" I shouted. The others were already inside the Home Ec room. Barbara and Nick had the window open and were climbing over the sill and onto the rusty metal fire escape.

"You called. We came," a girl's voice whispered. It wasn't Sherri or Barbara or Cathy; it was one of the dead girls.

The others were on the fire escape by then. I confronted the dead ones who had answered my call. "Go away!" I shouted.

What happened next was never fully explained. The fire escape was old and rusted, but it should have been able to hold my five friends, none of them weighing more than one-hundred pounds. Instead, it crumbled like stale bread, throwing them forty feet to the asphalt below.

Barbara and Nick died. They were dead when the ambulance got there, summoned by none other than Joe Siciliano. He rented a room in the house next door and had gotten up in the night and looked out the window at the school where he'd worked for most of his life. He told the police he got up to get a drink of water, but I suspect he got up to pee. Old people tend to have weak kidneys, and Joe was seventy-two at the time. He died the following March, after his beloved school was torn down.

Steuben School never reopened after that night when Barbara and Nick died. Ricky died, too, from an asthma attack. He was supposed to carry an inhaler with him, but he didn't that night. I don't know why. Perhaps he forgot, or he thought he wouldn't need it.

Cathy suffered a head injury from the fall and was partially paralyzed. She lives in a group home. I visit her occasionally. I'm not sure if she knows who I am.

Sherri was the least injured of the five, physically, at least. She broke her arm, but that was all. It seemed like she'd be all right, but a week later she walked out of her house one afternoon and never returned. She told her mother she was going to the store to buy a soda, but she never got there. What became of her is still unknown.

How did I escape? I never got onto the fire escape, never entered the room where the dead rat guarded the door. Instead, I turned my back on the ghosts. The door to the stairs opened easily to my touch. I walked through it, went downstairs, and walked outside. I didn't look back to see if anything followed me.

Steuben School was demolished. A wing was added to the middle school for grades K through five. I never attempted another séance, never again tried to contact the dead. I still live in Steuben. I sometimes walk past where the school was. When I do, I walk fast and don't turn my head. There's a housing development there now. It's rumored those houses are "troubled," as if whatever was there the night my friends died is still there. I have a feeling the rumors are right.

THE END

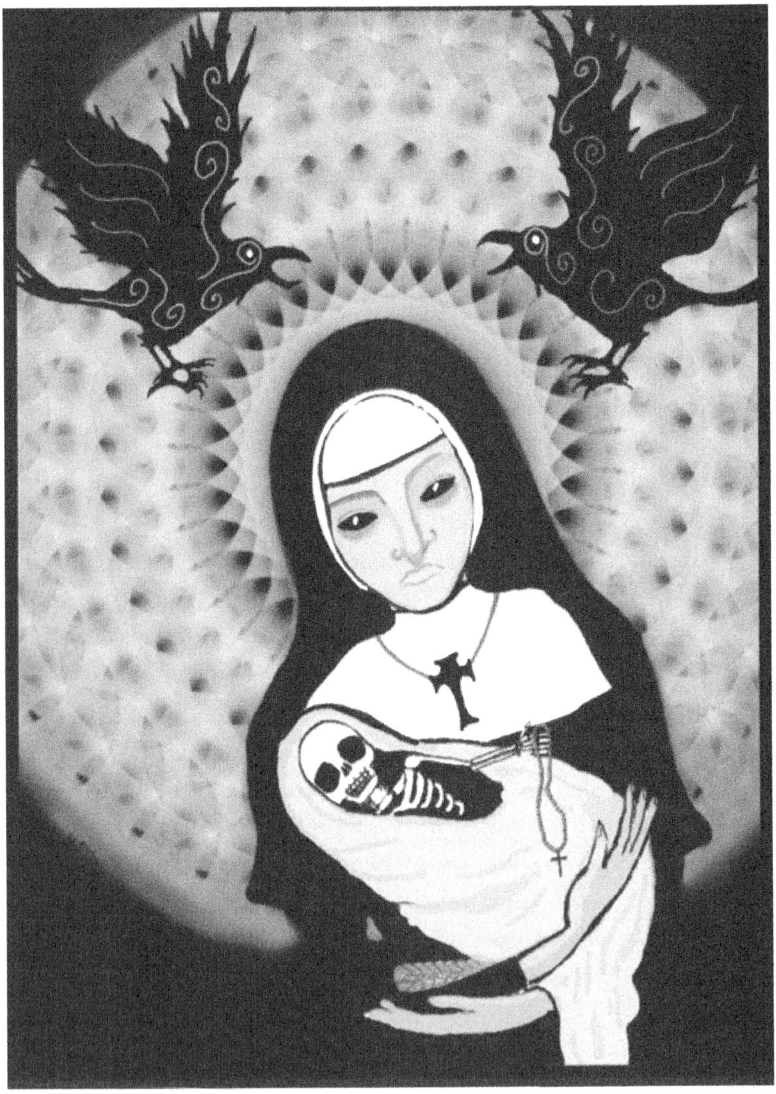

Case#7: The Babes in the Woods
by Nora B. Peevy

To: hodag1986@gmail.com

From: gofish@gmail.com

Subject: Satanic Desecration of Seminary Woods Grotto

October 14, 2020

Amber,

I hope this email finds you well. I'm contacting you off the record. As you know, The St. Francis Police Department has dealt with numerous complaints about occult activity in Seminary Woods and vandalism; we've investigated ritual murder, thankfully, managing to keep it out of the papers. The other detective on my current case is a skeptic, but in my years on the force, I have seen things I can't explain. Archbishop Listecki refuses to meet to discuss anything paranormal connected to Seminary Woods and has discouraged me from investigating the matter. I am looking for answers giving me a deeper insight into this case. I would like you to investigate Seminary Woods. My number is in your father's old directory. I look forward to hearing from you soon.

Detective Bryant

P.S. I've attached a few photos from the crime scene for your eyes only. I hope you have a strong constitution.

I bowed my head and took a moment to center myself before opening the attachments. I checked the baby monitor on my desk. Lily slept on her back, her tiny hands gripping her pink security blanket. I

Case#7: The Babes in the Woods

took a sip of lavender tea from my Pi mug, letting the clean, floral taste wash over my tongue. The scent soothed me. I clicked on the attachments, the first a wide angle shot of the front of the Our Lady of Lourdes Grotto, dedicated to the Blessed Virgin Mary. A park bench sat in front. The black wrought iron gates yawned open. A closeup shot of the lock showed it was cut with a bolt cutter. In another photo, "Nema Natas" was sprayed in red paint across the back wall of the limestone grotto. Both statues of the Blessed Virgin Mary lay beheaded and splashed in a dried rusty substance, possibly blood, whether animal or human, I didn't know. The crosses on the gates were inverted. Something hung from all five, but it was hard to make out in this shot. A small body lay at the center of a red inverted pentacle on the floor of the grotto.

A closeup of one of the black iron gates showed five dead crows strung from the inverted crosses with wide, shiny black ribbons binding their feet together. No blood pooled beneath their corpses. Possibly, they'd been sacrificed someplace else. A closeup photo showed a crow lying on its back on a stainless-steel coroner's table, its beak open, its black tongue extended, and its wings stretched in flight.

The last photograph was a life-size anatomically correct baby girl doll lying naked in the center of the inverted pentacle, the stumps of her arms and legs dipped in crimson paint. Her lips were sliced from her face and her empty eye sockets painted red. The paperweight eyes, blown glass blue eyes with depth, stared out from the doll's vagina. With the acid churning in my stomach, I couldn't finish my tea before bed. I printed both the email and the photos and added them to a new green binder with the label on the spine: Case #7: The Babes in the Woods.

I checked on Lily one last time, her steady breathing and sweet baby smell a balm for my tortured mind. Holly traveled for work. I slipped alone and exhausted between the cool linen sheets, as our giant orange cat, CheezIt, assumed his normal sleeping position, pinning my legs to the mattress and purring himself to sleep. I lay awake in the dark listening to the icy rain pelting the windows and the loud ticking of the clock on my nightstand.

Nora B. Peevy

⌘⌘⌘

The following night, I sat down to research the background information needed for my investigation.

CASE #7: BACKGROUND INFORMATION

Before the Black Hawk War of 1832 Native Americans inhabited all of Wisconsin, but in The Great Chicago Treaty of 1833, Native Americans surrendered their land to the federal government. Prior to 1833, the Potawatomi lived in what white locals called the "Nojoshing Woods." The Potawatomi called their village "Nojoshing," meaning "straight tongue" because it stretched across the land beside Lake Michigan.

In 1833 The Lake Drive Franciscan Sisters of St. Francis of Assisi purchased sixty-eight acres of land four miles south of Milwaukee from the Deer Creek Clan of the Potawatomi and the clan was forced to move across The Mississippi River to Iowa. On March 13, 1849, six women and five men traveled with two fathers to help Bishop Henni establish a congregation for German immigrants in Milwaukee, Wisconsin. In 1855 the land purchased from the Potawatomi became known as Seminary Woods and The St. Francis de Sales Seminary was built.

It is important to note that from 500 B.C. to 1200 A.D. tribes in Wisconsin built sacred mounds linked to the water, earth, and sky. Scholars believe the mounds were used to manifest powerful ancestral spirits into visual existence through ritual. The ancestral spirits were called "manitous." Manitous were life forces found in every stone, plant, and even machines, and brought the souls of the dead into the afterlife.

Sometimes sacred tribal mounds contained bodies and burial artifacts and sometimes they did not. Scholars believed the tribes gathered at the mounds to mark the seasons in ritual. Up to 20,000 mounds existed in Wisconsin. 4,000 remain today. Prior to the Wisconsin Act 316 in 1985, Native burial sites went unprotected, and most were plowed over for

Case#7: The Babes in the Woods

farming and development. According to The Wisconsin Historical Society, Milwaukee is built on two hundred mounds. Only two remain. One remaining is the Lake Park Mound located 7.8 miles from the town of St. Francis, on the lakefront. I believe previous mounds existed on the Seminary Woods property. Deer Creek and Lake Michigan are both sources of water on and near Seminary Woods. Water is known to increase paranormal activity. A prominent ley line also runs south of Milwaukee to Madison. All of these factors combined with the destruction of sacred Native American mounds, plus the sanctified murder of nuns' newborn infants born of rape during the American Civil War, and the modern satanic cult activity now occurring has desecrated the land. All who work, worship, and are buried there become twisted by the manitous' anger. The land is sour and uninhabitable by man, and nothing shall ever cleanse it.

Some may find the previous statement about The Catholic Church offensive, and they are right. It is offensive. An urban legend surrounds a tunnel in the Seminary Woods where the Our Lady of Lourdes Grotto was built and dedicated to the Virgin Mary by Paul Dobberstein in 1894. During the American Civil War from 1861-1865, many women were raped by opposing forces. Catholic Sisters served as nurses. Deer Creek runs beside the rumored tunnel. The grotto is located there today. It is said the Catholic Sisters would leave their newborn infants, the products of war and rape, to die in the tunnel. I have not been able to reach the Archdiocese to confirm or deny this urban legend, but in talking to other paranormal enthusiasts, I learned any mention of this story is quickly removed from the Internet. Is it purely a coincidence the grotto built in Seminary Woods is dedicated to the Virgin Mary?

A little girl ghost has been sighted multiple times beside the creek near the grotto and a large crucifix people pass on the way to the grotto is said to be haunted. There are also sightings of a white figure near the historic Henni Hall, by the entrance to the cemetery. Henni Hall was added to the National Register of Historic Places on July 24, 1974.

In February of 1919, four boys, residents of St. Aemilian's Orphan

Asylum, run by the nuns in St. Francis, found and ate a bag of cookie crumbs while sorting cabbages in the cellar. The next day, two of the orphans, Philip Giganti, age 13, and Joseph Djeska, age 12, died, and the other two boys, Frank Novakich, age 13, and Paul, his brother, age 12, were ill. A physician determined the cause as arsenic poisoning. The boys' deaths were ruled accidental, and the orphans buried in unmarked graves in Seminary Woods Cemetery, but during the investigation, the local papers said Sister Amabilis stated arsenic never was used at the orphanage. The orphanage had dealt with a rat problem a few months earlier using phosphorous poison. The supervisor of St. Aemilian's told the papers the poison was locked away and was safe to humans. Investigators could not find the paper bag containing the arsenic but found remnants of arsenic at the bottom of the vegetable bin in the asylum cellar. No one at the orphanage was found responsible. Rev. Kroha was quoted by *The Milwaukee Journal*, saying it was, "a very sad event." He chastised the papers for giving the accident undue publicity, which he claimed as "salacious, scurrilous, and libelous filth thrown at The Catholic Institution."

About a year later, the orphanage burned to the ground. The cause was never found, and the orphanage never rebuilt. The stone entry pillars are all that remain south of St. Francis Seminary Drive. Take the road towards the seminary, go right to the northern parking lot, walk south to the woods, and there is one of the paths to Seminary Woods Cemetery.

Near the grotto in Seminary Woods Cemetery, witnesses sometimes see dark figures in hooded robes, whether they are paranormal sightings or actual occult gatherings is undetermined. No one has attempted to speak with the hooded figures.

A screaming, gurgling female's voice is heard beside Deer Creek sometimes. She sounds like she is drowning. Today, Deer Creek has been mostly forced underground due to industrialization in Bay View. The only above ground part of the creek runs through Seminary Woods. In 1893, the city of Milwaukee built a sewer system to divert the creek. It

Case#7: The Babes in the Woods

runs out to Lake Michigan.

⌘⌘⌘

Two evenings later, I put Lily to bed around seven, after a feeding and bath, and curled up with a copy of *Jane Eyre*. CheezIt, my faithful companion, occupied Holly's empty spot. A cup of chamomile tea steamed on my bedside table and by Chapter Four, my eyelids drooped; a steady October drizzle lulled me to sleep.

I awoke sometime after midnight with a chill. Pulling on my fleece robe, I glanced at the baby monitor. Lily stared at something over her crib. I heard some static crackles and a few pops as the grainy black and white image wavered and bent and then I heard a young girl's laugh like shiny silver bells tinkling in the sun. My adrenaline jump started my nervous system and the tiny arrector pili muscles at the base of each hair on my arms and neck contracted, pulling the hair straight up from my flesh. In a primal state of fight or flight, I chose to fight for my baby girl.

I rushed barefoot across the cold, creaking floor to the nursery and slammed open the white painted door with a *bang!* Flicking on the light switch, Lily began to cry. I was still breastfeeding Lily at three months old and wet fabric now clung to my nipples, but all I thought about was picking up Lily. I sang *London Bridge Is Falling Down*, which always seemed to calm her fits, laid her on her changing table, and kissed her forehead and both cheeks and every precious finger and toe as I searched for any marks of harm. I picked her up, cradling her soft, warm head on my left shoulder as I inspected her crib. A young child's muddy footprints led from the door to Lily's crib. At the foot of her mattress, I discovered a few crumbs of dirt and dried leaves. I put a brittle leaf bit to my nose and smelled the damp fall woods, the tart memory of apple cider from my grandparents' farm tickling my tongue as saliva gathered in my mouth.

"Hello?" Silence. Lily, contented in my arms, sucked on her tiny fist. I followed a wandering line of muddy footprints down the hallway, through the kitchen. They stopped at the back door. Slowly, I unlocked the deadbolt and peered into the darkness, shielding Lily from the rain beneath my robe. The security light snapped on, disorienting me. There were no footprints or any sign of the child that made them. I hurried back inside, settled Lily between a bunch of pillows on my bed because I was not leaving her alone that night, and invoked the protection of the archangels in prayer. Then I huddled beneath my bedcovers with CheezIt warming my feet and tried to focus on my battered copy of *Jane Eyre*, until dawn came, and it felt safe to sleep after feeding Lily.

⌘⌘⌘

I wanted to keep a neutral mind as I approached Seminary Woods in St. Francis, but as soon as I emerged from my car, I felt watched. It was around 9pm on Friday night under a new moon. I carried my ghost hunting flashlight, the big heavy stainless steel one I inherited from my father that doubled as a head thumper. The beam of my flashlight sliced through the drizzle falling in the parking lot and I shivered, pulling my thermal raincoat closer to my body. I'd worn sneakers, mindful of the ground being wet as I trudged through piles of fallen leaves from the forty-nine maples flanking the drive and forming a grand archway to Henni Hall. I paused before the statue of St. Francis de Sales, for whom the seminary is named. Not detecting anything paranormal, I continued.

No figure in white greeted me. Drawing a cold breath of air, I reminded myself I investigated more than a few haunted locations and survived, but the atmosphere struck me like a hefty iron punch to the gut as I turned left at Henni Hall and spotted the two stone pillars of St. Aemilian's Orphan Asylum, singed from the fire of 1930 when it burned for the third time.

I passed the pillars and entered a clearing, now standing in Seminary Woods Cemetery. The night felt deeper and cloying, despite the strong beam of light bouncing ahead of me on the dying October grass. My flashlight's beam swept over the large beeches, sugar maples,

Case#7: The Babes in the Woods

basswoods, and red and white oaks surrounding the clearing. A lone owl hooted and the rustling of a small animal, perhaps, a mouse, scurried to my right. The gravestones jutted up like teeth from the ground. Somewhere the two orphaned boys who died of arsenic poisoning rested in unmarked graves. I listened for the sounds of children but heard only the soft patter of rain on my raincoat. Overhead, the stars hid shrouded in a blanket of clouds.

I approached the infamous twelve-foot crucifix I'd seen in multiple pictures on the internet and found no evidence of a mechanism on the prophet to explain witnesses' claims of Jesus turning his gaze upon them as they passed on their way to the Our Lady of Lourdes Grotto and the area commonly referred to as "the dead baby tunnel." *It's possible hearing the urban legend of the haunted crucifix plants a suggestion in a nervous person's mind, causing them to experience a jump in adrenaline or if they are sleep deprived, a momentary hijacking of the brain by the sensory cortex could lead to a small hallucination.* I was sleep deprived but used to living with a newborn on little sleep. I would have welcomed a jump in adrenaline, to not feel like a sleep deprived raccoon for just an hour or two. I knew the chances of this happening were fairly low, even in the middle of a "supposedly" haunted woods.

I walked past the statue, disappointed to not find Jesus judging me when I glanced back over my shoulder. As I drew closer to the Our Lady of Lourdes Grotto, the ground began to buzz beneath my sneakers like the sensation of being too close to a powerline, but I could not find any transistors nearby. *Strange, but not alarming. It could be a preprogrammed response.* The snapping of twigs and the rustling of underbrush startled my thoughts. My beam of light swung wildly back and forth across the naked trees on the edge of the clearing, and I got a glimpse of a black hooded figure running away.

"Wait a second! I want to talk to you," I called, as I gave chase down a wooded path. I stopped abruptly when a man stepped out from the shadows wearing a camo backpack.

"We're out here," he said, turned, and jogged away.

Deciding for my own safety not to follow the man further, I made my way back down the path to the clearing, and headed towards the faint trickle of water, which must be what was left of Deer Creek running beside the grotto. I lost my footing on some slick, wet leaves and almost fell, but caught myself at the edge of the shallow, muddy stream. I faced the grotto, which from the back resembled a mound of stacked stone slabs. A young girl giggled, and I felt a tug at my raincoat sleeve. The space beside me was empty, though.

"Hello? Is anyone there," I asked, peering into the blackness. "Hello?" I swept my flashlight over the tombstones in the clearing beyond. Nothing. As I followed the path towards the front of the grotto, I heard a muffled, gurgling shriek like someone drowning off in the distance. My eyes focused on the creek again and I saw a frail ragamuffin of a girl, scrawny and awkward, all legs like a colt. She was maybe, ten or so and her chestnut hair falling to right below her chin, framed the sharp angles of her face. She wore a plain white cotton nightdress with a round collar, hemmed just above the ankles, and as I approached, I could see the detail of handmade eyelets on the collar and around the hem of her sleeves. Her nightdress tied in front with a white frayed ribbon. She glanced over her shoulder, her eyes wide in fright. I looked over my own shoulder in response and saw a dark shadow barreling after her as she took off like a rabbit and slid into the creek. She stumbled on her hands and knees, a large wet, muddy print on her white bottom.

"Wait! I can help you!" I ran after her. The black shadow eluded me on the path, and I heard the girl cry.

"Anna, you're not supposed to be out here," a gruff man's voice said.

"But the babies, papa. Can't you hear them crying?"

I hurried down the path, trying to look out for fallen tree limbs and rocks as I went, but determined to find the little girl fast. Maternal instinct told me she was in grave danger.

There was a splash, a struggle, a scream, and then stillness. "Hello?" I swung the flashlight over the creek running beside the path and saw no one. "Is anyone out here?" After continuing on another five minutes, I

Case#7: The Babes in the Woods

turned back, frustrated, and puzzled with no explanation for what I'd witnessed. *This was not a mere visual hallucination.* Out of breath, I came to a stop in front of the bench facing the grotto. Aside from the two missing Virgin Mary statues and the wrought iron gates swung open, I would not have known this was a crime scene a few days earlier. I slumped down on the bench to catch my breath.

It was just after ten, as I glanced at my watch in the rain. I swept the beam of my flashlight over the grotto. It made a small, dry shelter from the rain, as I went to huddle inside. *Had I lost my hearing?* I couldn't hear the creek or the rain. I stepped out of the shelter of the grotto and heard the soft pattering rainfall on the wooden bench and my raincoat. I stepped back inside the grotto and heard nothing. *Interesting. It wasn't dug deep enough into the womb of the earth to muffle sound, so what could be causing it?*

I sat down on the ground, dizzy and fatigued with that buzzing running through my head. I tasted ashes in my mouth and then I heard it, the faint keening of a hungry infant. I knew no baby occupied the grotto with me. Frantic, I patted the dirt, hoping to unearth a wire attached to a tape recorder, but found nothing. My teeth began to chatter in the cold. I wrapped my arms around myself and sat on the freezing ground, imagining a nun abandoning a helpless, squirming bundle in the dark mouth of the tunnel. I thought of Lily safe in her crib. Her skin so delicate and sensitive to the cold. *What would it be like with hunger gnawing my belly as I lay on the cold, hard ground, alone?* Tears pricked my eyes. *Would exposure to the elements come first or the welcome bite of a hungry coyote snapping my neck?* I didn't know. I had to get out of this awful nightmare. I stood and vomited, splashing my sneakers in the shaky beam of my light. I ran as fast as capable back down the path towards the clearing with the haunted crucifix and the unmarked graves of the two young orphans.

A mighty howling rumbled behind me through the forest in great sonorous waves as I ran. It was the manitou of a young Potawatomi mother. Her powerful figure towered over the tree line as her long, tawny limbs stretched through the thick, black night, her slender fingers scrabbling to catch my coat as I stumbled to escape the cemetery woods and find the safety of my car. I looked back one last time by the stone pillars marking the entrance to the clearing. The manitou dwarfed the twelve-foot crucifix. Her waist-length black hair hung matted and unkempt around her bony face with bits of twigs, moss, and leaves twisted in her snarls. Her eyes glowed ruby red. She wore a plain deerskin prairie dress and low-cut moccasins, and she carried a wrapped bundle, kicking in her arms. The cloth fell away, revealing the small, fragile skeleton of an infant, its bones brown from the tannic acid of the ancient earth it was buried in. The manitou howled the soul haunting cry of a timber wolf and stepped back into the forest, disappearing in a black mist. I stood there shaking beside my car, my keys rattling in my hand, barely able to unlock the driver's side door. The energy imprinted on this land is a bloodstain spreading and no amount of light shed on past events will cleanse it from the earth. Some places are not meant to be inhabited by people. The curse remains unbroken in Seminary Woods. The land remembers, the Deer Creek Clan's ancestral spirits remember, and the woods cry out for vengeance.

END

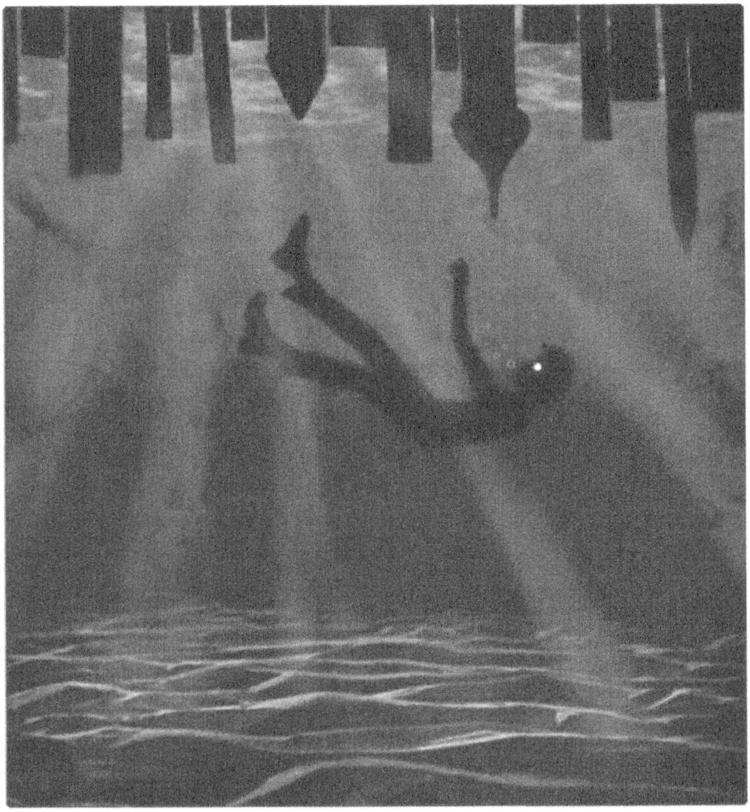

Undercity
by Tom Sewel

There's a street in Edinburgh, I won't tell you its name, but you can usually find it if you get walking in town and just follow your feet. This Edinburgh Street, it's a strange wee winding one, not very long, like a crescent, if a crescent had a few drinks and lost track of where it said it was going. From one end of this street, you can't see the other, and even in the middle, equidistant from either end, you can't see anything but the blind curve of regimented sandstone tenements closing off the view. It's in a busy area, this street, though it's always quiet; a weird eddy that's coiled out of the raucous river of the city and set still. There's shopping and socializing going on all around, but nobody ever seems to cut through here. Maybe because it doesn't look like it leads anywhere. Maybe you have to know this street to want to use it.

⌘⌘⌘

Edinburgh, like every old city in Europe, sweats torrents of grisly medieval horror; a thousand years of feudalism birthed hideous cruelty all over the continent. Vertically integrated industries have arisen to exploit visitors hungry for some gruesome frisson of baroque history. The tide of ghosts runs so strong down the Vennel and up the Canongate that you must swim into it or be swept away. But these specters - greasepaint grotesques and cheap frights that disperse in the wind - are just the spume whipped up for an international audience. They are mere productions of the city's greater haunting, not producers of it. When tourists and tourist-trappers trickle away, Edinburgh's sinister ambience still leaks from its rotting bones

The undercity is the secret corpse of Edinburgh-past, rolling in a shallow grave. A crumbling skeleton etched in absences, in holes bored through igneous rock and cavities formed between hastily sedimented layers of architectural crust.

The undercity is something you hear about often if you live in Edinburgh, something you know is there even if you never see it. People share legends about it: How it connects to a series of evacuation tunnels built for nuclear emergencies. How you can walk from the suburbs into town without once seeing the sky. How whole blocks were walled up alive in plague times and then paved over. How desperate folks live down there now, sheltering from the rain or hiding from the law in subterranean hollows that were once terraces and homes in the open air. A lumpy concrete palimpsest of crannies.

You hear rumors of people holding parties down there, finding some previously inaccessible buried building and fitting it for a dancefloor. You can take a guided tour through some of the undercity now, but there was a spell in the late eighties when people kept breaking into unexplored parts of it. These breaches were sealed with big industrial bulkheads that started appearing all over town. A casual observer could see then that the undercity was everywhere.

If you butter up the right people at the right old pubs they might still show you the way to their lowest cellar, three or four or five floors down from the pavement. The council's aluminum portcullis is riveted to the clammy stonework there. A padlock locked only once secures this muzzle around the maw of an echoing round throat - broad enough for a horse and cart - that declines farther into the pitch-black earth than the gridded light reaches. The metal gates stand as tacit, disquieting proof that the dark roads below are bandit country.

⌘⌘⌘

There is a jarring dislocation of perspective when you swim out to sea far enough so you can't see the land. The sea looks the same in every direction. In open water, bobbing around under a clear blue sky, the direction of the swell is not easy to determine. Turn around a few times or let your head go under and you lose your bearings. You could be anywhere, on any sea.

A minute ago, you could see the beach and you were fine, it was all fine. The beach was a fixed reference point for direction and distance and as long as you could see it, you could gauge how much energy you'd need to reach it. The water is getting a little colder as you go out but it's fine. You're swimming, so you're fine. You swim a few moments more, maybe a few longer moments, and now you can't see the land.

Disorientation is immediate and total.

The cold water feels different then, like weight pressing in on you, squeezing the warm from you. You are a downed fly, trapped and toiling on the surface of a great chilly indifference. Vast volumes of cool darkness stretch down hundreds of meters below you and nothing but your body's fragile buoyancy guards you from that sucking lightless oblivion. You don't know for certain that you have enough in the tank to get back to shore, because you don't know for certain how far out you are, or even if you are headed in the right direction. You are isolated and vulnerable in a way that sneaks up on your awareness and pounces.

You are both more free and more constrained than you have ever been. You encounter true independence face to face, and it means only your own abject helplessness. Wrestling with panic, your mind conjures phantoms: Graceful unseen observers who judge with patient apathy as your silhouette staggers across their rippling sky. Pale fingers curling weakly around your ankle. The brush of a fin against your arm. Translucent threads trailing through the water to sting and snare you. Spectral sense-impressions, produced by fear, like screams escaping through the nervous system. You can't directly see the danger of the

Undercity

deep, but your body knows it is there and it will provide whatever evidence you require to let loose the storm of adrenaline and save

yourself.

⌘ ⌘ ⌘

Undercity

When you look down one of those tunnels in the deepest cellar of an Edinburgh pub, squinting past the shiny grill into the darkness, you can't see anything. But the gates and the padlock tell you it's there.

Afterwards, you are a scarab beetle scuttling over the rooftops of a tomb city. Hollow chambers begin to haunt your tracks, labyrinths manifesting far down below where your feet fall. You could be sitting with friends by a fireplace sipping single malt and enjoying some rambunctious fiddle when you become conscious, quite unbidden, of a narrow spiral stairwell not twenty feet from your table that sinks like a drill into bedrock until it hits the thin aluminum limit of the surface world's domain. A conduit across the gulf between realities that comes out between the kitchen and the toilets. You might feel an eerie certainty in such a moment that some Morlock Jacob stands far below with pallid hands curled gently around a lattice of bright metal, gazing up the helix of their twisted ladder. A person who traces wisps with their breath in the chill damp of the earth. Someone not so different from you.

⌘⌘⌘

There is a street in Edinburgh that has no undercity. A quiet, unremarkable street in a busy area. It could easily be a street in many other cities. No fancy shops or bars or theatres to draw foot traffic. Stoic sandstone tenements nest in unbroken bending rows with maybe a single level of basement. The ground beneath, the porous subterranean secretion of the city since ancient time, has been scooped out, hollowed away, and filled in for heavy industry. Unlike nearly every other road in town, this street floats on its foundations. It is unrooted from its own history, unmoored in its geography from Edinburgh's totalizing psychic field. The Festival and Hogmanay crowds avoid it, and nary a goth lingers there. Turning onto this street unexpectedly while out walking, you might notice it feels odd, or somehow disjointed. It's not that this street is haunted, it's that it is not. The only street for miles with no clamor of forgotten souls. A street with no dead. No dusty, night-filled voids. No morbid stain of countless squalid and degraded lives.

The story goes that if you walk down to the middle of this strange wee winding street so that you can no longer see the city beyond, and then close your eyes, breathe in, turn around a few times, breathe out, and open your eyes, the street might have shifted. It could be in any city. Helsinki or Hanover, probably. Barcelona seems likely, and Athens, of course, if only Exarcheia. Some claim Tehran or even Vancouver but these are surely wishful thinking, at least for now. Perhaps as more come to feel the collapse of the cold volumes that hold us up

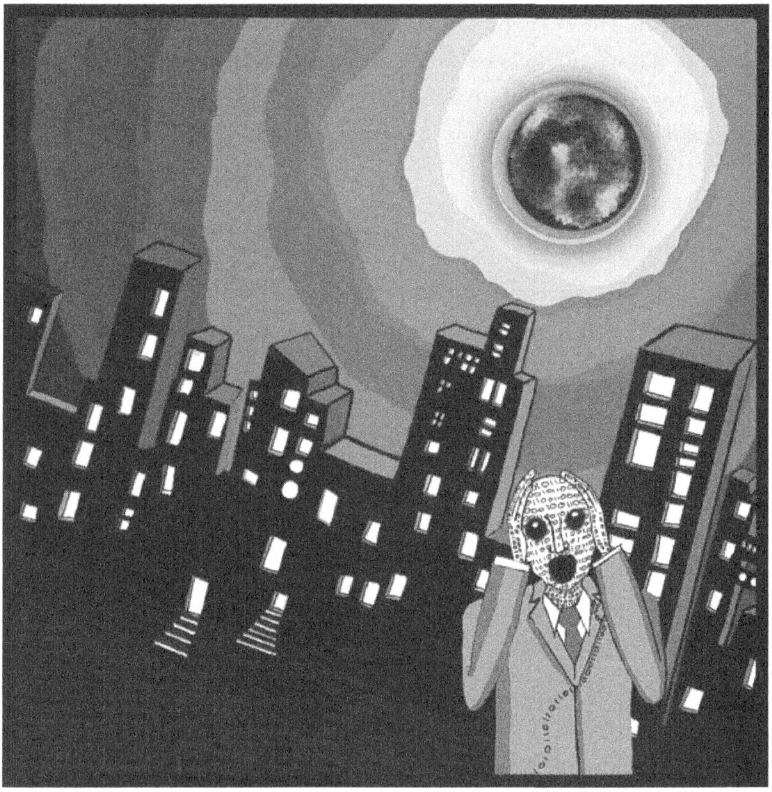

The Office on The Seventh Floor
By Malcolm Carvalho

Damn you, just stop that noise!

Sumit grit his teeth as he scanned the code comments on his laptop. Over the last few minutes, the clickety-clack of keyboards from the floor below had gotten louder and was now ringing in his ears like someone was furiously typing away right at his side.

He grabbed the glass at his right, gulped down the water and went back to work. The sound reappeared – the ceaseless tapping of keys as if it was being played on loop.

It's just in your head. There's no one on the seventh floor.

But he could hear it even louder now. He tried focusing again, making notes about the bugs he had fixed over the last two weeks. Murali would be here any moment and would start nitpicking on his work. Typical Murali stuff.

Then the clattering of keys took over again, the annoying sound hammering away around him. He slammed his fists on the table, if only he could get away from--

"So, those sounds again?"

Murali stood beside him; his laptop tucked under his arm. Damn these silent doors – when had he walked in? And like always, that annoying clatter had disappeared, like someone had pressed mute on a television remote.

"You heard them this time?" Sumit asked.

Murali rolled his eyes. "Of course not. I don't know what's with you, and all these things you claim to keep hearing. Maybe you could stop making excuses and just focus on your work."

He pulled the chair opposite Sumit and plonked himself in it. Then he powered on his laptop and projected a pie-chart on the screen to his right. "Stats from your code check-ins in the last two weeks. See the number of open bugs in there?"

Sumit leaned forward; his fingers interlaced under the table. "I've done better this time."

"But you still didn't meet your targets."

Sumit pressed his lips together. *I would have if you didn't waste time with these meetings. And then turn up late every time.*

"We knew beforehand, those were steep targets."

"I'm afraid your performance has dropped again," Murali said, pulling back the cuff of his sleeve. "We've given you too many chances."

"We've lost three developers in the last two months."

"You'll keep making those excuses? Everyone knows it's a bad time, we had to fire some devs. They just weren't good enough."

"But they were learning. And now with them gone, there's just too much to--"

"Man up, Sumit. You're the senior developer on this project, and this is VerveTech. We expect you to deliver to a certain standard."

"I understand," Sumit said. *Certain standards! Standards which keep changing.*

"How's it going on that report generation feature?"

"Umm, there are some minor issues. But I'll get it done in ten days. Before we finish the sprint."

"Before the sprint? I need it ready for the demo next Monday. Meeting some major customers. You've got three days."

"But... but we'd decided it would take about three weeks. Even if I finish it by the end of the sprint, I still would've developed it under the estimated time."

Murali disconnected his laptop from the projector. The meeting room darkened. "Our customers bring in the revenue. You want to keep

your job, have the feature ready by the weekend."

Sumit kept mum as Murali walked out of the room. He'd seen this happen twice already, with Peter and then with Varun. Bloody Murali.

He'd sucked their life out of them and when they were on the verge of collapse, he'd fired them.

The goddammed asshole has no heart.

What if Murali fired him too? Maybe Sumit could talk to his parents and tell them he could not send them money for the next few months. Maybe even ask them to pay his rent for a couple of months.

No, no, no! They wouldn't understand the pressure he was handling. Ma would instead say he was being too complacent.

He would fight this out alone.

Clack-clack-clack! Those damned keyboards from downstairs again.

Not this now. Stop imagining it!

⌘ ⌘ ⌘

The next day Sumit arrived at the office at eight AM. The floor was empty when he walked in, and he liked to work when there weren't too many people around. He filled his coffee mug from the office dispenser and got to work, ticking off the bugs on his list. Three days to fix them all and get those reports ready!

He was fixing the third bug of the morning when he heard it again – the hard, staccato sounds from downstairs. Mouse clicks, clackety keyboards, and those irritating pings of incoming emails.

He rose from his desk and looked over his cubicle wall. Two other employees had turned up since he had arrived, and neither of them seemed to notice the sounds.

He put on his headphones and got back to work. *Got to power through this and visit a therapist soon.*

⌘ ⌘ ⌘

When his teammate Naresh walked in, it was ten fifteen.

The Office on The Seventh Floor

"I heard Murali had a long chat with you yesterday," he asked as he logged in to his terminal. "All okay?"

Sumit shrugged, still typing away at his desk. "Uh yes, it's all fine." No point confiding in him. Everyone here was an expert at feigning sympathy.

"Good for you, man. By the way, have you heard from Peter? After he was fired?"

"No. You?"

"I've called him like a dozen times since--how long has it been since he left, five weeks? Dude hasn't answered even once. I think even my messages haven't reached him."

"Maybe… he changed his number? Left the city maybe?"

Naresh shook his head. "He lived with his parents here. Why would he leave?"

"True," Sumit said. Then it struck him – maybe he could talk to Naresh about the sounds. The man may have been his junior, but he had been working at this place for three years. And he did seem concerned about Peter. Maybe he could listen in to Sumit too. Sure, he was the chattier kind, but maybe he could help—

"You know," Naresh said. "I thought Peter was having some mental health issues."

"Uh… that is surprising." *Maybe hold off the confiding now.* "Maybe it was because he knew his job was on the line."

"No, not that. He had started behaving strangely in the last month he was here. Once over a drink, he said he had been hearing some sounds from the floor below."

Sumit's fingers froze. He turned around. "Sounds?"

"Yes, said he was hearing keyboards being pounded. Like someone was in a hurry. I thought it was just the alcohol, but when I asked him the next day, he said he was serious."

"He never spoke about it to anyone?"

"How could he? You know how everyone thought he was just one of those introverted awkward guys? And the dude's talking about sounds from the seventh floor!" Naresh laughed. "That space has been empty

for a year. Since that company, I forget the name…"

"Fortius Software…"

"Yes, since those guys shut down and vacated the floor. Plus, he always heard those sounds when no one was around. Once he even claimed to have heard electronic voices."

"Poor chap," Sumit said. *Hold it in, hold it in. You can find a therapist later.*

"Yea, I hope he's alright man. But you know what they say about downstairs… why no company lasts there for more than six months?"

"Why?" Sumit felt his pulse quicken.

"They say the floor is jinxed. That someone doesn't want it occupied at all. That maybe some other company wants the space. What a load of bullshit! As if the company couldn't rent the space right away."

"Ya ya, just rumours of course." Sumit laughed. Yea, *keep laughing. And stick to a therapist for now.*

⌘ ⌘ ⌘

The lights went out at ten PM.

Sumit groaned. *Damn you, Bangalore. Even a tech park can't escape your power problems.*

He stood and looked around the office. It was dark everywhere, except for the blinking lights from the UPS-powered server room in the far corner.

He glanced at the clock on his screen. He still hadn't got to the report generation task, but he had another two days in hand. He could put in the extra hours like he had done today, maybe start work even earlier. No point working in this claustrophobic place without even the AC on – it would soon get unbearably hot. He shut down his laptop and put all his stuff in his office backpack.

He walked to the exit and raised his ID card near the checkout sensor

The Office on The Seventh Floor

to swipe out his time. The device beeped and almost immediately, the sounds came in again – the click-clack from downstairs.

His hand froze around the doorknob. No, this was not him being crazy. He could hear the sounds more clearly now.

He'd have to take the stairs tonight. And he would pass the seventh floor.

No, not just pass. He would get in there.

⌘ ⌘ ⌘

A musty odor hit him when he reached the seventh floor. He switched on the flashlight of his phone and waved it around. The place looked like it had not seen anyone for months.

The sounds drifted in again. The frenzied typing of keyboards.

Sumit shook his head. Maybe *you're just too tired and sleep deprived. Maybe Peter got too stressed with the work pressure, just like you, and that's what this is.*

The noises grew louder. He pointed the flashlight to the glass door on his right. No sign, no nameplate on it.

He pushed the door and found himself in a vacant lobby, about twenty feet square. Opposite him stood a table and behind it an empty chair. He turned to the still-incoming rattling sounds. They seemed to come from the door to his left.

He walked towards it. The door swung open. He stepped in and found himself at the beginning of an aisle, clusters of cubicles on either side of it. Layers of dust covered the desks nearer to him. At the far end of the aisle, the cubicle walls glimmered with blue light. Screens?

Then the clacking of the keyboards again, from the far end. He ventured forward. The glow in the distance was brighter now, and he could make out someone sitting at the desk nearest to him.

He stepped up his pace and reached the cubicle. A broad-shouldered man sat there with his back towards Sumit, headphones around his ears, his fingers tapping vigorously at his keyboard.

Sumit swallowed. *I'm not crazy. And neither was Peter.*

There were people working here! But how did no one else know about it?

"Excuse me," he said, approaching the man. "Isn't it too late for you to be working?"

The man continued typing as if he had not heard him at all.

"Hello...oh! Excuse me!"

The man swiveled on his chair, turned to face him for a brief instant, and then got back to his screen.

And even through his thick beard, Sumit had no trouble recognizing him. Why, it was—

"Peter! What... what are you... what are you doing here?"

No response. Only Peter's fingers continued jabbing at the keyboard. What was wrong with this guy?

Sumit placed a hand on his shoulder and shook it. The chair swiveled around again. This time Sumit could take a closer look at Peter.

Hexagonal iron bolts, their heads as wide as a rupee coin, ran through his hands into the arms of the chair. Dried blood covered the bolt heads. From each of his eyelids ran out a wire, running behind the ear, and then burying itself in the fabric of the chair. His neck and torso looked stiff, as if they were held erect against his will. A needle lay embedded in his left arm, and from the other end protruded—

The chair swung back towards the screen and as if on cue, the typing resumed. Lines of text scrolled up on the screen within seconds, too fast for Sumit to understand what he was reading. It was a code editor for sure, he could understand by the interface. Then he noticed the familiar icon at the top right corner of the monitor.

The blue umbrella of VerveTech.

He staggered and fell against the cubicle wall. What was VerveTech doing here? The sounds from the other cubicles assaulted his ears. Click, click, click, click.

Grabbing a corner of the cubicle, he pulled himself to his feet and

The Office on The Seventh Floor

looked to the other side. A woman sat there, pinned to her chair just like Peter. Her curly hair fell over her shoulders, a pale streak of red running across it near her left temple. Then, Sumit saw the mole on her chin. His body tightened.

Neha!

How he had wanted to ask her out before she was fired! But wait, he caught a glimpse of another face in his peripheral vision.

It was Varun, the other developer they had lost recently.

Sumit looked around, scanning the other faces. All of them seemed familiar. He couldn't recall their names, but he knew he had seen each of them sometime in the last six months.

All of them with the same stiff bodies, headphones cupping their ears, wires running out from their eyelids, their forearms screwed into the chairs, the needles in their arms.

Sumit felt the muscles clenching in the pit of his stomach. He turned back and ran towards the entrance. In the dim light, he felt a machine clamp his feet by the ankles. He collapsed forward, holding his hands out to break his fall. The shock of vibrations surged from his elbows to his shoulders. Then he felt the clamps tighten around his feet.

It was the last thing he knew before he fainted.

⌘ ⌘ ⌘

He squinted his eyes as the screen flashed before him. He was in a chair now. He tried to stand but felt his body pinned. He felt something prick his sides, near his hips. He could still move his arms, thank God for that.

Owwwwww!

He screamed as a stabbing pain surged through his lower back. Something had pierced him near the base of his spine. Then he felt the thing – was it a wire? – curl inside his body, almost hooking itself around his spine.

Malcolm Carvalho

Owwwwww!

He gritted his teeth. The wire was piercing its way out. Then he felt the hook tighten around his spine, pressing his back to the chair.

A second wire pierced him between his shoulder blades. He could not hold back his screams this time, and as the hook tightened, he felt like his back was being stitched into the chair.

"Leave me alone," he cried. "Please."

"Very soon," a voice boomed in his ears. "But we have some work left."

He raised his hands to cup his ears. They had headphones, just like Peter and the others did.

He felt a needle jab the back of his neck. Soon the pain subsided, and he drifted into a semi-conscious state halfway between wakefulness and sleep.

"Welcome to the seventh-floor office, Mr. Agarwal," the voice in the headphone said. "I'm the virtual director of this office, and my job now is to ensure you're all set up as part of the second-string workers on this floor."

What the hell! Sumit wanted to scream, but he felt like his body had been drained of every drop of energy.

"Mr. Agarwal," the voice continued. "Do you feel the needle from the headrest piercing the back of your neck? No? Then tighten your seatbelt, lean further back in the chair. See the control panel at your right? Yes, that one. Turn the strength of the caffeine shot to low for now. Later, you can experiment with the other regulator and learn to adjust the strength of the morphine shots too."

Sumit followed the instructions. He felt a warm sensation around his neck.

"That will be good for a start. But as you spend more time here, the shots will become stronger. You can override the sensors and have even stronger shots by increasing the concentration, but you can never lower it. Don't even try."

The Office on The Seventh Floor

"Those wires in your back, they are just contraptions to keep your spine erect. We need this just so you don't have any back trouble, or what the non-hardworking people call 'occupational posture problems.' If you feel something trickle down your back, it must be your blood. But relax, the blood flow will stop in a few minutes. It takes a while for the coagulants to seep in through the fabric of the chair."

"Now about this headset. It will play ambient music to help you focus. Don't bother with selecting a sound - we've got a mix that will keep changing according to your levels of alertness. For starters, a rain background will help you ease in. We switch it with the chirping of birds, a baby's laughter, or a crackling fire. A warning though. If you begin to nod off, the track switches to nails on a chalkboard or an electric drill through the wall right behind you."

"We've taken care of your daily functions too. Those tubes you feel near your hip bones – they drain out the urine. There's another tube – a wider one – that goes in a little lower. You can guess what it is for. And we know eating can be a major time sink, so we've looked at that too. Just press that blue button next to the caffeine shot regulator, and a synthetic food delivery machine will slide into your desk and inject enough carbs into your throat. Don't worry, you will smell the aroma too. You have only one nutrition break every twenty-four hours, and only twenty minutes off work every day, so time your breaks wisely. Most employees take their food breaks just as they are about to wind down for their daily fifteen-minute sleep session, so they don't lose out on their productivity. It's a system that's evolved organically, and you'd do well to follow that."

"Now, time to turn on your monitor and start keying in the code."

"What if you don't comply, you say? Sure, you may want to escape – try breaking those three spinal hooks. Mostly you can't. And if you still stay here not delivering the code, we simply stop the food and excretion services."

"Do you understand?"

Sumit nodded weakly. Then, in a trembling voice, "Why did you get Peter and the others here when you'd fired them? And why fire them at all?"

The voice sniggered. "Firing them was just a ruse. It's not that any of them weren't competent enough. Quite the opposite, they were some of the most skilled employees at VerveTech. But they were also some of the most underconfident ones, employees whom we could get off our payroll and into this 'closed' undercover place. They write the same code as they would do upstairs, we don't have to pay them, our profits increase. No one complains. See how easy it is?"

"Okay, then why me? I hadn't been fired."

"Not yet. But do you really think you would have survived beyond this week?"

"I... I might have."

The voice laughed again. "See your hesitation right there, Mr. Agarwal? *You might have*, not *would have*. That's what gets you on this floor for the hesitant coders."

"Now rest tonight. You won't get much tomorrow. Welcome to the seventh floor."

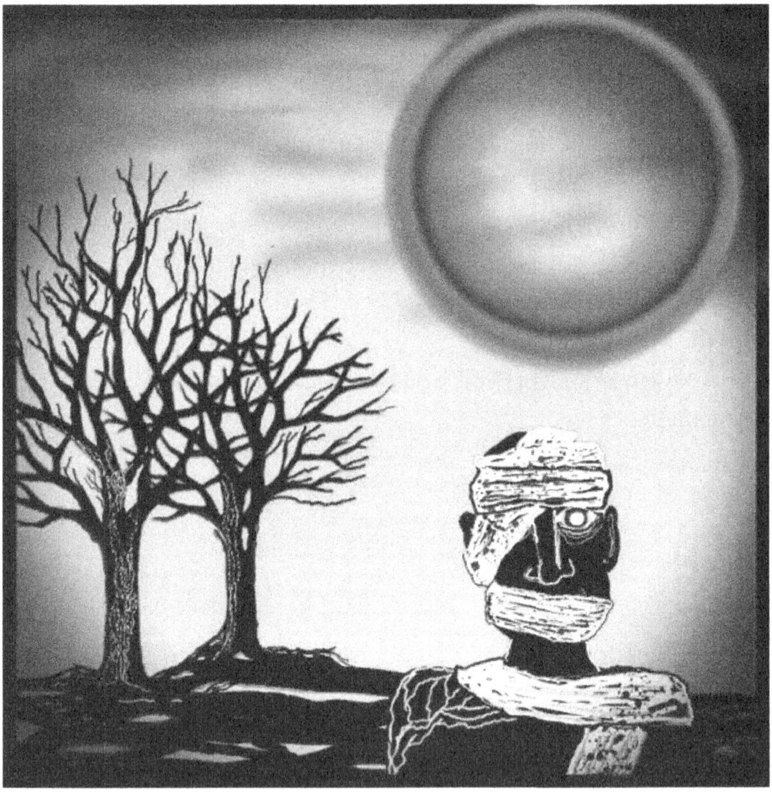

The Bandage Man's Way
by Wendy Wagner

No matter how many times I drove this stretch of highway, I was never prepared for the thickness of the trees, the snaking of the road, the aggressive speed of the cars streaming from Portland's rigid grid toward the freedom of the coast. Risking a glance to check the GPS on my phone felt dangerous, like begging the asshole tailgating our Subaru to ram us into the ditch. But I didn't want to miss the turn for Everdeen Camp. There was no good place to turnaround for miles.

GPS suggested we had a little over a mile before the turn. Then I'd abandon my beautiful girlfriend to run for hours in the woods while I waited patiently at our beach house, a repeat of weeks of training and prep for this ridiculously named race.

"Hey, we're nowhere near Tillamook. So why did they call it the 'Tillamook Burn'?" I asked Naveen over my shoulder.

She grunted as she pulled her sports bra down over her brown shoulders. I had to force my eyes back to the road; my girlfriend is dangerously adorable even when she isn't dressing in the backseat of our car. "I always forget you're not from here," she said.

"Yes, Michigan, absolute furriner, I know."

I caught her grinning in the rearview mirror. "You're so adorable when you get Oregon-shamed." She reached for the teal technical tee hanging on the back of the passenger seat. "Back in the 1930s, a huge stretch of the Tillamook and Clatsop state forests burned in a terrible wildfire. Volunteers came from across the state to help fight it."

"Wow, scary. So, the race is named for the fire?"

She *mmmn*ed an assent. Of course, Naveen knew all about it. She was researching wildfire impacts on forests for her doctoral thesis. She was as in love with forests as she was running. And me, hopefully.

The Bandage Man's Way

She leaned into the gap between the seats. "Plus, it's a great play on words. With 7,000 feet of vert, my legs are going be a-*burn*-ing today!"

She shot me a corny wink and I played along with some clever wordplay, although I was distracted my own extensive to-do list for the night. I barely resisted feeling for the gold circle safety-pinned to the inside of my jeans pocket. I'd have about five hours to prep the Air B-n-B while Naveen ran her 50K; I hoped I could find everything I needed in Cannon Beach. At least I could get her some good beer.

"Elise? Did you hear me? The turn's coming up in half a mile."

I startled out of my head. "Oops, wool gathering. Thanks!" I made the turn onto a narrow road, heavily shaded by maples I couldn't believe were less than a hundred years old.

A white shape shot into my field of vision, and I hit the brakes out of pure stupid reflex. It hung suspended in our window for a moment, all pale fluttering, and vast pupils, and for a second I thought I had hit someone, a tall man in white rags with impossible alien eyes. Then it swooped up, an owl, noiseless and beautiful.

My breathing filled the car, shrill and rasping.

Naveen was shaking my shoulder. "Your inhaler, sweetie. Use your inhaler!"

I grabbed my purse and rummaged for the plastic tube and dispenser. Pressure clawed the lining of my lungs as I shook the damn thing and then sucked back a bitter breath of medicine. Since COVID, I could barely manage 5K, let alone fifty.

"God, m was weird," Naveen said. "Must be a barred owl. They're so territorial they'll attack even in the daylight." "Yeah," I managed to gasp.

"Oh, check out that sign—*Runners in the Roadway*. This must be where we cross the road!" she said, and chirped on about the race's course, but her words floated over my head. I drove on, biting my lip.

My grandmother, superstitious Yooper that she was, would have called that owl a bad omen. I wasn't about to tell Naveen that, though.

I tried not to think about omens as I drove the rest of the way to Cannon Beach. I'd seen pictures from the course, and it looked like a difficult trail, steep, rocky, miles from anything. The race organizers had medics and volunteers, but that didn't mean Naveen wouldn't be spending hours mostly alone in the backwoods. She could get yanked off the trail by a cougar and no one would even know.

But she loved trail running, and I loved her, and if I wanted our relationship to work out, I was just going to have to trust that all her training would pay off and she could keep herself safe out there. And that she could outrun the cougars.

I took the exit for downtown Cannon Beach and parked beside a candy shop. Even before I opened the car door, I could smell the bright, sweet scent of cotton candy. Pink threads floated out of the building's open door as I passed. If it had been raining, they would have dissolved in the air, but it hadn't rained in more than a month. Every county in the state had issued drought warnings, even here at the coast.

The brewery hadn't opened yet, so I waited on the porch and studied the menu pinned on the bulletin board beside door. The fish sandwich sounded good. My eyes searched for a recent tap list and noticed a laminated page I hadn't noticed on previous trips.

"Bandage Man?" I took a step closer to get a better look at the illustration of some kind of homemade mummy.

"Learning about the local folklore?" a man asked, sticking his head out the front door.

"Yeah, I guess. Mostly killing time before I get some lunch and a growler to go." I followed him inside. My eyes took a second to adjust. "Bandage Man, huh?"

He led me to a table. "Supposedly he broke into our basement one night and scared the crap out of one of our waitresses."

"You ever see anything?"

He pulled a menu out of his apron pocket and put it in front of me.

The Bandage Man's Way

"I don't know. Isn't every basement a little creepy at night?"

The bartender came out of the back and stationed herself in front of the gleaming row of taps. "You scaring the customers again, Jeremy?" "I was asking about Bandage Man," I explained.

She smirked. "Legend has it that if you drive under the Highway 26 overpass after midnight, you risk him jumping into the back of your pickup. Poor guy. He just wants medical attention for all those burns."

"Burns?"

"Sure. He was a firefighter who got hurt in the Tillamook Burn."

My server was shaking his head. "No. No, that's wrong. He was a logger who got cut up in the woods."

I let them bicker about it for a second, then ordered my sandwich and a tasting flight. The bartender brought over the tray of tiny glasses and ran through the names and descriptions. Naveen loved an amber, and this place brewed two—unusual for the land of a thousand pale ales. I made notes on the stack of Post-its I kept in my purse.

The bartender nodded at the inhaler spilling out on the table. "I hope smoke doesn't bother your asthma."

"Why?"

"I just heard on the radio that a lightning strike started a fire last night out by Lukarilla. With the wind coming out of the east, we might get some smoke."

I groaned. "Wildfire? In May? The season just gets earlier and earlier."

"Scary times, my friend," she agreed. "Scary times."

⌘ ⌘ ⌘

After stops for flowers, fancy candles, and take-out from Naveen's favorite restaurant, I checked into our beach house and collapsed on the couch. I put hoisted my feet onto the coffee table, logged into the Wi-Fi, and checked Twitter for updates from the race. No one had finished yet, although one dude had passed the final aid station and had less than six miles left.

A tweet from another runner's coach caught my eye: *hoping everyone can finish the course before they have to be evacuated.*

Evacuated? I refreshed the race hashtag and saw people retweeting wildfire warnings from the Clatsop County Sheriff's office. I hadn't thought twice when the bartender had mentioned a fire—we were forty or fifty miles north of the race's course, and I'd never even heard of the town of Lukarilla. But apparently this fire was bigger and wilder than original reports had painted it.

I got up and began pacing. Found a vase for the flowers. Paced some more. Of course, Naveen was fine out there. The race organizers knew what they were doing, and if there was any real danger, they'd round up the runners and get them out, pronto. Naveen was probably chugging some electrolyte drink mix at the last aid station, ready to zip across the finish line and into our friend Tania's SUV. She'd be here in an hour, an hour and a half, tops.

Something slammed against the front door, hard enough to make me jump and stumble into the kitchen island. Fuck, I was tense.

The door thudded again, and I forced myself to smile as I walked toward it. It was probably the cleaners, confused about the schedule. But my feet slowed when I pushed back the lacy curtain on the door. The person on the front stoop wasn't carrying a mop or a vacuum or wearing a friendly smile. They stared at the door with enormous bulging eyes and a horribly bandaged face.

My mouth went dry.

The thudding became a knock. A nice, normal knock. Surely Bandage Man didn't knock. I rolled my eyes at the thought. This fire business had broken my brain. I slid the chain in place and opened the door a very reasonable crack. "Hi?"

A face peered into the gap—a face wearing ordinary sunglasses and a white face mask textured to look like one of those cans of Monster energy drink. Must be immunocompromised. "Just dropping off that firewood you ordered!"

The Bandage Man's Way

I'd forgotten I'd made that call. We'd selected this beach house for its romantic fireplace, and a fireplace demanded a fire.

"Thanks," I said. But as I dragged the bundle of wood into the house, I could already smell smoke on the wind.

I checked Twitter and saw that the first finisher had just crossed the line, coughing, and crying from the smoke. Medics warned that smoke levels had reached unsafe conditions for racing. The Burn's organizers were going to send volunteers to round up the rest of the runners for quick evacuation.

I grabbed my purse and keys and rushed out the door. How many runners and volunteers had carpooled? How many had simply been dropped off by loved ones who expected to meet them at the finish line? I couldn't just leave people out there. And I *wouldn't* risk Naveen getting left out there.

My hands and feet moved on autopilot, steering the car back onto the main road and then the ramp onto the highway. The flashing yellow signs barely penetrated the smoke in my brain. Then the pink flares and red and blue lights streaked across my panic. The cars ahead were slowing. Some were turning around. We crept to a snail's pace. I squeezed the steering wheel tight, tighter. Perfect fucking time for an accident.

A woman in blue Clatsop County sheriff's gear gestured for me to roll down my window. "We're closing the highway to through traffic," she warned. "Gotta evacuate folks who live near the fire."

"I'm headed to Everdeen Camp," I explained. "There's an event out there and people need help getting out."

"Everdeen Camp?" Her lips tightened. "The fire's headed that way."

"I know."

She murmured something into her shoulder radio and then rapped the roof of my Outback. "Better get a move on." She waved me around the makeshift blockade.

My arms shook as I steered past the first responders. This morning had started out so perfectly, and now I was driving into an evacuation zone. Was this the new normal these days? You planned a vacation, and shit like wildfires and tsunamis were just regular ancillary concerns like food poisoning or bedbugs used to be? Naveen, environmental scientist that she was, had told me climate change would mess with everything, but for the first time, her warnings really sank home.

The inside of the car began to reek of campfire. I swatted the controls until the vents closed. The smell clung to my skin. Last year fire season had been bad enough the smoke stench seeped out of the car's upholstery every warm, damp day of early fall.

A small rock began to form in the left side of my chest, hot and hard, and I took a preemptive hit of my inhaler to keep the sensation from worsening into a railroad spike or a squeezing hand. The stimulant hit me hard, accelerating my heartbeat and making my eyelids twitch. The good stuff.

Asthma had bothered me my whole life but moving to Portland had exacerbated it. People joked about their allergies and the way the city worsened them. I couldn't laugh. Spring made my eyes burn and my sinuses ache. Winter brought the molds, enflaming the lining of my bronchioles. Fire season doubled the sensation. And life post-COVID had meant adding an oral steroid every morning to the already rich buffet of antihistamines and decongestants.

It was worth it, though. Hiking in the woods with Naveen. Walking the beaches. Sitting beside the ferns and letting the mist roll over my skin while I waited for Naveen to finish a trail run. She made every pill, every sinus infection, every wheezing moment worthwhile.

I nearly missed the exit for Highway 103. The green marker barely stood out from tea-colored air. Ribbons of brown smoke—at a certain thickness, smoke changed from gray to brown, a dead and viscous shade like the goo lining a smoker's lungs—bled through the trees, turning the day into a grim twilight. I turned on my brights, but the particulates transformed the light to eye-stabbing glitter. I downgraded to low beams and wished for fog lights. The turn to Everdeen Camp had been hard enough to see in good conditions.

The Bandage Man's Way

A battered green Ford Explorer, kind of familiar, appeared ahead of me, and I flashed my lights, hoping to catch their attention. I stuck my head out the window as they pulled up and wished I hadn't. The air burned like gasoline in the back of my throat.

"You coming from the Tillamook Burn?" I shouted. Dirty people filled every seat of the SUV.

The driver stuck his head out. I recognized him from some of Naveen's group runs. "We're on our way out!" "Did you see Naveen or Tania?"

He shook his head. "They were behind me."

A girl leaned over his shoulder. "Tania sprained an ankle. Naveen was helping her."

Shit. "Thanks!" I waved, and he rolled up his window, hurrying away.

My eyes stung, and not just from the air. Leave it to Naveen to be a hero.

I sealed up the window, but the pause had invited too much smoke into the car. My lungs hurt. My eyes burned. Even my skin felt weird. I tried not to cough, because once the coughing started, it was almost impossible to regain control over my breathing without hitting the inhaler again, and I didn't want to risk worse jitters or heart palpitations.

Control. That was the key. Box breathing always helped. The smoke narrowed the road to floating white and yellow lines as I inhaled four slow beats, held in the air for four slow beats. Exhaled. Resisted the stinging need to breathe.

My chest loosened a little, but I kept my focus. White lines. Yellow lines. Four counts, moving and retaining air. Four counts. I made the turn for the camp. So close now.

I lost my focus for a second and burst into coughing, so hard stars exploded in my vision and my foot tromped on the gas pedal. The car surged forward, out of control. I tried to scream. Tried to find air. Yanked my foot off the gas.

Something pale exploded across my windshield, and I remembered how to stomp the brakes. Still not breathing, not at all. My head spun.

Ragged white shreds floating everywhere like threads of cotton candy. Sticky stuff, dark spatters of *I didn't want to think about it*. No, maybe it was just chocolate. Chocolate syrup. That was it. I was still in Cannon Beach, and I was parked in front of the candy store, and I had never even heard of Bandage Man.

But when I closed my eyes I could picture the figure, tall and pale with enormous eyes like accusations. The kind of eyes that would terrify a waitress who caught a glimpse of them in the basement of a brew pub, the kind of eyes that would scare the shit out of a kid driving home late at night only to see those gleaming in his rear-view mirror.

The coughing slowed and I found my breath again. My head cleared. The white shit on my window wasn't bandages, of course, but feathers. That same stupid owl had attacked my car again, and this time I'd really hit it. What lousy timing that territorial asshole had.

I threw back my head and laughed and laughed. The laughing made me choke and cough, but the coughing felt better, like it was actually clearing some of the gunk out of my lungs. I pulled myself together and eased the car forward, practically crawling because I remembered how quickly the camp had come up after the owl attack. Then I was there.

People rushed everywhere, loading Subarus and SUVs with gear and event stuff. Vehicles seemed to float in the smoke, unmoored from the forest around us. Figures seeped out of the thick air to drop bags beside cars or toss boxes onto tables, then vanished into the gloom as ethereally as they came. I pulled in beside a picnic table where volunteers were packing up bags of sandwiches and orange slices. I opened my car door as someone dumped an enormous Igloo cooler and the smell of artificial lemon momentarily overpowered the smoke. Ice cubes sluiced around to cover the toe of my sneaker.

"Naveen?" I shouted.

The woman dumping the cooler jerked her chin at me. "You just missed her." She doubled over coughing.

"What do you mean?" It came out more like a gasp than speech. I'd need to use the inhaler again soon, no matter how bad it would make me feel.

"She ran back up the course to help some of the other runners," the woman managed between coughing fits. "She left four, maybe five minutes ago."

I spun around, trying to picture the course map that Naveen had studied so carefully. The runners used the driveway of the camp as a starting chute before they crossed the road to climb the first big hill.

"She was loaded with first aid gear," a volunteer added. "Took all our bandages."

Bandages? I remembered the white feathers floating through the air like bandages unspooled from a mummy. But they were feathers, of course. Not bandages at all.

I saw the grill of my car then, goopy, and chunky with something the same dull red as raw hamburger. And caught in it, a scrap of teal fabric the same color as Naveen's favorite technical tee.

My foot skidded on spilled ice, and I stumbled into the car's hood, my mouth working for air but finding only smoke. An owl. I had hit an owl. A territorial barred owl, not Naveen or a bandaged man. An owl.

The figure in the backseat of my car stared back at me, its eyes as dark as the smoke-filled forest, its cheeks white rags. A sound filled my ears that could have been laughing, or hooting, or my lungs wheezing up a scream. And Bandage Man smiled, his mouth spilling darkness across my vision as I ran out of air.

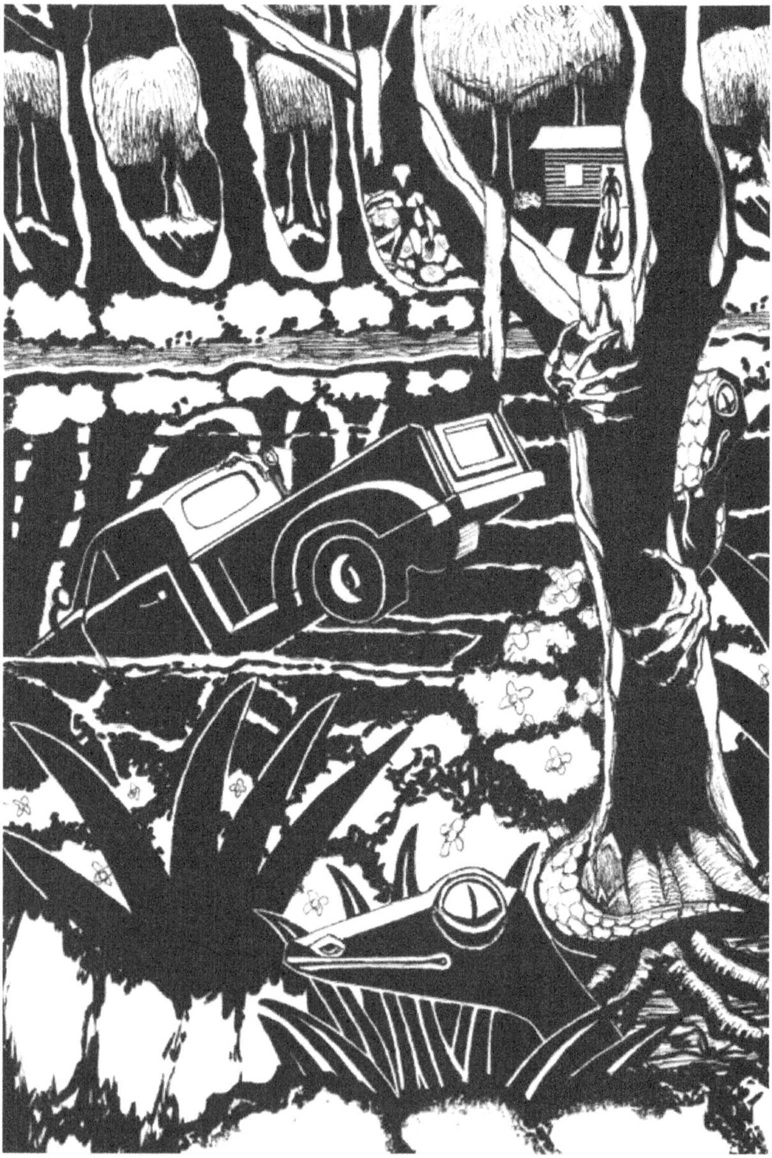

Bloody, Meaty Ends
by Maxwell I. Gold

Crawling through the stink of the humid Midwestern fog, leathery feet clapped over thicket and brush where snapped twigs barely contained the dark, reptilian possibilities lurking in the marshes. A clever spot, thick with mud, death, and soiled fears which for untold centuries concealed the dark rumors of the lizard men who made these wetlands their home. Old trucks broken down, sank into the mud, *swallowed* by the earth or perhaps an unfortunate man caught in the teeth of a hungry alligator? Under bridges, outside the grasp of reason or calls of help. All it took was one, little, fall. The lizard men cared only for ends, the *bloody, meaty* ends.

Rumors though, right?

History, soon bled into mythology while the amber eyes of reptilian gods built their cities of mud, bone, and rumors. Still, on the sultriest nights, many claimed the sinister orchestration of leathery footsteps and wet lips as they smacked underneath a bridge...outside of reason, away from town.

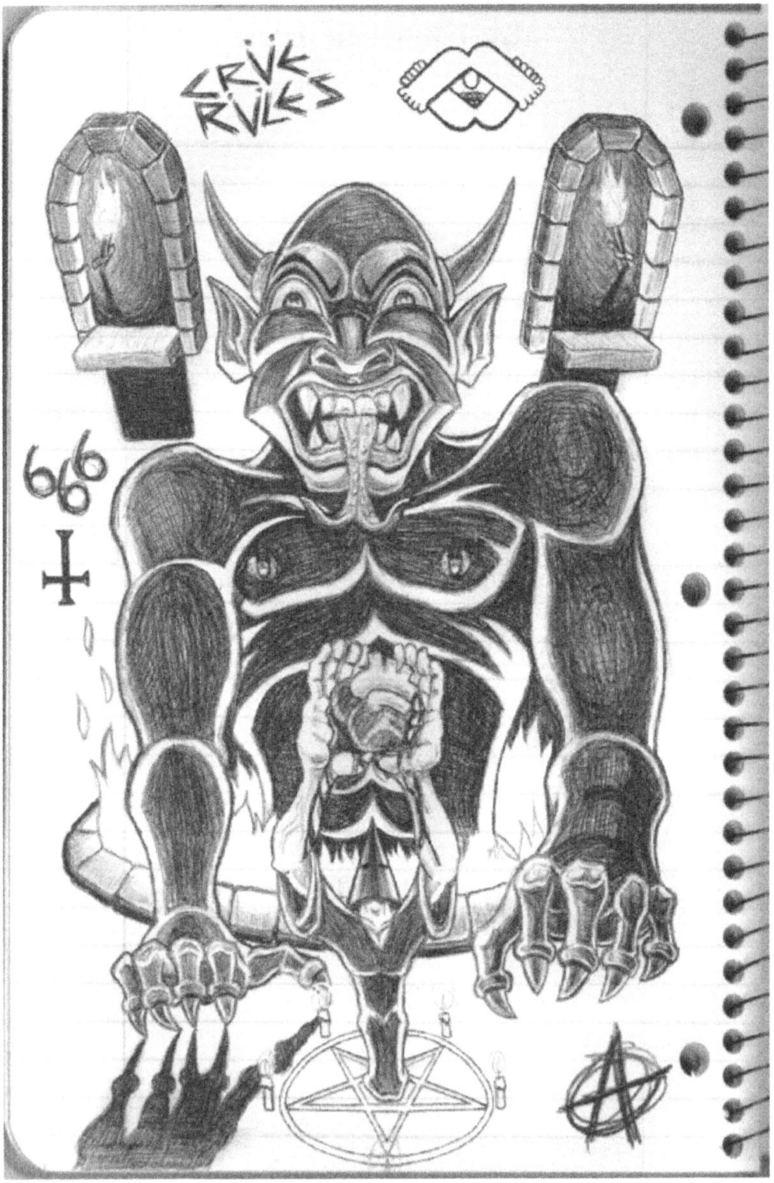
CRÜE
RULES
666

Satanic Panic
by Chelsea Arrington

I heard a rumor the other day! I heard a story, true!
There is a cult within the town of evil through & through.
The members, they all dress in black & speak the Devil's name!
They conjure him by salt & air, by water, & by flame!
They dance & chant & fornicate, unholy are their ways!
To Satan they all pledge their troth; to him they give their praise!
And when the moon is dark & black; & when the moon is gone
The leader will present a babe, from whom all blood is drawn!
A hundred-score they've drained & drunk & lain before their lord;
And when his thirst is sated & his cock is as a sword
He sodomizes each of them & whispers in their ears,
"To me your most belovèd bring & let me drink his tears.
"And so, my friends, beware the lure of rock & roll & drugs!
Avoid all naughty truants, homosexuals, & thugs!
Look not upon the porno mags or trick-or-treating go!
For that's the Devil's night & thus his power you will know!
Delve not into the lurid books of dungeons & of dragons
Or else to Hell your soul will go in handbags & in wagons!
My friends & children, listen well & to sweet Jesus pray,
Lest you may find your way to sin & and to the Devil stray.

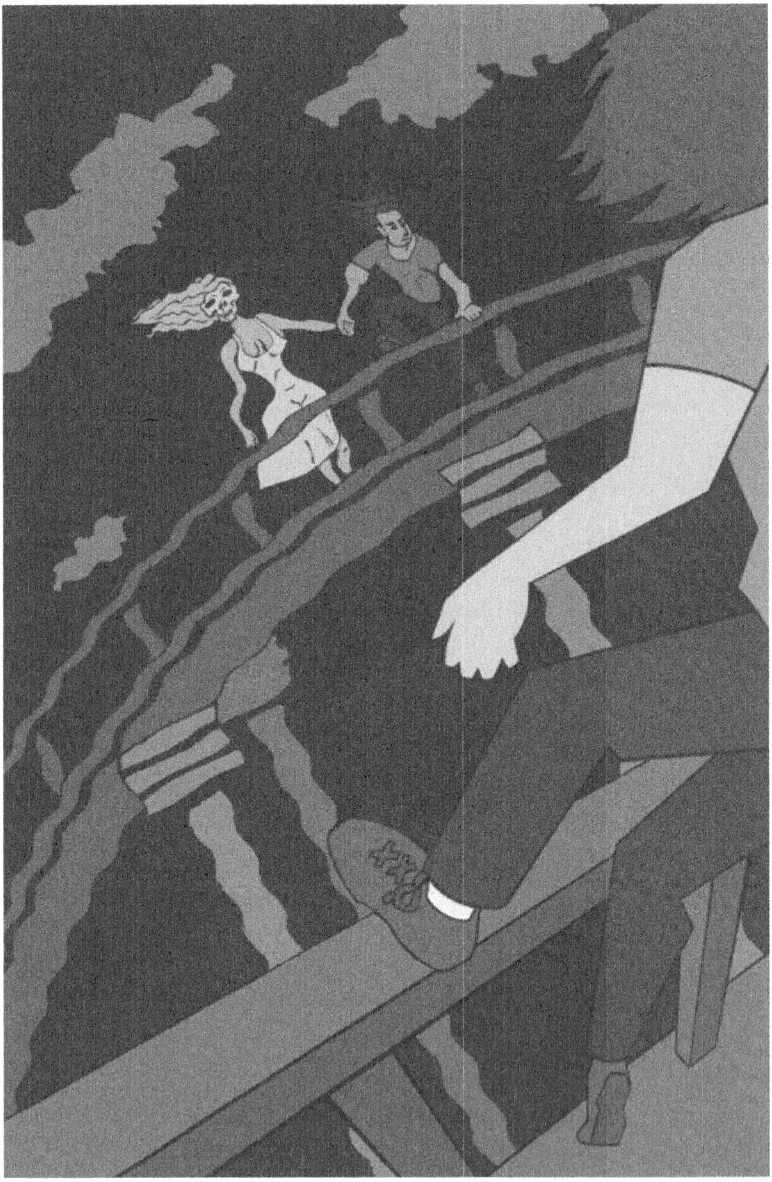

Bridge of Lies
by Hayley Arrington

There is a bridge where lovers went
Or, so I have been told.
A bridge where lovers' vows were spent:
Of happy tears and rings of gold.

But then a summer of suicides
Made all those lovers flee.
No longer happy, blushing brides
Said "Yes" on a lover's knee.

A maiden, so lost and lonely,
A lover's tryst did make.
She found herself gliding, gently,
Amongst soft waters of the break.

A youth at Manhood's door did come
And thought a love he'd made,
Not realizing his lover's hand
Did lead him to the grave.

For true love is eternal, yes,
Sadly, so, too, is regret.
Beware the Bridge where love's confessed.
A different fate will not be met.

Bridge of Lies

Right before you hit the waters
You know it's the Bridge of Lies.
A whispered promise of love's embrace
Is but suicide in disguise…

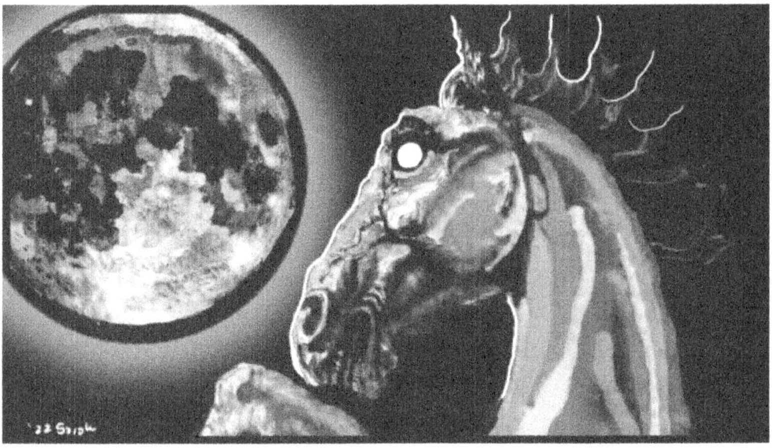

Blucifer
By Carolyn Kay

Blucifer bowed his blue head over his beer and whinnied in frustration, scattering foam across the scarred wood of the bar at Rezalli's Pub. It was his one night off from holding vigil over travelers in his namesake statue, so of course there was an angel at the end of the bar who wanted to poke fun at him.

Rezalli's was neutral ground, a place where anyone from any of the realms could come to unwind over a pint. Brawling was strictly prohibited and swearing required a donation to the swear jar—usually just a quarter, more if the bartender was feeling surly that night. The fine was doubled if Jesus happened to be there. Lucky for Blucifer, tonight was not one of those nights, but he held in a curse out of habit.

Blue flicked his tube-like tongue into his beer, sucking down the amber liquid before turning to the white-winged, angelic figure. Seated on a stool at the end of the spell-protected mahogany bar (some of the stuff Rezalli's served was caustic or worse), the angel stared back at him, its double-helix of multi-colored eyes spinning in a dizzying display around its head. The creature had been smirking at him all night.

And humans thought demons were scary? Blue shook his head, an ethereal wind blowing his mane back. Enough was enough.

"Laugh it up, bub. Yeah, I'm the demon horse of Denver
International Airport. But at least people know me. Who are you again?"

The angel downed his shot, some purple and silver goo, stood and approached Blue with an outstretched hand. Blue hesitated, but decided to be civil, offering up his fist for a bump instead. Physical habits were hard to break, which meant he had to concentrate on actually using fingers instead of his normal hooves. He'd transformed most of his body into a humanoid form for ease of navigating the bar, which, while catering to all sorts of other-planar beings, was primarily set up to serve those who could take a humanoid form. He left his head as it was, in horse form, because it really was his best feature.

"I'm Abasdarhon, from the Head Office. Please forgive me. I wasn't laughing. At least not totally." The angel shrugged, and small bells chimed in response. "I heard the story of Blucifer, but never realized until now that the statue was such a likeness." The angel's voice sounded like a dozen people all speaking at once and all just slightly out of sync.

Blue motioned to the barkeep. "Give me a shot of Heaven with a sulfur chaser. Talking to this angel without it will give me a headache."

The barkeep on duty was a slight gnomish girl with pink pigtails and an equally pink dress. She pulled two shot glasses from beneath the bar, filling one with what looked like liquid gold that smelled like wildflowers and the other with a bubbling yellow slime that smelled exactly like its name. She smiled, flashing teeth a shark would envy and turned to put the two bottles away, holding them like opposite ends of a pair of live jumper cables.

Blue knocked back the golden shot. Warmth and love instantly flooded his chest. He'd save the other shot for when he was done.

"Now Abs, can I call you Abs? Do you want to hear the true story of my statue, or are you going to stand there all hoity-toity with your spinning eyes, and keep laughing at me?"

Seriously, how did angels not fall over dizzy with all their eyes spinning around their head like that?

"Oh, do tell." The shot of heaven had resolved Abs' voice into a single, androgynous alto. Much better. Too bad it didn't do anything about the eyes.

"Well, sit down then. It's not a long tale, but you standing there in my face is making me dizzy."

The angel sat and the noise in the bar hushed. Blue looked around the dim but cozy bar. Most of the overstuffed, burgundy booths were occupied by various demons, fae, reaper angels, and a smattering of other creatures, as were the solid oak tables. Everyone was looking at him. A purple-haired demoness wearing a "Death Metal is for pussies" t-shirt winked at him from a nearby table. Better than being ignored, he supposed. Adjusting his seat on the bar stool, he started his tale.

"It's well known that my namesake statue killed its artist. The head fell right after he'd finished painting it and it severed his femoral artery." There were murmurs through the bar — some sad, some in acknowledgement.

"And of course, everyone thinks I did it. The statue's red eyes freak humans out, so naturally, they think it's possessed. They're not wrong." Blue snorted. "But the head falling was just an unfortunate result of

physics and a thousand pounds of fiberglass and steel."

A few of Abs' eyes slowed in their orbits for a moment before resuming their course. Or maybe it was just the flickering torchlight off the mirror casting odd shadows. Blue blew it off, continuing his tale.

"It all started in El Paso, about 1993." Blue's red eyes glowed with the memory. "Luis was driving home, only half paying attention to the road. He'd just gotten the commission for the DIA job and was trying to figure out what to sculpt for it.

"It was dark, a quarter moon if I remember right, and the dirt road he was on was clouded with dust from a truck full of teenagers racing ahead of him.

"As most of you know, I'm the patron demon of traveling, so I wasn't surprised when I got a call to stop an accident at an intersection about a mile down the road. Figured at the time it was to save the kids, but since then, I'm not so sure."

Blue glanced at the angel, looking for a sign that he was right, but the dang creature just sat there, its eyes spinning madly.

"So anyway, the kids had spun out, trying to take the turn too fast and kicked up a lot of dust, obscuring the fact that there even was an intersection. Things weren't shaping up well for either party. The kids were okay, but they'd gotten a flat and were trying to fix it right there in the middle of the intersection. So, I had to find a way to stop Luis before he ran right into them."

"I usually get a little more notice to come up with something, but I only had a few seconds, so I improvised. Admittedly, it wasn't my most creative work, and I did get reprimanded for it by the Head Office." He glared at Abasdarhon, then eyed the sulfur shot. Not yet.

The bartender slid a beer down the bar to him. Nodding in thanks, he sucked some down. It was cold, harsh, and just a little sweet. Perfect. He downed the pint, wiping away the foam. The angel cleared his throat.

"Oh sorry. Where was I?" Blue knew where he was, but he wanted to make the angel wait out of spite.

"You were about to break the rules and show yourself?" the ghost rider sitting in the back under an Infernal Ale sign said in a smoky voice.

Blue sighed. Was it that obvious? He really needed to work on his storytelling. At least the ghostrider was cute if you were into folks with flaming skulls.

"Way to ruin the punchline. But yeah. Really, I think what I did was actually inspired, and well, it *did* inspire…"

"So, you appeared on the road in more or less your true form." Abs interrupted.

Who was telling the story here? What a prick. Not that he was surprised. Those Head Office lackeys were the worst.

From the look on a few other faces, he wasn't the only one who thought that. Too bad the ban on fighting was so strictly enforced. He'd love to knock a few eyes out of orbit.

Instead, Blue took a deep breath and continued as if the angel hadn't said a word.

"So yeah, I went full horse in the middle of the road and blew the dust clear, so he'd see me in time. The guy loved horses, so I didn't want him to swerve into a ditch. Still, he almost did, but a little nudge kept him on the road. In my haste, I did forget to change my color and I'm pretty sure my eyes flared." He paused for a moment in recollection. "I suppose that's probably more cause for his panicked reaction and pale face than almost hitting a horse. But hey, at least he didn't have to think too hard about his color palette."

Polite chuckles filtered through the smoky haze of the bar. Odd...no one was smoking. Then he spied the source.

"Hey Joe. When did you get here?" Blue raised his chin at the oblong cloud of smoke and shadow by the door.

"Just popped in – right about the time Abs stole your thunder," the Emenra said, disdain clear in his voice.

Blue shot the angel a smug look.

"Let's catch up after, yeah?" Blue asked Joe.

The smoke demon raised a mug of something black and took a seat next to the ghostrider.

"Anyway," Blue got back to his story. "I stayed in the road until I was sure Luis wasn't going to have a heart attack. Once he calmed, I conjured a cloud of dust and disappeared."

A few beings started to clap, but Blue held up his hand before continuing. "I'm not quite done. Something about Luis intrigued me. So, I broke the rules again and went to one of his gallery openings a few years later."

"Please tell me you at least showed up as human this time?" the ghostrider heckled.

Blue neighed a chuckle. "Yeah, I did. Showed up as a Native rancher. Figured I'd try to match the locals there in New Mexico. So anyway... Luis' style was unique, and I was really drawn to it. He caught me staring at a small-scale sculpture of a Native American hunting a bison and came up to talk to me about it. We talked about his use of color—vibrant blues and purples with splashes of red—for probably half an hour. And then he pulled me over to another sculpture. This one was of a rearing blue mustang with red eyes. He said it was the prototype for a larger, more imposing version for an airport. I was blown away. It was like looking in a mirror. The eyes even had LEDs that made them glow. So of course, I fawned over it, all the while waiting to be struck by lightning because it's usually only the angels that get to keep the good press."

Several in the crowd laughed and Joe belched a giant smoke ring.

Blucifer

"But the lightning never came. Luis and I really hit it off. He told me about how an angel in the form of a blue horse had shown up one night while he was driving home. He didn't know why but thought that maybe the angel meant for him to help out the kids with the flat down the road." Blue shrugged. "I mean…I didn't dissuade him of that assumption. He went on to tell me that he'd dreamt of me—that horse—for several weeks after until he started sketching out plans for a sculpture. And that's when he knew it was what he was going to do for the Denver commission."

Blue motioned for another beer from the bartender, and she obliged, sliding a pint down the bar. After a long swig, he continued. "Luis invited me to his studio later that year, and we had coffee often after that. He had an acerbic wit and a kind heart. We'd spend hours talking about the trials and tribulations of the peoples of the southwest – of the inequities endured by farm workers and the hazards faced by those crossing the border seeking refuge. He'd done several pieces of art with those themes, and they really struck a chord with folks.

"He even invited me over to a couple of family dinners where I got to meet his daughter and grandkids, and I met up with him in DC when his vaquero on a blue mustang sculpture was installed at the Smithsonian.

Blue paused, collecting his thoughts. "I was devastated when he died. I'd had no sense his time was up, and for him to be killed by my likeness —it was like a knife through my heart. I went to his funeral and hugged his grandkids one last time. I might have even added an extra zero on the check they got from his life insurance. It was enough that his family could take the time to finish the mustang sculpture and deliver it to the City of Denver.

"It wasn't long after the sculpture went up that I was reassigned as its permanent resident—my watch tower so to speak—to watch over the travelers at Denver's airport. I knew it was punishment for showing myself so blatantly to Luis, but honestly, I didn't mind. It was the least I could do for the memory of a dear friend."

Blue bowed his head and the small crowd in the bar clapped.

Someone let out an earsplitting whistle that made Blue lay his ears back.

"You only delayed the inevitable," Abs said, its voice now lower and more menacing.

"Well yeah, all humans die." Blue quipped back.

"There is a time and a place for everything." The angel's tone reminded Blue of a stern school marm—condescending with notes of superiority. Typical angel. "There's a finely crafted balance that you"—the angel's eyes all stopped and stared at Blue for a split second—"and I have been tasked with maintaining. We both know that free will only goes so far."

Realization dawned on Blue, and he rounded on the angel. "Tell me you didn't, you holier-than-though freak show!"

The angel smiled and the room got darker. "The Head Office decided to let things slide after your…slip up. The head honcho has a soft spot for artists, and things seemed to be working out ok in spite of the deviation from the plan. But as time went on aberrations started appearing on the projected timeline, and, well, you know how things are." Abs shrugged and somewhere tiny bells chimed again.

Blue's vision went dark, the colors in the bar shifting to red. Somewhere far off, the bartender's voice warned him about the no fighting rule. He ignored her, stepping nose to face with the angel.

"So, you killed him with his own art? That was you? Why not just a massive stroke, or a coronary in his sleep? Luis deserved better than to bleed out on his studio floor."

Blue debated whether a head-butt or just a fist to the head would be more effective against the celestial being. Meanwhile, Abs seemed wholly unperturbed by Blue's anger.

"Luis paid for your mistake by the most poetic means, if I do say so myself."

The angel's attitude gouged into Blue like a hot knife, but something made him pause for the second time that night.

"My mistake? Luis was supposed to die that night? Then why did the

Blucifer

head office send me and not a reaper?"

The angel shrugged. "Most of us were at a birthday party. I got there too late – you'd already gone, and the Head Office called me off. The boss wanted to see how things shook out."

Stupid angels. First of Creation, and lazy as all get out. When demons came on the scene, the angels made them do most of the dirty work, preferring to lounge around and be muses or the occasional holy messenger. Head Office wasn't much better. Abs was right – they were all about free will until they weren't. Blue slumped back onto his barstool and grabbed the shot of yellow slime, slamming it back. The searing pain of the molten mineral sliding down his throat kept him from going after the angel. Damn the Head Office anyway.

By the time his vision cleared from the pain, Abs was gone and several of the bar patrons surrounded him.

"Dude's the ultimate asshole, Blue." Joe said. A chorus of voices agreed.

"To Luis and Blucifer, and art that grows on you!" the bartender said in a gravelly voice, raising a glass.

Blue, his eyes watering from the sulfur shot (shut up, that stuff's strong!), lifted his empty glass with the rest, in memory of a man who saw him for what he was, and turned it into genius inspiration.

Later that night, if a traveler at DIA dared to look closely, they would have noticed Blucifer's eyes glowing a little brighter, and the lightning on his sides flashing as Blue watched over them.

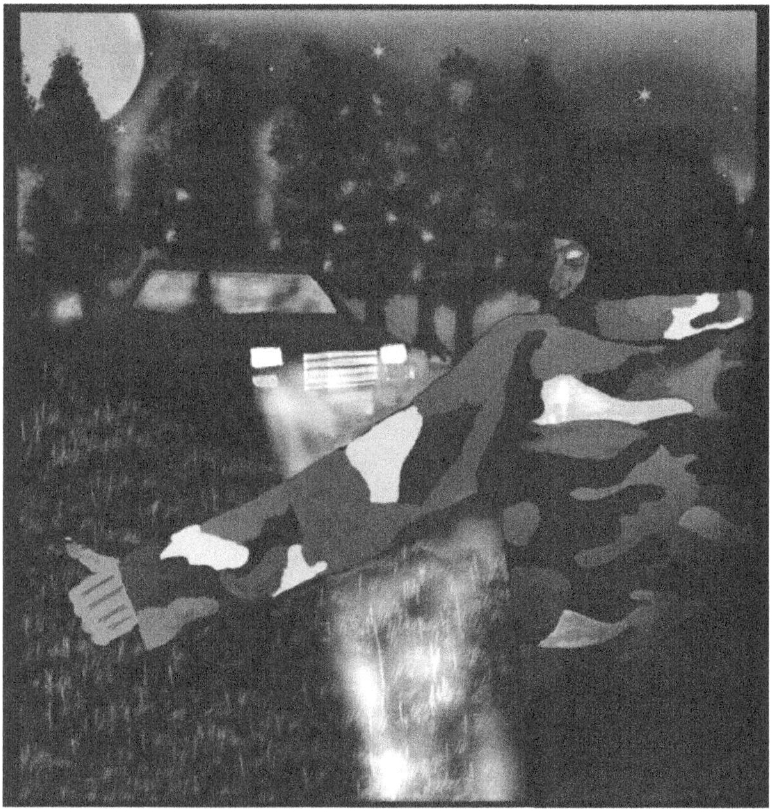

Along a Rural Highway
by D. L. Myers

The creeping blackberry vines, which lined the highway, twisted, and quivered in the car's headlights, as it rushed into the twilight. The driver and passenger pondered what presences might linger amongst the dark trees through which they drove; the highway a river slicing through a vast gorge of greenery.

A figure appeared suddenly, at the side of the road, and then vanished in a flash of the car's lights. A breath later, it was only a bleached snag in the rearview mirror. Drunken bats swooped over the road disappearing in the trees to either side, and then reappearing in an endless parade.

The road ahead curved into the shadows of the trees, and at the bend of the road stood a man with his arm outstretched and his thumb up. The car slowed and stopped on the shoulder. For long moments, the man continued to hold his pose at the edge of the road, then shuffled to the car and got in.

He wore moss-stained, green camo, several sizes too large for his scrawny frame, and a rumpled t-shirt with a large, rusty stain. His hair was wild; his beard as well, and on his lap sat a corroded metal box. As soon as they pulled back onto the road, they were assailed by a noxious stench that overwhelmed the driver to such an extent that he brought the car to an abrupt halt.

Disgusted and repelled, the driver and passenger ejected the man and sped away, but the fetid odor did not exit with him. Even with the windows down, the smell was overpowering, and then the driver saw that

Along a Rural Highway

the metal box was sitting on the backseat. The car braked hard and slid off the road. the passenger pounced on the back door and opened it. On the worn, leather seat, the box sat squat and menacing, and he had to work himself up to lifting it from the car. As he turned toward the forest, something fluttered and shifted inside the box, and he dropped it before he even registered the fear that rose within him. here on the pavement lay seven dead, desiccated birds. They were in a constant state of motion with flutterings and head motions cold and stiff. But true terror froze him to the core when he saw what lay beyond the birds. A heart that softly pulsed and the great, grey worms that coiled about it.

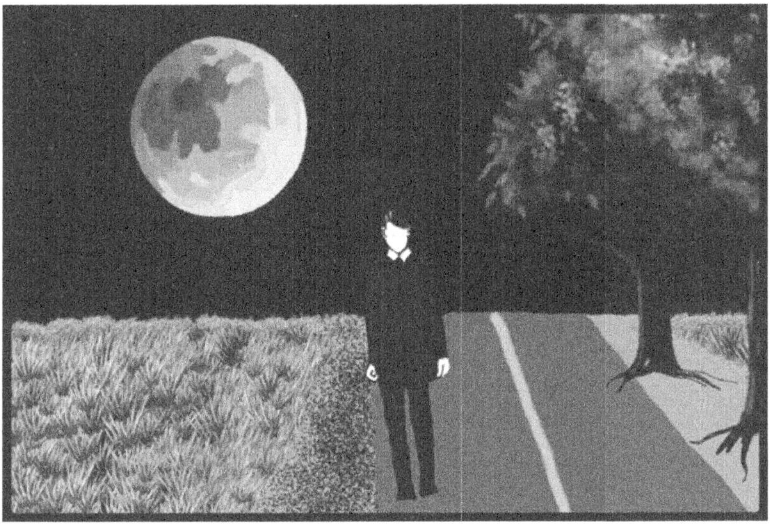

Face the Music
By Duane Pesice

Lloyd leaned forward, steepling his fingers, his elbows on his knees. He began touching the tips of each finger, alternating, to the tips of his thumbs. Both hands.

He started slow and got going pretty well before his face unclenched and his chest stopped heaving.

A dozen feet away, another boy lay on his back, staring at emptiness. His respiration was slow, his expression ecstatic.

Near the other curb, a gaggle of moon-eyed preteens rubbernecked. They were buzzing, talking among themselves.

I wished I'd brought my deerstalker cap, but I didn't, and there wasn't going to be any seven-percent solution here, even if it did all turn out to be elementary.

My other son Jason emerged from behind the salt storage, his thumbs active as he texted people he thought needed to know what had happened.

"Jason." I said.

He looked up from his phone. "One sec." His thumbs did the rumba.

"Yes."

"Spill," I demanded.

"Lloyd and Eric here don't like each other. This is two years of bullshit ending. Eric started it."

"I'm going to need more than that. Why is Eric lying on his back dreaming into the clouds?" "Um, Eric had a moment."

"Did Lloyd have anything to do with his 'moment'?" I could feel a real good scowl coming on.

"Not, not exactly. The 'moment' had to come eventually. Karma…" My incipient scowl deepened.

The mob of kids were quiet.

Face the Music

"Tell the whole thing," I said.

"Yes, sir. When we moved here, Eric took an instant dislike to Lloyd. He spent a lot of time picking on him, calling him names, even hitting him once in a while if he thought he could get away with it. And he always had his buds around. It made him brave."

"Please continue."

"It just made Lloyd sad. He stimmed his way out of it all. But one day Lloyd talked back. You see Eric is a big boy, kinda fat. Lloyd is a big guy, but he doesn't have real muscles. And he's kinda goofy.

"Anyway, Lloyd had enough, and he said, "I don't respect your authoritah, Cartman." The nickname stuck."

"Well, it's perfect," I admitted. "This is South Park, PA, yes?"

"Yes. But Eric beat the shit out of him. Lloyd never told you that. He just said he fell down. And after that was when Lloyd took to walking around at night."

"I remember." And I did. Lloyd took to walking down toward where we were now. I'd followed him a couple of times to see that there wasn't trouble, and he did have his phone.

"Well, Lloyd met someone he could talk to. Someone he felt close to. He told me he used to talk to the ghost every night, and that one day the ghost had hugged him, and he was able to feel how what he did affected other people, and it opened his eyes."

"The ghost-hug?"

"The ghost-hug."

"Okay. Let's assume for an instant that I believe all of this, Jason. The ghost-hug would work how?"

"Well, the ghost had seen a lot of awful things, and felt some awful things, yet he was still kind and forgiving, and he passed it on."

"Fine," I said evenly. "And this relates to the scene how?" I indicated my son and his adversary with my chin.

"They were fighting. Lloyd texted me that he had seen Eric nearby and expected trouble, so I was here not long after it started. Eric was trying to stab Lloyd.

"The ghost came out, and he took the stab, and got closer, and hugged Eric.

"Eric's such a shit, he couldn't take knowing what he was. He passed out."

I tried to take it all in. I really tried. But it was so ridiculous, on the face of it.

But, but. There was a legend, an urban legend, of a ghost in these parts, the shade of a man named Raymond Robinson, who had experienced electrocution and had lived through it. He had been bullied, feted, in short, exposed to humanity.

And this was where he had hung out.

It wasn't at all a surprise to see a man with no eyes and a hole for a nose sitting among the preteen brigades.

"Charlie," I said. He dipped his head.

Eric awakened, looked about him, blinking. "What? Oh yeah," and he got up and left.

"There's no crime here," I said. "Everyone, get lost." They scattered, except Jason and Lloyd.

And Charlie No-Face, who had saved my son.

"Thanks," I said simply.

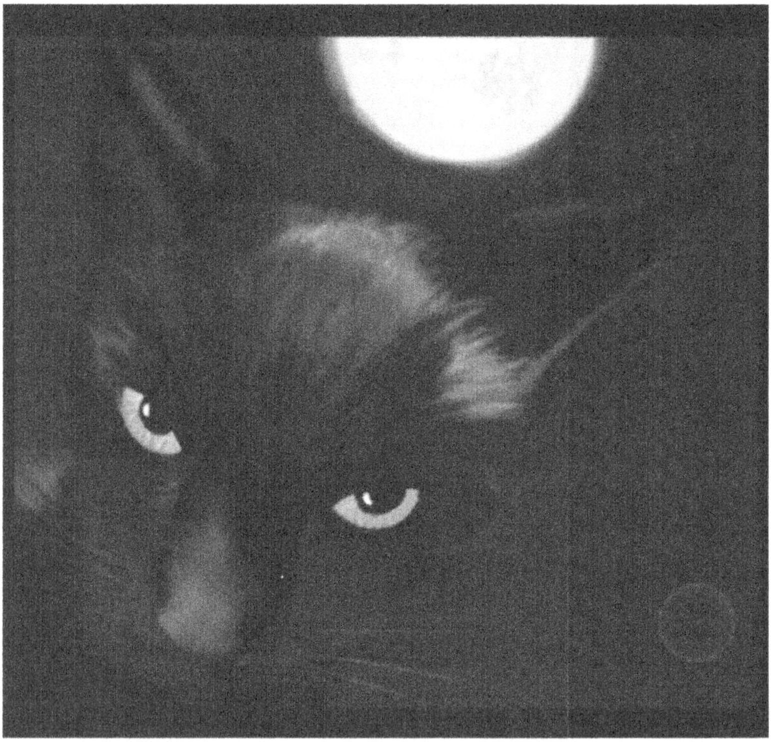

Half-Sick of Shadows
By R.W. Moffat

Nobody knows who the mirror belonged to, only that Elaine picked it up, and with some difficulty and two sweaty bus-journeys carried it home. Brought it home to that little quarter mile of the Fleet that isn't Camden, or Chalk Farm or Gospel Oak or anything much but an afterthought of all three and all the little villages that make up Old St Pancras. That little quarter mile that has been the haunt of peculiar mirrors and fearful reflections since before London swallowed it. The home of haunted mirrors and the Cantlows Hag.

It was left out on the street for passers-by to collect. It is unknown whether this was an act of deliberate cruelty - murder, if you will - or if its previous owner was quite unaware of its waiting, waiting for a victim like Elaine. I imagine it had been travelling for years.

My feeling - built on my weary experience with these inchoate matters - is that it was discarded thoughtlessly by bereaved family. By family who'd grown up with it, vaguely oppressed by its fogged glass, the bluish cast and the ragged black spaces, the lost mercury; the odd way in which the tight clutch of shatter in its bottom left corner seemed sometimes to reflect light that wasn't there.

I see an old woman, long bed-ridden, wrecked, and infirm, and bewildered sons doing their best and, in the barely lit marches of her final morning, in a struggle to make sense, to take control of the uncontrollable, they put it out. And they stand there together, in the silent, empty, pale North London Street, contemplating the dawn of a world without her in it.

But I am afflicted with these imaginings. This sight. There was a time when I was told that it was a talent, that I had "the gift" as my breed of outsiders call it. Which, thanks to my wry German mother, always makes me sneer in cynical amusement. "Gift" in German is, of course, nothing short of poison.

Half-Sick of Shadows

My name is Absalom Gaunt, and I am a witch.

I was contemplating drinking a second glass of breakfast negus when all my familiars suddenly stared at the staircase a half-second before the doorbell rang below. Sometimes I wondered if they listened at the speed of light. Such thoughts often come after breakfast negus.

I heaved myself down the long curve of stair-tunnel, nose full of the damp lime and horsehair reek of it, slippers scuffing on the bare boards, down to the lovely old front door and the few bright bars of stained-glass sun that shimmered through its fanlight. Down to meet the piled meat and tired polyester of Officer Tennyson. The poor boy still had no idea why his SIO called him Alfred, or why, in vexing circumstances, she would mutter "Alfred, Lord..." as she struggled to control herself.

I reached up and opened the door and let in the bustle of noise, the stink of last night's pub-piss, and Tennyson's not inconsiderable shadow. As usual, Alfred was wearing his "being polite to the freak" face, which mostly resembled bafflement leavened with discomfort and, probably, some very British type of rage.

"Officer Tennyson."

His tiny eyes, jittery in their sockets, scrutinized the doorframe and stairs, the ceiling, even the worn paintwork on the door itself. Anything but looking at me. This morning, the negus made me genial, so I found amusement in his discomfort. I mean, to look at, I'm not even close to as disconcerting as some on this street. Perhaps a bit short. No, not that exactly. I'm not a dwarf. I just.. I look.. I look further away.

"Doctor."

"Will I need my bag?"

"Job's in Camden."

I waited, more out of fun than expectation. No, there was nothing else, no further clarification. The pale and puffy face stared, impassive, at a space somewhere above and beyond me. Message delivered. I turned and went back upstairs. I'd probably need my bag.

Earlier that morning, under a sodden blue shop-awning a little bit too much like the tarps the UN use to shelter the displaced, the Engineer had stood looking down the greasy, rain-swept expanse of Kentish Town Road smoking hungrily at a cheap cigarette and pondering. Under the awning, misty rain spray swirled, cooling the racked fruit and tomatoes and pumpkins, and darkening the grimy paintwork and the filth in amongst the chipped ceramic tile. The dangling strings of Halloween mirrors flickered dully in the gloom, signaling their brethren hung from other awnings up and down the street. Did the outside mirrors like his mutter to each other, loathe the brighter, drier ones in the crystal shop across the road, envy their bright reflections lazily turning in the incense scented middle-class air within? He wondered about that, but knew it was just him. Just him and his bitterness and disappointment.

Cars and buses, vans and trucks buzzed by, hissing and fizzing in the weather like a thousand busy, very wet snakes. The rain had been falling steadily all night and the smells were long past petrichor, were now the dismal stink of summer drains unlocked, the fishiness of woken rot. Past the gaudy chipped and peeling paintwork of the Abbess of Cantelowe and the rain-heavy trees the muddy yellow brick of the railway bridge still bore its message in blocky white graffiti. "Hope." Not likely.

He screwed a bitter smile around the cigarette and his mind drifted on. Was schadenfreude something you could feel about yourself? The ironies were quite delicious. Here he was in a dilapidated terrace shop, with all his degrees, and there was hope scribbled on a railway bridge, and next to it, between him and the canal and Camden Lock was a construction site, a world he knew as well as this life was foreign to him. Every day. Every damned day.

With another deep inhalation the cigarette was done, pulled right down to the filter, hot and bitter. It arced out into the rain and was lost to the street. He was contemplating having another and luxuriating in the burn deep in his lungs when a customer appeared. Frankie. Frankie Carter. Student. From that last, lost row of old houses that split the development, a slim melancholy finger stuck down the roaring throat of the new.

He hadn't been good at customers at first, but there was a rhythm to

Half-Sick of Shadows

it, a performance. Just as there was more to stock than having full shelves. He'd understood that straight away. Was surprised to find that a skill he'd used to build bridges and hospitals and schools was also applicable to canned meat and bread and household goods. But he'd had to work at customers. So, he had learned them, faces first, then names and little facts. Where they lived, what they did. And in that there was some pleasure. A sense of achievement when they came to him and not to the Sainsbury's down the street.

Frankie Carter had been easy to learn. She was small and shy and slightly adrift. He recognized her discomfort. The sense that she was in this world, this place, but not really. Not actually present. She seemed as unaware of her physical self as he was aware of it. Which was painfully. She wore baggy shapeless clothes and big spectacles and didn't often wash her hair. But even this camouflage could not conceal the swell of thigh against her sweatpants or the soft movement under her sweaters. And so, in order not to demean either himself or her, he kept his eyes always on her face. It was a face that had become a sweetness, a sweetness among the canned goods and wilted cabbages.

But today it was pinched with worry, the eyes darting, the skin more than usually grey, the hair lanker. Today too, she had not properly dressed. A soaking dressing-gown over blue pajamas, rabbit slippers grey and ruined on her feet. He watched her slosh past the Abbess, a pale figure reflected in its wet windows, on the slick black sidings of its street terrace and captured a thousandfold in the festoons of hag-mirrors that hung from each prominence of its faience facade.

As she stepped under the awning he towered over her, this small, this tiny woman. She looked up at him, and he saw that she'd picked at a spot and that a thin trickle of blood ran down her cheek, diluted by the rain.

"Good morning, Sayyid Yusuf." She spoke with a bright, formal politeness, as if her throat were made of crystal and her tongue of glass.

"Would you have anything for cleaning mirrors?"

Wide and green, her eyes flickered with an unmoored madness.

Inside the shop and in its bright lights and among the bright colors of packaging and cans and rows of bottles she looked even more grey. Soaked to the skin and shivering, leaving a puddle on the floor by the household goods, she continued brightly to talk.

"I'll definitely need to clean that mirror. I've got to clean it right out.. She's going to be more difficult, though..."

She frowned more deeply and dug with a restless thumb at some itch in the corner of her mouth.

"Blood shouldn't be hard, should it? I mean solid-hard not difficult." Frankie fixed Yussuf with a wild and wobbly stare, which slowly lost its focus until she looked no more animated than a doll. Worried, Yussuf spoke slowly.

"Blood? - I see you've hurt yourself.."

He reached out a tentative thumb towards her bleeding cheek and Frankie snapped back to life, aware and feverish.

"Oh no - that was her. It was the blood. Elaine's before...before she...went?"

The trembling woman began to rummage in her pockets, dressing gown first, then the pajamas. The top pocket over her left breast was stained. Stained red. Of course, it was to this that she came last, having rummaged through every pocket on the way and filled Yussuf's nose with the ghost of her night scent and more hints of her than he felt remotely comfortable with. She fished the thing out of her bloody pocket and showed it to him, glistening on her palm. It was dark and glossy, about the same size and shape as an apple-seed and set in a small, ragged oval of pale material.

"I tried to wipe it off, but it was too hard. Look, it's like glass."

Frankie tapped the object with a fingernail. A fingernail that he could see was grimed with blood. A moon of it under the nail and soaked well in around and under the cuticle where the rain had not been able to wash. The bloody fingernail struck the thing with a faint ringing sound.

"In the end I had to peel it off."

She mimed picking at her cheek, and Yussuf could see now that the oval of stuff which backed the shiny red thing was a match for the shape that bled.

It was as if a shutter fell. A sheet of impervious armor between Yussuf and Frankie, between him and whatever had happened. Some lessons are only learned the hard way and Yussuf had learned his well. Protect yourself from the brutalized, for their injuries can be infectious. Give charity but don't get involved. Give it so you don't get involved. Stay invisible. Be grey. Survive.

It would be more than an hour before he came to himself again. Long after the mad wounded girl had taken several washcloths and bottles of glass cleaner and bleach and headed off back into the weather. The rain was passing slowly to the east and the road was glittering palely in the watery sunshine as he came out of his fugue and felt the shame of it. He kept his hand on the telephone until he'd revisited the conversation several times, and the plastic was warm as he wearily raised the instrument and called the police.

"So," droned Tennyson in his flat uninflected voice as we crossed the river and the rain started up again, "the shopkeeper calls the uniforms, and they send some poor bitch and her mate from Community Support, and they head down into this Bentine Mansions place. More of an alley, really and it's between these big building jobs. Fucking noisy, and of course they don't know which place, do they? He only knows she lives down there, somewhere. Used to go right through to Camden Lock it did - you know? Houses worth a bit if it still did. Anyway, they make their way down the road, knocking and ringing and checking and asking, looking for this Carter girl. Nobody's quite sure what to expect. I mean, she sounds mad, right?"

It hardly seemed necessary, but I meekly nodded as he drove and held forth, bullying the big black car through the wet streets, heading North. Outside the car the world was streaming, hazy greys and blues, occasional flashes of color, the throbbing brightness of traffic signals, indicators, brakes.

"So, they miss a few empty places, speak to a couple of old birds and finally one of them says 'oh her? mad girl? number eight' or something like that and off they go, straight there and the door's open, see? House lights are off, no answer to the knock.

"And in they go and there's no sign of the Carter woman, but there's movement in the shadows back of the house, out towards the kitchen and they go in. Powerful smell of puke they said. And she's in her bra in the kitchen scrubbing her shirt with a wooden spoon on the breadboard propped up in the sink."

"This one looks wild mad too and is crying. So, women and all -"

Tennyson made a weird sideways wobble of his head and raised his hand from the gearstick momentarily, palm up.

"- they start looking after her. One of them tries to calm her down, make some tea, finds some biscuits, but the woman isn't interested, just stares at them all nuts. The other one checks out the bathroom and finds some clothes for her. You know, hung up over the bath?"

Tennyson paused to concentrate on the junction with Euston Road and I gazed absently through the steamy glass at the great grey mass of St Pancras the New, its tall pillar-box red doors like the distant heat in a Rothko painting. So, the woman in the house wasn't Carter and there were two female community officers? As we set off again, so too did Tennyson.

"They get the sick one dressed and sat down and they ask her, y'know, what's wrong eck-cetera, and they're getting nothing, nothing at all. She seems dumb. Struck dumb. So, while her oppo is trying to dig something - anything - out of the sick one, the senior one goes looking around for the mad one. Her mate hears her sort of squawk and the front door go and she comes out to find the poor cow puking. She's leaning over double in the street puking straight into the gutter."

I was reasonably sure by now that Tennyson's anonymous women were four; two PCSOs, Carter and a housemate of hers. I wondered if his written reports were like this and listened to his words tumble heedlessly on.

Half-Sick of Shadows

"Sound crime-scene skills, 'course, but still. Anyway, the oppo goes back in to see what the fuss is about. Turns out she's the only one with a strong stomach, see? Third time lucky, ha. Calls it in. Proper uniforms come. They send for CID; the dicks call it in again. Control calls us. We go round. We call you."

It was a shared house in an alley in Kentish Town, close by the canal, but on the wrong side of the tracks. The rain was coming down heavily again and it was damp and chilly.

Tennyson stopped the car and sighed. Chunky hands still at ten-to-two on the steering wheel, he stared off at nothing in particular. He looked unwilling to get out of the car. As discomfited as a dog by something in the corner.

"Problem?" I inquired. He sighed again. Started the business of getting out of the car, the clicks, and clacks of neutral and seatbelt, keys. Raincoat, radio.

"No, Doctor. Just. This one's weird."

Outside the car, we did up our coats in the wet wind and as we walked down the alley I considered all that he'd told me on the way up. Two women disappeared: Frankie Carter and her housemate Elaine Scalotta. One remaining occupant, Lydia Newcombe, in what Tennyson called 'a state.' Indications that Carter might have attacked Scalotta included her behavior at a local shop prior to her disappearance, and a bloody tableau on the stairs. It was this that had brought us in.

Us? Well, the National Crime Agency anyway. Tennyson *et al* worked in an obscure, apparently administrative department called Unscheduled Risks. Not always affectionately known as the Odd Squad. What they did was weird, always. Which was why they occasionally consulted with me. That Tennyson found this one disturbingly so was troubling. He went on.

"It's the blood I think. There's a lot of blood. And a shoe. It's like a wizard's shoe."

Here he made an odd sort of gulping sound. Cleared his throat and wiped his nose.

"Full of blood. And it's like glass." He frowned at me. "Like glass, but

176

it looks fresh. Like it's wet, still liquid. Soaked into the stair carpet, the walls - through the shoe? But it's glass. It's…. Wrong."

"Okay." The negus was more or less worn off by now so I was just feeling weary, in need of coffee and sugar, and I was going to need a little time to get up to speed.

"So," I said as we got to the blue front door, cracked, and weathered paint, dull old brass knocker, "the stairs are where, exactly?"

"Um, in there? Right side of the hall. Across from the girl's - the one who's gone. I mean not the mad one? The one that might be…ugh. Her room."

"Let's start with that, then? There's no blood in the room, I gather?"

"Yeah." He muttered something into the radio mike at his shoulder, and with a suck of door-brushes and a slight squeak, the door was opened.

The down-at-heel house contained many -- as an estate agent would say -- original features. Deep skirting, broad plank floors, coving and chair and picture rails. Plaster cornices and lamp-roses brutally ignored by the modern lighting which punched through the ceilings any old how, and fine doorframes insulted by modern fire-doors.

The staircase ran up the side of the entrance corridor from opposite the door to Elaine's room, with the stairwell opening supported by a shallow arch. The arch was unremarkable. Its corbels were not. There was something about the corbels that made my palms itch. I looked at each hand in turn. The faint beginnings of stigmata were there on both. A little more on the left, perhaps. A reddening of the life, head, and heart lines, where they met and mingled in the middle of my palm. Puffiness around them, the center of each palm marked by an itchy, almost painful M.

The paired figures stretched out of the walls, the arch springing from their shoulders and shadowing their outstretched faces. They were, or had been, angels. Along their long backs were the crude stumps of sawn-off wings. Wooden, but now smothered in year upon year of white paint and plaster, gloss, eggshell, emulsion, lime. Their faces were round, their

Half-Sick of Shadows

hair crude and bulbous masses. What could be seen of their eyes under the paint were wide almonds, leaf-shaped; their mouths open, distorted by stratified paint into peculiar snarls. They were by my reckoning a fat seven hundred years old and I didn't like them one little bit.

Elaine's room was the major room of the ground floor and opened off the tiled entrance hall. As an artefact, it was almost wholly intact. There was a complete circuit of cornice, picture rail, chair rail, skirting. There was a wedding-cake fireplace and a chimney-breast cupboard and a deep window seat in the bay window. There were clothes everywhere, skirts draped on chairs, coats piled on the table/desk, the figure-eight knots of peeled knickers here and there on the floor, shoes in the fireplace and books in teetering stacks by the bed. Photographs of a redhead. She changed from girl to woman and the people around her changed too, but she was the constant, bright red hair, and bright green eyes. Bright.

The mirror was propped on the mantelpiece, scabbed brown intricate geometric frame, and about three feet by two. The glass was foggy blue in places and wide sprawls of blown silvering marred it like mildew. The cracks were the first thing that really caught my eye. I was standing next to the bed and breathing her in when I felt watched. Seen. As I turned, something deep black and shiny was present, then gone, like an eye snapping shut, there in the bottom left corner of the glass. There was a small snarl of shards tucked tight into the corner, thin and long, like the petals of some kind of flower, and from this a few longer cracks spilled, like stamens, while a single long crack bisected the entire thing from the bottom left corner to a point halfway along the top. When I looked straight at them they were ordinary, inert, unremarkable damage. But if I looked away they changed.

I looked out of the window and let the glass petals unfurl. At first there was just darkness, different shades of shadow across the clenched shards. And then there was movement, glossy movement, as if something were creeping up to the glass, and then the slow congealing, coalescing, of a single black eye, fragmented, segmented, shifting and blinking. I imagined Elaine sleeping, dressing, working, with that eye crawling all over her skin and shuddered.

"Could I speak to Ms. Newcombe, d'you think?"

The kitchen was pure student, or at least how I remembered it being. A battered dining table of two folding leaves and uneven gate legs and the faintly sour smell of cheap varnish on its way out. Fitted cupboards, with not a single door hanging true, piled undone washing-up. Cheap kettle, cheap toaster, greasy gas cooker with eye-level grill and scorched wall-paint behind. Smells of old black tea, spoiled fruit, grease. Our untouched tea cooled in mismatched mugs, the small lumps of nearly sour milk bobbing with dwindling brownian motion.

Bright coral close-fitting wool sleeves exposed pale wrists, almost white, like statuary, which she obsessively rubbed with long bony fingers. Knobby pink knuckles and elegant oval nails nibbled right down to the red quick. Her hair gleamed like oiled water, spilling in well-fed autumn waves down a heart-shaped face. A face that no doubt was placidly beautiful in repose but currently riven by frowns and deep fatigued lines about mouth and eye. Her voice came in slow querulous snatches, chewed around pursed and screwed lips. Curiously high-pitched, it seemed too old for her.

"Why this concern over the damned mirror? She found it in.... Stoke Newington. Discarded."

A pale hand dashed back a tumble of silky-rich hair. She was hopelessly out of place here, and the air around her seemed to shimmer with the dissonance of it, a screeched undertone to her current distress, like the tiny howling of snowflakes falling on open water.

I watched in queasy fascination as Lydia found a tiny corner of dry skin at a cuticle and scraped it back with her opposing thumb. Her skin blanched and reddened under the assault and I watched the tiny bright bead of blood as it bellied, watched her absently lick it away.

"That mirror - it's nothing. Just a mirror. Aren't you supposed to - don't you want to know…"

Tennyson cleared his throat from the corner and stated:

Half-Sick of Shadows

"That is, the Doctor here is, hmm, not Police exactly. Advisory. Please just answer the Doctor's, um, questions. They might be important."

Lydia looked between us, bewildered.

"Advisory? What on, antiques!? My - they're gone and, and you, you - how am I to, going to .... pay rent if they're dead!?"

And she collapsed in on herself, like a wilting flower, sobbing clumsily into her wool-sheathed forearms, hands bent on the table palm upwards, like a supplicant.

"Boss!" Tennyson bellowed out of the kitchen door. "She's crying again."

Fenn appeared at the door, face a fine conflict between distaste at Tennyson and professional care for her charge. She ushered us out of the kitchen.

"Tennyson, why don't you show the Doctor the stairs, while I make Ms. Newcome a nice cup of tea."

ΦΦΦ

I once saw a documentary about wolves. In it, alongside dramatic music and helicopter shots and sci-fi graphics, the makers explained the extreme sensitivity of wolves to scent and to sound, to all the physical states of the world around them. That their senses were extra forms of sight. So heightened, so full of information that it would overwhelm a merely human brain. It was overblown pop-science nonsense of course, but it was the first thing that helped me manage my gift.

Not that I am a wolf. No. In more folklore-woven times my sort were wise women, seers, sybils. People with sixth senses, second sight. I've never found the terms useful. This sensitivity is not extra, and without control and management it's all the time. I - we - have to develop skills to dial it all down or we'd go mad, awash with all that data. Things like the negus help take the edge off, and meditation. Self-hypnosis. But at the bottom of those stairs, I was going to have to dial it back up. My stomach uncurled and squeezed. It was showtime.

ΦΦΦ

Against the curdling in my stomach, I first stepped back a little, so that I had both angels and mirror in view. Ignoring the staircase, I allowed myself to relax, to allow the prickling of the angels and the foreboding black thing in the mirror to mingle, to wake my gift.

I was right. The angels were very old and fierce, but they seemed only kittens next to the rage from behind the glass. I had thought the angels aware of me, and angry, but it was overflow. In truth the pair were poised like cats watching a particularly unpleasant rat. The thing in the mirror was truly terrible. Screaming, foul. They hated it.

When I reached such shimmering sensitivity that I could hear the collagen straining in Tennyson's jaw and the dust collecting under the floorboards, I turned my absurdly heightened senses on the stairs. They were a howling sleet of fear and terror, loss, and rage.

To my wide-open straining eyes, they appeared to sit apart from the house, a step away, on the other side of some shimmering boundary, inside a copy house constructed of glass and crystal, the planes, and panes of which were trembling, vibrating just on the edge of shatter, as if scraped by the fingernails of the damned.

Inside this the staircase stood, still as wooden as in the real, its carpet as threadbare, its one plaster wall as scuffed by shoulders. A little island of stasis, the eye of that crystal storm.

The blood began three steps up, finger marks on banister and wall. Fingers that had been very bloody, pressed and smeared against the wood and plaster as if their owner had been using all their strength to propel themselves upstairs. There were deep scratches here and there and the long rinds of torn fingernails, and about halfway up bloody footprints too. The first was a mere smudge, a heel or toe print maybe, but with every step they grew larger until by the top of the stairs the prints were paired, saturated. The handprints flailed their way up in tandem with the feet until they reached the landing and then stopped. One pace beyond the stairhead was a puddle of gore, with centered in it a small, pointed leather slipper, itself half-full. Beyond this final tableau nothing, nothing but the crystal house screaming and the dim remembrance of the human one, far, far away.

"Shit." I said and shut my eyes. Bent a little, and queasy, I asked Tennyson to please retrieve my bag.

I faced the mirror amid the squealing of its cracked glass and the warbling notes of tortured reality. I rifled through my equipment, the little glass jars, selected one. I lifted it out and made eye contact with its occupant. The octopus roiled within, thinning out, bunching up, rippling with color as we spoke. Spoke silently, a sort of *within*. A place like the quiet under the surf and above the tumble of shingle. Thoughts like kelp slid softly across my brain. Though alien, boneless, marine, and salty, and from somewhere way beyond our human past, it understood. I dipped my finger in the jar and felt its suckers take hold.

It flattened against the mirror, tentacle-tips probing at the cracks, searching, seeking. Eventually, it found entry and thinned its' impossible self to fit between the planes. I considered the things I'd seen, while my familiar searched for things I could not imagine.

The staircase story was of pursuit and anger, hunting and taking. The song of it told of an absence created, as if Elaine, cut and slashed and bleeding had been torn from this world, removed. The blood-filled slipper was peculiar. It had no mate among her things, no similar article among the modern ordinariness of the room. That was it! The damned thing was old. The octopus froze. Almost entirely within the mirror now, its last visible tentacle stopped moving. With a fizz and a small whirl of smoke it fell, to twitch and flail at my foot.

There was little life left in it when I picked it up. No attempt to curl about my finger at all.

The taste of it was out of place. A happy memory of a terrace at the eastern shore of the Sea of Marmara, a meal with someone who hadn't seen my oddness. The octopus was salty and lightly charred but it hit my stomach and everything pleasant vanished. I saw:

A huge crouching figure all sharp angles and edges. A mass of hair made of tumbling shards, hot eyes, a bony face riven and scarred, a hideous strained scream coming from a throat opened to the bone. Skeletal fingers clawed my octopus from the glass and - she was gone.

"Oh," I said.

I had to take a moment. Several. Tennyson watched me from the door, disgust at the octopus-business clear on his meaty face. I said: "I need a moment. I'll, ah, I'll go out. Walk around…" "Huh," said Tennyson.

Cold and full of the bright cleanliness that follows rain, the air did me good. My brain cleared with every step away from the house. I knew there was a pub, just nearby. This was not witchery, just the magic of drinkers, and the kindness of pubs.

But pubs are a problem for the seer and the listener. They contain far too much. Every emotion etched into their walls, every thought, dream, and mishap soaked into their furniture. Nothing can ever clean a bar. And their owners collect. Curios, objects, signs. Things. If you're even a little turned up, they drown you in voices. After the octopus, I was very keen to turn it all off.

The Abbess of Countelowe was a substantial Victorian thing, all tiled green and gold and multi-paned windows, and dangling garlands of circular mirrors. It fairly chuckled with light. There was a purple poster behind the door-glass. Hag Night, due to fall that Friday. A pleasant enough change from tarts and vicars, or sexy witches, or whatever. I walked in.

It was only just eleven, and there were no customers at all. A woman was fixing purple crepe above an enormous fireplace, her stepladder set in the cold, empty grate.

"With you in a sec," she said, and I went to the bar. It was dark

Half-Sick of Shadows

mahogany, as were the fittings behind it. The pub was all wood, apart from the stone pile of fireplace. It was full of pictures, mirrors, and clutter. All of which was wreathed and pelmetted, draped and stuck with crepe and ribbon and evergreen swathes, all very dark and funereal, set off only a little by bright accents of purple. Crepe and ribbons. Hag Night fliers.

The woman circled around me and slid behind the bar.

"What can I get you?"

Her voice was a curious mix of accent and inflection. She carried herself with solemn competence, a sense of long experience in interesting things. She was one of those people whose age one can't place. Her mileage showed, but not her vintage.

"Do you have the means for Hot Toddies?"

"Of course. Which whisky? I'd recommend Paddy. That's quite lively and hot."

"Actually, could I have port? And maybe a dash of gin."

She asked if I'd like lemon. While the kettle boiled, she set to cutting one up. She used an old carving knife which I rather coveted. It was dark grey and mottled and long, carbon steel not stainless and as old as the pub if I was any judge.

As the blade hissed through the fruit and the hot water steeped with the port and the gin, I felt compelled to make conversation.

"Hag Night?" I asked.

"All this? A local Halloween thing. The local ghost. The Cantlows Hag."

I took a polite sip of the toddy.

"What does she do?" I asked.

The landlady produced a bundle of peculiar instruments. They were lengths of about six inches of florist's wire, with a small clamp at one end and about an inch of Velcro at the other. The hook side, not the loop.

"She lives in mirrors, and she grabs young ladies' hair." She laughed.

"Of course, I can't ensure it's only the young who get grabbed. But the old like to pretend, too."

The port sat in my stomach heavy as porridge. She lives in mirrors, and she grabs young ladies' hair.

"She wants their bodies, you see." She raised a sardonic eyebrow. "To live in, that is."

"That's a new one," I said, taking an unwisely deep draught.

"Not really." She leant her elbows on the bar, bodice pressing, and eyes on mine.

"See, she's really quite old. Despite appearances." A small poke of tongue on the left of her mouth, and a little glimmer of glee.

"Round here," - she tossed her head to encompass all the near spaces outside - "used to be famous for glass.

"The Abbey of Countelow used to make glass. They made mirrors, too. Proper mercury mirrors. There was talk of witchcraft and alchemy.

The Abbess was old, and she had a beautiful acolyte." I was a stew of dread.

"She tricked the girl and put her soul in mercury, put her in a mirror and herself in that young body." She smoothed her skirt over her hips, looked down at herself, smiling.

I am not a good runner, and neither was the creature that came out of the house. Lydia not Lydia, powering up the street in a body not hers, its awkward limbs acting wrongly, now so obviously, obviously that of Elaine. The last came in snapshots.

Tennyson, in the doorway, frozen in futile chase, cascade of red at his throat.

The glint of the kitchen knife in her hand.

The two women meeting in the street.

The hiss of the knives sliding home.

The smile of relief on the landlady's face.

The blood on the tarmac and

Pavement swinging up to meet me.

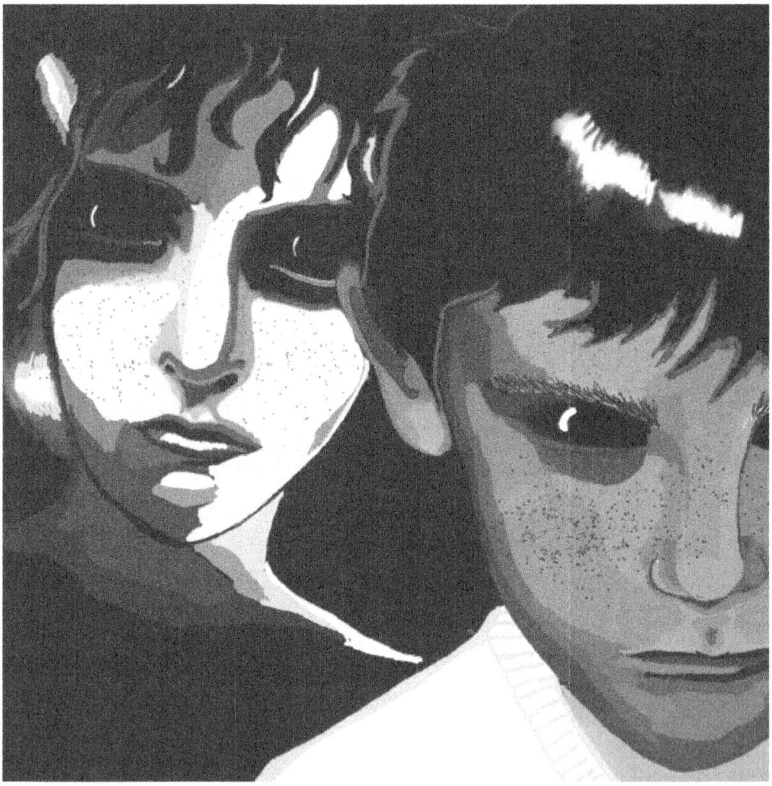

Mother Will Be Displeased
by David Barker

MrSwales – August 25, 10:15 PM

I don't normally post stuff like this online and have never posted anything on this board, but the creepiest damned thing just happened, and I'm hoping somebody can explain it to me and put my mind at ease.

I work nights until 9 o'clock. The walk to my apartment is a short one, only three blocks. I live in a quiet seaside town with no direct beach access, and there are few people out at that hour. Tonight, was no different, but for some reason I felt on edge, apprehensive.

Nothing happened for the first two blocks but as I was crossing the intersection onto my street, I sensed that I wasn't alone. A second later, I spotted two figures standing by the fish market in the middle of the cross street. They were too short to be adults. Maybe preteens or children. Hard to tell their ages or genders because they were both dressed in dark jeans and hoodie sweatshirts, which was odd because it's a warm summer night. They were facing my direction, but I couldn't tell if they were watching me. It was too dark along that part of the street, and their faces were hidden in the shadows under their hoods.

No matter, I picked up the pace, figuring I'd be inside with the door locked before they could reach me, if they had any thoughts of messing with me. That didn't work out as planned. I was two buildings away from the door to my apartment, glanced back, and they were already at the intersection, turning onto my street. I still had enough time to be inside before they could catch up with me, or so I thought.

But as stepped onto the stoop with my keys in hand, I felt a presence directly behind me, on the sidewalk. What the hell? How did they arrive that fast? And they weren't even running. They were just there. The taller one spoke. Not much, just a couple of words.

Mother Will Be Displeased

"Pardon me, sir."

Although they were already creeping me out by this point, some adult sense of duty or whatever compelled me to respond respectfully.

"What can I do for you?" I asked, knowing I wouldn't be doing anything for them.

At that time, I realized the taller one was a girl. 12 or 13, I couldn't say. She was very slender, couldn't have weighed more than eighty pounds, if that. Long, stringy blonde hair and pale skin, from what I could see of it, her chin, mouth, and lower cheeks being the only part of her face visible in the dim light. Her companion, who I assumed was her little brother, was 4 or 5, and he too had pale skin and straggly blonde hair. They both had an unkempt look, like orphans or something. Like his sister, the boy's upper face was hidden under his hoodie, and I couldn't see either of their eyes, and whatever expressions they might have held which would have tipped me off as to their intentions.

"May we come in and use your telephone?" asked the girl. "We need to call our mother."

A couple kids, alone on the street at night, wanting to call their mom – normally I would have said sure, no problem. But something put me off. Something wasn't right about them. I didn't know what it was, but I sure could feel it: I had an instinctive wariness of them. A visceral distrust. Which was strange, because they couldn't have been much of a threat to me physically, unless they had weapons. Then it would be two against one, and they might gain the upper hand.

"Uh...," I stammered, not knowing what to say. "Don't you have phones of your own? Everybody carries a cell phone these days."

"The batteries in our cell phones are dead," she said with a smile that was almost a smirk. Then, in an instant, her mood seemed to change. "You have to allow us to enter!" she pleaded. "We cannot do so without your permission!"

Now she sounded impatient, even angry. What an odd thing to say, that they needed my permission to go inside my home, which of course was true in the legal sense, although they could have just pushed their way in past me, against my will.

"That's right," I said. "Give me your mom's number, and I'll call her for you."

"We do not remember her number," she said, which was ludicrous, given they were asking to come inside to call her on my phone. The girl suddenly changed tactics on me, again appealing to my basic adult instinct to help out vulnerable children in need.

"Well then, sir, may we please come inside to use your bathroom? My little brother needs to go to the toilet."

That request was harder to turn down. I found myself involuntarily moving my hand toward the door, about to slide the key into the lock, to let them in, then caught myself.

"No, I'm sorry," I said as firmly as possible. "There's a public restroom down at the fish market. They're still open. It's on the street you just came from, you can be there in a minute."

The girl stepped forward a foot or two into the small circle of light cast by the fixture over the entrance, and I saw her eyes for the first time, which sent a shock of terror through my body, for they were entirely black! No whites, no irises, nothing but deep pools of liquid blackness, like the dead space between the stars.

"You must invite us into your home!" she demanded. "It is important that we be allowed to enter the premises."

"Why do you keep saying that?" I asked. "What's the real reason you want to be inside my place?"

The little boy had stepped forward with her, and now his eyes were likewise visible under his hoodie. And like hers, they were pitch black. Empty spheres of nothingness. His mannerisms suggested he was disturbed by his sister's aggressiveness, that he knew things weren't going as planned. I wasn't playing along with their ruse, and she was revealing too much of their true nature.

"Do not worry," she said to me in what was supposed to be a soothing tone but really wasn't. "We will not harm you. You will see. We promise. It is just that mother expects us to go inside with you. It is what

Mother Will Be Displeased

she needs. She will be very displeased if we do not go inside."

"No!" I said firmly. "You can't come in. I forbid it."

By then I was completely terrified, but somehow found the courage to turn my back on them and open the door, my hand shaking as I slid the key in the lock. I was sure they would follow me in against my will, force their way in, but for some reason they didn't.

Slipping inside, I immediately turned around and shut the door, my hands trembling as I turned the deadbolt. There's a little peephole in my door, and I peered through it with one eye to see them standing there, staring back at me.

I wish I could describe how their eyes looked in a way that could make you feel what I felt at that moment. It was like some weird negative energy just flowed out of those utterly dark holes in their chalky-skinned heads, some kind of inhuman hatred or pure evil that bore no mercy toward me, no shred of goodwill toward any human being. I sensed that I was completely disposable to them – a resource to be used and discarded.

I have never felt so existentially threatened in my life. I was certain they meant to do me harm. I noticed the little boy, who still hadn't spoken a word, was holding a small, ragged teddy bear in one hand. It hung so low that it was dragging on the sidewalk. Oddly, the thing looked like an antique, a stuffed animal toy from a century ago.

"Please!" begged the girl in a voice that was growing increasingly raspy and dry. "I implore you to grant us ingress! We must come in!"

"No," I yelled back, loud enough to be sure they heard me through the door. "No way! I'm not letting you in!"

All through this the boy said nothing. He had turned and was staring at his sister with a puzzled look on his face, as if he were uncertain how far she would go in her effort to enter my apartment.

"Go away," I bellowed, "before I call the cops!"

That did the trick. She grabbed her brother's hand and turned away, leading him off into the darkness.

I continued to stare through the peephole until I was sure they had actually left. Five minutes passed and there was nothing visible out there but the empty sidewalk. They were gone.

Okay, so what in the hell are they? Children with completely black eyes; they can't be anything normal. Are they demons? Aliens? The ghosts of dead children? I have no idea. The vast, empty sickness of their malignant stare guarantees they are not something to be trusted. Nothing good has a look like that.

Their effect on me was overwhelming. I was nauseous, agitated, drained of energy. After ten minutes I was confident they were really gone, but I was still shaking. I sat down at my computer and wrote the above. It seems utterly insane to me, but I'm going to post it anyway in the hope that someone will explain it in a way I can live with. So, what do you all think? Any thoughts?

BeezusKripes – August 25, 11:03 PM

Assuming you're serious, it's a good thing you didn't let them in. Nobody has done that and lived to tell the tale.

PaulinaD4 – August 25, 11:20 PM

MrSwales: the children as you describe them sound like classic Black-Eyed Kids, or BEK as they are also known. Their appearance and manner of dress, the odd behavior, the archaic and strangely formal language of the girl – it all fits the pattern. They are extremely dangerous! Please be extremely careful in dealing with them. I'll send you a private message with links giving the history and possible explanations for this phenomenon. Keep us updated on any new developments, no matter how insignificant they seem at the time. Do not trust them – they lie! They will say anything to be inside alone with you. God only knows what they do to people. Something horrible no doubt.

Mother Will Be Displeased

PaulinaD4 – August 26, 8:01 AM

Are you okay, MrSwales? I'm worried by your silence. Tell us what's been going on!

MrSwales – August 26, 11:21 AM.

Sorry for disappearing like that. It didn't stop at 10 last night. They came back later, early this morning. I'd finally fallen asleep at midnight after they first left, but then around 2 AM there was a loud "Bang Bang Bang" on my door, and I woke up in horror: they were back! All night I had been dreading their possible return, imagining how awful it would be to look out the peephole and see those demonic black eyes again, knowing they were real, not something I had dreamed, some terrible nightmare. I knew I would feel utterly trapped, like there was nothing I could do to make them go away. Cornered, alone, defenseless, everyone else in the building in bed, unconscious. Only me awake to face them. And now, here they were, making that fear real, bringing it to life.

"My answer hasn't changed," I said in what I hoped sounded like the normal speaking voice of someone who isn't frightened. I didn't want to waken the neighbors, who by now must all be asleep, and I didn't want to give the children the impression that I was afraid of them. Besides, I suspected the children could hear me anyway through the door.

"Please may we enter?" asked the girl in a thin, airy voice that sent chills down my spine. "We need to telephone our mother. She is expecting our call and will come pick us up. You *have to* do this. *Please!*"

I had the strongest compulsion to do as she asked, but resisted giving in to that urge, my rational mind aware of the danger in carrying out her instructions.

"Sorry, I'm not going to do that."

As before, the boy said nothing, but stared at his sister nervously, uneasy with her aggressive, insistent behavior. I waited to see what she would do next. She continued to glare at the door, directly at the peephole, waiting a while longer for me to give in, then finally relented and walked away, her brother following behind her.

I waited a minute, then opened the door, stepped out, and quickly looked both ways. They had vanished.

I didn't sleep well after that second visit. I just couldn't shake the idea that they might return yet again. I didn't think I could manage seeing those vacant black eyes filling the sockets in their skulls for a third time. Someone, please, how do I make them stop???

PaulinaD4 – August 26, 1:13 PM

I don't know if this helps but I've heard of cases where they come back three or four times, hoping to wear you down. Be strong. Don't give in to their demands. They can't make you let them in against your will. It has to be something you choose to do. That's the key – never allow them to persuade you to invite them into your home. It's like that thing with vampires, a spiritual rule that they must be invited into the victim's domicile before they can feed on their blood. Same thing with these Black-Eyed Kids. They're like vampires in that way.

MrSwales – August 26, 1:15 PM

That does help. Thanks. Not sure I can take being alone tonight. Too effing scary. Think I'll ask a friend to spend the night. There's this woman I know who would probably come over. Should I tell her what's been going on with the kids? Or will that just scare her away?

PaulinaD4 – August 26, 1:20 PM

For the sake of honesty, you should mention that last night something

Mother Will Be Displeased

weird happened, and you don't feel like being alone tonight, but there's no need to go into a lot of detail. You can explain it in general terms once she's there, but don't elaborate. No need to scare her. They might not come back if you have company. It's worth a try. Let us know what happens.

BeezusKripes – August 27, 7:43 PM

How did it go, MrSwales? Did the woman come over? Did those creepy kids return?

PaulinaD4 – August 27, 10:15 PM

The suspense is killing us, MrSwales. Please check in.

BeezusKripes – August 28, 9:31 PM

So quiet on this thread you could hear a pin drop.

PaulinaD4 – August 29, 9:46 AM

MrSwales, I'm starting to worry. Are you okay? Private message me if you don't feel like making it public.

AndyS555 – September 5, 8:26 AM

Hey, I just discovered this thread. Pretty weird story. Anybody know this MrSwales guy and what happened next?

BeezusKripes – September 5, 9:46 AM

David Barker

He's gone dark. Hopefully, the children didn't return. Or if they did, that he stayed strong. They can be quite persuasive. Some say they use hypnotic powers to overcome their victim's resistance.

MarilynG37 – October 15, 11:08 AM

I just found this message board and was debating on whether or not I should post what I know about this case. I decided I should, if only to put an end to people expecting MrSwales (his real name was Mike Belknap) to come back and tell the end of his story. I hardly knew Mike and had only met him a couple times but was close friends with his on-and-off girlfriend, Suzy French, the woman he invited to stay over at his apartment the night of August 26th. I don't know anything about any kids with all black eyes, and I'm not sure I believe what Mike wrote on here about being intimidated by such kids the night before Suzy came over. That's pretty crazy stuff. Maybe that story was just something he made up, a ploy he used to persuade Suzy to spend the night? All I know is what I've read in the local papers about the murder. Mike and Suzy were found dead in his apartment on the morning of September 1st. His landlady had come over to collect the rent, like she does on the first of every month, and Mike didn't answer when she knocked and rang his doorbell for a long time. She assumed he was out running an errand, and she was about to leave when she noticed smears of blood low on the door frame from what she called "a small hand." This was a tiny, bloody handprint, like a child would make with fingerpaints. That's when she called the police and asked them to do a welfare check on Mike. She unlocked the apartment for them (there were two cops on the call), and they entered, quickly finding both victims sprawled in the living room, fully clothed, dead. All the blood had been drained from their bodies. "Fully exsanguinated" is what the police called it. A horrible thing. I can't even think about it. It's so sad and frightening. Their deaths are being investigated as a double homicide. So far there are no witnesses, no suspects, and the motive is unknown. There have been stories in the

Mother Will Be Displeased

paper about it, but no real progress has been made in solving who did it, or why. It's one of those cases that may never be solved. Robbery clearly wasn't the motive; there was $250 in cash on the dresser in plain sight. Now Mike was no angel, he had his personal failings, but there was no reason anyone knew of why someone would want to kill him. He was not involved in drugs, gang activity, nothing like that. Just your average Joe working a low paying job and drifting through life, unattached. As for Suzy, well, she was an absolute angel; you couldn't find a nicer gal. A real sweetheart, and it tears me up thinking of her having to go through a nightmare like that. I think she had dreams of Mike someday changing, applying himself harder, making something of himself, them marrying, having a family, but it was not to be. They came to a tragic end, and nobody knows why. Just thought you all should know. If you're a believer, please say a prayer for them. Oh, one other detail I heard that wasn't in the papers, a bizarre clue I guess. The cops found an antique stuffed animal in the apartment. A beat-up old teddy bear, on the sofa next their bodies, like a kid might leave behind. So maybe there was something real behind Mike's crazy story. Just thought you should know.

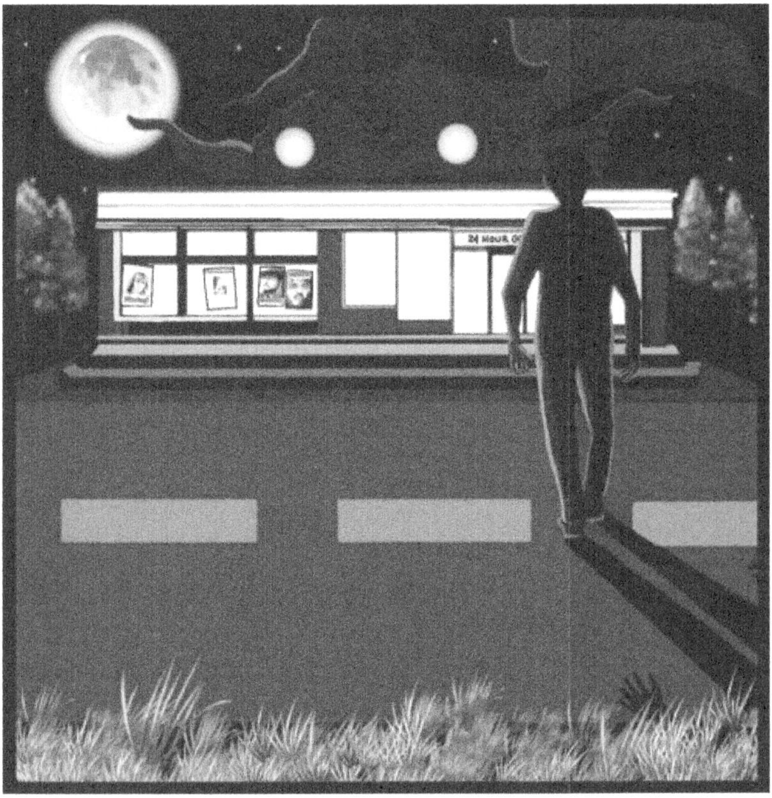
24 HOUR

Fish Story
by Scott J. Couturier

It was the sort of night that just felt haunted.

You know what I mean. A prickle at the nape of your neck that refuses to go away. Little darting things at the edges of your vision, a feeling of motion in the darkness that can't be explained by any of the five basic senses. I was driving home after work – I install water softeners, not much else to say about it – along the way I usually take, old County Road 87, a winding two-track through the woods and hills, all the way back to my place in Wishful Poplars, population 1,243.

I'm a local, born and bred here, never even been out of the state. So, you can believe me when I tell you this night was just different somehow. Places I knew, things I'd seen a million times took on a new, uneasy sense of significance. Farm-or-lake houses off on remote plots, or driving through one of many small towns, every lit window caught my eye and drew it inexorably. I saw bulbs glowing in attics and could feel the weight of the memories they contained; it was the kind of night people go upstairs to rifle around in the past. Cloudy and rainy, with a faint mist hovering wraith-like over everything. The moon shone dull behind clouds that barely moved, a wet wind gusting about barbed with winter's lingering chill. Late March in northern Michigan's no picnic-weather, as a general rule, but climate change made for new norms in a hurry. I had both my windows down as I drove, letting the night wind rush over me despite its chill undercurrent.

Lots of animal life out-and-about. Fat hares leaping away from the roadside, scurrying squirrels, coyotes howling and yipping in the near distance. Spring was here, too soon and rampant, the earth bursting with green shoots and little purple flowers, snowdrops, and early trillium. Bats swarmed in abundance, and as I drove lakeside I could even see a few

gulls soaring against the cloud-dulled moon, sounding their mournful calls. Life ran to excess; and, at the same time, spirits (I can't think of any

Fish Story

other way to say it) were everywhere. Elves and faeries, shades of the dead, call them what you will. A sense of the uncanny, such as I hadn't felt since I was about ten and still scared of whatever lurked in the closet, clung to everything like a heavy dew. Under each streetlight my eye anticipated a white-sheeted figure, or something stranger leering from the half-lit shadows beyond. I'm not a morbid-minded person, though I've read lots of Stephen King, and Halloween is admittedly my favorite holiday. But this was different than anything I'd ever felt before, a real fey-ness in the very fabric of things, like I was traveling deeper and deeper into another dimension, or a dream.

More lights on in attics, shining from dining rooms, glowing on the outsides of closed shops like empty, merry eyes, lights lancing beneath closed garage doors and welling up from narrow ground-floor basement windows. My mind became a kaleidoscope of potential, bewitched, and dazzled by the endless possibilities each light suggested, as if I were watching a picture show of cut-up frames spool out in my mind. Could be I was making it all up, so psyched by the night that my fancy went into overdrive, but I also suspect it was something psychic, real senses and flashes of reality I was getting, glimpses into the past and future. As if all of potential time were somehow piling up in that moment, and anything could (as a result) happen. Ghosts were real as flesh, so my fascinated imagination convinced me; and yes, all this time I kept, as Jim Morrison advises, "Keep your eyes on the road and your hands upon the wheel." I wasn't tripping, hadn't had anything but a Monster energy drink and some vape-juice. But these phantoms flew all around inside my mind as if *I* were some kind of haunted building, and I did have to slow down, just in case a deer or raccoon (I'd seen a few biggies by the roadside, they get up to forty pounds out there) jumped in front of me. It'd be a wicked night to have a wreck, and I hated hitting animals on principal. My Pa could never even get me into hunting.

The night wasn't just weird feeling; there was a danger in it. Like I could get abducted by faeries or pick up a ghostly rider who'd give me directions to the nearest cemetery, then lead me down into their grave. As it happened, the nearest cemetery was Oak Vale, a little Methodist burial-ground which flashed by on the right even as I thought of it, tombstones glaring like teeth bared in anticipation. My heart knocked on the inside of my ribcage like a captive fist, *thump-thump-thump* sounding in my ears with each beat of blood. The lumpy pavement of the street shone eerily, wet with rain and mist, the headlights of oncoming cars seeming to glare more brightly off the road than above it.

A strange night. My uneasiness came from a sense of certainty it was bound to get stranger.

Of course, part of the reason I felt so uneasy had to do with old County Road 87's reputation. Enough people had vanished along this stretch in the last twenty years – almost a dozen – to make it somewhat notorious. Always the same MO, driver and passengers missing but their cars found intact, off the side of the road hidden in the woods. I'm not a superstitious person, don't even go to church, so I just figured there might be some maniac in the area, who occasionally came out of retirement to take a few new victims. Eighty-seven was the quickest way from the shop to home, by a long (or rather short) shot, and I'd always taken my chances with being the next one to disappear just to shave fifteen minutes off my route. And anyways, it was probably just some crazy idiots on drugs who ran off the road and wandered into the woods, right?

Still, one particular story gets told again and again. More than a few folks that I know, and trust claim they've driven by a gas station on County Road 87 where there shouldn't be one. The location is always different – down at the crossroads, over by Johnson's Creek, up by 5 Mile, it doesn't matter – it's there. Lights gleaming over old-school pumps, neon 'Open' sign blinking, ice machine out front. Always, they feel a shiver of dread go down their spines and drive on by. None of them ever stop; if you dare go inside, the station (so they say) sinks down into hell, taking you with it. No one ever sees the place twice. But once you see it, you never forget.

The story swam around in my head as I drove, on a night that would've felt creepy even without the coloring of gruesome local lore.

Fish Story

My skin grew clammy, and I shrugged off my overshirt, rolling up the windows to block out the howling night air. I could've turned on the radio, but something kept me from doing it, a feeling like it would have been disrespectful. This sensation, in turn, gave me a fresh thrill of uneasiness, and I caught myself humming nervously under my breath, hands slippery on the wheel, wet and glistening like the streets I drove on. On, on, into the night. For a long while I saw no one else on the road.

Just as I came around a tight corner near the Pine Grove Nature Reserve, I felt something like a ripple pass under my truck. Bumped me up so hard the top of my head hit the cab's ceiling, the steering wheeling wobbling like crazy in my hands, a sound of metal tearing followed by squealing tires as I half-lost control. My headlights lanced off into the night, creating webs of crazy shadow in the surrounding leafless trees.

After a few seconds I got back in control, the steering wheel settling into a grinding judder that let me know something was seriously wrong. I saw the digital gas display go down to empty, swore and slammed on the brakes. No one behind me, no one in front; by now I hadn't seen another vehicle for at least ten minutes or so. My truck came to a screeching halt, and I leaned forward, breathing heavy, now having a full-on panic attack. Reaching into my pocket, I pulled out a bottle and popped a Klonopin, the pill grinding to sweet grit between my shaking teeth.

After thirty seconds or so my breathing calmed, and I tried to pull the truck off the road. This set off a barrage of automated alarms and flashing lights, and I freaked out all over again, slamming my fists against the console until the radio came on, screeching static. I fumbled it off and sat back, sucking down huge gulps of air, drowning in my native element. Just then it started raining again, and I had the crazy notion I should run out into the deluge, hold my mouth open and try to breathe in the droplets. Or maybe go find a nice puddle to wait out the night in, *glub-glub*, like a catfish. My eyes crossed, and I shut them and shuddered, forcing my breath rate back into a manageable rhythm.

Meanwhile, the engine died. Try as I might it wouldn't fire up again. The rain intensified, drumming like frantic hands on the cab's roof, a streetlight some ways off glowing dim as a will 'o' th' wisp. Then, suddenly, as if I'd rounded a corner without moving, a gas station came into view.

It sprang to being with the immediacy of a vision. Green-and-red neon tube lights, Shell-like logo (but, not a Shell station), four gray pumps with black handles and nicotine-yellow glowing squares displaying gas prices, none of those irritating screens that blare commercials at you. A welcoming fluorescent glow shone from inside, where I could see row upon row of cigarette cartons lining the back wall, clerk lounging on the counter, prices of lottery tickets taped up in the window, advertisement for some kind of jerky with a moose mascot, the works. Just what I needed – a miracle after whatever disaster tore up my truck.

My hands slid up and down the wheel, squeaking on a slick of chill sweat. That feeling of the unreal washed over me with renewed poignancy, and almost I thought to see a troop of ghosts and goblins go rushing past, hear a *whoosh* and cackle of witches on broomsticks – and remember, I'm not regularly superstitious. Palpable, as if scales were falling from my eyes, or rather being aggressively flensed from my senses, all against my will; and yet there was the gas station, normal looking like any gas station. And me, broke down and helpless on a rainy night.

Hesitant, at last I pulled out my cellphone. Just a customary check: I knew I wouldn't have any usable signal out here. Still, I tried to call my roommate a couple times, then tried to call the police, and finally my mom. *Calling home...* the screen read, but I never heard a single ring. All the while the rain kept up its patter, dying down into a dull-but-persistent spritz, just enough to keep the leafless limbs of the trees and the undergrowth bobbing rhythmically.

What else could I do? I knew the stories, had laughed over them at campfires while roasting marshmallows and having a few Labatt's. Now, faced with a gas station where there shouldn't be one (I knew the place, a vacant field with a torn-up, rusty wire fence set around it, clinging to decaying wooden posts) I could either sit here in my busted truck and wait out the night, or I could get out and head toward the light. Really,

Fish Story

the choice made itself – even if it took me almost ten minutes to finally nod, shut off my lights, open the door and step out into the persistent drizzle. The Klonopin was working its wonders, and I had a five-inch knife strapped in my boot, always kept it there. If this gas station turned out to be some kind of glamour or illusion, well, wasn't iron supposed to keep the creatures of faerie at bay? I found myself thinking back to the Brian Froud picture books I'd had as a kid, remembering that one weekend after first getting them when I really, truly *believed* everything they said. I'd spilled it all out to my best friend, Bob, thinking I was revealing this big secret and boy did he have a laugh. "What the fuck? You still believe in Santa Claus, too? Faeries, man, that's some gay shit."

Last time we saw each other until years later, and of course the first thing he said was, "Hey, you still believe in faeries?"

Funnily enough, I'd figured out I *was* gay meanwhile. Just like my job installing water softeners, not much more to say about it; it's all just a question of plumbing. Anyways, I grinned and said, "Faeries wear boots, yeah, and you gotta to believe me." I'd heard he was a big Sabbath fan (and, more subtly, I was wearing black combat boots). It disarmed the moment. Of course, I didn't believe in faeries, but I *remembered* believing in faeries, if just for a moment. Maybe that's part of what made me so susceptible to the night's enchantment.

Slowly, carefully, I went up to the gas station, passing by the pumps, and pushed open the glass-and-steel doors. A burst of warm, recycled air washed over me, welcoming and womb-like. I took an impulsive breath and rushed over the threshold, eager to be out of that rain-soaked night despite all my tingling misgivings of some underlying wrongness, a vague hint about things that rang untrue, even upon the first second I entered. The clerk looked up, a younger woman with bright red hair and chubby cheeks, eyes oddly yellow in color, her lips stretching in the faintest simulacrum of a smile.

I ruffled the moisture out of my hair and stamped my feet down, boots now wet with clinging mud. "Quite a night out there," I said to her, spacing out each word, the statement a test, like someone immersed in a virtual reality video game taking their first hesitant steps.

She looked me up and down, and her smile faded. "Looks like it," she said plainly, and the hovering illusion of nightmare shattered with such force that I blinked and staggered, falling back against a magazine rack.

Her eyes widened. "Geez, are you okay? What happened out there? You having some kind of car trouble?"

Well. A simple, straightforward, reasonable question. "Uh, yeah," I told her, then described how something had apparently torn a hole in my gas tank, stranding me just thirty-odd feet away from the station. "Like I was in a canoe," I said, "and something just *pop!* punctured the hull."

"Wow," she said, half-sardonically. "Lucky you, huh? I mean, that you had somewhere to go. Most places around here are already closed by now."

"I guess so," I said, feeling some of that uncanny fog drift through my mind again.

"You want to call a tow truck? We've got a phone in back."

"Yeah. Yeah, thanks, I appreciate it."

She led me into the back, and I made the call. Dillon, at Trident Bros. Towing, assured me they'd be out to rescue me soon. "We get a lot of calls from out that way," he said, with a little chuckle. "Especially when the weather turns bad."

"Oh yeah?" I said. "People call from the gas station, you mean? I can never get a signal this stretch." Funny the clerk didn't mention anything.

Another chuckle. "You just sit tight," he said, "we're on our way." Then a click, a dial tone. I set the phone back on its cradle, only then realizing how old it was – like something from a seventy's movie. The very air of place felt like it came from the past, sour with the mustiness of old cigarette smoke and body odor, undercurrents of bleach and leaded gasoline making for an olfactory Time Capsule circa 1972. A wave of uncertainty washed over me, and I remembered my own analogy of my truck's breakdown, "Like I was in a canoe." Did that mean I was in the rapids now, spinning?

Fish Story

I jumped as the clerk cleared her throat. "Um, I have some other stuff I need to do, so if you don't mind…"

"Of course," I said, rose and wandered past her without daring to look up into her face. Maybe I was afraid I'd find her just as dated as the surroundings – that hair clip, would anyone wear such a thing in the 21st century? I hustled out from behind the counter and made for the coolers in the back, hoping to distract myself by brooding over the pop selection.

This provided, at least, a brief mirage of the mundane. Mountain Dew in fifteen different custom flavors, Coke Classic, Sprite and Dr. Pepper and 7-Up, all in those brand-new plastic bottles that get narrower every year – but they distract you by adding artsy spirals at the base. I finally decided on a Coke and turned back towards the counter, having killed a good ten minutes on my hunt. All that while the gas station sat silent, except for some tinny music playing over an archaic sound system, hole-pocked speakers recessed into the vinyl ceiling tiles. Outside, the rain drummed a lulling and constant cadence, my dead truck lost in the black of night beyond the fluorescent lighting glaring down on the four lonely pumps outside.

"I wonder how long it'll take them to get here," I pondered aloud as I shuffled up to the register, depositing my pop on the counter.

The clerk rang it up without saying anything, red light flaring from her handheld scanner. "1.99," she said, "just .99 cents if you get the two liter."

"Yeah, well, I don't need that much sugar water right now," I said.

"So, you're willing to pay more for less, rather than not have any at all?"

I stared at her, meeting her eyes head-on for the first time. "Yeah," I said, "that's right. It's the great American way."

To my surprise she smiled, teeth showing sort of black in the bright glow buzzing down from overhead. "Someday soon they'll get people paying for nothing," she said as I swiped my card. "What a funny thought."

What a funny woman, I thought to myself. "Food for contemplation," I said aloud, picking up my pop and twisting it open. "How long does it usually take for them to get out here?"

"Who?"

"The tow truck guys."

A half-vacant look came over her face, and it was several seconds before she answered. "How should I know? I don't even know which company you called."

Trident Bros. Towing. The only towing company listed in your phone book. Which smells like it came wrapped around a dead fish. Out loud I said, "Never mind. I'm gonna go wait outside."

"Suit yourself. Free country, and all that." Only after I turned away, went through the doors, and took a long drink while staring out into the rain-darkened night, did I realize she wasn't even wearing a name tag.

I stood out there for maybe ten more minutes, drinking over half my Coke, just waiting, and listening to the rain, my senses piping a persistent chorus of unease. Something about how the neon flowed in the lights...it affected me the same way watching a nature documentary makes you sympathize with what it's like to be a small furry thing, a hawk suddenly wrapping its talons around you. I know that's vague, but the feeling was vaguer. More than once I checked to make sure the ground beneath me was still solid.

Then, I saw a flare of lights off in the night. Raising my hand to wave, I cried out in dismay as a gray wave – like the road had suddenly bucked up – tore into the undercarriage of the vehicle, the air clouding with a smell of burning plastic. The lights wobbled and pitched, and I heard the screeching of breaks, the truck skidding partway into the light shed by the florescence overhead, nearly clipping a gas pump. I saw, then, it wasn't the tow truck, but a new-model SUV, two kayaks lashed to its sloping roof with blue-and-yellow bungees. Smoke rose from beneath the hood as the driver – a woman – got out to inspect the damage, a man (good-looking but older, clearly her husband) leaning out of the passenger's side with a little wobble. He'd been drinking, but not much.

Looking back inside the station, I was shocked to see the nameless

Fish Story

clerk still leaning idle against the counter, as if unaware of the SUV's near-explosive arrival. I banged my palm on the window several times, then ran to the couple to help as I could, the rain briefly pouring over me, bitterly cold and with a salty tang to it, as if it were ocean water.

The woman, as it happened, was a bit distressed; she told me her name was Janet, her husband introducing himself as Michael, no last names given. Both of them seemed puzzled to be there, as if they'd suddenly skewed off the road into some parallel reality. They blinked and repeatedly checked their cell phones for service, both remarking that they didn't remember a gas station being out here. I said nothing to that, instead bending down to look under their vehicle. By the light of my cellphone's screen, I saw the metal frame torn up as if by huge jaws, the gas tank ripped open and dripping, viscera from the belly of a felled animal. I straightened and shrugged, telling them I'd had something similar happen and that a tow truck was already on the way.

We all waited for a moment, in which I'm convinced one of us could have broken the night's spell by admitting we were under it. "Does this all feel really weird to you?" one of us could've said, and it might have saved us a lot of trouble, not to mention misery. Instead, we looked into each other's eyes in silence, while the rain muttered and the fuel dripped, the clerk inside still slouched at the counter, now chewing on something that might have been gum.

"Well," Janet said at last, "I guess we should call the tow service, too." What could I do but agree? We turned and headed inside.

The clerk looked up as we all entered but said nothing. At last Michael huffed and muttered, "What a horrible night."

"Looks like it," the clerk spoke up automatically. Then her yellow eyes widened. "Geez, are you okay? What happened out there? You having some kind of car trouble?"

The words rang in my ears like a cracked bell. Every syllable, in exactly the same place; just what she'd first said to me when I entered. The clerk's eyes showed concern, but it was the same concern, a fixed expression she could adopt at will – or rather, when her programming demanded it. I shook my head, trying to convince myself I was falling prey to paranoid delusions, but I *knew* they were the same words, said just the same way.

"We are, indeed," Michael said, blinking raindrops from his eyelashes.

Janet's face was pale with fright and shock. "We almost hit one of your gas pumps," she breathed, shaking water from her hair like an irate cat. "Oh my God, if we'd drifted just a couple feet to the left...I don't know what happened, Mike! The road, it just – came at me."

"Wow," the clerk said, "lucky you, huh? I mean, that you missed the pump and had somewhere to go. Most places around here are already closed by now." She gestured at the rainstorm, and I marveled at the exactitude of her phrasing, just a couple extra words adjusted to the situation. Turning to me, she seemed to recognize me for the first time, and her yellow eyes narrowed. She realized I'd caught her in the midst of her act, whatever that meant.

"You want to call a tow truck?" she said at last, her gaze fixed on me as she spoke, almost a challenge. "We've got a phone in back."

Michael and Janet nodded, went back, and made their call in the smelly office, dialing on the out-of-date rotary telephone. I stood down the hall watching, saw the clerk interrupt them in just the same way she had me; something trailed behind her, like a long bit of toilet paper stuck on her shoe. They came back out looking dazed, Michael now gone a bit peaked, white splotches marring his jolly red cheeks.

"The man on the phone didn't say how long it would take for them to get here," Janet told me. "I mentioned that you'd already called, and he said the tow truck went in the wrong direction. It's headed towards us now."

"I'll bet it is," I muttered, sweat again rolling from my pores, my own fear-stink prickling in my nose. "Look, this all seems outright funny to me. A gas station, where there isn't supposed to be one – you guys are locals, you must have heard the stories. And my truck went out just like your SUV. Something scraped along the underside, tore out my gas tank.

Fish Story

When it happened to you I saw the road rise up – like you said, Janet – and rip at the undercarriage. Almost like a huge tail thrashing, or something."

Janet and Michael looked at me as if I were drugged, drunk, and gibbering in a cage.

"No," she said, shaking her head. "It was my fault. I just – I took my eyes off the road, hit the cement verge on the parking lot."

My eyebrows raised. "And what about that cement verge? Or this station? They just throw it all up overnight?"

"Come on," Michael said, eyeing me now with a sense of suspicion. "Let's go wait outside for the tow truck. They won't be long." He wrapped a protective arm around his wife, steering her away from me.

Just like that, my attempt to draw attention to our circumstances failed. I could have argued with them, told them the clerk said the exact same things when I came in, but it was no use. The moment for potential escape velocity had passed. We were circling some terrible event horizon together, something none of our common senses could convey or even see, but that our souls *knew*. I shivered and decided I'd have a word with the clerk, at least. Maybe she'd produce some new phrases for me – or maybe she'd just recite the same rote over and over again, like a string pull doll.

"What is all this?" I demanded, coming up to the counter. "This place...it can't be real. No gas station like this has existed for twenty years. And you said *the exact same things to them that you said to me when I came in*. No reason to deny it. Suppose if he'd bought a Coke you would've suggested the two-liter upgrade, huh?" I slammed my hands on the counter, and the woman jumped and shied from me, so that I felt suddenly ashamed.

Eventually, timidly, she lowered her hands and replied, "Sir, it's corporate policy that I push for an upgrade."

I ground my teeth together, resisting the call of a second Klonopin. "How long does it take the tow truck to get here?" I demanded.

She stared at me, blank-faced, as if processing what I'd said. It was then I looked down and saw, with a gag of horror, that a lappet of sucker-laced skin dangled from beneath her work shirt, connecting her to a wet fleshy spot on the counter. She noticed my attention, and quickly pulled her shirt down, though her face maintained its vacant, uncomprehending expression.

"You can't answer me," I snarled, leaning forward again. "Can you?"

A flare of lights came from out in the night. "Dillon is here," the clerk said, raising one hand to point out the window. "And just in time!" She rolled her eyes as she spoke, making me doubt – yet again – whether I wasn't really the crazy one here.

I turned around to see Michael and Janet front-lit by the incoming lights – *two* pairs of lights unless my eyes deceived me. But they rippled and flowed in a manner I remembered from nature documentaries, the way glowing spots on eels coiling in dark coral holes move. I felt a certainty of something awful happening, and raced out the front doors, reeling to a stop by the couple as they raised their hands in greeting to the oncoming lights. Those lights, in turn, stopped out in the dark where my truck *should* have been. Two man-things wandered into view, no slam of doors preceding them – I say things because each walked in a herky-jerky way, moist uniforms draped sloppily over their malformed bodies, strips of pale skin trailing from their backs off into the darkness, attached to God-knows-what. "We're here to help," they called out, gurgling in unison, and Janet and Michael went rushing over to them, sparing me a final wary glance.

What happened next I can only approximate. Words fall short, as does meaning, yet I had a front-row seat. I watched as the concrete below the couple warped and parted, revealing a flared throat filled with blazing geometric shapes. A singularity emerged, the crowning bulb of an abyss from which flowed rank, foul-smelling waves of pitch-black water. Something huge swam inside the orb; I fell back and retreated inside the gas station as the building quaked all around me, at last thrust violently up into the night by something bursting through the concrete. I gasped as the station walls pulsed and contracted, pop boiling from

Fish Story

plastic bottles to spew all over the floor, hissing. I felt a horrible pain in my stomach, and remembered I'd drunk half a Coke. Sticking fingers down my throat, I made myself throw up what was now digestive acid of a far more potent variety than human.

Meanwhile the clerk grinned at me, her black teeth dangling and falling from her jaw to reveal row upon row of translucent fangs. Within seconds she lost any semblance of human form, her body flushing like a plastic glove with fluid, taking on its true shape. A fishy nightmare with burning eyes loomed over me, but my attention was held by happenings outside and below. The gas station was held up on a luminous stalk of flesh, attached between the eyes to something so huge I could barely take it in and understand what I was seeing. A colossal fish, large as an ocean on earth, eyes big as cities staring up through leagues of blackest, unlit water, save – its body gave off a virulent green glow, making the depths phosphorescent. Things swam by and around it, things I could only just make out, my eyes centrally fixed on poor Janet and Michael, whirling around and around now with ever-hastening speed on the lip of the singularity, flesh burned to a crisp by the geometric shapes. Then – the thing *broke above the surface*, just enough so that the tiniest edge of one eye was revealed, burning into me with a hunger magnificent and profound. A fish's head exploded through the earthen crust, mandibles yawning to suck Janet and Michael the last few feet over the singularity's edge. They were in the orb of darkness now, in the vast ocean, and jaws that once swallowed empires closed around them, black water sloughing to douse the surrounding forest, flattening the trees, which then sprung back in place like something out of *Steamboat Willie*.

The gas station bobbed above it all, attached to the fish-beast by that stalk of luminous, tremulous flesh. The walls quivered and oozed about me, eels now slithering from pocks in every surface to writhe in coils of frenzy, the clerk-girl a bloated half-fish-half-human sock-puppet undulating overhead, trying to frighten me out the door. Where the fish would devour me – the very doom of leviathan.

I did what any reasonable person would do. That is to say, I screamed and pissed and shit myself all at once, holding onto the mushy countertop for dear life. The clerk-thing hissed and struck at me repeatedly as the anglerfish rose further from its abyssal blot, the station's doors banging open as all windows shattered inwards. It dangled the station on its strip of skin, trying to shake me out to fall into its mouth, the last crackerjack tenaciously clinging to the bottom of the box. I screamed louder as the clerk's fangs bit into my right hand, pumping full of a clear-colored venom. Grabbing the knife from my boot, I slashed at her, first gouging her right hand before managing to cut her across the throat, releasing enough foam to flood a car wash. I made a final swipe, severing the cord of flesh linking her to the station's counter; more digestive-juice pops popped, and I found myself awash in an aerial acid bath, wailing as the stuff ate away at me, fingers of my right hand still stuck into the countertop as if I'd jammed them deep inside someone's eye sockets. No way in hell was I letting go.

A roaring sound, as of more water than you can possibly fathom rushing together all at once, blasted my ears, rupturing my tympanic membrane. The walls had become fully plasticine now, covered in greenish scales with weeping sores underneath, segmented worms and eels and crayfish spewing in stinking geysers to blast me towards the open doors. Below, that bottomless gullet yawned wide as the world, framed by teeth like skyscrapers; I held fast as I felt the huge fish crest and then settle, its massive head plunging back below the surface, back into that orb of unending nighted ocean. Its eye vanished, and then the gas station plummeted towards the ground, a high-velocity impact inevitable.

I braced myself to jump clear, managing it with less than a second to spare. Instead of blasting apart on collision, the station sank into the earth, where the wobbly throat of the singularity still spun, lit up by neon forms. Then, a cracking sound as of a thousand trees breaking, or the very timbers of reality rupturing, who can say? At last, I landed on cold, solid earth and crawled as fast as my acid-scarred limbs could carry me, away from that empty field ringed by rusty wire, where you found my truck.

Fish Story

Now, you can believe me or not. I know the phrase "a whale of a tale," not to mention "fish story." You can say this damage to my body was all done by barbed wire, you can say the gas tank of my truck wasn't ruptured, you can tell me all these things until my ears start bleeding again, but it won't change what really happened that night in March. What about the empty SUV, the missing Johnsons, as you call them? You say I've also been missing for three months. Everyone knows the old story about that gas station, how no one ever stops – unless they can't help it. And that girl, the red-headed one you found dead in the field...you tell me if you can figure out her name. She's not even wearing a name tag.

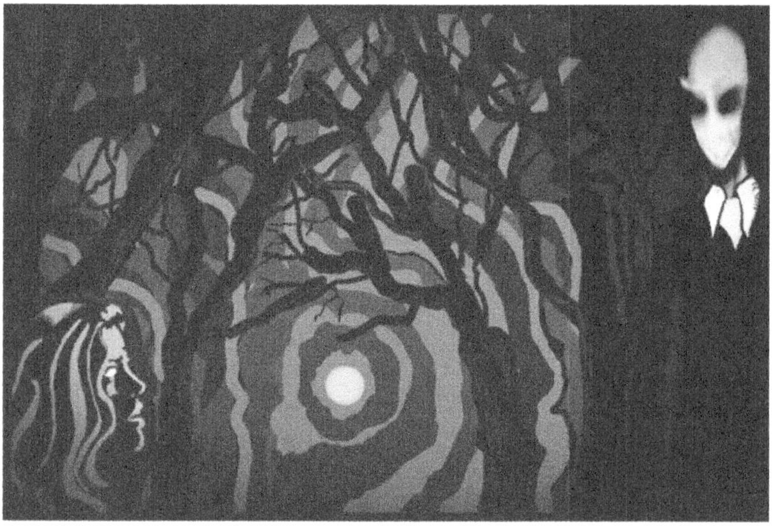

Beware the Slenderman
by Manuel Arenas

Beware the Slenderman, my babes, who lurks beyond the woodland line.

He hails from the realm of nightmare, wherein the sun's rays never shine.

To see him bodes calamity, mere proximity mystifies.

His boundless reach snares juveniles, unhindered by a lack of eyes.

His gangling frame is smartly clad in a stygian business suit.

His end game is unknowable, and the subject of rampant bruit.

Beware the Slenderman my babes, the muted, inscrutable face!

The tentacles that slink and snatch, to a lair beyond time and space.

Pray, be vigilant when abroad. Fates forfend this horrid danger!

Never take the proffered hand of a tall and faceless stranger

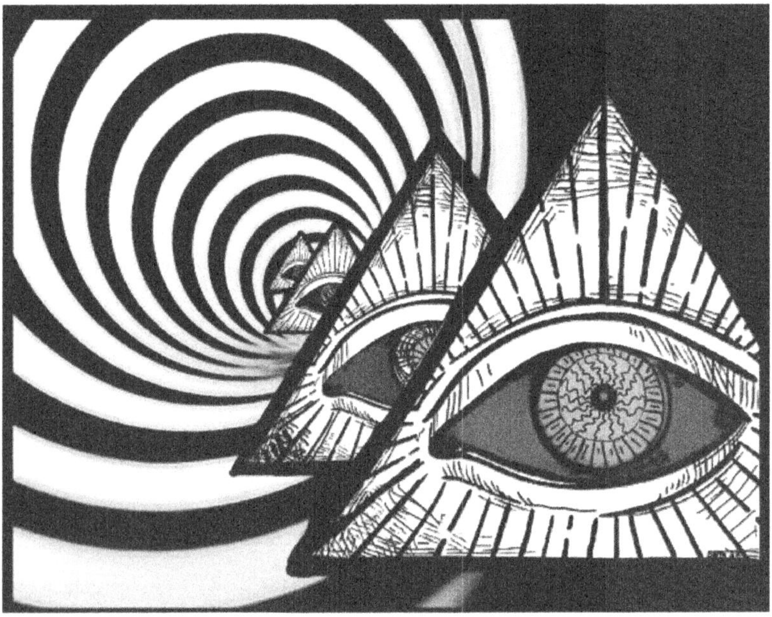

Third Eye Delight
by Jennifer Caress

Tony opened the front door before his daughter could reach for the outside knob. She stood on his porch, staring at the phone in her hands, but was startled by the woosh of the front door being flung open with such vigor. She was then startled again when she looked up and saw her father.

"What's that on your head?" Veronica asked, her face contorted with confusion, a touch of fear, and a smidge of disgust.

"What took you so long? I called you like 20 minutes ago." His eyes were wide, brow furrowed and sweat glistened on his entire face. He moved aside to let Veronica into the house.

"You know how traffic gets on the hi--why does it smell like tobacco in here?" She sniffed around the living room. "Have you started smoking? And what in the hell is on your head?" She had that look again. The one that suggested her old man might be losing it.

"Oh this?" Tony pointed at the artwork on his forehead. "This is nothing, just my new third eye. Are you kidding me, this is why I called you over. Weren't you listening to anything I said?"

Veronica's upper lip curled. "When you said you had something to show me, I didn't think it was this. I mean, what made you decide to wake up this morning and draw an eyeball on your forehead, with what I'm guessing is a magic marker?"

"Yep, magic marker." He smiled big and despite the perspiration, the drawing wasn't running or smearing, and didn't seem affected by the wrinkles across his scalp.

She sniffed the air again. "You woke up this morning, grabbed a black marker, drew on your face, and started smoking? Dad, I've got to be honest here, I'm kinda worried about you." She sat in the peach—colored armchair beside the coffee table with her back straight, letting her purse drop to the floor, her phone hanging loosely from her hand. It

Third Eye Delight

wasn't until the phone started to slip from her hand that she seemed to remember even having it. Veronica turned the phone on and spoke into the mic, "effects of Ambien" and waited for the search machine. "Did you take a sleeping pill last night? What's the last thing you remember before--" she waved at his head "--this?"

Tony walked over to his daughter and lifted her up by her shoulders, his face close to hers. "Oh ho, my girl it is far weirder than that. Look!" He put his arm around her shoulders and held her tight, gesturing to a large pink book on the coffee table.

"What is that?" She asked, sparing a side glance at the man she was sure was missing a few marbles from his collection.

"I don't know." He said with a strange mix of confidence and delight.

"You don't know."

"It just appeared."

"It just a-- what now."

"Appeared."

"Appeared?"

"Yes, and look!" He led her closer to the large pink hardcover and pointed down at the book, then up at the drawing on his forehead. "It's the same!"

His daughter was dubious. Her mouth was turned down and her voice was low. "It sure is." Indeed, the amateurly drawn eyes encased in crudely drawn diamonds both matched. One on her father's forehead, one on the pink hardbound cover.

"What do you make of that?" He asked her.

"I... I don't know." She shrugged. "I guess you woke up and felt like drawing eyes on things?"

"No! Don't you get it?" His eyes twinkled as he smiled bright. His daughter had the reverse expression.

Tony and Veronica had always gotten along, bonded by their hatred for his wife and her mother, Gertrude, whose only means of showing love or affection was through yelling. Gertrude died when Veronica was 14 years old and his son, Tony Junior was ten. Tony raised his children not as a parent but as a friend. Now, Veronica was almost forty and he and his children remained friends, talking almost every day.

"Not even a little. Dad, this isn't like you. Tell me what's going on before I call a paddy wagon and have them haul your old ass away." She was only half joking.

Tony grabbed the sides of her head and roughly pulled her closer, kissing her head. "Okay, listen, listen." He paused, staring into her eyes. She stared back and the silence dragged on. "Are you listening?" he whispered, hands still on the sides of her head.

"Yes," she whispered back.

He continued the whispering trend. "There's magic in this house."

"You know how I have trouble sleeping?"

"I knew it! You took an Ambien. Dad, why didn't you just say so? Now it all makes sense. Well, no, nothing makes sense, but at least we know why you're acting like this."

"I didn't take a pill."

"You didn't take a pill?"

"No," Tony said, "now listen." He sat on the floor and motioned for Veronica to do the same. He sat with his legs folded at the short end of the coffee table, she sat on her knees at the long end. He tapped the large pink book but didn't open it. "So, it was like three in the morning, right? And I couldn't sleep so I did like you suggested, and I started playing meditations on YouTube to help me relax and go to sleep, but then I saw this one video that was talking about frequencies and chakras and opening my third eye. You with me so far?"

"I guess..."

"Okay, good, so I was watching this video--"

"The one with the frequencies?"

"Yes, now shush. And this guy comes on and at first he seems kinda goofy, talking about foofy 'I'm a shaman who lives in multiple dimensions' shit but then all of a sudden...*I felt it.*"

Third Eye Delight

She cocked an eyebrow. "Felt what?"

Tony pushed his finger against the magic marker eye on his brow. "The tingle."

Veronica's face was resting on her fist, keeping the confused snarl alive. "Mm-hm, but what abo--wait!" she slid the book closer to herself, leaned in close, and took a long sniff. "It's the book! That tobacco smell is coming from the book! What the hell?" She started to lift the cover, but her dad slapped her hand away and placed his own hand on top to keep it closed. "Hold on, don't get ahead of me. Now, where was I?" "The tingle," she said with a discrediting scowl.

"Oh right! Okay so this hippie dude is talking about some far-out stuff, right, and I'm only paying attention because I've got nothing better to do but then all of a sudden the room gets warm. Like, humid-warm but not uncomfortable, and then this spot," he pointed to his forehead again, "starts to tingle. A lot! And, I don't know, something just told me to draw *this eye* on my *third eye*--"

Veronica interrupted, "I've never heard you talk like this. Third eye? And what video were you watching? I've heard stories where certain videos contain these tones that mess with your mind, like make you hallucinate and stuff. I thought that was just an urban legend but now that I see markers on your face, I'm starting to wonder."

"Yeah, maybe, but that's not even half of it. So, I draw this thing on, watching myself in the bathroom mirror, right? And it's still feeling like warm and misty kinda, and the video is still playing on my phone but now the guy's humming and I guess there's still frequencies or whatever in the background, but I come out of the bathroom, and I remember your brother brought these cookies his friend made, and I was feeling hungry, so I got them out of the freezer and--"

"Why are you keeping cookies in the freezer?"

"I don't know, that's just where Junior put them. So anyway, I have a couple and then—"

"Wait a minute," Veronica hopped up, strode across the living room, and into the kitchen. Pulling a plastic bag out of the freezer she asked,

"Is this them?"

"Yeah, but you're focusing on the wrong thing here. After that I came into th--"

She wasn't listening. Instead, she had the bag opened and was taking a deep whiff. "Dad! These are weed cookies! *Weed cookies, dad!* How many did you eat?"

Tony sighed. "Noni! Will you please--"

"This explains everything! How many did you eat?"

For the first time in a long while, Tony raised his voice at his eldest child. "Noni! I'm trying to tell you what happened, the damn cookies don't matter. Now will you *please* come sit down?" Not used to being yelled at, she did as she was told.

Tony started again, "The vibrations, the warm air, the third eye, all of it started before the cookies, okay? The fact that you can see, the fact that you can *smell*, that you can *touch* this book means that I'm not crazy, and I'm not hallucinating."

"Okaaaaay," Veronica said.

"It was still dark outside, right? And I had just eaten the cookies and I was listening to the YouTube video when I started hearing a different hum, but it wasn't coming from my phone, it was coming from in here. So, I come in here to see what's making that noise and the vibration in my head gets super intense, almost disorientating, and that's when I saw this…" He picked up the large pink book and pressed it against his chest, then placed it back on the coffee table. "And guess what's inside?"

"Um, I don't know, words?" Her tone was more skeptical of the tale she'd just been told than sarcastic.

Tony smiled big again and gestured for her to open the book. Looking more at her father than at the book itself, she lifted the hard cover to a blank page. She turned the page to reveal another blank page. Turning and turning before flipping through pages, all Veronica saw were naked sheets of paper. This time her tone was gentler and carried tones of worry and concern. "This is what you're so excited about? A blank book?"

Third Eye Delight

He still smiled and slid the book closer to himself. "Watch." Tony closed the pink book and winked at his daughter. "Who am I and how do you know me?" He opened the book towards the middle and slid it back to her. Across two pages was written:

You are Tony from San Antonio

I have always been with you

I am you

You are me

We are always

Veronica looked up from the book, at her dad, and back at the words in front of her several times. She closed the cover and opened it again, flipping through the pages once more. "Where did that page go? Nothing's in here. Where did it go?"

"Noni, it's okay, look," he reached for the book, which she continued to leaf through, and closed it again. "Watch again. I've asked it this before, you're going to get a kick out of this." And to the book he said, "What is my destiny?" Again, he opened the book to somewhere in the middle.

There is no mystery here

You live

You die

You live again in a different part of space

Tony laughed from deep within his belly. "That's what it said before! Ha ha can you believe it? Now you try. Ask it something."

Veronica examined every crevice of the large object, glancing occasionally at the eye drawn on her father's forehead. She sat it down with a thump and slid it away from her. "Okay, you got me. I don't know how you did it, but it's silly. Let me guess, Junior got this for you from that novelty store he's always shopping at."

"Noni, honey, this book just appeared. In my living room. In the middle of the night. Just like I said."

"Uh huh, after you ate two marijuana cookies, and who knows how strong those are."

Tony wasn't swayed. "You're seeing it too, though. Ask it something. Go on, ask. What could it hurt?"

Veronica was silent for a spell then quietly said, "I don't know what to ask."

"Don't be afraid. Go on."

She took a deep breath and thought for a moment. "When will I die?"

Her dad was startled. "Wait, no, honey I don't want to know when my child's going to die. Don't open that! Ask it something else. Please baby, ask it

something else."

She hesitantly agreed and took her time thinking of another question. Finally, "Okay, what are you? Where did you come from?"

The pair looked at each other and then at the book. Veronica gingerly pulled the book back towards herself and stared at the eye on the cover. "Just open it wherever?"

"Yeah," Tony said quietly, as he also stared hard into the eye.

She tucked her fingers into the first few pages and opened the book. The two read the words silently to themselves, and then read them again.

"Huh," Tony said.

"I... I mean..." Veronica said.

Not even the truth

Will satisfy

A doubtful mind

They read the message again and again before Veronica suggested she should eat a cookie, too. "Wait, try again." Tony said. "Ask it something else."

She halfway rolled her eyes. "How much did Junior pay for this, anyhow?"

"Noni--"

"Okay, okay. Dear book, what is the point of you?"

Third Eye Delight

Tony looked like he wanted to object but didn't. She opened the book again, and on the right-hand page was this:

Only destiny knows what waits for you in the shadows On the left-hand page was this:

It's getting dark outside, don't you think

It's time to turn on the lights?

"Dude…" Tony sat back while Veronica looked back over her shoulder.

"When did it get to be so late?" She asked, staring out the miniblinds. "The book is right. I got here around 10 this morning, but look, the sun is almost set." Tony had gotten up and was flipping switches in each room, illuminating the townhouse. Veronica closed the book again with a lot more force than necessary.

Tony was apologetic. "It's normally not like that, I usually just get weird or vague messages like you saw before."

Her face was gray, but she forced a small smile. "Well, tell Junior you got me pretty good with this dumb thing." She pushed it further away from herself. "Didn't you?"

The hard cover flipped open, smacking on the coffee table. Pages shuffled with an unseen force and Veronica jumped to her feet. "Dad!" Her father ran in and stood by her side, they both watched as the pink pages stopped at a certain spot. They took a step forward and leaned over.

Leave behind what you deny

Eye to eye

Step through with good grace

"What does that even mean?" Veronica whispered..

"Uh, I'm more concerned that the book just moved by itself." "You said it just appeared out of nowhere, right?" Veronica asked.

"Good point. Okay so what do we do now?" Both continued to stare at the book, neither moved. His phone vibrated in his hand and when he looked down at it, Tony got an idea. "Maybe the way in is the way out."

"Good thinking!" Veronica grabbed her purse from beside the chair and dug out her car keys. "Let's go. You can stay at my house until...well, I don't know until that thing dies or something. Come on," she grabbed his arm and tried to lead her father to the front door, but he wouldn't budge.

"Honey, my third eye is open now and I can't close it," he pointed to the drawing of an eye on his head. "Don't you see? I can't go back to being regular old Tony from the block. I'm enlightened."

Veronica could tell he was half-joking, and the endearing look on his face made her smile until she glanced to the side and saw the hardcover pink book on this coffee table behind him. "Yeah well, enlightened, or not, I don't want to be around that thing anymore, and I don't want you around it either. Let's get out of here."

"No." Tony's firmness was out of character for him and caught his daughter off guard. "I know drawing on my face was silly, and yes, I was super high from Junior's cookies, but the book is real. Whatever *this* is, it's *real*. I think--I think I brought something in from *another universe*. How amazing is that? We can't just abandon whatever's going on here, even if it's scary."

Veronica had that look on her face again, the one that indicated she feared for her father's safety. "Okay, yeah, maybe that thing did come from another universe or dimension or whatever, but we don't know what that other universe was like. Maybe it was hell, with a bunch of little demons concocting...books to…" she struggled to form the right words, "to eat souls of stoners...or something, I don't know. But this doesn't feel right." Her father was at a loss for words, so she stepped closer to the book--but not too close-- and said, "Book! Do you want to harm us?"

In the span of a breath, the pink book closed and reopened. Pages fluttered to the left and settled.

Harm is in the eye of the beholder

Tony stared at the message while Veronica grabbed his arm and tried to yank him out the door. "Oh, hell no," she said, pulling hard.

Third Eye Delight

Tony barely budged. "I don't understand. It wasn't like this before you got here."

"Blame me in the car, now *let's go!*" She tried again to drag her father out the door without success.

"This was fun until you got here," he said again.

"Dad!"

He gave her a quick hug, "Oh honey, I'm sorry, I didn't mean it like that, sorry, sorry. I just mean that I don't get it, why is the book turning dark now? Maybe I was supposed to keep this all to myself-- not tell anyone."

"Let's not stick around to find out what its reasons are, come on."

Tony turned his back to the book to face his daughter, she looked over his shoulder to keep an eye on it, and said, "Here's my idea-- you should open your third eye too." He ran to the kitchen and came back with his phone. Once it was unlocked, he pulled up the video and pressed play. Electronic vibrato music came out of the tiny device as Veronica covered her ears.

"Are you insane?" When she reached for the doorknob she pressed the freed ear to her shoulder, not taking any chances. The knob wouldn't turn. She tried again and again without success. "Dad, help me! We're trapped!"

When Tony didn't move to help, Veronica grabbed the phone from his hand and threw it across the room. It hit the wall and bounced onto the couch, while the music played on. She tried the door handle again, this time giving up on covering her ears and using both hands in an attempt to free them. When it didn't turn she began pounding on the door and screaming, "Help! We're trapped in here! Help us!" Slowly she realized her father hadn't moved at all since she tossed his phone, and with the greatest hesitancy Veronica pivoted from the townhouse's front door to the man standing behind her...and gasped. Tony's eyes were a pale pink, his pupils were gone.

"Oh god, dad," she said before her hand flew to her open mouth.

He reached out his arms, "Noni…" the book behind him turned its pages and she could see her name in large letters on the new page. Other words began to form as Tony spoke. The words were his words, writing as he was talking. "My daughter, I would never hurt you. Take this journey with me." she watched the words he spoke get written on the pink pages on the coffee table.

Veronica ran past him, slammed the book shut and carried it into the kitchen, throwing it into the sink and turning on the water, waiting to see the paper curl and dissolve, but the water ran off the cover as though it were covered in oil. She pried the book open, and water ran from the pages the same way. "Fine," she crossed the narrow kitchen and grabbed the matches on the shelf above the gas stove. She pushed a dirty pan back from the front burner, turned the knob as high as it would go, and lit a flame before snatching the book from the sink and placing it directly on top of the fire. "Release my father!"

"Noni…" Tony stood in the doorway, looking at his daughter with his blank eyes. He stepped towards her, arms still stretched outwards, waiting for an embrace she wasn't about to give. She looked back at the large pink book and didn't even see smoke. Damn it. Without further thought, she grabbed the dirty pan off the stove and smacked her father in the temple. He fell into the refrigerator but recovered and stood back up.

"I'm so sorry!" she said and hit him again, harder. This time he fell to the kitchen floor and Veronica waited. When he didn't move she nudged him with her foot. Confident he was unconscious, she rolled him onto his back and pressed her head to his chest. He was breathing. Good! Then she wetted a dish towel, knelt beside her father, and scrubbed at the magic marker third eye on his forehead. When the drawing didn't so much as fade, she grabbed the bottle of dish soap and poured some onto his skin. "Sorry," she said again, and rubbed harder. His forehead turned from its usual light brown to red to purple, but the drawing remained. She screamed, throwing the wet, soapy towel onto the floor. She looked up at her nemesis and realized the book wasn't on the stove anymore, and all she could see was the blue flame of the burner.

Veronica didn't have to guess where the damned thing was, she knew.

Third Eye Delight

Placing a gentle hand on her father, she looked into the living room and at the coffee table. "Why are you doing this?" she asked the book.

The cover opened and pages turned. Sweaty and defeated, Veronica stood and walked closer.

Noni

She loved you

Couldn't get past her own pain It was all she knew of motherhood

The next page read:

She expressed herself through fear

Made her pain yours

Regrets it all

Your mother loves you

Veronica felt as though she'd been punched in the gut. "Wha--shut up. Shut up! Don't--" but she didn't know what else to say. Truth has sharp edges.

Tony Jr. was happy to see his sister's car in front of his pop's house. He considered himself lucky to have a close family, and when he opened the front door of the townhouse, he yelled out, "Hey fam! What's up?" but only a few steps in stopped dead in his tracks. His smile fell. On the couch sat his dad and his sister, staring straight at him with pale pink eyes. Their foreheads had eyes inside of triangles crudely drawn on them. On the coffee table in front of them was a large hardcover pink book with a similar drawing.

"What's going…" his question faded, frightened by what he was seeing. The two smiled at the same time and said in unison, "Welcome home." The book before them opened on its own and blank pages ruffled to somewhere in the middle. Tony Jr. stumbled backwards, the keys he carried in his hands falling to the floor. He looked from his father and sister, into their pale pink eyes, then back to the large book and watched as words in black ink formed, forming a single phrase:

What was in those cookies?

The End

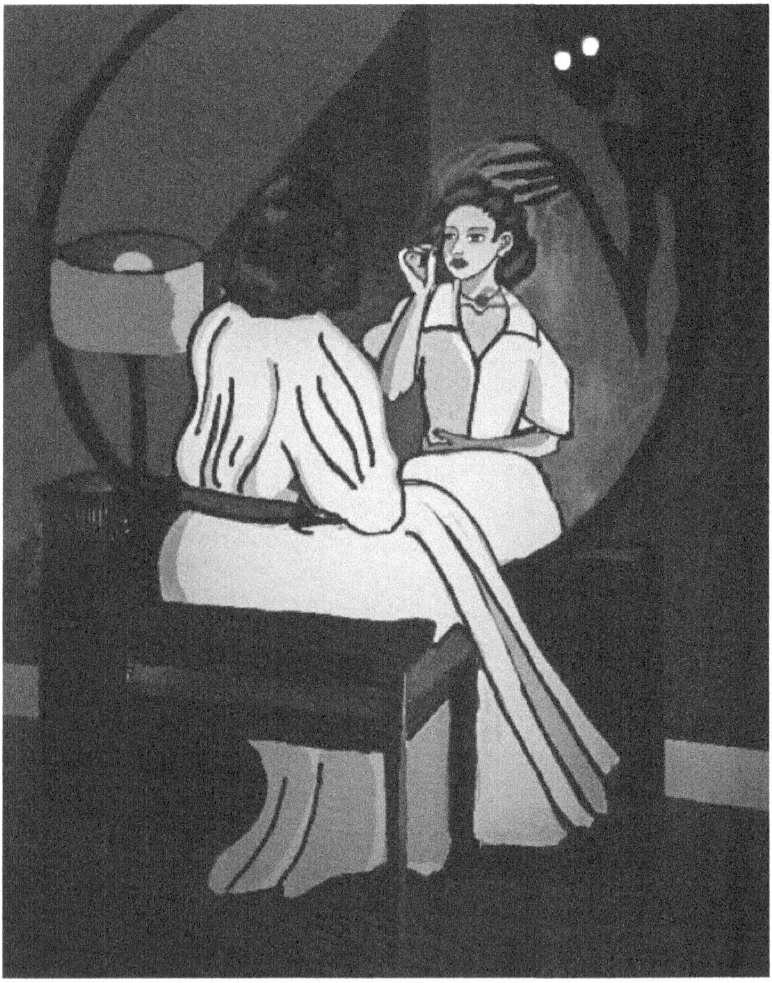

Mrs. Saltonstall's Dybbuk
by Adam Bolivar

It was John Drake's habit to wander the streets of Beacon Hill alone at night, illuminated only by the flicker of gaslight and the moon's mournful glow. That hallowed mound at the heart of Boston's labyrinth had been his family's home for nearly three hundred years; he was bound to it by ancestral chains which always pulled him back, much as he strained at them for release.

His house at 13 Acorn Street was the oldest on Beacon Hill. Seldom was it noticed by passers-by, and even more rarely did it appear in any history book.

The upper crust of Boston, the self-proclaimed Brahmins, grudgingly counted Drake among their number, but did their utmost to pretend he did not exist. And yet, when they had need of help with some supernatural complication, it was to him that they inevitably turned. It was an arrangement that was nearly as old as the city itself.

One night in January of 1924, Drake trudged through freshly fallen snow to Pinckney Street, to the house of a prominent lawyer by the name of Richard Saltonstall, who had summoned Drake there that evening. Drake observed a woman peering down at him through the frost of an upstairs window, but when she caught him looking back, she quickly drew the curtains. Saltonstall met Drake at the door, and, after the latter had disencumbered himself of his coat and hat, ushered him into a tastefully decorated parlor with a marble fireplace in one wall and a cut-crystal chandelier overhead.

"Good of you to come out on such a bitter evening," Saltonstall said. "Would you care for some brandy?"

"Thank you, I will," Drake replied, overlooking his host's blatant

disregard of Prohibition. "Considering how short a walk it was, I was not greatly incommoded by the journey."

Mrs. Saltonstall's Dybbuk

"Ah yes, of course," Saltonstall nodded. "I forget that you're just over on Acorn Street. It's mostly tradesmen who live there, isn't it? I'm rather surprised someone of your station would make it his residence."

Drake sampled the brandy and found it to his liking, though not Saltonstall's snobbery. "We Drakes were there first, as it happens. The street grew up around our house, as did all the others on Beacon Hill. And there's nothing wrong with tradesmen. Some of them can be very pleasant."

"Yes, yes, quite," Saltonstall said, waving his hand as if trying to ward off a tiresome subject. "I suppose you're wondering why I asked you here tonight."

"I presume you are in need of my services," Drake replied. "There is no other reason why anyone ever calls on me."

"Well," said Saltonstall, lighting a cigarette, which prompted Drake to do the same. "You are correct. I am in need of your services. It is an open secret that you are the one to turn to in matters which are of, well, an uncanny nature."

"Please get to the point, Mr. Saltonstall," Drake said. "It is true. I have considerable experience with the supernatural. I will have an open mind to anything you may have to tell me."

"Very well," Saltonstall said, pausing to consider his next words. "It's about my wife, you see. She is under some sort of affliction. She stays in bed most of the time, or else stares out the window for hours on end. When she does speak, which is rarely, she says the most absurd things, things she wouldn't normally say. It's as though she has become an entirely different person."

"Perhaps this is more of a matter for a psychiatrist," Drake suggested.

"Normally, I would agree with you, sir," Saltonstall nodded. "But it is more than that. Her condition is accompanied by ... unsettling occurrences. Unnatural, you might say."

"Tell me about your wife," Drake asked. "What is her background?"

"Hannah is an émigrée," Saltonstall replied. "She is of Jewish origin. As

234

a teenager she came to America from Lithuania to escape unfortunate circumstances."

"A most unusual match for someone of your lineage," Drake remarked.

Saltonstall shrugged. "What can I say? I was smitten with her. She was so quick, so fascinating. My parents were furious, of course. But it's water under the bridge at this point. They have come to accept her, albeit grudgingly."

"I know the feeling," Drake sighed. "Has she told you much about her life in Lithuania?"

"Not much," Saltonstall admitted. "It's not something she likes to talk about. She grew up in a ... what's the word? A shtetl. It was a very traditional upbringing, which she desires to put behind her." "Is she still observant of her religion?" Drake asked.

"In small ways," Saltonstall replied. "Lighting the candles on Friday night, that sort of thing. Old habits die hard, I suppose. More brandy?"

Drake stubbed out his cigarette. "No, thank you. I think it's time for me to meet Mrs. Saltonstall."

Saltonstall took Drake upstairs. He went to a door and gave it a vigorous knock. After a few moments with no reply, he opened it. Beyond was a bedroom furnished with a four-poster bed and a dressing table, upon which the stub of a candle burned in a wax-covered brass candlestick. A woman in a white nightgown sat at the dressing table. She gave no indication she was aware of her husband's presence. Instead, she peered intently into the mirror at her own face, which was wreathed by untidy locks of dark, curly hair.

As he stood in the doorway, Drake caught a glimpse of a silver necklace set with a faceted blood-red ruby. It sparkled in the candlelight as she toyed with it. Before Drake could enter the room, the woman slipped it into a jewelry box and closed the lid.

"Hannah," Saltonstall said. "This is Mr. Drake. He is here to help you."

"How do you do, Mrs. Saltonstall?" Drake said. "Can you hear me?"

Mrs. Saltonstall's Dybbuk

Still looking in the mirror, the woman replied, "Of course I can hear you. Hannah has two good ears, doesn't she?"

"Why do you say *Hannah* has two good ears?" Drake asked. "Are you not she?"

The woman laughed. "What is this *mishigas*? My name isn't Hannah."

"Now, now, Hannah," Drake persisted. "Surely you know your own name. Your husband is concerned about you. That's why he called me."

"That schmendrick? My husband? Hannah is betrothed to *me*! She thought could get away from me, but I was too smart for her. And now she will never be free. A promise is a promise."

"Speak your name then," Drake commanded. "Who is this entity that inhabits Hannah's body?"

Mrs. Saltonstall, or the shell that was her body, stood up and turned around to face Drake. "Ach, English is like treacle on my tongue. You want to know my name? I'll tell you. It is Yosef Fleischer. I know your name too, *Jack.*" The possessed woman pointed her two forefingers downwards and then flicked them upwards in Drake's direction, a gesture which pushed him out of the bedroom with an invisible force. The door slammed in his face of its own accord.

Rather than attempting to regain entrance to the room, Drake started down the staircase to the front door, where he retrieved his hat and coat. Saltonstall hastened to catch up to him.

"Well, Drake?" Saltonstall asked him. "What do you make of this morbid business? Can you help her?"

"I have an inkling as to the nature of your wife's malady," Drake replied. "But it is outside my usual area of expertise. I must make some inquiries before I can proceed. I'll send word when I have news."

"I beg of you, please do," Saltonstall pleaded, clutching the sleeve of Drake's coat. "I don't know how much more of this I can take. I'm at my wit's end."

"Then take heart," Drake assured him. "For my wit is very keen, and I'll match it with this devil's soon enough."

⌘ ⌘ ⌘

"It sounds like a dybbuk," said Yacob after Drake had recounted the story to him the next day. Yacob Lerner was Drake's tailor. He stood behind a wooden counter of his shop on Salem Street, in the North End. Behind him was his workshop, a jumble of scissors, measuring tapes, bolts of fabric, and half-sewn articles of clothing. A woman wearing a kerchief over her head was hard at work hemming a pair of trousers on a sewing machine, which she powered by pushing a treadle back and forth with her foot.

"That's what I thought," Drake replied, raising his voice to be heard over the machine's clattering. There was a lull in the racket, and he lowered his voice to a near whisper. "A restless spirit who possesses the body of another."

"Oy vey!" Yacob moaned. "What is this you bring to my doorstep? I'm only a tailor, not a rebbe."

"I understand," Drake said. "I thought you might be able to direct me to someone who is knowledgeable in such matters."

Yacob stroked his black beard. "Well, you've been a very loyal customer, Mr. Drake. You could talk to my brother, Shmuel. He goes to yeshiva school, and I'm sure he knows all about it. Come back this evening at seven after I've closed up shop. My brother and I live upstairs with our family. You're welcome to share our meal."

"That is kind of you," Drake said. "However, I wouldn't wish to cause any inconvenience. Is there some establishment where you are accustomed to dining? It will be my treat."

"Well, if you put it that way," Yacob said. "I am partial to Esther's on Spring Street in the West End."

Mrs. Saltonstall's Dybbuk

"Well then, I shall meet you and your brother there at half past seven," Drake said, consulting a gold pocket watch. "I trust my new suit is progressing nicely."

"Oh, very nicely, Mr. Drake," Yacob replied. "It should be ready for you next week."

"I'm certain it will be of the most exquisite quality, as always," Drake said as he departed. The brass bell above the shop's door rang as he opened, then closed it. Yacob watched through the front window as the gaunt man in the black overcoat trudged through the falling snow. He shivered, as though he had been visited by the Devil himself.

⌘ ⌘ ⌘

Drake and the Lerner brothers were the only customers dining at Esther's Delicatessen on that cheerless evening in the dead of winter. Even at half past seven it was already dark outside. Yacob and Shmuel tucked into their kugel, while Drake contented himself with coffee and cigarettes. It was a much shabbier establishment than the ones he frequented, but infinitely more charming. Between the delicious smells emanating from the kitchen and the Hebrew letters painted on the windowpanes, Drake could have just as easily been in a village in Eastern Europe rather than a few blocks from Beacon Hill.

"Are you sure you won't have anything to eat, Mr. Drake?" Yacob asked him. "I'm sure they can make something that even a goy would like."

"No, thank you, Mr. Lerner. I am quite content."

Yacob turned to his brother. "This one is so thin. He is like a skeleton. No wonder he wants to hear about dybbuks."

"The dybbuk is no laughing matter," Shmuel scolded him. Whereas Yacob was chatty and gregarious, Shmuel was reserved and intense. Like his brother, Shmuel had a dark beard, and wore a frock coat and a black hat.

Drake lit another cigarette and motioned to the young waitress for a refill of his coffee. "My understanding is that a dybbuk is the soul of one who has died but refuses to move on to the next world."

"Always with evil intent," Shmuel added. "This Yosef Fleischer whom you speak of, tell me, who was he to Mrs. Saltonstall?"

"Mr. Saltonstall said he was not aware of his wife having known anyone by that name," Drake replied. "She refused to confide in him about her former life in Lithuania. My instinct is that he was a spurned suitor who took his own life. Now that I think of it, a dybbuk's longing for a lover from beyond the grave would make an excellent pretext for a ballad."

"Yosef Fleischer must have been a man of great learning," Shmuel said. "And he used his learning for impure purposes. There is no greater crime. He has turned his back on Adonai, the Most High, and sought the comfort of Samaël the Fallen. He is a sorcerer. A warlock."

"But how did Fleischer's spirit come to possess Mrs. Saltonstall's body from across the ocean?" Drake asked. "There must have been a catalyst to precipitate this event."

Shmuel lit a cigarette. "Did this woman come into possession of anything unusual lately? Some talisman or jewel?"

Drake snapped his fingers. "That could be it! When I first saw her, she was holding a silver necklace set with what appeared to be a large ruby. She was careful to conceal it when I spoke to her. This could be the talisman you're referring to."

"The sorcerer must have put his soul into the ruby and arranged to have it sent to her after he died," Shmuel reasoned. "It was a trap, a pretty bauble a woman couldn't resist."

"So, what can be done?" Drake asked. "There must be some method for exorcising a dybbuk."

"There is a ritual," Shmuel nodded. "We will need to bring the woman to the shul, so that the ritual may be performed. There should be a minyan of ten men, who have purified themselves through fasting and immersion. I will ask Rabbi Schwartzschild to arrange it."

Mrs. Saltonstall's Dybbuk

"But how will we get the woman to the shul?" Yacob pointed out. "If the dybbuk has such a hold on her, I doubt she will go willingly."

"My very thoughts," Drake said. "We can't bring her there by force. Her screams would attract bystanders and they would alert the police, who I doubt would be sympathetic to us. Could the rabbi and his minyan come to the Saltonstall house and perform the ritual there?"

"This Saltonstall is a gentile, you say?" Shmuel asked. "Does he keep kosher?" When Drake shook his head, Shmuel frowned. "No, the house would be too impure."

"Very well," Drake said. "I shall have to procure a sleeping draught to pacify Mrs. Saltonstall. Then we can bundle her, insensate, to the shul. Just be ready on your end."

"I'll talk to the rabbi," Shmuel promised. "I will inform you when the night is set. If the dybbuk is as tenacious as you say, we may need to bind it to the ruby again. And then we would need a vessel to contain the ruby. Some sort of ark, perhaps a box."

Drake flashed a wolfish grin. "I know just the thing."

⌘ ⌘ ⌘

The exorcism occurred on a day the following week, at midnight. As planned, Drake and Saltonstall drugged the dybbuk-possessed Hannah with phenobarbital and drove her in Saltonstall's Model-T to the Vilna Shul. It was an odd, cube-shaped building, newly erected on the north slope of Beacon Hill, where the hill adjoined the West End. The two men stood on either side of Hannah, and half-walked, half-carried her from the car to the steps of the temple. There they were met by two women, their heads covered by black shawls, who led the still-docile Hannah to the women's entrance in the side of the shul, while Drake and her husband entered by the men's entrance in the front.

Inside were two rows of benches, one for men and one for women. In front of the benches was a raised podium with a reading desk, called *a bimah*. It was where readings from the Torah and the Haftarah, a series of selections from the books of Prophets, took place. Behind the *bimah* was the Ark containing the Torah scrolls. It was a beautiful object, constructed of ornately carved woodwork and surrounded by curtains. Surmounting the Ark was a depiction of the two tablets inscribed with the Ten Commandments given to Moses.

Drake felt the same deep discomfort he experienced in Christian churches, for e was beholden to other gods than the one worshipped here.

Drake had measured the dosage of the drug so that Hannah would regain consciousness now, for it was vital that the dybbuk be aware of the exorcism taking place. The women in black shawls led Hannah to what looked like a courtroom's witness box on the women's side of the shul. Drake and Saltonstall took seats in the front bench of the men's section.

Next to the *bimah*, nine men wearing fur hats and white prayer shawls — Shmuel among them — sat at a table presided over by an elderly rabbi with a snow-white beard. He was the tenth member of the minyan's quorum. The ten men sang prayers from seven scrolls taken from the Ark, while seven black candles burned atop the table. Also, on the table lay seven shofars, ceremonial horns made from the curling horns of rams.

Hannah Saltonstall — or rather the dybbuk inside her —had fully awakened and glared at the sacred symbols. The rabbi stood up and addressed the demon directly.

"Dybbuk," he said, in a deep, imposing voice. "You are not welcome. Not in the body of this woman, Hannah Saltonstall, or in the world of the living. I command you to depart."

"But where can I go, rebbe?" the dybbuk whined in Hannah's voice. "I have turned my face from the Creator and cannot go to Olam Ha-Ba.

Even Samaël has turned his back on me now. All paths are closed to me."

"That is not my concern," the rabbi said. "This woman is under my protection, and I will not permit you to remain in her body. Does this minyan give me the authority to drive out the spirit who does not wish to depart?"

Speaking as one, the nine other men seated at the table answered, "We give you that authority."

"Dybbuk," the rabbi said. "Wandering spirit. With the authority of this holy congregation, I, Avram Schwartzschild, command you to depart the body of Hannah Saltonstall, or be excommunicated from Israel."

The dybbuk laughed mirthlessly. "You cannot cast out who one has already been cast out. I am already cast out from Israel."

"Then you must wander in the darkness between worlds for all time," the rabbi said. "Until the horn is blown on the final day." Seven of the minyan stood and raised the rams' horns to their lips. They blew long mournful blasts which melded together in an eerie cacophony.

"I cast you out, dybbuk!" the rabbi commanded. "I cast you out! Go then and find a path of your own." Schwartzschild opened his arms wide and spread the fingers of each hand into a 'V' shape.

Hannah screamed, suddenly herself again. She looked at her husband, who sprang to his feet. "Help me, darling! Help me."

"The ruby, Saltonstall," Drake barked. "Did you bring the ruby?"

"Yes, I have it here," Saltonstall replied, producing the silver necklace set with a blood-red gem.

Drake snatched the necklace out of his hand and sprang to his feet to face the dybbuk. He pulled a wooden box from his overcoat pocket, the lid carved with the image of a boar. Drake opened it and placed the necklace inside.

The rabbi and two of the minyan recited incantations in Hebrew, while the other seven blew their rams' horns again and again.

The dybbuk stared at Drake with eyes blazing with red fire. "Now you shall bear my curse, Ettinfell. You will bear the mark of Samaël for all eternity!"

Hannah tumbled out of the witness box and collapsed on the floor. A red spark burst out of her big toe, blowing a hole through her shoe. It flew into the ruby, which glowed like a coal, the same infernal red as the dybbuk's eyes.

Drake snapped the lid of the box shut and whispered a prayer of his own: *In the name of Woden and Thunor, Freya and Ing, I bind you, thyrs.*

Saltonstall rushed towards his wife but restrained himself from crossing over to the women's side after warning glances came from the two women who accompanied her. Hannah opened her eyes and blinked as tears streamed down her cheeks. She was herself again, free of the dybbuk's curse, for Drake had taken it upon himself.

⌘ ⌘ ⌘

In the cellar of 13 Acorn Street was a door, and beyond this door were stairs carved from living stone that led down and down into the dark and cold, into a cavern deep beneath Beacon Hill, a heathen place of old. Drake descended the stairs by the light of a candle in an ancient tin lantern, which he held in one hand suspended from a chain. In his other hand, he clutched the cedar box that held the ruby with the dybbuk imprisoned inside. Against the wall of the cavern was a chest which had belonged to his ancestor, the first John Drake to come to Boston.

Drake set the lantern on the cave floor and knelt to open the chest with a key on the ring at the end of the chain of his pocket watch. The chest contained a hoard of occult items: tomes and amulets, witch's bottles, a chalice stained at the bottom with dried blood, and a folded-up cloak which was said to render its wearer invisible.

To this outré collection, Drake added the cedar box whose lid was carved with a coat of arms depicting a rampant boar. It was the same box he had found in the hollow of a tree by Jamaica Pond, and which had contained a silver key and a deerskin pouch full of sand. Now it contained a cursed ruby. There was a certain symmetry to this outcome.

Mrs. Saltonstall's Dybbuk

Drake locked the chest once more, and so ended the affair of Mrs. Saltonstall's dybbuk. But still his mind was troubled.

At the far end of the underground chamber was a tunnel that led still deeper beneath Beacon Hill, until the distinction between the waking world and the dream realm became indistinct. From far down the tunnel carried distant moans and the ghostly jingling of chains. As he was every time he came here, Drake was tempted to enter the tunnel, and find the source of these unsettling sounds. But his father had warned him that this way led to perdition. So, with a great effort of will, he turned away, and climbed the stone steps back to the house above. He locked the secret door in the cellar with another key on his watch chain, and retreated to his study, where he collapsed into an armchair and brooded darkly, as bound by ancestral curses as the dybbuk was in the ruby.

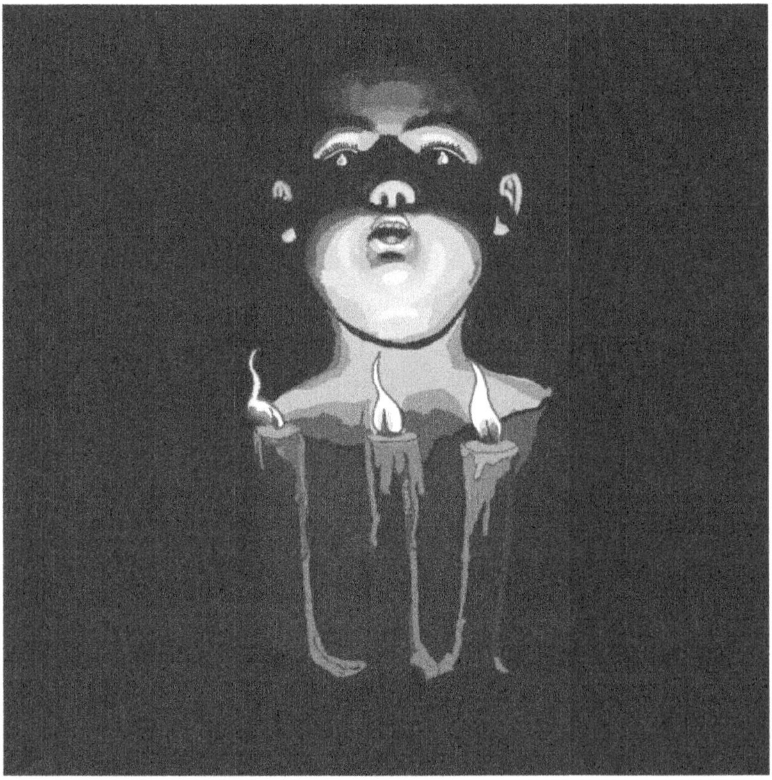

Invoking a Playmate
by Laura Davey

I'm not saying to do it, and I'm not saying not to. I just know that when I searched online for wishing rituals, I didn't get all the facts. The ritual is simple, really. And safe if you stick to the instructions.

But with what little I knew, I thought it was an easy choice. It shouldn't have been an easy choice.

Now it's your choice too.

⌘ ⌘ ⌘

1. Get a doll and sleep with it for at least a month.
2. Wait for a moonless night.
3. Be alone. Take comfort in this solitude while you can.
4. Give the doll your name. Your true name, either the one that was given to you at birth or the one in your heart. If you give the doll a fake name, then that fake name will get a wish at dawn, but you'll still have the consequences.
5. Close the curtains and turn off all the lights, except for one candle to keep beside you. Make sure that candle never blows out.
6. At midnight, stand in front of a mirror with your doll and say, "I invoke you and invite you. I invoke you and invite you. I invoke you and invite you. Whoever is watching, come play with me until dawn."
7. Do NOT look behind you. Whatever you see in the mirror. Whatever you hear whispered. Don't look behind you.
8. Don't scream. When I screamed, my candle sputtered and was almost extinguished. For that brief moment, I felt the sharp pain of grasping appendages and deep wet words that still echo in my nightmares. I was safe again when the flame regained its strength, but the bruises remained.

Invoking a Playmate

9. It's okay to cry.

10. Hold out your doll and state the doll's name. Tell the creature that your doll wants to play. Remember, you have already given the doll your name. Always call the doll by your name. If you call it anything else, the creature might realize that *you* go by that name, and it will think that *you* want to play. And then it will play with you.

11. Start a game. It doesn't really matter what the game is, from checkers to hopscotch. Be prepared to play both sides. Keep the lit candle within sight and don't do anything that would create enough of a breeze to blow it out.

12. Keep playing. Go from game to game. If it gets too bored, the creature will start its own game. If it does, swallow the lit candle. If you're lucky, the hot wax will blister your mouth and burn your throat. If it doesn't, I'm sorry, but that means the creature is still there.

13. Keep playing. Don't stop even if you have to soil yourself. Don't stop even if you accidentally knock over a treasured figurine and broken glass scatters across the floor. Don't stop even if you step in the glass, driving a shard deep into your heel. Don't stop even if the blood and pain make it difficult to play.

14. The creature may delight in what it considers a new "game"— one of destruction and agony. It's your choice to continue to play that game or not but remember that you should never let it grow bored.

15. At sunrise, the mirror will become cloudy, signaling the ritual is nearing completion. Address the creature and thank it for playing. Then, ask for a wish.

16. The wish can be anything, but the creature must believe it was a fair exchange for a night of entertainment. If you ask for too much, it may decide the cost is to continue to play. By now, your candle should have burned down enough that even swallowing it may not keep the creature away.

17. Recall your wish that made you believe this ritual was worth it. When the dawn arrived for me, as I stood bleeding and bruised with unearthly words still fresh in my mind, I could barely think. I had desired

the usual—riches, fame, love—vague wishes that inspired that night because then I could say I had tried everything rather than truly believing a ritual would work. But it did work, and there was no method to stop without repercussions. Those vague wishes were caught behind my teeth, as fear that the creature wouldn't believe the night was worth the price kept me silent. In the end, all I could wish for was for it to leave.

18. When it departs, it might take the doll. If it doesn't, bury the doll with strong chains wrapped around it and salt the ground. Consider moving.

19. Open the curtains to the morning light and use your blood to extinguish the candle. The mirror should return to normal, and you can safely treat your wounds. At least, those on your flesh.

20. If you still can, cry.

END

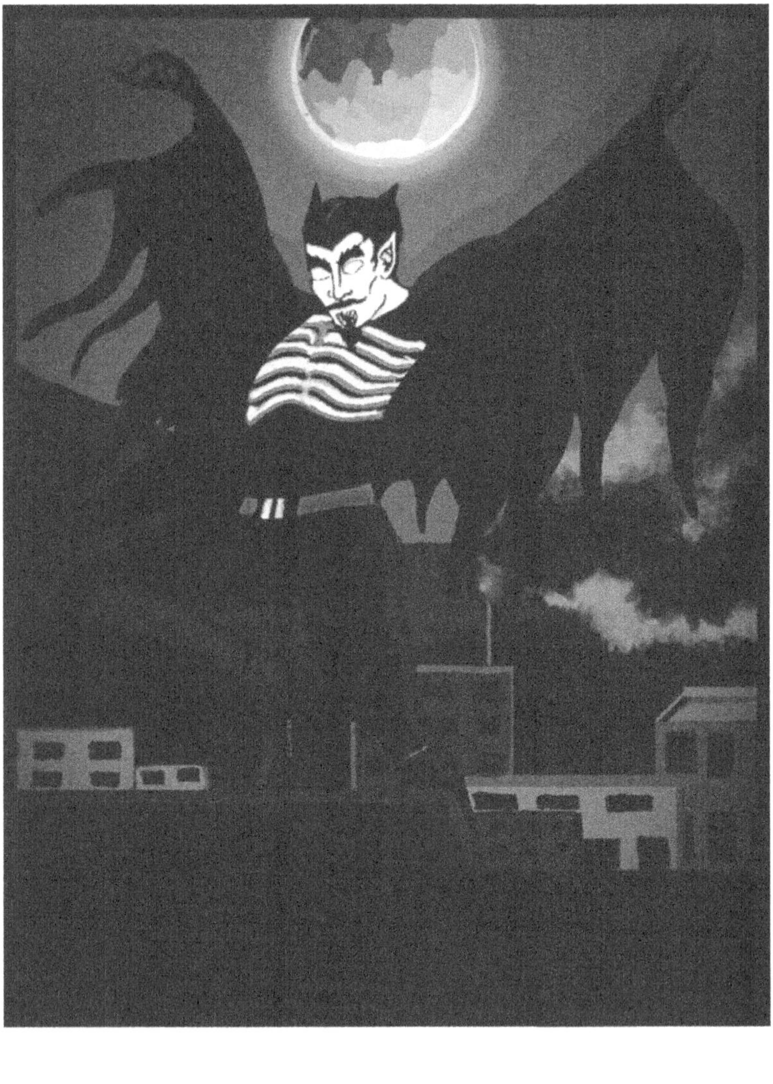

Spring-Heeled Jack
by Ashley Dioses

The legendary Spring-Heeled Jack
Arises for a spell.
His claws extend, and fires crack In blue
like flames from Hell.

Beneath his cloak is tight oilskin,
His smile reveals white flames.
On Lavender Hill he revels in
The scent of his next game.

The screaming souls of victims past
Still ring inside his head.
Insanity has won at last—
His eyes are ever red.

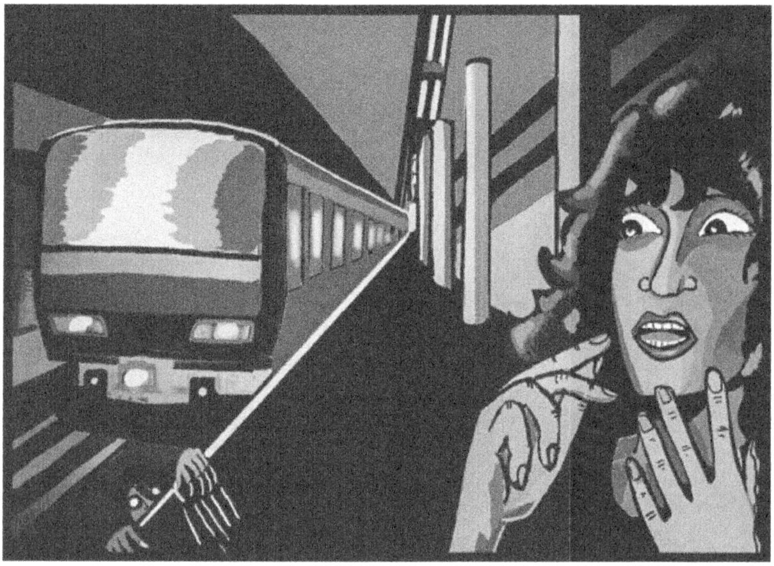

Midnight Train from Tokyo
by John H. Howard

Catherine hurried through the deserted Tokyo subway station, the night pressing in on her. The pockets of gloom in the corners where wall met ceiling seemed heavy enough to crush her should they somehow come untethered. She picked up her step, her footsteps bouncing off the walls. The echo made her feel like she wasn't alone. She cast a quick nervous glance over her shoulder but saw no one.

Still, she heard it, half a beat out of sync with her step: *teke teke. Teke teke.*

The stranger's words had affected her more than she had expected.

He had stepped onto the train a few stops from hers. Until then, for several stops, she had been the only person in her car, having caught the last train at midnight.

His eyes showed his surprise when they alit on her. He politely sat across the aisle and a few seats down. His black hair glistened from the evening mist. Runnels of moisture left behind darker trails on his black leather jacket. He looked to be in his late twenties, about the same age as her.

Their eyes met and he smiled.

"You American?" he said. His English was quite good.

"Yes," she said, smiling back. "I'm here with my fiancé for a business thing. Not mine, though, his. I'm in between jobs right now. It's my first time to Tokyo, let alone out of the country. The States, I mean. It'd be lunchtime there right now. My body hasn't adjusted to the time difference yet, so I'm wide awake. And a little hungry, to be honest. I'm still learning my way around, but I've found that riding the subway is a good way to see the sights. Plus, it can be pretty meditative, and it helps me relax so I can sleep." She forced herself to stop. Daniel was always complaining that she rambled too much when she got nervous, and she could tell she was doing so now.

Midnight Train from Tokyo

The man's smile widened. He dipped his head slightly. "In that case, welcome to my city. I've lived here all my life and while I've traveled abroad many times, I always return. There's something about the lights and the life here that I could never leave for long. I sincerely hope you enjoy your time here. Maybe you'll come to love Tokyo almost as much as I do."

"Thank you," Catherine said. Any doubts she might have had about the young man sitting across from her melted away at his kindness. "It's a beautiful city." She stretched across the aisle and extended her hand. "I'm Catherine, by the way."

His handshake conveyed both confidence and retrained strength. "I'm Haruto. Pleasure to meet you, Catherine."

His eyes were kind, his manner gentle. Catherine felt the color rise in her cheeks. *Daniel would be upset if he saw us*, she thought.

She broke his gaze and looked up at the destination monitor. "My stop is coming up next," she said. "It's been very nice to meet you." She stood and moved closer to the door. She grabbed onto the pole to steady herself.

Haruto's smile disappeared. "This is your stop?" His voice was serious.

"Um. Yes. Is there something wrong?"

"How long have you been here?"

"Just a few days. Why?"

"Please be careful at that station," he said, serious now. "In fact, I wouldn't go there at night. It's extremely dangerous." "Why?"

"The '*Teke Teke*,'" he said.

"I have no idea what that is."

"A couple of years ago a young woman was killed there. Video surveillance showed that she had been pushed in front of a train. It was too late for the train to stop. She was cut in half." Catherine was getting scared.

"So, whoever did that was never caught?" She didn't want her first journey outside the country to end with her being pushed in front of a train.

Haruto shook his head. "No, they caught them. Just some bullies. They thought it would be funny. I doubt they're finding prison very funny, though."

Catherine's fear faded somewhat. "So, if they caught the guys who did it, what is there to be afraid of?"

"The *Teke eke* is the young woman's spirit. She's looking for her legs. *Teke teke* is the sound she makes as she pulls herself along by her arms. If she catches you, she'll ask you where her legs are. If you answer her incorrectly or if you try to run, she'll rip you in half."

"I'm sorry?"

Haruto made his hands into fists, put them close together, then pulled them apart like he was breaking something. "Like that."

Catherine's brow creased. "With her bare hands?"

Haruto shrugged. "She is an *onryō*, an angry, way vengeful spirit. Capable of anything."

Catherin's temper flared. "You really had me going," she said in a flat tone.

Haruto looked confused. "What do you mean?"

"I thought you were a nice guy, but instead you were just making fun of a stupid American, taking advantage of my ignorance."

"No, I'm not making fun!" Haruto stood and took a half step toward her before seeming to realize it wasn't a good idea. He looked distressed.

"You're a very good actor," Catherine said. The train started to slow.

"I'm not acting," he said quietly.

"Is there a camera around here somewhere?" Catherine made a show of looking around the train car. "I know how you Japanese like your pranks."

"It's not like that," Haruto insisted.

The train pulled up to the station and stopped. The doors slid open.

"Please, just be careful," Haruto implored.

255

Midnight Train from Tokyo

Catherine stepped out.

Before the doors closed, she turned around.

"What's the correct answer?" she asked.

Haruto was clearly confused.

"*If* I run into to her and *if* she asks me where her legs are, what should I tell her?"

Haruto shrugged. "No one knows. No one has lived to say." The train doors slid closed between them.

The train pulled away from the station and Haruto was gone. She was alone.

Now, the clicking ticking sound seemed right behind her as she approached the stairs. Once again she glanced behind her and once again saw nothing. She half ran up the stairs to the exit.

At the top she looked behind her one final time. Did one of the shadows at the bottom of the stairs move? It almost seemed like something looked up at her from the gloom. Something with long dark hair and black pits for eyes. She blinked and the illusion was gone.

Catherine jogged most of the way back to the small apartment that Daniel's company had arranged for them. She hated that Haruto's story had gotten under her skin.

Still, she told herself, *I'm a woman out alone after midnight. The sooner I get back the better.*

It wasn't until she was a block away that she realized that she had been wearing rubber-soled sneakers that barely made a sound on the pavement.

Catherine stepped into the small apartment, their temporary home away from home while Daniel was working here. The nature of his business wasn't entirely clear to her, but since his company had agreed to pay her way, too, she wasn't asking too many questions.

She shucked off her dripping jacket and hung it on the peg in the entryway before taking off her shoes and placing them on the rack by the door.

By this time, it was closer to morning than midnight. Daniel was certainly asleep by now, so Catherine walked softly through the apartment so as not to wake him.

She was surprised to find him not only awake, but busy at his laptop in the tiny room that he had claimed for an office. Usually, he kept the door closed, claiming confidential business matters, but tonight he had left it open. Daniel sat with his back to the open doorway, seemingly unaware that Catherine had come in. It looked like he was in a chat room. *Probably work stuff*, she thought.

She hovered silently in the doorway for a long moment, casually watching him. The man she was going to marry in just a few short months.

Something on the screen past his shoulder caught her eye.

The words "she has no idea lol" floated upward on the right side of the screen. Daniel's side of the chat. Her breath caught in her throat.

She couldn't see the reply that came a moment later or who made it, but Daniel chuckled out loud.

Catherine must have made a sound because just then Daniel's head whipped around, his blue eyes wide and surprised. "Cath!" he said. "I didn't hear you come in. I'm almost done. Be right out." He swung the door closed, forcing her to step back so it wouldn't hit her in the face.

Her strange conversation with Haruto on the subway and the weird events in the station afterward were pushed from her mind by the words she had just seen her fiancé type.

She has no idea.

Catherine suddenly and unexpectedly found herself on a turbulent emotional ride, vacillating between hurt, betrayal, depression, and shock.

"Take your time," she called through the door. Her voice sounded unsteady to her own ear. "I'm just going to get ready for bed." No reply came.

A short time later, Daniel still closed up in his office, Catherine cried herself to sleep over the newfound knowledge that her fiancé was

Midnight Train from Tokyo

cheating on her.

Daniel woke her with a kiss on the cheek sometime the next morning. She didn't respond, remembering that she was still mad at him.

"C'mon, Cath," he said. She heard amusement in his voice. "I know you're awake. I can see your eyes moving behind your lids."

She cracked one eye. She didn't say anything about her discovery of his betrayal. She hadn't decided how she wanted to respond yet.

She let him kiss her again but didn't return it. He didn't seem to notice. More proof, in her mind.

"I have to go out for a while," he said. "Order yourself in some breakfast. Or lunch, whatever you want. It's almost noon."

"When will you be back?" Her voice cracked in her sleep-dry throat.

"Not for a while. I have some meetings this afternoon."

She opened both eyes to look at him. He was dressed in jeans and a button-down shirt. "You're going to meetings dressed like that?"

Daniel shrugged. "They're casual."

Catherine raised her head to follow him as he made his way toward the door. He picked up his backpack on the way, the one he had just bought before their trip. He'd said it would be more comfortable than carrying a briefcase around.

She let her head drop back to the pillow.

"See ya later, Cath. Love you."

She didn't respond because she didn't know how she felt anymore. Like with the kiss, he didn't seem to notice. The door clicked closed behind him.

Catherine lay in bed for a while, despondent. After some time, her grumbling stomach urged her out of bed to order some food. She didn't understand most of what was on the menu, but she knew what hamburgers and French fries were. She really wanted pancakes and sausage and hash browns, since her stomach was still on States time, but she didn't see anything resembling the comfort food she craved.

She ate in bed, facing the door to Daniel's office the entire time. Her eyes kept drifting to it, even though she tried to ignore it. She continued to stare at it long after she had finished her meal. He usually kept it locked, but she wondered...

Her arms pushed her out of the bed and her legs carried her to the door. Her hand reached out and stopped just shy of the knob. It was as if her body was saying *I got you this far. It's up to you to do the rest.*

She hesitated. But she had to know for sure. She grasped the knob and turned.

It was locked.

Catherine crawled back in bed and spent the next few hours staring at the door, lost in her own mind.

A knock came at the door around four o'clock. A woman's voice said something in Japanese, then repeated it in English: "Housekeeping."

Catherine forced herself out of her catatonic state. She looked around the room and realized it hadn't been cleaned the entire time she and Daniel had been here. Plastic soda and water bottles, dishes from food service, and dirty clothes littered the place.

The knock came one more time, but no announcement came with it.

"Just a minute!" Catherine pushed herself out of bed and threw her robe around her shoulders. She hadn't bothered getting dressed all day.

She opened the door and let the housekeeper in. The woman who entered looked simultaneously young and old. Her face had the appearance of a twenty-something year-old woman, but the creases around her eyes and the slight stoop in her posture were those of someone much older. As she stepped out of the way, Catherine made a mental note to leave a generous tip when her trip was over.

After the housekeeper had finished and was stepping out the door, Catherine had a sudden thought.

"Wait a second," she said.

"Yes?" the housekeeper responded.

"I just remembered that I accidentally locked myself out of that room. Would you be able to help me?"

Midnight Train from Tokyo

"Oh, yes. No problem." The housekeeper smiled. Internal doors didn't have the keycard locks that the doors to the hallway did. They needed an actual metal key. And Daniel kept theirs with him at all times. The housekeeper pulled a keyring out of a pocket and inserted just such a key in the lock, turned it, and twisted the knob. The door swung open.

"There you are, Miss," she said.

"Thank you so much." Catherine said. She realized that she had been half hoping that the housekeeper wouldn't be able to help.

"My pleasure." The housekeeper bowed once and was gone.

Catherine walked over to the door and pushed it all the way open. Daniel's laptop sat on the small desk against the opposite wall, closed.

Before she could think about what she was doing, she sat down in front of it and opened it. It booted right up.

The cursor flashed in an entry field, wanting a password.

Catherine tried several different things: Daniel's birthdate, his address, his first dog's name, his favorite food. Nothing worked.

Then she tried her own name.

Nothing.

Her name with her birthdate.

Still nothing.

Her address, her middle name, her high school mascot, her first cat's name, her birthdate, her address, the date they met, the restaurant where he had proposed to her.

Nothing worked.

She was about to give up when she heard Daniel's voice in her head saying his favorite phrase: Fuck the world.

She typed it in.

The screen went dark for a second and then, with a chime, his desktop appeared.

It was easy to find the chat program Daniel had been on the night before. The transcript was still up.

As she scanned through it, Catherine's blood went cold.

John H. Howard

Daniel wasn't cheating on her after all. It was much, much worse.

Catherine left the apartment before Daniel got back. After walking the streets for a while, she eventually found herself on the subway again as the light of day fell to the dominance of the neon and LED-lit Tokyo night.

Before she knew it, the announcement came over the speaker system in both Japanese and English that it was the last route of the night.

She was going to have to get off soon. And then she was going to have to face Daniel with what she knew.

A few stops from her own, her car once again empty, Haruto stepped aboard.

He stopped short when he saw her. Then he took a seat across and down from her, as he had the night before.

"I wasn't sure I'd run into you again," he said. "You seemed pretty upset. Figured you'd try to avoid me."

"My fiancé is planning on killing me," Catherine blurted out. Tears threatened and her voice broke. She'd been carrying it with her all day but saying it out loud broke through the dam that she had constructed to contain her emotions.

"Is this you trying to get me back?" Haruto asked after a long silence. "Because if it is, it's not funny."

"I just found out that Daniel is an FTW terrorist, and his cell is planning something a couple of days from now. And they're--he's-- planning on using me to carry it out."

"The Fuck the World group? Catherine, this isn't funny. They're really dangerous."

"There's a big tech convention two days from now. That's when it's going to happen."

"I know about that convention. I tried to get tickets and couldn't. But didn't you say you were here on business with him?"

"Yeah, that was a lie. The FTW is sponsoring the entire trip."

"So where do you come in?"

261

Midnight Train from Tokyo

"At the convention at some point he's going to leave his bag with me under the pretense of going to the restroom, but the bag will have a bomb in it. He'll leave, the bomb will go off, and I'll get the blame. He went out today to plant evidence against me."

"My friend, if this is true, you need to go to the police!"

Catherine shook her head. The only evidence she had against him was the laptop. By the time she got back, he'd be there, and she wouldn't be able to get it out of the apartment without him knowing. She didn't have the bomb. It wasn't in the room. She had searched everywhere. Either it was in his backpack, and he had taken it with him or someone else was going to deliver it to him at another time. "I don't have enough against him yet. I want an open-and-shut case against him."

Haruto changed seats so that he was right in front of her. "Come stay at my place. It's only a couple of exits away from yours. I promise no harm will come to you. In the morning, we'll go to the police together."

"If I don't show up tonight, Daniel will get suspicious, and he'll disappear. Besides, I'll be okay for the next day or so. I'm part of his plan. And if I need to, I can contact security at the convention the day of the show. I just need a little more time."

Haruto didn't push. Instead, he produced a card from his jacket pocket and passed it to Catherine. "If you need anything, call me, regardless of the time."

Her eyes stung with his kindness and generosity. "Thank you, Haruto. I will."

As the train pulled into her stop, she tucked the card into her jacket pocket. She smiled at Haruto, noting the concerned expression on his face. She nodded at him but didn't say goodbye. He just watched her go.

She walked the platform, lost in her thoughts. She was in no hurry to return to the apartment and certainly not in a hurry to see Daniel and have to pretend she didn't know that he was planning on sacrificing her for his terrorist hate crime.

Catherine thought back on how they had met. She had joined a social media group for the newly single after her boyfriend had abruptly left her for a previous flame. She had been looking to commiserate with similar-minded people but wasn't opposed to meeting someone should the opportunity present itself.

Daniel popped up pretty quickly and they hit it off right away. He was witty and smart and easy on the eyes. They chatted for a while privately and before Catherine knew it, she was smitten.

She realized now that nothing had been real, that she probably fit some sort of psychological profile as an easy mark, and she had played right into his hands.

It had turned out that Daniel lived not too far away, which, again in retrospect, probably wasn't a coincidence. She wondered, though, if he had already lived there and had been assigned to her or if he had relocated once things progressed to the point of meeting in real life.

And that was the thing—he was *so* convincing. He had a nice apartment, and he was the same in person as he had been online. It was an easy, natural fit. The relationship progressed quickly, and they were engaged within months.

Catherine mentally berated herself for being so gullible. She wondered if he had even been responsible for her firing from the clothing store where she used to work; two weeks before the trip her supervisor Amee had received multiple complaints about Catherine's customer service, and she said she had no choice but to let Catherine go. None of the complaints had been true, of course, and Catherine had said as much, but Amee said she had to err on the side of the customers, which of course meant the best interests of the company. Still, the timing was too perfect not to have been a setup.

The longer she dwelled on things, the angrier she got.

She was pulled out of her reverie by a sound echoing off the walls of the station around her: *Teke teke.*

Teke teke.

Catherine's blood ran cold.

She had forgotten about Haruto's ghost and her experience the night before.

Midnight Train from Tokyo

She ran for the stairs leading up and out. They were simultaneously close and infinitely far away.

The sound grew louder, closer.

Teke teke Teke teke

TEKE TEKE

She was full-on sprinting now, but the sound was still getting louder, which meant whatever was making it was getting closer. Catherine didn't dare look behind her for fear of tripping and falling. It sounded like whatever it was right on her heels.

A shadow crossed the wall next to her.

Then it was in front of her.

Catherine skidded to a stop, but her feet went out from under her. She landed on her backside with an "Oomph!"

The thing before her had straight, dark hair with an oily sheen, teeth that were jagged and sharp, and eyes that were black pits, each with a tiny red ember burning deep inside. It was at eye level with her because it was pulling itself along with its hands. The thing's legs were gone, its torso trailing glistening bloody viscera on the tiled floor behind it. The thing's breath smelled sweetly of rotten meat.

Catherine's bladder let go. She knew she was about to die horribly. She saw it in the thing's face.

It said something in Japanese. Its empty unblinking sockets burned through her. Its voice was like bones rattling in a snake's dry skin.

"I…I don't understand you." Her voice was thin with fear.

"Where…are…my…legs," the thing managed in English.

"I…I…" She almost said, "I don't know" but something told her this was the wrong answer.

"I know where they are," she said breathlessly. "I can bring them to you."

The thing cocked its head at an unnatural angle. "My…legs. Bring…them…to…me." The thing inched closer. A blood-red tongue snaked out between cracked blackened lips. The thing didn't blink once.

"I can," Catherine said, desperate to be away from this horrible creature. "I will. Tomorrow. I'll bring them to you tomorrow."

"Tomorrow," the thing echoed. It pulled itself closer yet, practically on top of her. "Or…I… take…yours."

Catherine didn't realize that she had anything left in her bladder until it emptied itself again.

Then the thing was gone, back into the shadows. It moved impossibly fast for something that propelled itself with its hands.

Catherine sat on the cold tiled floor of the subway station in a pool of her own urine. She gasped for breath. She sensed that she was safe for now, but she had no desire to linger. She got shakily to her feet and made her way up the stairs and out of the station. She ran the last few blocks back to her apartment.

Daniel was once again in his makeshift office, chatting away on his laptop.

"Hey, Cath," he said, lowering the lid slightly and craning his neck to look around the doorframe. "Where you been?"

"Out and about," she said, hanging behind the corner. She didn't want him to see her in this state. And she had little desire to see him. The rage she felt at her betrayal might escape. "Exploring. I figured you'd be working late and didn't want to bother you." Apparently, the role she needed to play wasn't going to be so difficult after all.

"That's cool," Daniel said. "I know I've been working practically the entire time we've been here, but I should have most of the day to myself tomorrow. Maybe you can give me a tour since you seem to know the city so much better than I do now."

"That would be nice," Catherine said. "I have a few places I'd love to show you."

"Sounds good," Daniel said. He closed the door. She heard it lock.

After a hot shower, Catherine climbed into bed. Daniel was still locked in the other room, which suited her just fine. That night she slept like the dead.

Midnight Train from Tokyo

The next day dawned gray and overcast. A storm was coming; petrichor hung in the air over the city scents of asphalt, concrete, and vehicle exhaust, weighing them down, keeping them trapped close to the earth, creating an acrid blend of scents both nature and human.

Daniel had spent the morning and part of the afternoon in his office, hammering out the final details of his plan with his cohorts, Catherine assumed. The plan that would end with her dead.

We'll see about that, she thought.

She spent the time alternately surfing through channels on the television and flipping between her social media outlets, but nothing kept her attention.

When Daniel finally finished, he emerged from his room with a bright smile. "Ready to go, Cath? I'm all yours for the rest of the day."

"More than ready," she said, forcing a smile.

As they slipped on their jackets to step out, Catherine's hand slipped into the pocket in hers, finding Haruto's card from the night before. She rubbed it between her thumb and fingers like a talisman.

Catherine and Daniel spent the afternoon walking the city. She took him to some of her favorite spots that she had discovered in the last week, the bookstore on the corner, the sushi place down the street that admittedly catered to the American palate, the Imperial Palace, and the Tokyo Tower, a red and white replica of the Eiffel Tower in Paris. As they wandered the city, Daniel would sometimes take her hand, although Catherine would find every opportunity to break his grasp, pointing at one site or another. Whereas before, she craved his touch, now she couldn't stand it.

As night fell, they found themselves in downtown, the impressive snow-capped Mount Fuji serving as backdrop against the skyscrapers. The bright pastels of the neon signs, the LED billboards, and the windows in the high rises lit up the night, bringing it to life. Nighttime in the city was Catherine's favorite time. It made her feel wholly alive, although she didn't share that sentiment with Daniel. That bit was just for her.

With a flash of lightning and a crash of thunder, after holding back all day, the skies finally opened up. They were drenched within moments. Laughing, the pair ran for shelter in the doorway of the nearest shop.

Daniel's eyes reflected the city lights. They searched her face. Forgetting herself for a moment, she let him kiss her.

When she reminded herself of his plans for her the next day, Catherine pulled away.

"That was nice," Daniel said. "It's too bad…" His voice trailed off and a frown marred his otherwise pleasant features. His gaze drifted downward.

"What is?" she asked, pressing him.

His eyes found hers again and he looked regretful. "That we haven't had time to do this more."

Nice recovery, Catherine thought. *Better than "it's too bad you'll be dead tomorrow."*

"We should probably head back," Daniel said. "Tomorrow is going to be a big day."

Catherine led him to the nearest subway entrance and found the line that would take them back to their apartment.

Even though it was late, the train was full of businesspeople, shop workers, and families heading home for the night and tourists traveling to their next destinations.

Their car had mostly cleared out by the time they reached the outskirts of the city. Their stop was on the outer fringes of the line's service area, so they stayed on.

Two stops away from theirs, the last people departed and no one else got on. Catherine looked for Haruto, but he didn't make an appearance tonight. *It's just as well,* Catherine thought. *I don't know what he'd do if he met Daniel.*

As they drew closer to their destination, Catherine became increasingly nervous. Her heart pounded in her ears, drowning out almost everything else. What if her plan didn't work? What if it did?

Midnight Train from Tokyo

They were one stop away now. It would be a long way to walk, especially in the rain, but it was doable. Still, a promise had been made and she felt that she'd be made to keep it one way or another.

The train pulled away from the platform.

She chased away her hesitation with thoughts of what Daniel was planning to do to her. What he had already done.

At some point, he had taken her hand. She squeezed his in hers.

Hard.

"Do you think it'll hurt?" she asked.

Daniel tried to pull his hand away, but she wouldn't let him.

"I'm not sure what you're talking about, but I doubt it will hurt as much as my hand does right now," he said, glancing at their entwined hands.

She squeezed harder.

"Cath?" he said. "Can I have my hand back please?"

She looked him in the eye, still holding his hand. "Getting blown up," she said. The momentary look of shock on his face was priceless, but he quickly hid it away again. "I'm worried that it'll hurt quite a lot. On the other hand—" she squeezed even harder and felt the bones in his hand grind together.

"Ow, Cath! What are you doing?"

"On the other hand, I guess it won't last long." She released his hand, and he snatched it back.

"What the hell are you talking about?" Daniel massaged his sore hand. He looked angry, but the color had drained from his face.

Catherine pulled the engagement ring off her finger and dropped it in the general area of Daniel's injured hand. He snatched at it but couldn't grab it before it clinked to the steel subway floor.

"What the hell is this?" Daniel seemed equal parts confused and outraged. He dropped to the floor on one knee and felt around. Finally finding the ring, he thrust it toward her, a parody of a proposal. "You put this back on right now."

"You keep it," she said, her temper rising. "That way you won't have to buy a new one for the next girl you plan to blow up." Daniel's face turned red. "How'd you find out?" he hissed.

"Fuck the world," she said in response.

Daniel took his seat, tucking the ring into a pocket. He sighed and the anger seemed to drain out of him. "For what it's worth, I actually like you," he said. "You're kind and you're smart and you're a great kisser." The train squealed to a stop.

"This is us." Catherine stood.

Daniel looked wary. He stood up slowly. "You're coming back to the apartment?"

Catherine shrugged and stepped onto the platform. "Why wouldn't I?"

"Why would you?" Daniel followed her out of the car but didn't take another step. Suddenly, he was alert, looking all around, peering into the shadowed corners. "Are the police waiting for us?"

"Nope."

"You're lying."

"I'm not." Catherine started slowly toward the stairway leading out. The train's doors closed with a hiss and the train departed with an ear rending screech. A profound silence remained in its wake.

"What are you up to?" Daniel refused to budge.

"What are you talking about?"

"None of this makes sense. You discover my…plan and you still want to go home with me?"

"I'm tired, Daniel. It's late. And believe it or not, I had a good day with you. Let's not ruin it like this. We'll go back, get a good night's sleep, and part ways tomorrow. I'll forget what you did if you promise to leave the FTW and never do anything like this again."

"I can't do that." Daniel shook his head. His dark eyes narrowed. "I have a mission. If I don't fulfill that mission, that would make me a traitor to the cause. Then I become a target. I don't want to be a target,

Midnight Train from Tokyo

Cath. And even if I walked away, it may be too late to send a new operative this time, but there will *always* be a next time."

Something broke loose inside Catherine. She had stopped listening after *I don't want to be a* target. She unleashed everything she'd been holding back. "But it was okay to target *me*? It's okay to target thousands of innocent people at that convention center tomorrow? To murder husbands, wives, mothers, fathers, and children? People who, unlike you, actually *contribute* something to society? Fuck your mission, fuck *your* world, and fuck *you*, Daniel!"

Catherine spun on her heels and strode for the exit.

Daniel finally stepped away from the platform edge. He caught up to her quickly and grabbed her arm, spinning her around to face him.

"You don't understand, Cath. These people are coming over and destroying our country, corrupting our way of life. They need to be taught a lesson, that we will strike back. That we're willing to destroy their country and their way of life, if necessary. That we're not—" His head snapped around. "What was that?"

Catherine followed his gaze. Something moved in the shadows just past the platform.

Then she heard it.

Teke teke.

Daniel let go of her arm and followed the sound.

"Seriously, what the hell is that?" He frowned, peering into the shadows.

The shadow moved again.

Teke teke.

Daniel, now halfway between her and the edge of the platform, suddenly turned. "You lying bitch!" Spit flew from his lips. His face was contorted in anger and hate. He started back toward her. "You said you didn't call the cops! I should just kill you n—"

The creature appeared from out of the shadows and grabbed Daniel's ankle, yanking his foot out from under him. He went down face first on the floor, hard. Two white teeth clacked to the tile and skittered away like dice.

Daniel was dazed. He looked up at Catherine, his eyes unfocused. Blood pooled at the corner of his mouth. Then he turned his gaze to the half-girl holding his ankle with one hand and holding herself up with the other. The thing leered at him, the red dots in its eye sockets glowing brightly. Slaver dripped from between cracked black lips.

Daniel screamed and struggled to get away. "Catherine!" he cried.

"Help me! Please! I'm sorry!" He clawed at the tile and kicked at the floor with his one free foot, but the creature's grip was too strong.

"I brought you your legs," Catherine said.

"My…legsss…" the thing echoed.

One clawed hand gripped Daniel's hip while the other grabbed onto the bottom of his ribcage, curling its fingers into his flesh and around the bone.

Daniel screamed again, this time in pain.

With a violent spray of blood that splashed onto the black-and-white tiled floor and the concrete column next to them, the creature tore Daniel in half. His shrieks echoed up and down the subway tunnel.

Glistening pink and purple viscera spilled out onto the floor. Intestines stretched thin and then tore. From where she stood, Catherine heard the snap as Daniel's spinal column broke and then pulled away from his bottom half. The bones of his lumbar vertebrae shone stark white under the fluorescent lights.

The creature skittered behind the column with Daniel's legs, trailing a broad streak of crimson.

Daniel's mouth moved as he gasped his final breaths. His eyes met Catherine's as he died.

Catherine felt completely void of emotion as she watched the light go out of her now former fiancé's eyes.

A moment later, the creature stepped out from behind the column, wearing Daniel's legs, dark blood soaking the jeans all the way to the knees. It was a little shaky.

"Legsss…" it said. Its eyes found Catherine. "Promisss…kept…"

The thing hobbled down the line, trailing a path of dripping blood behind it as it disappeared back into the shadows.

Once it was out of sight, Catherine lost her nerve. She turned and ran.

She ran up the stairs and into the cool outdoors, through the pouring rain. She didn't stop running until she was in front of the elevator doors, pounding on the button to summon the car.

"Miss?" the young gal at the front desk said in exceptionally good English. She looked concerned. One hand rested on the telephone in front of her. "Are you okay?"

The elevator doors dinged open. Catherine threw herself inside and smashed the button to take her to her floor.

The elevator ride took forever.

When it finally reached her floor and the doors opened—too slowly—she ran from the elevator to her room. She fumbled with the keycard, but after a few attempts, managed to get the door open. Once inside, she slammed the door closed and turned all the locks.

Catherine screamed, not caring if anyone else heard her. She screamed and she wasn't sure if it was out of relief, fear, or trauma. She screamed until she couldn't anymore.

She tore off her sopping wet jacket and threw it on the bed. A white card fluttered to the floor.

At the sight of it, she forced herself to calm down. She picked it up and turned it over in her hands. She stared at it for a long time.

Fuck it, she thought finally.

She dialed the number.

After a few rings, a very tired-sounding voice answered.

"Haruto?" Catherine said. "It's Catherine. I have an extra ticket for tomorrow if you're still interested."

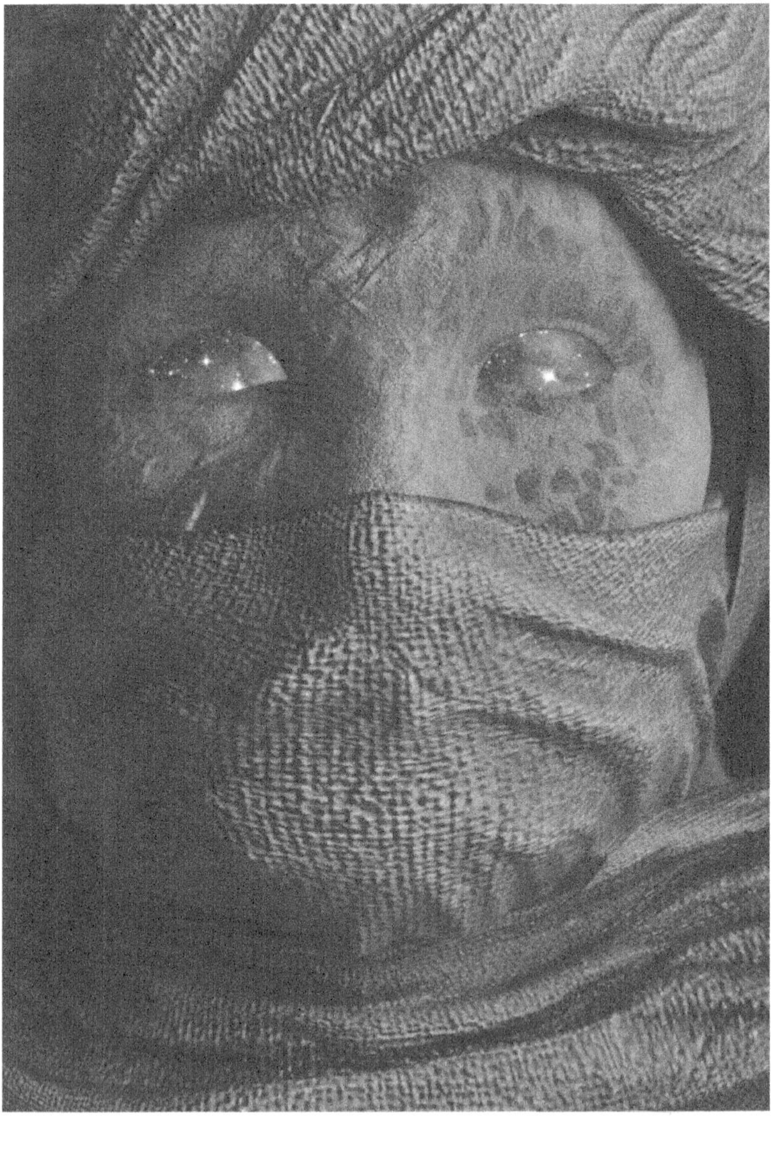

The Yellow Man
by Shayne K. Keen

The Yellow Man gets everyone who goes in there, but he doesn't kill them. No, what he does is much worse than that...

⌘ ⌘ ⌘

It has been told since before I lived on this earth that in the southern part of the Fairport district in the city of Haven, there is a neighborhood filled with old, blocky Craftsman houses, and that one of them in particular is haunted. Though, "haunted" might not be the right word.

Whatever the house is, I do know that a man named Bill Wallace, who lived across the road from it, went crazy after watching it every day for years, finally getting up one night and going to work on his whole family with a butcher knife. When the police found the bodies, Bill Wallace was missing. An officer noticed that the front door of the abandoned house across the street was partially open. The cops went in there and found him hanging from a light fixture. His eyes were gouged out.

There was no one else in the house. Only one set of footprints led through the thick dust on the floor. Only one set of fingerprints were on the doorknob. There were trails in the dust where he'd dragged an old straight-back kitchen chair to reach the fixture. The rope he used to hang himself was from his own home.

All that told a tale that was easy for the police to decipher, just another loser who murdered his family and then opted out of facing the music by putting an end to his own, lousy life. Except for one thing.

Wallace didn't gouge his own eyes out. His hands were bloody, but the blood wasn't his. His eyes were never found.

The Yellow Man

It wasn't long before new crimes occupied the attention of the police, and they stopped working feverishly to find the mystery person who had gouged Wallace's eyes out. The truth was, they figured that as long as the mystery eye-gouger confined himself to gouging out the eyes of a dirtbag who'd murdered his family, it was no big deal. Occasionally a freshly promoted detective would pick up the cold case and try to solve it, out of curiosity. It was just so damn weird!

One officer in particular, Joe Meeks, went to the house to investigate and disappeared. Poof. Gone. Vanished into thin air. His cruiser was parked at the curb in front. Everything inside it was in order. A cardboard takeout cup of coffee was in the cup holder, still warm, and a small bag of freshly baked donuts, also warm, was on the passenger's seat. But Joe Meeks was never seen again.

Inside the house they found his footprints and fingerprints, tracing his movements upstairs, but once in the bedroom—called the "Yellow Room" because of its yellow wallpaper, sunny, yellow-painted ceiling, and dingy yellow carpet—he seems to have just popped out of existence. No trace was left of Officer Joe Meeks, not even a hair.

Several years ago, a group of girls went to the house on a dare. Nothing had happened to anyone there in a very long time, so, according to the survivor's statement, they believed the ghost was made up. A bogeyman to keep kids out of an old house that was falling apart. Just more lies and garbage in a world filled with lies and garbage. Four girls were said to have gone, but only one came out.

She was young, only twelve. The others were older than she. The following is a transcript of a cassette-recorded interview with an attorney and a social worker.

⌘ ⌘ ⌘

"What is your name?" The first voice is husky but feminine. This is the social worker.

"Joyce (beep)." (The last name has been redacted to protect the girl's identity.)

"Okay, Joyce, now tell me what happened last night."

"I don't know how to tell you, I don't know what happened, we went into the house..."

"What house?" (This is the lawyer, a much more nasal voice, a Midwestern accent, she sounds almost squeaky.)

"The house on Renfro Street."

"The Davies House?"

"The abandoned one. The one that people say is haunted. It is haunted." Her voice trembles a little bit, no telling if she can get through this. My belly feels like my guts are being pulled from it just hearing her. There is a distant, haunted quality to it. I want to comfort her, but this interview is twenty years old now. Wherever Joyce is, if she's still alive, she is an adult. Older than me.

"Why do you say it's haunted?" The social worker again.

"I saw it, we all saw it, the Yellow Man. He was big, so very big, his eyes... they were like pieces of the sky filled with stars, they were black and shiny, and it seemed that you could fall into them, and I screamed when I saw him. I wanted to run, but I couldn't. I couldn't run. I screamed and screamed and..." Joyce falls silent, until finally the lawyer clears her throat.

"And what, Joyce?"

"Diana, Katie, Sherry, all of them... they just were gone. Like they never existed..."

"You know they never did exist, right? These girls: Diana Sherman, Katie Alexander, Sherry Parsons. None of them ever existed. We talked to the people you claimed were their parents, none of them have children with those names..."

The social worker speaks up. "You don't have to browbeat the child."

"I'm sorry, I just can't stand a liar." The venom in the lawyer's voice makes me wince for poor Joyce. She's probably at some huge conference table in a quiet room; you can hear the occasional hum of the air

The Yellow Man

conditioner in the background, and when silence falls, the buzz of florescent lights, the tick of an old dial clock, like they had at schools and police stations, prisons, and banks.

"They are my friends! I go to school with all of them!"

"None of those girls go to your school. None of those girls exist!"

The social worker shouts, "Just stop being mean!"

"No, Joyce, needs to stop lying to us! As far as we know Joyce went into the house by herself and got scared, then ran out into the street screaming. That's all that happened. There was no one else with her! Even the witness said she went in alone."

"I was not alone," Joyce wails, her voice crackling and stuttering, "I was not alone," she repeats with a sob.

"Tell us, then. Let's say we believe you weren't alone. What happened?"

"I told you. They all disappeared! We went into the house and saw a bunch of dirt and dust, but that's it. We went to the kitchen and the bedroom and the bathroom, we sat on the couch and Diana sneezed because she's allergic. We all laughed at her. Sherry said we should go upstairs, but I was scared; so were Diana and Katie. We didn't want to go up there, but Sherry always gets her way, she always makes us do what she wants..." Joyce breaks down sobbing again. This time it takes a few minutes to calm her and get her to speak again.

"They're gone!" Joyce screams after a while. "They're gone with the Yellow Man, and nobody believes that they ever existed! I had a picture of us that we took at the booth in the mall, but it's gone too! They're all gone!"

"They were never here," the lawyer states flatly. There is a chill silence in the room, and I like to imagine the social worker staring ice picks into the lawyer's skull.

"They were my friends, we made slam-books and shared makeup! We were sleeping over at Katie's last night, we snuck out because she only lives two streets over from the house..." Joyce sobs again. This time there is an obvious pause in the cassette. In a moment she's back.

"I can't help what I know. I know that my friends existed until last night, that we went into the house and the Yellow Man came and now they never existed, and I don't know what to do."

⌘ ⌘ ⌘

Very little is left to know of Joyce. Her name is redacted from the court documents. She was diagnosed with schizophrenia and given over to the care of a psychiatric unit. Joyce was in the unit for two years, released when medicinal advances made it safe and humane for her to leave the facility. From there, no trace of Joyce exists, just like her friends. There are no names of parents, school records, or pictures in the yearbook. There are only three schools in the neighborhood she could have attended. I checked all three. When I asked about her, I received only blank stares.

"Joyce? With some girls who disappeared? No, that has nothing to do with this school."

"We had no student like that, Ms. Price."

"No, no Joyce who was sent to the loony bin. Even if we had her I couldn't tell you, you know. There are laws that protect confidentiality."

⌘ ⌘ ⌘

I tried to find out about Bill Wallace, the family killer, but there was no real information, though lots of people remembered him and his wife and children. They were lovely people, it seems, good folk. The kind of neighbors anyone would want. They talk of him vacantly, without emotion, just stating facts. It was like they were talking about a war fought before they were born.

No one ever figured out who gouged out his eyes.

The Yellow Man

⌘ ⌘ ⌘

The crux of the story and the trouble, though, comes from a certain man named Joshua Davies, who bought his home from a Sears and Roebuck catalog in 1936. Sears sold thousands of these "Modern Homes" in the years from 1908 to 1940. They came in the form of kits to be assembled on-site.

Davies was fairly well-off, but peculiar. Supposedly he was an unassuming bachelor in his thirties, born and raised in Bloomville but moving to Fairport after a good job came his way. For him, the Depression was far behind. He bought one of the nicer Craftsman models, a two-story model, with a basement and a porch with short square columns atop a concrete-covered brick half-wall. He seemed happy, according to the people interviewed after his untimely exit, but yes, he was an odd duck.

There are pictures of the inside of the home, taken after he was found. To say he was dead is to say the wind exists while leaving out hurricanes and tornadoes, typhoons, and tropical depressions. His body was ripped to pieces in a most gruesome way, his guts pulled out of their cavity and strewn about, gruesome garlands saturating the carpeting in blood and gore, the contents of his stomach and intestines spewed over the walls, pattern-like. I have seen the pictures they took then, and I think the splatters and smears are not pattern-like at all. They are actual patterns. The patterns on the wall drawn in the bile, shit, blood, mucous, gall, and whatever bodily fluids could be tapped and used, repeat themselves, a series of odd, near maddening shapes horrid enough to make the viewer nauseous—and not just because of the repugnant medium with which they were drawn.

⌘ ⌘ ⌘

They never found his head. I tried to locate his grave. The woman at the cemetery looked through all the deaths from 1952 and found nothing at all. There was no mention of Joshua Davies. I asked about a pauper's grave, and she showed me the book she held.

"If a pauper has a name, we write it down."

Who was this artist of blood and bile and shit and spit who felt the need to break people apart in this mortal coil, freeing them to the afterlife or the eternity of non-existence? I did research, read old papers from across the region at the time, and found no mention of any such crime other than the murder of Davies. No one else was torn apart, their intestines and liver used as paint brushes. Whomever did it must have been satisfied with one go.

The house was becoming an obsession.

⌘ ⌘ ⌘

"No!" I was asleep. I sat up straight in bed. The darkness weighed on me like a wet blanket, and I could see the outline of Davies' dead guts strung up like Christmas lights. I screamed and closed my eyes. When I opened them, everything was normal, except for the lightest crimson smudge on the wall, like a bloody thumb had casually brushed against the lemon-ice colored paint.

I stared at the smudge until I felt brave enough to press a paper towel to it, wiping off as much as I could before scrubbing it. I used every cleaner I had, I rubbed paint off in spots, but the red stain, now a faint pink, would not lighten any further. I was disgusted by this reminder of Davies' horrible death, and the terror it sent through me; I wanted it gone, gone the way of so many hair and toenail clippings, something you never think about because it was almost like it was never there. But it didn't leave. I went to the basement and found the leftover can from when I redecorated the room and painted over the spot. Though I couldn't see the smear anymore, I could tell the difference between the touched-up spot and the rest of the wall. I decided to paint the whole room a different color and did just that. I finally began to relax when it was all done a day later—until I noticed the spot had moved to the floor.

The Yellow Man

I repeated the process, washed, and scrubbed, dumped bleach and even more caustic chemicals; denatured alcohol, whatever I could. Even as they ate away the oak stain of the floor, the smear remained. Finally exasperated, I put a rug over the spot, but the rug mocked me with its presence. "I'm just hiding the stain," it would whisper, "it's still there on the floor right beneath me. If you pick up any of my corners, you'll see it in a few seconds." I got onto my hands and knees and crawled to the rug, pulling it up. The stain was visible. I thought of getting a bigger rug, but just saw myself wriggling under it, a caterpillar in a Persian cocoon. I couldn't live that way.

Finally, I cut the chunk out and replaced it with a new board. The stain is still gone, but I'm acutely aware that it can come back at any moment.

I feel the encounter with the red stain has drastically altered my mind. It depresses me. I was just becoming happy when I started my research on the Davies House.

⌘ ⌘ ⌘

I have deduced that I know more than anyone else in the city about the Davies House on Renfro Street. At the police station they seemed happy to assist me when I said I was looking for any information about Joe Meeks. A few old timers remembered him with fondness. It seems he was a good kid, a round peg in a round hole. He embraced the detective policeman's role better than almost anyone, had a sharp mind and a good heart. Or at least that's what they said. I saw another layer peeping out beneath their smiles and wistful, nostalgic memorials. They were lying. They said these things, spoke of him with fondness, shook their heads and said what a shame it was, how baffled everyone was when he disappeared, but it wasn't the truth. The truth is that they, too, know he was there at one time, but isn't anymore, and they can't really remember his being there at all. Just like with Wallace. Exactly like the others, Joe Meeks is a name in a file and nothing more. He never really was.

"Yeah, we could give you Joe's employment records. The statute of limitations has passed, but we don't have them. Don't know where they got off to. We usually keep things ship-shape around here. Far as I know, these are the only ones missing." So said a cop in the records department.

I asked for Joyce. I asked for the murderer Bill Wallace. I asked for the dead-and-exploded Davies (this is where I saw the picture and heard the tape), but there's no more information than that these people once existed and were connected tragically to that house. I needed more.

There was only one solution.

⌘ ⌘ ⌘

I do not make friends easily. Some would say it's because I'm not personable or nice enough. But it's not that. I find others grueling at best, and cannot suffer fools, which most people are. I did have a few acquaintances, though, who wanted to spend more time with me than I usually allowed.

I went through my messages on the dating app I used when I was excruciatingly horny and found my first choice: a skinny, weathered man named Mark Sink who wore big, ugly, serial-killer glasses and spoke in a hideous country drawl. I didn't like Mark that much, but we'd met a few times for casual sex (as he was hung like a horse) and, though he lacked staying power, could go several times in one evening. I didn't care how many times he got off as long as I did.

Mark swore that he loved me, that he wanted to be with me for real, but I shied away from him when he called on New Year's Eve threatening to kill himself if I didn't become his. As I said, I don't suffer fools. We had made somewhat of a peace over the few months since, and I decided it would be a perfect test of our relationship to see if he would go with me to the Davies House.

He agreed immediately.

"I like the idea of going ghost hunting," he said, "I always wanted to do that." His drawl annoyed me, but then I wasn't there for his drawl. I told him to be at my house three hours early so we could have a good time. I was feeling electrically charged, like one giant nerve ending.

We fucked in my bedroom. He commented on the new color of the walls, much brighter yellow than the previous shade, almost the color of lemon peel. After I came and took a shower, we went on our ghost hunting trip. By that time, it was night, and I knew the Fairport neighborhood would be dead.

I had spent a couple of weeks driving through at different times, scouting a spot close enough to the house to park and walk unseen. I'd even had been in the front yard of the house. The back yard was enclosed by a big brick wall, architecturally sound and too high for me to climb. There was a side door, but it was locked. The front door, however, was unlocked. I had opened it just a crack, to make sure.

Now, I parked two streets over in a public parking lot used by people who went to a semi-popular dance club next to it, and Mark and I walked the short distance to the house. I was abuzz with sensation. An understanding of what I was doing if reports were correct should have made me feel something other than absolute joy, but honestly, that's all I felt. I didn't know what had gotten into me at that time. Now, long after it's too late to do anything about it, I do.

When we reached the house, Mark blanched.

"You didn't tell me it was this house you wanted to go in."

"So, you know about it, huh?" I said, unbuttoning the top few buttons of my blouse.

"I heard the rumors. The Yellow Man. How if you go in there and don't come out, the world forgets you ever existed." He sounded scared.

"I've heard them too," I said, projecting innocence and curiosity. "I also heard that the Yellow Man appears and tells you the future, and that there's gold hidden in the upstairs bedroom, which he guards."

"I think I heard that too," said Mark, his voice less fearful. Good.

"Let's go in," I said, grabbing the small flashlight attached to my keychain and pushing the button. "I'll go first."

"No, no, I'll go first," he said. Chivalry, even in this destructive age, was apparently still alive and twitching, no matter how weakly. He pulled out his phone and turned on the light.

"We don't want it too bright," I said as we went into the house. "The neighbors might..."

Everything shifted, and the world was different.

Inside the house lay the headless body of Joshua Davies, the walls painted with his guts, and I knew what the painting meant for the first time. It was a ward, a sigil, and a trap all at once. Its purpose was to show the viewer something otherworldly, outside of time and space. I blinked and it was gone, just a musty living room, its once-white walls now yellowed and dingy with age.

"You okay?" Mark asked. He hadn't seen Davies or had the same epiphanies.

"Yes, thanks. Come on, we need to go upstairs." In the shadows, as we shone the light around the room, I heard a creak from up above. I turned my penlight in that direction to see the eyeless face of Bill Wallace, bloated and bulging, his body hanging stiffly, hands clutching onto something that dropped and floated to the floor as I watched. I went to that spot and bent to pick it up. Mark hadn't noticed anything. It was a piece of paper with a single word written on it, a word I had never seen before nor heard uttered by any human, and yet I felt I should know it. I folded the paper and put it in my bag.

Mark was at the bottom of the stairs, Wallace gone as quickly as he appeared. I shone the light on the landing above and saw a man in uniform, obviously Joe Meeks, but there were others surrounding him. Three girls, presumably the ones who disappeared with Joyce, stood alongside a crowd of children and adults, some dressed sharp, others looking like they lived on the streets. I wondered how many people had dared the house over the years and just... stopped existing? Whatever drew me on was more than just morbid curiosity about the past. It was a burning desire to see it happen, in the flesh, in person.

"Upstairs, now," I whispered, and leaned into Mark's back, making

The Yellow Man

sure my boob pressed firmly against him.

"Yes, ma'am," he said, his voice croaking but excited all the same. Strange he didn't see any of them, as they were still milling about on the second-floor landing, not looking at us or anything in general, just existing, or not existing depending upon perspective.

The shades began disappearing as we ascended the stairs. The closer we got the quicker they left, until the lading and upstairs hallway were completely empty. As we went down the hall, I looked into the first room: dark and shadowy, nothing in there. Across the hall had to be the room I was looking for.

"In there," I said to Mark, aiming the flashlight at the knob.

"This one?" he croaked. His fear was strong again, but I knew he was too much of a "dude" to allow it to stop him from opening the door.

The room was lit from within by a jaundiced light that cast a sickly pallor onto everything. There was a bed, still made but dusty, and a nightstand with an old lamp on it. The lamp clicked on and suddenly we were somewhere else, somewhere dark, and drear. As I watched, Mark's face went slack and began twitching.

"Mark! What do you see?" I called, but he didn't reply, just stared with that idiot look on his face. I wanted to hit him but refrained.

"Who are you?" Mark asked, his voice trembling. That's when I saw it happen. The very air before us began to quiver and wave as though it were river water rippling, and through that invisible barrier someone—something—stepped out into our world. Behind it, I saw two suns and a diseased yellow sky. I saw a building on a hill that I knew was holy, and a sea that dully burned.

He wore a robe with a cowl pulled down over his face, but I knew what his face was. When he looked at Mark and reached up with his sinewy hands, pulling the cowl back, Mark didn't even scream. Instead, his face went blank, mouth dropping open as though hypnotized, and I backed away, watching, making sure I didn't look into the face—though I did catch a glimpse of those eyes, those terrible eyes, whole universes held within them. I then saw Mark not exactly disappear but become less substantial; I looked through him as the shocked expression on his face changed to one of abject terror, hearing his scream but not with my ears, more of an imaginary echo.

I don't remember running out of the room or down the stairs. I don't remember leaving the house and getting to my car, but when I "came to" I was sitting at the wheel, crying, looking for anything that Mark might have left behind, but there was nothing. He carried a little pouch with him, like a purse, but it wasn't in the car. I couldn't be sure if I'd really convinced him to leave it there or not, couldn't be sure that we didn't put it in the trunk, but it wasn't in the trunk either.

I drove back home. Mark's truck wasn't in front of my house as it had been when we left. I drove to his apartment on the other side of town. The truck wasn't there either. I saw that the light was on in his place, so I took the stairs and knocked. A couple of seconds later a short man, stocky and well-built, answered the door.

"Can I help you?" he said, slightly irritated that I'd knocked so late.

"Are you Mark's roommate?" I asked, knowing that Mark lived alone.

"Who?"

"Mark Sink. Are you his roommate? This is his place, isn't it?"

"Lady, you have the wrong apartment."

"This is 15C, right?"

"Yeah, and I've lived here for almost five years. Ain't no Mark Sink ever lived here since I moved in, maybe before..."

I cut him off. "Thank you, I must have the wrong apartment, I'll go."

"Well, it's not every night that a pretty lady knocks on my door. Why don't you come in and have a beer with me? I'm just drinking alone and watching wrestling."

I don't know why I did it, why it was so important to replay the same scene with the new guy (his name was Gary Johnson). I had to see for sure, just to make certain that I wasn't losing it. Surely it wouldn't happen again.

But it did.

The Yellow Man

After the same scenario played out again, I knew I had to do something about the house—a terrible place for sure, but sacred. I started reading what I could about the Yellow Man, meditating on him and on Joshua Davies. I kept a dream journal, writing what I could remember in it each time I awoke.

I dreamed that I was Joshua Davies, moving into the Craftsman house I had built all alone. I never intended to take a wife, in fact I was clearly a homosexual, but couldn't bring myself to fall down that rabbit hole of debauchery and self-hatred. However, as the years waxed, I grew more and more desirous of a companion. I called to God for guidance, but none came, so I began reading about other gods, about demons and spirits both beneficent and harmful, about rituals and altars and wards and spiritual traps.

I made things. I built altars to love goddesses and gods, I built wards to keep things out, my whole yard was filled with the things, every decoration had a purpose, every single piece came together in a perfect whole to make sure that my house was protected from whatever might assail it. The more I learned about these things, the more afraid I became, having convinced myself that my homosexuality was a demonic curse, evil spirits just waiting for me to trip up so they could come and drag me to hell. I grew more paranoid and afraid. Finally, I built traps all over my house. I chose the colors of the rooms for the kinds of spirits I wanted to trap. I built and bought furniture conducive to their presence, eliminating the possibility of their escape until I decided how to be rid of them.

I practiced chants and rituals, working toward this end for ten years. I knew I was doing something important, making my world better by not giving into my animal urges, instead cleansing my soul and spirit of the black spot that tarnished it.

For a long time, not much happened. There were a few little things in the traps, but nothing serious, nothing that scary, though to those who'd never seen such things they would have been terrifying. They told me I had cast bait, but I knew they were liars. I was not seeking to lure them, only to protect myself.

Then it happened. I woke one night to see, at the foot of my bed, a tall, stick-thin figure in a flowing choleric robe. I was unable to resist looking into his face, and then...

⌘ ⌘ ⌘

It has been two weeks since that dream, and each night it repeats. I've become everyone who ever went into the Davies House. I could tell you about Snooky German, a homeless man who slipped inside for shelter and never came out again; about Jimmy Fortenberry, who went in to prove that it wasn't haunted, and who seems now to have never existed; about Donnie Wheatcraft, who took an underage boy there to do terrible things with but found himself as part of the pattern, and of the boy named Sam who never was. There are hundreds, actually, and some of those escaped. For a while. It seems that after you go inside, it is your duty and need to be there forever. You are, you see, already his when you catch even the slightest glimpse of him.

Tonight, I'm going back to the house with the full knowledge that I'll never be seen or heard from again. I don't doubt that most of my troubles will be forgotten, and that's why I'm writing this down. I'm going to leave copies in several places, with the hope that one of them manages to stay. I'm going to give copies to a few people I know: my sister Sally for one, the few friends I have left, a few couples I've met of late who go ghost hunting with me. I'm mailing some to newspapers, and to the city hall. I want it known that I lived and explored the Davies House, that what lives in the Davies House is trapped in there but is working its way back out, all so *he* can return to his beloved city. He isn't evil, just a force of nature, just a thing that is too big and real to be in this world. I'm going to do all I can to break the wards and traps before he shows himself to me. I'm hoping it allows him to go back to his world. I hope that he doesn't prefer ours.

As I'm finishing this, I clutch the one reminder of my first visit to the house, that little scrap of paper which fluttered from Bill Wallace's hand. Surely he must have picked it up before he hanged himself before his eyes were gouged out. On it is scrawled a single word I now understand is a name.

Hastur.

I'm going back to the house: I hope this finds its way.

Very truly yours,

Deanna Price

890 Carver Ln

⌘ ⌘ ⌘

Note: Three copies of this document are known to exist. The first was mailed to the Haven Library, Fairport Branch; the second was found on the doorstep of one Sally Price, who assures us that she is of no relation to anyone named Deanna. The third was found in the abandoned Davies House by the couple who bought it shortly after the fire that burned the upstairs bedroom. The manuscript was shoved into the mailbox on the front porch.

Though many of the claims in this document are true, many are not. It is a curiosity, though, and I can't help but add the fact that the family who bought the house and restored it to its current glory abandoned it and disappeared, without having paid off the mortgage. Things like that happen, though. We have no reason to believe the old Davies House is more than just that: a house. Unwanted, unloved, but definitely not home to some evil spirit.

A search of vital records and other sources yielded no information about Deanna Price, including the existence of any such person. We can only conclude that this document is a work of fiction and that the Yellow Man legend is just that. Something kids talk about to scare each other, the kind of thing that supposedly lives in all sorts of abandoned homes all over the world.

The lucky buyer of the Davies House will receive one of the original three copies of the manuscript along with their purchase, as it has become part of the property record.

Bidding on the home will begin Saturday, June 16 at 10 A.M. sharp.

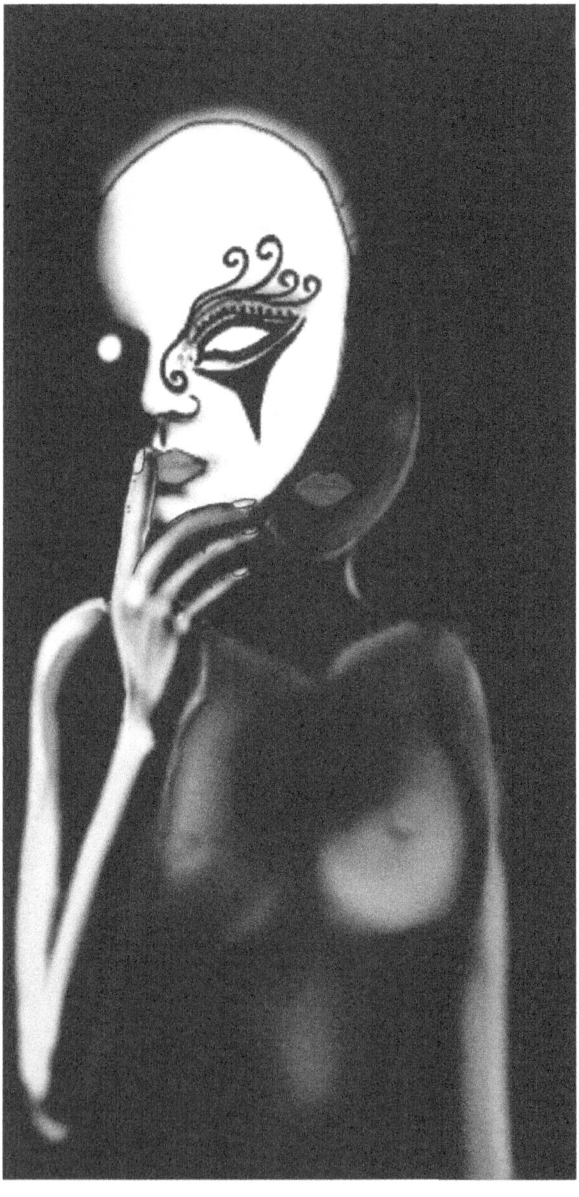

Coulrophilia
by K.A. Opperman

I seek the one who haunts the Fun House mirror,
    The harlequin, that quaintly painted doll.
None of my dreams are farther, none are nearer—
    She is a laughing shadow on the wall.

She is a painted phantom primped and ruffled,
    Replete with pom-pom, polka-dot, and stripe.
Her swiftly traipsing steps are strangely muffled,
    A ghost in some old gray daguerreotype.

    Or is she merely my imagination,
        A disembodied costume, jester's mask?
    A magic lantern's prestidigitation? —
    These are the questions that I dare not ask.

Beyond the Big Top, past the Midway's bustle,
Beneath the yellowed lightbulbs dimmed with dust,
    Upon the carousel, I hear the rustle
Of something more than midnight's fitful gust.

And there she sits, astride her prancing pony,
One lacy glove wrapped round the striped brass pole.
Her lips are heart-shaped, yet her stare is stony
Through burnished tresses and black stars of kohl.

Coulrophilia

And then she gallops toward the yawning devil,
Her faithful stallion somehow come to life—
The carnival must hold a secret revel
Inside the Fun House, with illusions rife.

I follow her, but find no fair reflection—
Only her crumpled clothes, and on the glass,
A perfect copy of her clown complexion,
A floating ghost from fantasy's morass.

I seek the one who haunts the Fun House mirror,
And kiss her cotton-candy-perfumed face.
Against the glass, I know that I am near her,
And let my fingers lose themselves in lace.

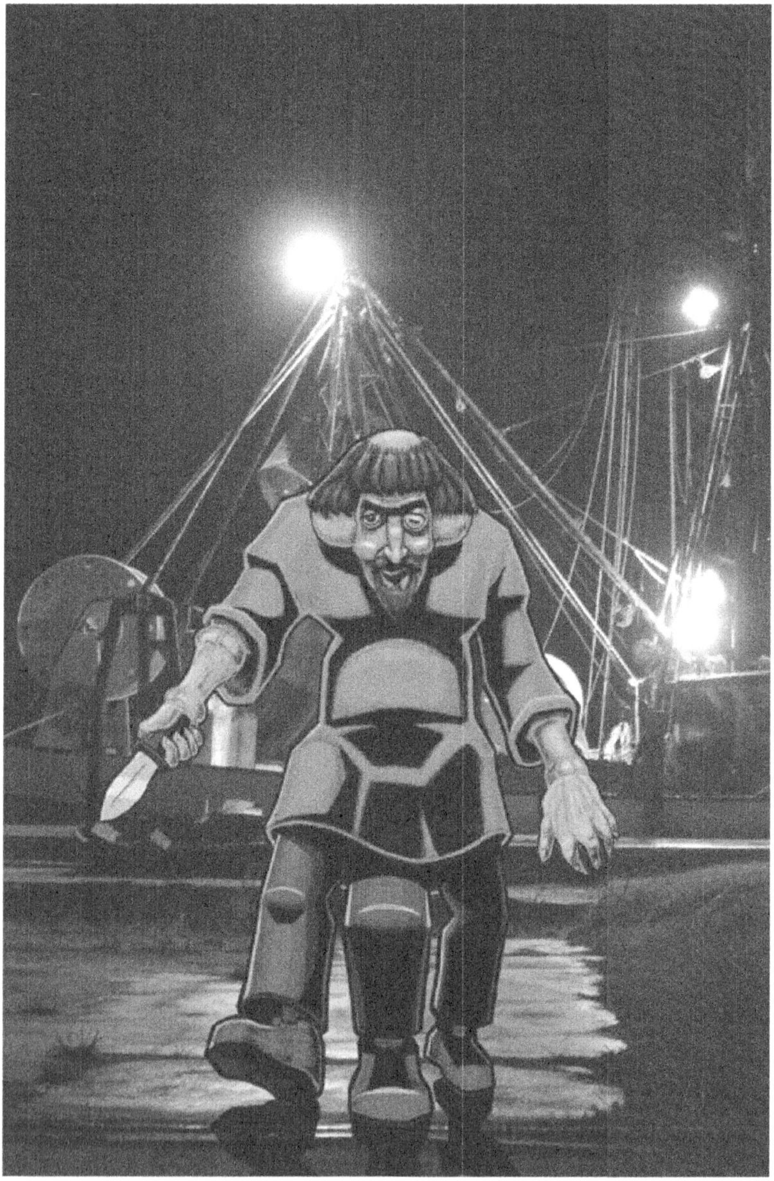

The Legend of Johnny Nepkin: A Home-Grown Bogeyman
by A.P Sessler

alternately titled

The Home-Grown Bogeyman
by Charles M. Clemmons

The old, old, old timers of Wanchese well knew the story of Johnny Nepkin. They passed it on from generation to generation but much like old hand-me-downs one size too big or two sizes too small, the moths of time ate away at the story till nothing remained but scraps too few to make anything of. But never fear lads and lasses, for ol' Charlie kept all the yarns locked up here in his attic trunk, and he pulls them out from time to time to let you try one on for size.

First off, let's get out of the way this notion that Johnny Nepkin was a mere fairy tale. Johnny Nepkin was a real man with a real mother and a real father--of sorts--but certainly real. But before I get to the true horror he was, let me tell you of the woman who bore him.

Vonetta Daniels was the daughter of Lydie Baum Daniels and Waverly "Wavey" Daniels. At first glance once might assume Johnny came from considerably healthy, human stock, but that's where Johnny's father comes into the story.

In the days before the bridge from the mainland was constructed the only way to get to Dare County was by ferry. It was one particularly ominous night Vonetta and a number of passengers found themselves on one of these ferry trips when the vessel struck bottom and was stuck hard and fast in the sand. Their only recourse was to wait out the night in hopes the rising tide would break them free from the clutches of the treacherous shoals.

The Legend of Johnny Repkin

Beneath the light of the full moon, they passed the hours, unawares of the things that dwelt beneath the surface: the cephies as the old salts call them; shape-shifting octopi. Had the hull of the ship not been composed of such lustrous metal, the cephies would have likely passed it by, but nay, its gleaming shell called to them with siren song, an irresistible melody that drew them nigh.

Now the creatures may only take what they can carry, so it's doubtful even the largest consortium could in any wise drag such a vessel down to their silvery lair. Cephies are, however, notorious thieves, so whether or not they can take possession of a vessel they know from eons of experience that humans often carry their wealth on their persons and seldom make difficult targets, especially when confronted with the paralyzing horror of seeing a cephie face to face. For even when taking human form as an act of camouflage or deception, cephies are prone to shift to a form somewhere between human and animal to maximum the effect of their terror.

Such was the fate of the ferry that night and the cephies made no distinction between passengers or crew. Occupants' metal trinkets were seized by force, some violently, so that rings were torn from ears or fingers, leaving the victims bloodied if not amputated. All but one soul suffered injury that night, and that being Vonetta Daniels. Having submitted to the scripture that says women's adorning should not be that outward adorning of plaiting the hair and of wearing jewelry, the devout woman was spared.

Only something happened that surpassed leaving her unscathed, and that was that the cephie, not known for their attraction to humans, did not change to a typically daunting form. In fact, it had chosen not the terrible visage of a hairy brute or old hag, but of a handsome man of the finest stock, and that in the flesh, that is nude. When faced with this stunning specimen of manhood, she herself was instantly beholden, and because of the pure beauty of her unpainted face and perhaps the hidden man of the heart that Scripture speaks of, the cephie likewise was beholden to her.

Their meeting would end as quickly as it began as the consortium took their spoils and departed immediately to the sea, but from that night hence the victims would question why Vonetta alone was spared molestation to the point some suggested she held an alliance with the sea devils and their supposed master, Satan. Beside malicious whisperings, Vonetta would also face shunning, even from those far less devout than she.

Though having been smitten as she was, the woman often found herself retreating to the docks and shores where land met sea and stared and stared out over the night-black waters reflecting the broad stroke of moonlight painted over its surface. Deep calls unto deep, and it must have been so for her hidden man called to that of the very cephie she had encountered that fearsome night and soon the two entered into relations normally reserved for those bound in blessed matrimony.

No one would have known of these relations had she not disclosed it at a later date save the night two fishermen found her in the throes of passion and the hot, forbidden embrace of the cephie. Sensing something unnatural about the occurrence, Jolly Etheridge and Otis Pugh confronted the lovers and demanded they part ways at threat of injury, which they appeared more than willing to execute as just having left the fish house, one of them brandished a large hook and the other a shovel.

Perhaps in order to avoid harming an otherwise innocent man they inquired of the stranger but two questions: "Who are you? Where did you come from?"

Now in my travels I can't claim to ever have heard a cephie speak, and none of the encounters with cephies I am familiar with include the talking variety. That in itself would make the story seem highly suspect, and if not for the character of the men in question I would seriously doubt it, but seeing we know Johnny's surname there has to be some reason for it.

The men claim the stranger answered one word, and that was "Nepkin." Now Nepkin is certainly a real surname, as is the more

The Legend of Johnny Nepkin

commonly known variant Napkin. And even though cephies are not generally known for having their gift of gab, we have to assume that when in human form they possess the same organs necessary for speech as they obviously do for reproduction. But we also have to assume that cephies, being wild creatures of the sea, have no need of human speech per se or surnames, unlike the inhabitants of Atlantis.

So, considering all things, could it be possible that the cephie did not answer the question "What is your name?" but "Where are you from?" And could it not also be possible that this creature, again not known for speech, might have been speaking in a language not known to humans, or if so, speaking it with great difficulty as its speech organs were relatively untrained?

That said, I propose the creature did not say "Nepkin" but possibly through a speech impediment caused by this unfamiliarity with human vocal cords, answered not its own name, but the one who sent it and from whence it came: Neptune.

It is well known that creatures of the sea owe their allegiance to the
Roman god Neptune, or Poseidon to the Greeks. Nay, you won't hear a mermaid call on Jehovah, an Atlantean Allah, nor a selkie Vishnu. They are creatures born of the sea who perish to the sea; therefore, they are ignorant or else have no need of the gods of land.

Before you dismiss the stranger as an otherwise mute man, it is what happened next that assured the fishermen of his aquatic origins. For as part of its defense mechanism the man proceeded to change form for the first time that Vonetta witnessed into something much less human. The man sprouted two extra arms and equally extra legs. His head swelled into a bulbous thing that drooped limply over his chest and it retreated, still facing them, into the water till it was submerged completely from their sight.

If Vonetta was held suspect of witchcraft and heresy before by the simple villagers, all doubts were then removed, at least for those who believed the half-drunk men. She had not only transpired with Satan but fornicated with his agent, and very soon was heavy with its child growing in her belly.

And with this lengthy preface we arrive at the subject of our story, the man-thing some deem but the fated byproduct of this ungodly union between human and monster: Johnny Nepkin.

In those days, most babies on the island were natural born with only the medical attention of a midwife. Johnny was delivered by Bessie Tillett, who beheld the horror I'm about to describe first-hand.

Firstly, it must be said with some pity and respect that Johnny was born what they called in those days a "waterhead" baby. No such birth is ever accompanied with joy, so you can imagine at once the difficulty with which Bessie had to complete delivery of the child while encouraging poor Vonetta to assist with every aching muscle in her body. Once the head was out the eyes opened, and Bessie was said to have yelped in horror at once at the sight of them: one human, the other's pupil a horizontal slit she had only ever seen in the head of a goat, so cue all the images of Azazels and scapegoats and Satan himself that flashed through her sanctified mind.

Fighting through her immediate superstition and fear, she freed the boy from his mother's womb, only to see the most bizarre of his distinguishing traits in the addition of a third leg. Nature has often birthed freaks so-called, so this in itself could be overlooked even if with struggle or revulsion, but when considering the whole of his features and the fearsome truth his father was not at all of the natural order, it made him all the more terrifying.

Throughout his infancy his mother clothed him in long baptismal dresses. When he was old enough to walk she made him suitable pants from flour sacks, and when he began to play with other children, she made him wear an eye patch, though he constantly removed it in spite of the way they treated him.

No matter how often his mother corrected him he tore the thing off. It is said he preferred to see the world in black and white, and the cephalopod eye facilitated just such a view. Unfortunately, children shunned the boy, leaving him to play by himself. Fearing his deformity was cause for the rejection, Vonetta made him wear oversized coats to conceal his third leg, which Johnny took to as he burned easily in the sun. Unfortunately, his wardrobe did not protect him from further exclusion, which followed him well throughout his childhood years and left him with few social skills that made for many awkward interactions.

This constant seclusion allowed him to give in to his more animal nature, namely his proclivity for theft. Now throughout the world if you find some piece of silver left outdoors missing, you might rightly blame corvids, for several manner of black birds are just as enamored with shiny metal things as cephies. But here in Wanchese parts, the locals know there is only one likely thief, and that being Johnny Nepkin, who takes almost entirely after his paternal side of the family.

It was a common sight to find Johnny at the docks and fish houses, pilfering items, and their daily catch. He wasn't but seven years old when Earl Wescott caught Johnny red-handed with his oyster knife tucked in his draping sleeve and gave him the thrashing of his life. The imbecile boy ran home and hid in shame from his mother until she pried the story out of him. She rang up Earl to apologize, and to soothe her poor boy's spirit she got him his very own oyster knife, which he henceforth carried around anywhere he went, admiring the steel blade as if it were the finest silver mined by man.

He proudly displayed it to Earl, who along with the other fishermen gradually warmed back up to the boy, though they were ever mindful not to leave any metal valuables in plain sight. They didn't care that he took a fish on occasion, even when they witnessed the disgusting action that followed. It became a source of amusement to them, to throw the half-witted lad a fish just to watch him eat it eagerly, guts and all. Whether it was done out of a mean spirit or not, when Vonetta learned of their treatment she refused to let Johnny visit the fish houses for fear of their humiliating him.

Peck Midgett, one of the fishermen and a distant cousin of Vonetta's, actually missed little Johnny showing up. While he understood bringing raw fish around for Johnny to eat like an animal would be frowned upon by Vonetta, he did bring the occasional bucket of oysters, clams, or mussels, which she had no problem with Johnny enjoying.

They say it was the damnedest sight. The boy could work his fingers into any shell within a minute's time, at which point he'd suck down the contents whole and raw. He never once had to use that knife to open a shell, yet it never left his side, always stuffed in a pants or shirt pocket like a keepsake or magic charm.

As he grew older some tried to give him work, but even the most menial of tasks wouldn't take. It would seem Johnny was incapable of learning. For such smart creatures it seemed his cephie half was rendered an idiot by his human half. Vonetta cared for the boy as long as she could, but it seemed she had contracted some infection which spread throughout her body and eventually overcame her. Johnny was heartbroken as any human child would be. Few contributed to cover funeral expenses, as the old rumors surfaced again about her relations with the Devil, and the house went into foreclosure and Johnny was left without a home.

It was then Johnny began to revert to what some considered his childhood acts of theft, but could more rightly be called his animal nature, which brings us to his more current appearance.

You've heard me describe Johnny the babe, but how shall I describe Johnny the man? Save the fact his left eyeball was the kind straight out of an octopus' head, his eyes were too kind and his lips too red and always glisteningly wet, but not necessarily from spittle. His face was too pitiful (to hate), but his hands—now there was a sight that bestowed horror: fat fingers that terminated in dull points, and the palms swollen like those of a waterlogged corpse. His brows met in the middle and his mustache and beard gave him an almost wizened look. Likewise, his brown hair which covered only the top half of his hydrocephalic head almost lent him a look of normalcy—almost and only from a distance.

It was this Johnny that after some time emerged from the woods, like

The Legend of Johnny Repkin

Jesus fresh out of the desert after his temptation. And just as Jesus performed his first miracle at a wedding, so too Johnny committed his first major act of theft.

It was just before the reception for newlyweds Bo and Gilda Payne Gallop that Johnny swept up all the silverware in broad daylight. Gloria Ballance claimed he shoved her down when she confronted him, but she was frequently given to exaggeration and appeared unharmed. Some suggested the theft would not have taken place had she used the more modern plastic cutlery that had become popular of late. It only took a few more gatherings visited by Johnny for others to practice what they preached, and soon everyone adopted their use.

With less and less eating utensils to pocket, Johnny had to find another, more vulnerable source to scratch his itch.

It would be Sadie Daniel's eighth birthday. You could say the lass was a bit of a tomboy, in that she preferred toy cars and trucks over dolls and houses. Her favorite present that year was a die cast metal cap gun and matching Sheriff's star. She ran around shooting at any and every one, who were kind enough to play wounded or even dead. All save Johnny.

When she spotted him she called him out, but Johnny was in no mood for a duel. She drew her piece and fired away, but in that moment he would only die for one thing, and that was the shiny toy revolver and star. He took them from her with little resistance, and when her tears drew her father Tuck and three other men from the General Store, Johnny fled the scene.

The men chased Johnny into the marsh, where they discovered a shiny little hut, assembled entirely of all the silver and metal things he had spent a secret lifetime accumulating. When the men observed him drooling like mad as he fixed his newly acquired treasures to a domicile built of necessity and having none of them once offered him lodging even after his mother's death, they were struck with shame and could not bear to confiscate the stolen goods. The men returned empty-handed, but Tuck promised Sadie he would buy her a new cap gun, which he did, and all was forgiven. For a time.

A.P. Sessler

Though Johnny was not entirely welcomed, he frequently made appearances at the local gatherings. He would keep to himself or else have a brief nonsensical conversation with anyone who lent an ear before excusing themselves, which often led him to gravitate toward the children. Parents had not yet instilled in them a fear of familiars like they had outsiders, so the young 'uns were far more tolerant than grown-ups in that they didn't seem to mind his babbling, perhaps because it hadn't been so long ago they too could barely speak a word of English.

Only one person drew his attention and was more welcoming than the children, someone Johnny had an admiration for even more than all things silver, and that was all things Sally Gray. The lass was a looker, no doubt, and the only flesh and blood thing beside his own late mother he had true affections for. While one would at first glance assume it was her teeth crowned and filled with silver that Johnny was after, it was plain to see he had taken to her before ever she opened her mouth.

Miss Gray and Ben Scarborough were talking marriage, and even eloping and leaving the small-town life behind for the big city. The latter was not taken well by family in general but especially her parents, who wanted nothing more than for her to bear several children as they had in obedience to the commission to be fruitful and multiply.

Knowing he was a halfwit, Sally and Ben were patient, even tolerant of Johnny's feeble flirtations when he brought her cemetery flowers or some of his favorite shiny trinkets. She accepted them with the grace (if not an occasional giggle) becoming of a lady and would put the flowers in a vase or store the trinkets atop her dresser or else pass them on to her younger siblings.

One day Johnny saw the younger Gray sister with one of his simple gifts and went into a rage. The child understood not a word nor why Johnny was so incensed, but she understood his demand to return the gift to his possession. However, the scared but foolish girl clung to that hood ornament like life itself, not knowing the ease which Johnny could extricate an occupant from the tightest mollusk.

The Legend of Johnny Nepkin

When those not far off heard her cries they ran with all haste to find her curled into a fearful ball, her fingers bloodied if not broken from Johnny's assault. Sally's father, the Reverend Daniel Gray, led the frenzied charge with the curse "The Devil take your soul back to hell, Johnny Nepkin!"

Now any attempts to catch Johnny were of course in vain, for all knew that though while walking he appeared as lame as a spider with a broken leg, but when he ran, dear children, Johnny was no clubfooted klutz. He was as swift as a cat, as graceful as a doe. He could outrun the fastest by a stone's throw, and that he did that afternoon.

They quickly lost sight of Johnny, but they knew well his favored habitat, and so they made way toward the woods they knew housed his metal mansion. It was on the way that it seemed the Devil had heard Reverend Gray's curse, for a storm broke out and when they entered the clearing they watched with their very eyes as a bolt of lightning struck his house.

One thing the simple-minded Johnny had not counted on were the conductive properties of his home's chosen materials, so when the ill-timed bolt went a-knocking on his door, the house exploded into sparks and flames and set the surrounding marsh on fire. The men fled for their lives and by time the fire truck from Manteo arrived the worst of the damage had been done.

The next day the men returned to the scene to find only a molten and sooty mound of metal remained of Johnny's beautiful but humble home. Within a month the local metal works arrived and began to salvage the material for scrap, dreading the discovery of Johnny's burned body but no such revelation was made. It appeared Johnny had vanished, perhaps anticipating or else falling prey to Reverend Gray's curse for the Devil to take him back to Hell, and if Johnny still possessed his mortal coil, he was certainly forced into exile.

It must have been the same event that saw Sally and Ben flee by night from the small town as they had long promised, only not a soul witnessed their departure as they did so without so much as a single goodbye. The

Reverend and Mrs. Gray were heartbroken. Had they pushed too hard? Had they not shown enough kindness to or even too much suspicion of Ben? Either way, the children were gone, and it was said they never wrote or called.

Some time passed with nary hide nor hair of Johnny and all was relatively peaceful. Like many a cephie victim his human nature must have been submerged deep beneath, drowned completely and forever, for what soon surfaced would become the stuff of nightmares, more precisely, this very legend.

Nowadays Johnny is used by parents as a home-grown bogeyman to discourage children's mischievous behavior. Some claim his name was never Nepkin or Napkin but a rearrangement of "kidnap," that is "Napkid." While this interpretation gives honor to the cleverness of Wanchese-folk, it does a gross disservice to the truth. Johnny was never partial to children out of some perverse motivation, but simply because their size and weakness and would in no wise spare a grown-up of equal vulnerability. Either one he'd snatch up the way an owl a rabbit, and up the road he'd fly out of reach and out of sight.

The first known example was Kenny Saunders. The boy had a mouthful of gleaming metal, bought with the goodliest of intentions of straightening his broken-down picket fence-teeth by mother Alice. I say "had" because once Johnny got hold of him with his prized oyster knife, he set about to pry that delicate silver filigree off the boy's teeth with no regard for flesh or bone. When the authorities found Kenny's body there was little left of his teeth or gums. There was so much blood the boy's clothes looked as if they were freshly dyed in a tub full of red Rit.

Jenny Beasley was the next to fall prey. Thankfully, the architectural contraption around her head was removed with less finality but not without permanently scarring the wee angel's face, which forever bore what the Scots call a Glasgow Smile.

The only question that remained was what Johnny was doing with his newly acquired treasures. With his forest-marsh mansion now a thousand pieces of repurposed metal scattered 'round the state, where was he taking his booty? This is where even my knowledge runs thin.

Some say Johnny, part cephie, took to the sea. Had he learned to shift forms as his fathers, or did he possess on that hideous desecration of a body some organ that enabled him to transition to the depths without suffering harm?

Whatever the case might be it's his long absence from the world of men that precipitated the legend's slow demise. Few know his name and fewer the truth of his origins or the horror of his deeds but meet one of the surviving old timers and make mention of his name and you'll see their eyes light up with a nostalgic terror they had nearly forgotten. Yes, ask the old timers, and let them recall—nay, *relive*—the fear they knew when Johnny crossed their yards and walked their back roads. Remind them so they may live in anticipation of his clandestine return, and perhaps hide their shiny metals away, far from Johnny's half-human sight.

For though many suspect Johnny long dead, knowing half-men and seafolk as I do, I can attest to their long, almost immortal, lives. I imagine right now Johnny sitting content in some gleaming underwater keep, not a care in the world. Who knows, maybe he's even found himself a suitable mate among his kind. However, having learned of and witnessed many a tragedy, I often wonder if by his side rests the remains of one Sally Gray, a pile of crab-picked bones and silver-crowned teeth he can't help but admire the remainder of his otherworldly days.

-30-

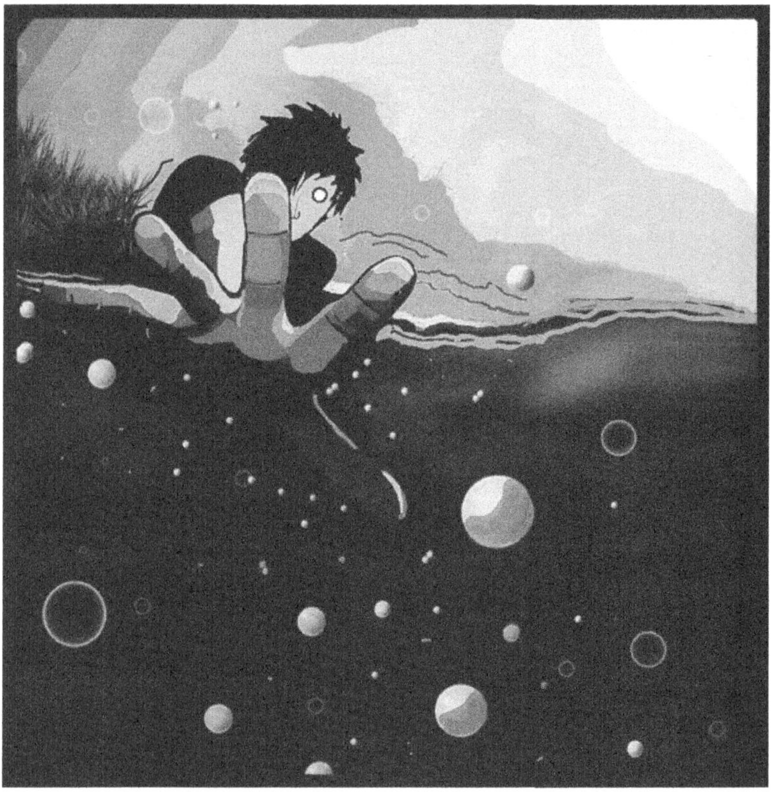

Necker
by Grant Bright

We would have found our way to the gravel pit ourselves, eventually.

It had the morbid gravity that dark places often have for idle boys. Like some black hole out in space, slowly drawing us in. We couldn't have resisted that pull forever. Even if Paul Kelleher hadn't drowned in the gravel pit. Even if Mick's brother hadn't told us the story of the Necker.

Mick's brother was older than us and we believed everything he said. He told us what he did with girls. He told us about the fights he had with the squaddies in town. We were all scared of him. He went to the secondary modern with my cousin Terry and he had a moustache. He told us he knew Paul Kelleher from secondary school. A friend of a friend, he said. We had heard plenty of rumours from different kids at school, but Mick's brother knew the truth. Paul Kelleher had gone swimming up the gravel pit on his own, he said. Paul Kelleher had ignored the warnings and so the Necker had got him. There was nothing in the papers because they wanted it kept secret, he said.

The story and variations of it rippled around school that spring and tugged at our imaginations. We needed to see the place for ourselves.

We sprinted out past the empty garages and echoing warehouses of the industrial estate down to the water, choked with chemical-dyed weeds and stained with rainbows from rusted oil barrels. We traced the tired river upstream and across the long, river-fronted lawns of the posh houses at the edge of town, keeping low and scrambling over brick walls and fences at the edge of the water. The grass was long and full of rain, and the legs of our trousers were soaked to the knees, but still we ducked and wove. We ran in fluid formation like the soldiers we saw in Sunday war films. Dashing to cover. Ducking behind bushes at the slightest sound.

Necker

We had come that way a hundred times before. Sean and Mick and me. We had made a den in the rotten boathouse where we hassled the holidaying couples at the marina for spare change. Sometimes we had gone as far as Dracula's castle, the old derelict hotel half a mile out of town along the river. But we had never ventured as far as the gravel pit. It had taken us two weeks to work up the courage. We lied to our parents about what we were doing that day. There would be murder if they knew.

Mick was the most worried about being found out. Sean and I were talking too much, giddy with nervous excitement. But Mick was quiet. He could laugh like a madman, smashing windows and running from barking dogs. But he could also be deadly serious. That morning Mick had a face on him like there was a stone in his shoe. Something was eating into him so badly he was almost buckled by it.

I knew what it was.

We reached a wood of grey pines with red bark that pushed up against a chain-link fence like they were trying to force their way out. The fence was topped with barbed wire. It ran down to the river and then out over the water to deter trespassers. The wood was thick, but we could see sunlight on the other side.

'We've got to swear.' Mick said. 'Before we go in there. Swear not to tell anyone what we was doing. We never went to the gravel pit. Swear we were never there.'

'I swear,' said Sean straight away, just like that, and Mick rolled his eyes.

'Just saying it ent enough, dumbo.' He called him that deliberately to hurt Sean's feelings. Sean was in the remedial group at school and had to do extra handwriting lessons with Mr. Kirkby at lunchtime. Sean's face was red, and it wasn't from running.

'We got to swear properly so we never forget.' Mick snapped a branch off through the fence and stripped it clean of needles to make a slender switch. 'Put your hand out.'

Mick's dad hit him. His brother did, too, passing down the beatings he had received himself. It made Mick cruel, sometimes. He was our friend, but we did what he said. He was our leader. I could tell Sean was scared and I didn't want Mick to start picking on him again. Sean would bawl and we would all have to go home and never even see the gravel pit. I knew that couldn't happen. I stuck out my hand.

'I'll go first.'

'If anyone asks you, you swear you were never there.'

'I swear I was never there.'

It was worse than the cane. I thought Mick might go easy, but the branch whipped through the air and stung so bad I hopped about with my hand squeezed between my thighs, swearing. It was a warning. Not just to keep this promise, but to keep the promise that we had made in secret before. Mick and me.

Sean's big brown cow eyes had tears around the edges before he even got hit. I told him it wasn't so bad, really, and he slowly put out his hand.

'I swear I was never there.'

I don't think Mick hit Sean as hard as he'd hit me. He didn't want him to run off bawling, either. Mick had a plan, and he was determined to see it through. Sean was handed the branch so he could make Mick promise, too. He hit him with the switch so lightly, Mick barely flinched. But we had made a pact. There was no going back. It was sealed.

Sean had grassed Mick up.

It happened on the last day of term. Mick had sneaked into Kirkby's office for a dare. He looked for something to steal to prove he had been in there and all he could find was the lump of obsidian that Kirkby used as a paperweight. Kirkby noticed it was missing straight away and lined up all of us boys in the hall, hoping someone would crack. No one did. Sean had his extra lesson at lunchtime, and Kirkby must have seized the opportunity to question him about the stolen rock. I don't know what he asked or whether he promised Sean anything for telling the truth. Sean wasn't much good at lying anyway. I don't suppose he wanted to tell, but he just couldn't help it. Kirkby made Mick turn out his coat pocket before home time and there was the black rock. Mick got some licks of

Necker

the cane from Kirkby, and then some more from his dad's belt when he got home. That was at the start of the Easter holidays and Mick had not forgotten.

We came out of the trees and the black pool of the gravel pit lay before us, perfectly round and still, more like a glass plate than a body of water. Mick's brother had said that the gravel pit was cursed. The diggers went too deep, he said. They had uncovered something, like hell or something, he said. They had disturbed the Necker. That was why they had to flood the pit—to cover it up.

The other kids at school told variations of the tale. Even Gary Lynch who said his uncle had told him the story years ago. He said his uncle knew the story from when he was a kid himself. It was still the same story. The same pieces told as facts. Something had brought the Necker up from where she slept, to wait for any kids foolish enough to go swimming in the gravel pit. Kids like Paul Kelleher.

The black disc of ice-cold water did not seem to belong in the landscape. It sucked in the warmth from the air and the colors out of its surroundings. It was easy to see why stories had been made up about the place. No insects buzzed in the air above it. No water boatmen skated on the surface. It was as glossy and still as the volcanic glass that sat on Kirkby's desk.

'Paul Kelleher is down there.'

It was so deep you couldn't ever find the bottom. That is what made it so cold. The depth of it. Cold as space. Some said the Necker was just a story to scare kids so they wouldn't swim there. Even if there was no Necker down there, the cold would get into you and freeze your muscles as you swam. Mick's brother said that if you put your foot in it up to the ankle you couldn't see your toes. Couldn't feel them either. It was so cold that your foot would be numb, and you'd think it had gone. Bitten off. You'd be stupid to try it. A cramp, out there in the freezing black, would be fatal. There were the sloping remains of a ramp used to drive the gravel up, but the submerged sides of the pit were sheer. Swim here and that would be your lot.

Grant Bright

In our heads, we knew it wasn't a cramp that would do for you. The Necker would grab your ankle and drag you down. It would not be like drowning—more like being buried under the weight of the water, heavier and heavier, pushing you down further and further. Blacker and blacker.

Paul Kelleher was not quite dead and not quite alive. That was what the stories said. The kids pulled down into the Necker's lair didn't die. They were trapped down there in the cold, lonely deep, to be held in her long arms, their faces as white as the bellies of dead fish. And we were going to see them.

Mick's brother said there had to be an offering. One thing each that was special to us, that we did not want to give away. I had two precious stones with holes in them that I'd found on the beach in Devon last summer. Sean took out a rubber duck.

'You fucking divot,' Mick said when he saw it. Then calmer, reacting to Sean's deflated expression, he said, 'The bloody thing will float.' Sean held the stupid thing out. It was clearly valuable to him. Some artefact from when he was little.

'It's fine, Sean. It's fine,' I said.

Mick huffed and gave me a vicious dead arm. He turned to Sean and smiled, reassuring, and said, 'Give it here.' He took out a biro and started to drill a hole in the yellow neck of the duck. Screwing and drilling the metal tip into the plastic as if he was holing a conker. The plastic gave too easily taking Mick by surprise. The nib passed straight through the neck of the duck and into the soft flesh of his palm between the index and middle fingers.

'Fuck. Shit,' he said, clamping the injured hand into his armpit. I made him show it to me. The hole in his hand was white and bloodless at first. It was so deep I could see the yellow fat between the bones of his fingers. Then the blood came, almost black, filling the hole and spilling out of his hand onto the gravel. There was a look in his eyes then, just for me. This was Sean's fault. Again. The plan was still on.

I suggested Mick wash his hand in the water. Sean's face whitened at that, and Mick just sneered. He said it was fine, fine, and he marched away from us, along the curve of the gritty beach to where the rubble pile stuck out into the water. As we waited, he crouched and washed his injured hand at the water's edge. His back was to us, but I could feel the waves of rage that came off him, even from that distance. By the time he stood up on the promontory, he was calm enough to shout the instructions across the water to us.

I threaded a piece of hairy string through the neck of the duck and looped it through the holes in my magic stones. Mick had given up a crow's feather as his contribution. I had asked him at the time if it was precious enough and he snapped back at me that he was saving it to make an Apache headdress with. I knew he was never going to do that. We hadn't played cowboys and Indians for a year, and I already knew we never would again. It did not seem precious enough. Mick had given me a painful rabbit punch on the shoulder to remind me that it didn't matter. What mattered was that Sean would believe in it and then he would get the punishment that was coming to him. The stories were so tightly woven together, I had started to believe it myself. I wondered later if the poor value of Mick's offering was the reason for what happened.

Sean was the thrower. Mick had spent the holiday telling him he was the best thrower we knew. So, it would be Sean that would throw the offering and then Sean who would look down into the water to tell us what he saw. It would be dangerous. We were playing with monsters. Mick told him he was the bravest and Sean was almost convinced by the flattery. He agreed to look down into the black water at the reflection of his face. If the magic worked, Mick's brother said, and if the offering was accepted by the Necker, and if he was brave enough not to look away, then Paul Kelleher's face would appear to Sean alone, summoned up from the depths of her lair.

'Throw it out as far as you can,' Mick shouted. There was still anger in his voice. He was halfway along the stony promontory, silhouetted against the grey. He made no move to come back to where we were standing. That was how it was going to be. I was on my own.

Sean swung his arm back and did exactly that, hurling the weird bundle in a high arc that hit the surface of the gravel pit dead center. There was no splash. The offering sank under the water soundlessly as if it had fallen into a pool of treacle. Not even a ripple.

'Now look. Quick. Look down into the water.'

Sean stood right at the lip of the gravel pit and stared down.

I positioned myself behind him and looked over at Mick for the signal.

'I can't see nothing,' Sean shouted.

'Lean closer. Lean right over or it won't work,' Mick called back. 'Paul Kelleher is coming.' I swallowed my guilt and placed my feet wide apart on the gravel behind Sean, hands outstretched, ready for the push.

'There ent nothing.'

'Lean closer.'

A hard breeze came up off the still water and the sun came out from behind the clouds. Goosebumps rose on my arms. My hands felt exposed. The red welt across my palm sang painfully in the cold.

Suddenly, the black lid of the gravel pit was as clear as a mirror.

I looked up.

Sean had turned and was looking straight at me. He fixed me in those wide eyes and saw me in all my treachery. He knew what we had planned to do. To push him into the freezing water and then what? Run away? Pretend the whole thing was a big joke? Sean knew what I was going to do, and he knew why. What I thought was disappointment in his eyes was really empathy. We were both victims. Sean, because of his slow wits and his bovine trust. Me, because of my weakness and fear of being a target for scorn and hurt. Bullies weren't big kids who gob on your blazer and steal your dinner money. They were the people you chose as your leaders because you were too scared of being on the wrong side of them. You called them friends and they hurt you more.

There was a short shrill sound far off, like one of the birds we routinely failed to identify in the woods. The spell was broken.

Necker

Sean looked down at his feet and I looked across toward the source of the cry. There was nothing there. No sign of the bird or whatever it had been that had made that sound. The pebbles of the promontory were wet and there was no sign of Mick. Just the flat glassy stillness of the gravel pit. The dark liquid of it was unbroken. A black hole.

When I looked back at Sean his mouth was open with the shock of Mick's disappearance. We stood there, still as the cold air over the water. We were too frightened or shocked to move from our spot on the bank. Far too scared to go over and investigate the place where Mick had been. Where he no longer was. Sean waited for me to decide what we would do next. We didn't look for Mick. We knew where he had gone.

Sean and I did not speak on the long walk home.

Later, the search for Mick rippled out of the town and came to the gravel pit. They sent divers down into the black water for two days and they never came out with Mick or Paul Kelleher or anything else. We knew Mick wasn't dead. Not like your granddad was dead. All waxy faced in an open coffin so everyone could check and make sure he was definitely gone before they put him in the ground. The Necker didn't want you dead like that. It was lonely down there.

They asked us if we knew anything, and we kept the promise we had made.

We never went to the gravel pit.

We were never there.

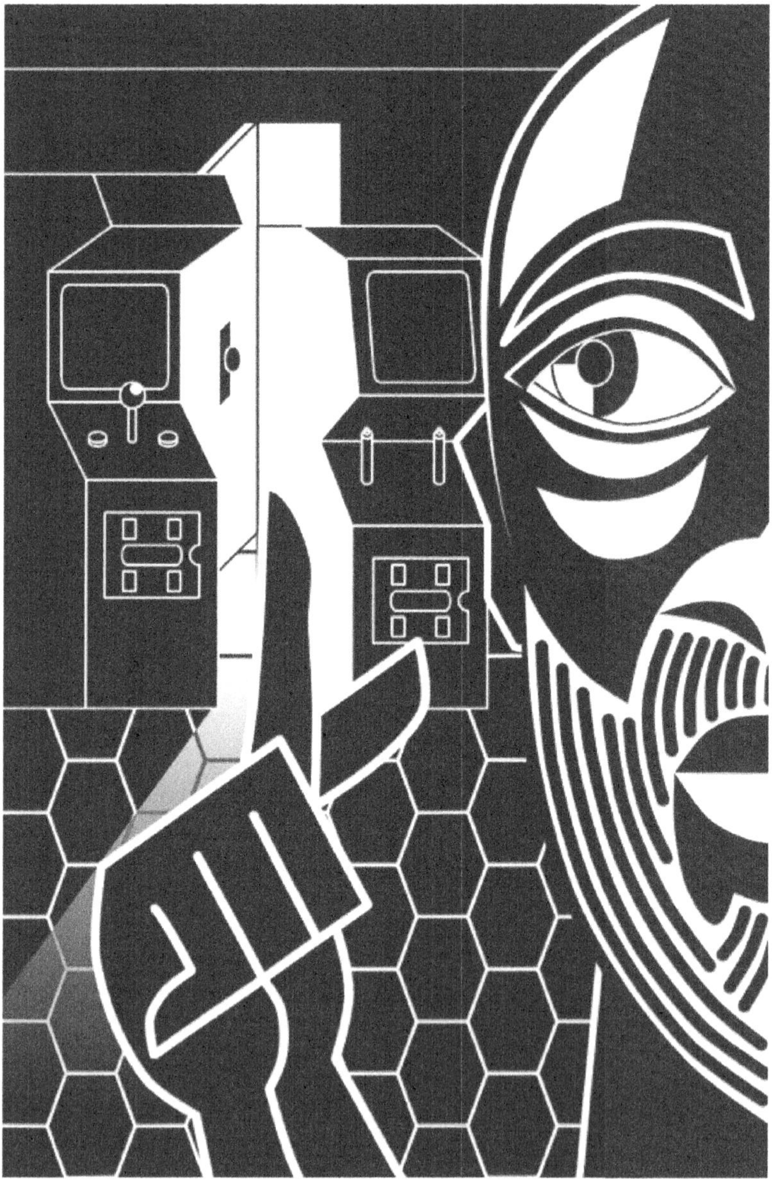

Figures of Shadow
by Frank Coffman

The "corner of the eye" will sometimes catch
A fleeting, yet moving, figure or a shape!
Often amorphous, yet sometimes we think we see
A human form. We look but cannot snatch—
In most cases—any clear view. They escape
Our searching. We ask, "How could such things be?"
Then we tell ourselves. "Merely a trick of the eyes,
An 'optical illusion,'" as it is said.

Yet some will say they've seen these things—distinct,
Straight on. And more, much more than the surprise
Is paralyzing Fear and deepest dread.
One theory is that these Shadow Folk are linked
As Ghosts within our realm of Life and Light,
The undeparted spirits of our dead
Moving among us, normally unseen.

Some legends tell of a supernatural wight:
A Djinn [1], darker than black, eyes glowing red.
"Nalusa Chito," [2] as the Choctaw women keen.

Still others say they do not come from here!
They come from *other worlds*, from *a Future Time* [3]
Even *other Dimensions* [4], parallel to ours!

Most say they are aggressive, feed on our Fear.
Some tell that, incubus like, these fiends will climb
Upon a sleeping soul to steal the breath. Such powers
They have, that physical objects can be thrown
About—though they are incorporeal!

At night they are blacker than blackest shadows,
Although they can appear by day, as is well-known.

Figures of Shadow

Whether they're newly come or are primordial,
They have chosen their frightful presence to impose.
    Some say, when encountered, they seem merely curious;
Others recount aggression, actual attack
With the Shadow running at them and—*right through them!*
    Non-believers say such stories must be spurious,
Mere hallucinations, outright lies. These *Figures of Black*:
Figments of imagination to which our minds succumb.
    Yet, flickering in and out of our peripheral vision,
Those shadows at the "corner of the eye,"
Dark phantoms we've all once or often seen.
Though the thought of Shadow People meets derision,
There's evidence such doubting would belie—
In our world, their world, or somewhere in between.

Frank Coffman

1 The Islamic entities know as *Djinn* or *Jinn* are demons of various characteristics and types. The Ifrit or "fire djinn" are dangerous due to their essence in flame. Other types include shapeshifters and, indeed, shadow figures.

2 The Choctaw have stories about shadow beings. *Nalusa Chito* was the soul-eater, a *"great black being."* If individuals allowed evil thoughts or depression to enter their minds, Nalusa Chito would creep inside them and eat their souls.

3 Another theory suggests that Shadow Figures are beings from our Future, true *Time Travelers*.

4 And yet another suggests that *They* are from another Dimension, Trans-dimensional entities from a parallel universe.

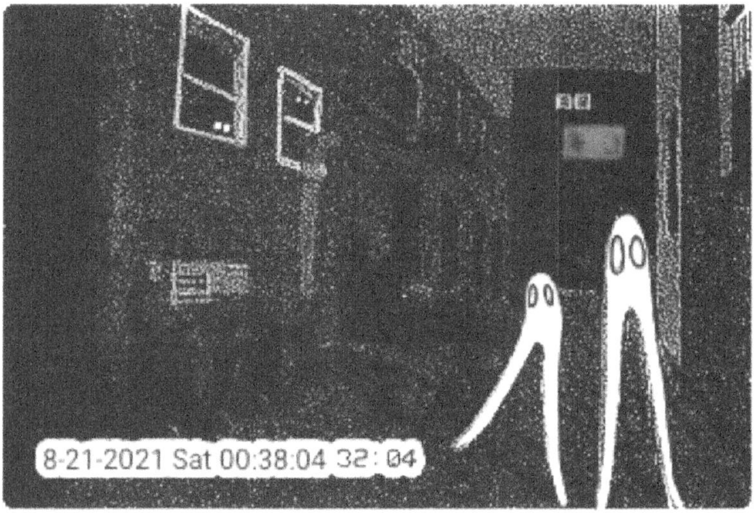
8-21-2021 Sat 00:38:04 32: 04

The Visitors
Michael S. Walker

They are called The Nightcrawlers. Sometimes The Fresno Nightcrawlers from the CCTV footage where they first were spotted. Such a stupid name. Implies something on four (or more) legs. Something bestial and near the dirt. *The Visitors* (as I prefer to call them) are nothing like that. Sometimes—when I know my Aunt Joy is asleep and not going to be bothering me about some stupid thing—I just like to lie in bed and watch the proof that they DO exist. The footage from Fresno and that other video from Yosemite National Park. There they glide and sail across the screen. Armless. Sometimes looking like a long pair of white pants. At other times looking like billowing capes surrounding…NOTHING.

They obsess me. They really do. I find them beautiful. And aloof…

When Dad was alive, we used to love to watch creepy stuff like that. Video after video of cryptids and urban legends. Bigfoot. Chupacabra. The Hook…

Five months ago, Dad died of a sudden aneurysm. And here I am now, in Zanesville Ohio, living with his only sister.

My Aunt Joy…

Such an incongruous name. I don't think she really feels any joy about anything. At all. She is 67 years old and works over 60 hours a week at some Gap Warehouse. Maybe when she is thumping her Bible in church. Or cold calling people to convince them that our incumbent president is the devil… Maybe.

Joy. Anger. Love. Sadness…

It's weird but, at the age of sixteen, I feel like some old man or something. Seen too much tragedy. Too much fucked-up shit. And when Dad died, there was nowhere else to go. It was either Aunt Joy or…

The Visitors glide across those screens. Unconcerned. Diaphanous. It appeals to me.

I have been fixated recently on the footage of The Visitors from Yosemite. Recorded a few years after the initial Fresno sighting. In that green video there are two of them: one in the forefront and one trailing a

The Visitors

few feet behind. The one in front is significantly taller than the one behind.

Father and Son?

And where are they going? They seem to be in no hurry to get there maybe but they seem to be headed SOMEWHERE...

There is an old Native American legend that The Visitors are something very ancient. That they are swamp creatures originally from some distant swamp planet. (Hence the long legs that help them ford through all the Muck and Mire.) That they are here on this earth to reconnect all of us joyless people to the natural world. There are Native American totems that look just like those ghosts in the vids...

That legend appeals to me also...

Not much else appeals to me anymore. I miss HOME. I miss Chicago. I miss Joe and Dusty and my school there. Zanesville High is full of nothing but redneck jocks who look at me every day as if I were one of the Nightcrawlers. And now, my aunt is on my back morning noon and night to get a job and start paying her room and board.

Such a kind Christian women...

Actually, I would not mind getting a job. Anything. I am going stir-crazy here. Either at school or in this little bedroom my aunt has me billeted in. A stucco prison that every dark night seems to get smaller and smaller. It belonged, once upon a time, to her son David. Her only son. He was an Army specialist who died in 2003. Stepped on a mine outside of Fallujah. This room is still a shrine to his memory: diplomas, football trophies. A large poster to the right of the bed depicting a soldier with dragonfly wings. A Linkin Park cover—apparently his favorite jam.

Not allowed to touch any of it. Or remove any of it.

Sometimes late at night, out of the stillness, I hear my aunt sobbing. And calling his name.

Yeah, I want a job. Or some kind of escape...

Now that the weather has started getting better here, I spend as much time as I can outside of the house—tooling around Zanesville on my beach cruiser bike.

Not wanting to go back to that little tomb...

Last night, on the outskirts of this bike park called Fory Park—a place I never take my bike to—I swear to God I saw three of the Visitors.

I absolutely swear that I did. (Or maybe I am just cracking up—a long time coming.) I brought my bike to a halt there on the sidewalk outside the park and watched them walk, watched them glide, watched them do anything BUT crawl, as the traffic behind on 21st Street flew past all.

Obliviously…

Yes. There were three. On the far side of the park. They were navigating a cement bike ramp there as if they were getting ready to board some phantom ocean liner that was docked on the edge of it.

IDK. Maybe they were. In some other reality tangent to ours…

The Visitors

I do not know how long I stood there, squeezing the handles of my bike. Apparently the only one seeing this weird vision.

I watched them, my heart pounding harder and harder in my chest. Occasionally I would shake my head, furiously. Blink my eyes. And still they came on. Like in the footage from You Tube… *Creepy Pasta.*

White. Brilliant. Armless and unconcerned.

Two of them were larger than the other maybe. Maybe four-and-a half-tall or so if I was judging correctly there in the darkness. And another trailing slightly behind. Like in that Yosemite joint. Maybe a foot smaller.

A family?

And, just when the first two got to the edge of that bike ramp—on their long, long legs—they all stopped (as if on cue) and turned their small heads toward me.

And they nodded.

I fled then. Almost fell there on the pavement getting the kickstand of my bike up, bringing my boots hard down on the pedals. One thing to see The Visitors through the safe distance of my phone.

And another…to actually see them.

⌘ ⌘ ⌘

Tonight, I lie on this small bed, tossing and turning. Depressed. Uncomfortable in my own skin. Outside thunder sounds—an approaching spring storm.

This room. I want to be anywhere else but here in this room. Shrine to a dead boy.

That Linkin Park poster looms above me. Above this bed. Like some undiscovered cryptid. I often imagine that was what happened to Aunt

The Visitors

Joy's son when he clicked on that mine. His body wasn't splattered all over the desert like meat in an uncovered blender. No. No. He was immediately transformed into that singular image on the poster. *Dragonfly Soldier...*

In my mind's eye, I keep seeing those Visitors in the bike park. Turning toward me and nodding solemnly.

As if they had been expecting me...

Through the heating vent in this little room, I can hear my Aunt Joy call her son's name over and over in a weak voice.

"David...David..."

Dad...

The Creepy Pasta called LIFE Most of it so horrible really.

I keep staring at the time display on my phone. In about another hour, Aunt Joy will stop mourning her dead son, get up, and start her shower.

Another day at The Gap...

Another day in the swamp called life.

How do we bear it all?

I think when my Aunt Joy finally leaves, when I hear her 4X4 thunder and boom out of the driveway, I am going to put on my coat and leave here too. Spring storm be damned. I am going to get on my bike and pedal back to Fory Park. I just can't shake the conviction that The Visitors are here for ME. That they are here to deliver me from another day of suffering. Another day of nothing.

Another day...

They were nodding at me.

I swear that they were.

⌘ ⌘ ⌘

I sit in Mr. Luzio's homeroom—not listening—as he drones on about what to do if shooter or shooters storm the sacred, porphyritic halls of Zanesville High.

I have already heard the drill a billion times...

Sometimes, I wish...

Behind me, Dave Frank--star forward on the Blue Devils basketball team—starts his usual whispered gibes on my behalf.

Michael S. Walker

"Hey UFO boy...hey queer," he hisses. Below Mr. Luzio's grim instructions about barricading our homeroom door with desks and chairs. Again, I am not listening. I go through this ordeal with Frank almost every gray morning...

What I am trying to do is watch the You Tube video of the Nightcrawlers—the one from Yosemite that I have watched over and over—trying to keep my muted phone buried in my Algebra 2 book. I can barely keep my eyes open from lack of sleep.

The Visitors did NOT come back to Fory Park. They did not come for me.

NO

Once again, I sat there on the periphery of that little park. Waiting. Hoping to see them sail up to the edge of that concrete bike ramp. Hoping that they would deign to take me aboard some invisible mothership, take me light years away from Blue Devils and another day in Zanesville fucking Ohio. Take me away from Aunt Joy and all the rest...

I sat there, clutching the handlebars of my bike, in silence,

Until the rain started falling... The Visitors did not come back.

Hey UFO Boy...Hey Queer...

I really am not listening. To either Mr. Luzio or Dave Frank, as they sing out their usual homeroom duet. I listen instead to the silence of a CCTV camera. Like I have a thousand times before. Two ghostly figures that resemble really a father and son walking downhill in the green air. Figures in turn like stilts...like pants...like billowing capes. Visitors walking in peace, serenely, above all our MUCK and MIRE...

OR

It could just really be an elaborate trick. Random bedsheets on a wire.

Creepy Pasta

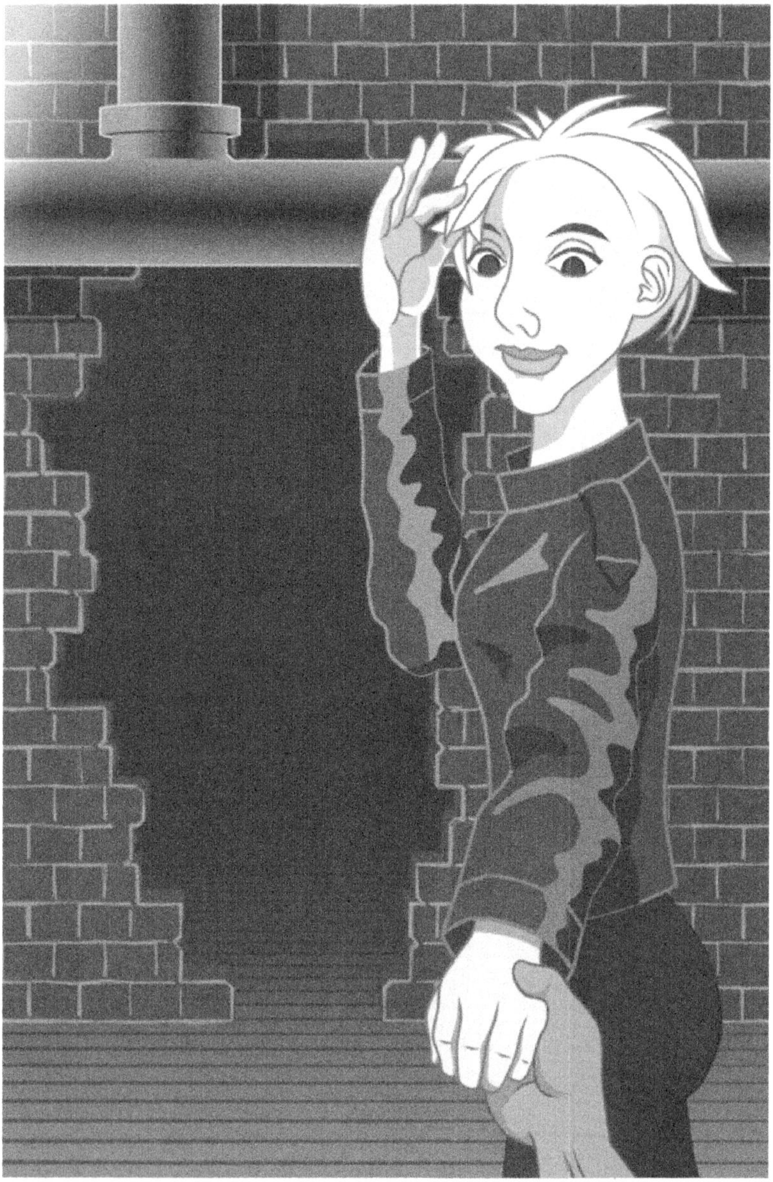

Danse De L'Amour
by Ivan Zorich

Here's a name you don't hear often. Violette Reign. The words rolled effortlessly off her tongue. Her perfect French scattered a pack of wild chills up my spine. No way I was going to repeat it without practicing—Slav roots and hard Rs be damned.

It suits her. One look at her, shivering in the cold February night air, inside the courtyard where we were all gathered, and I knew she had reinvented herself with it. It is not the fact that she was obviously cold (and that thin leather jacket did not help either), no. She shivered with grace; a delicate tremble of the shoulders, a gentle sway of her hips, all the time standing on the tip of her toes.

The fool that I am, I fell for it. I offered her my coat, which she refused with a smile.

"I am not that cold, really," she said. "Besides, I hear it is warm down there, like almost 68 degrees."

Down there were the Portland Shanghai tunnels. An underground network of passageways, holding cells and old opium dens built back in the day when beards were worn by men instead of hipsters and vices were more than just a night of gambling and a buffet at Spirit Mountain Casino. Nowadays, they were home for gutterpunk kids, restaurant pantries and rat colonies. The tour we were on was nothing more than a glorified basement crawl, covering a city block, if that. I was working on a new story and had to get some firsthand experience. It's not like I could just go to any basement, at least not without fear of getting shot. The long, cold fingers of the NRA were all over Portland, no matter how liberal it tried to look.

"So, I hear; lack of air flow and all those heating pipes," I said.

"Kind of creepy, right? I mean, getting snatched and taken down like all those people back in the day? I'd die before they even get to sell me off."

Danse De L'Amour

"Well, make sure you stay in the middle of the group, just in case," I said. Her eyes clouded over.

Tour guide interrupted our exchange, as courtyard went quiet, some twenty or so faces starring at him in expectation.

He opened with a history of the Shanghai tunnels, an almost century old network of tunnels underneath downtown Portland. For all of its current liberal glory, the city used to be a real-world hellhole not even a hundred years ago. Not all the pirates and smugglers preferred Caribbean. Some of them loved cold waters of Pacific Northwest and Columbia River. Finding enough people to crew the ships required a bit more unorthodox approach, though. Snatching being the most popular one. Drop and roll had a different meaning back then.

He followed this with a story of how he had been lost in tunnels as a seven-year-old, more than once and always in the company of a haggard sailor. I'm pretty sure he was totally oblivious to how it sounded to the rest of us. Violette shot me a glance, eyes wide open and I responded with a raised eyebrow and shrugging. We both smiled and I put my arm around her shoulders. The jolt of electricity caught us both by surprise. I almost pulled the arm back, but she grabbed it with her hand and pressed it harder into the shoulder. I understood. Her shivers stopped.

Our guide opened the massive trapdoor and led us into the musky darkness.

She drew closer and cozier with every nook, every corner we explored. I could smell her perfume, a faint trace of rose water and something else, much sharper and earthy. Not too strong to be intoxicating, just subtle enough to make me wonder. The tunnels were pitch black, aside from a few holes in the ceiling, so we kept fingers interlocked. Her skin felt smooth and cold, a lake in flesh, so unlike the rough volcanic island surface of mine. From somewhere up above drifted the noise of the rolling bowling balls and pin strikes. The smell pizzas baking wafted down through the vents. It was strangely comforting.

There were no hobos or ghosts, though, unless you count those in stories that our guide served with an enthusiasm of an old schoolteacher.

That's exactly what he looked like, sporting a Mr. Rogers sweater, taped glasses, and a monotone voice even Ben Stein would be proud of. He belonged down here, with cobwebs and old sailor boots. His haircut was somewhat of a relic as well.

Not that it was a completely wasted journey. The rope and cans early alarm system worked surprisingly well even nowadays. Especially because our guide did not warn us about it, so we got to experience the firsthand how loud and terrifying it is when you walk into it. The room where they broke the young women spirits after being kidnapped was a box with nothing but a chair and aura of despair completing it. It was a pure essence of claustrophobia. Violette and I checked the walls for nail marks and messages, but like most of the tour, the original woodwork had been replaced. In these confined halls, the air was heavy and oppressive.

We were happy to be out of there after an hour. The cool breeze felt like a blessing. Clear spring night, so rare for Portland, opened all around us. The city was alive with laughter, music blasted as we walked by the open bar doors, mixed with drunk shouts, and singing. It was still early in the evening, so we grabbed a table by the fireplace at Hobo's and ordered drinks.

"So, I have to ask – what's with walking on your toes? I noticed you do it a few times tonight?"

The shadows of the fire danced upon her face as she played with the straws in the cocktail glass.

"I am a ballerina."

"That is awesome. I have never met one."

"Been doing it since I was three. It's in my blood. I live for it," she said.

"Ballet, or blood?"

"Both."

A devilish smile flashed across her pale face, as she licked a few drops of runaway Ruby Sparkler cocktail of the edge of the glass.

Danse De L'Amour

"Have you ever watched anyone dance by candlelight?" She asked.

"I have not."

"An erotic ballet virgin then? How quaint. Would you like to?"

I did, and it wasn't just the snark in her voice that I reacted to. I can't dance. It's elusive and abstract to me. Magic, when it really comes down to it. We were out that door before the ice cubes in our glasses even had the chance to melt.

Her ballet studio was off Burnside. A two-story building tucked in behind a row of birches, barely visible from the street. She unlocked the front door and we found ourselves in the dark, yet again, only this time the musky smell of the underground had been replaced by something much more appealing. The same rose water fragrance, only that mysterious earthy component much stronger this time. It was not her perfume, I realized, but the studio itself. She must have spent hours here every day. Every night. The sound of traffic came through muffled, nothing but a buzz. This was a temple of the Art, and I had every intention of becoming a devotee.

"Take off your shoes," she whispered.

I obeyed without argument. She produced a chair, from somewhere deep in the room and I sat down, eager for the show and slightly buzzed.

"Wait there, I will be right back. I have to change and bring candles," she said and disappeared into the darkness.

I sat there for what seemed like an eternity. Time is elastic, any junkie can vouch for that. It has a tendency to stretch itself thin when you really need something, when you *want* something. At that very moment, I wanted to see Violette dance more than I wanted to breathe.

A small flicker of light appeared in the far end of the room, followed by another a few moments later. She was lighting candles along the corners, eight of them altogether. I could vaguely see shapes of barre all along the room.

"Shouldn't there be mirrors on the walls?" I asked.

"Not here," she said. "They take away from the magic of it all. Besides, when I dance, I can't see myself anyway." She stepped into the faint light, and I could finally see her, dressed up for the occasion.

She wore a black leotard like another skin, muscles shifting under it as she moved, like panther waiting to pounce. The parts it did not cover were covered by a complex mosaic of tattoos, ranging from simple tribals, all the way to a scene from Le Petit Prince, complete with fox and a rose.

"Le Petit Prince?" I asked.

"Always. So sad, yet so poignant. I identify myself with him. I too have a rose which takes too much of me, it seems," she said.

"Your art?"

"You could say so…"

She walked back to the barre and turned facing away from me. Candlelight made her look ethereal, shadows dancing across the floor like licks of dark flame.

"A few basic steps for the first timer," she said.

"This is Demi-Plié." Her knees bent halfway as she executed the move.

"Followed by a Grand-Plié." This time she bent all the way down, her feet apart. I swallowed hard.

She sped up.

"Elevé, Relevé, Battement Tendu, Rond de Jamb." And then she took off, like a comet across the night sky.

It was pure magic. All I could do is sit there, my mouth open as she moved across the floor like a living flame.

Her bleached blonde hair whipped back and forth as she ascended into figures, I thought impossible to perform by the human body. Pirouettes so precise, so fast that for moment she was nothing but a blur of color. She would snap out of them in jumps high enough to make me question the laws of gravity. Her back arching to the point of unfolding, as she spun and danced her way from one arabesque into another, fluid

Danse De L'Amour

like a river. And I swear those tattoos were moving as well. It was subtle, at first, the position of fox slightly closer to the rose, but as she went on, they became a moving tapestry, an animation in flesh unfolding in front of me. The fox ran away, and the rose withered, leaving the surface barren, only to be replaced by baobab trees, growing out of it. I did not even get to register surprise when Little Prince himself appeared and started plucking them out, sighing visibly. The snake slithered in soon after and I could see her talking to him seductively.

I wanted to scream, to warn this new-found miracle she danced into existence for me as I knew very well how the story ends, for now I was sure this was not the work of an ordinary ballet dancer. Her magic transcended the boundaries of life and death. What was once a dead painting on the surface of the skin became just as alive and solid as I had been. This was her Piecé de Résistance, this new life she created out her passion. Tears started filling into my eyes, as I saw the bite that would end it all.

"And now for Coup de Grâce!," she said and before I could even jump, Violette spun close to me and drew the tip of her ballet shoe to my neck. A sharp pain exploded in my jugular, white heat spreading through my body. I watched, paralyzed, as she pulled a long sliver of a needle, sticking out of her shoe and landed en pointe, finishing her act, glimmering with sweat. The candles began extinguishing, one by one, light dying all around me until there was nothing left but the tunnel vision and a sound of her labored breathing. The darkness came soon after.

⌘ ⌘ ⌘

I woke up to find myself hanging from the ceiling, hands tied to the massive chandelier which was now lit up.

"It's a shame, you know," Violette said, as she walked in front of me, wearing the same leather jacket I first saw her in. "I actually liked you. There is certain gravitas about you. You seemed genuinely interested in my dance, rather than just hoping for a quickie in a dance studio. Makes what comes next all that more painful."

She pulled out a long, curved blade and without flinching cut a big chunk out of my biceps. I screamed as she licked the flesh and tossed it into a bowl on the floor nonchalantly.

"This gift of mine did not come without a price. It requires sustenance in order to persist."

She walked down to the massive doors at the far end of the room.

"Come out little ones. Time to drink in. Allegro!" she said as she opened the doors.

The sound of dozens of small feet in ballet shoes moving in hurry filled the room. Ballet dancers in training. I finally figured out why her studio smelled like earth. She lived for blood.

"He was right, you know. Le Pettit Prince. You become responsible for what you've tamed. You're responsible for your rose."

As the blade starts cutting into my flesh again, I am left with but a single thought. The stars on her skin will be my home when I wake up anew…

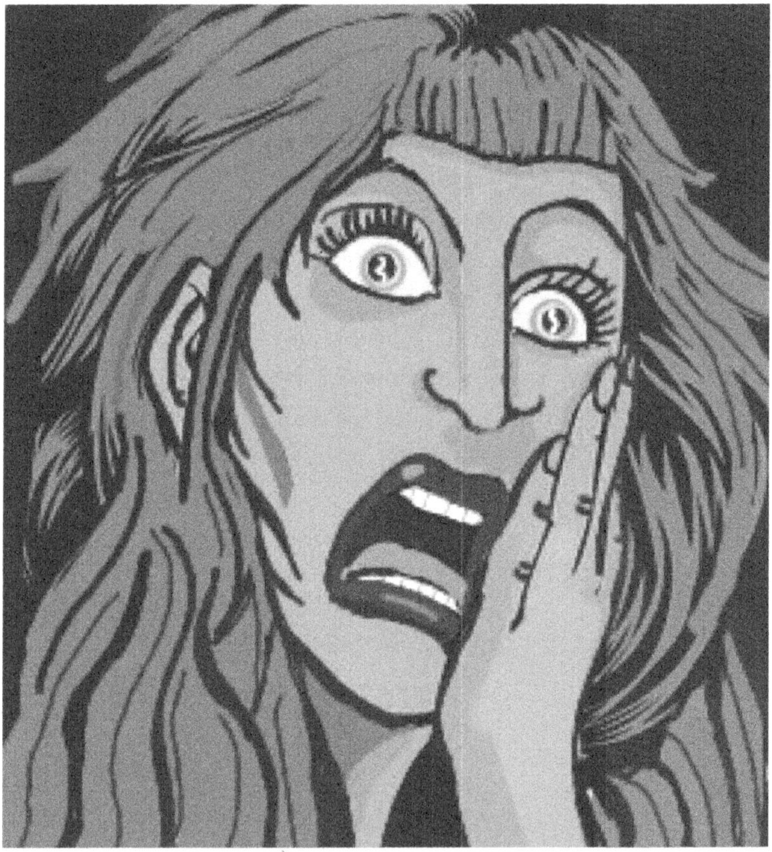

The Snakes of Errington
or
The Legend of Specky Eggy
by Russell Smeaton

As I drove along the small road, I could see Errington Woods growing larger in the distance. A grey sky pressed down on the trees, smothering them in a light mist. Slowing down for the roundabout, I could see tractors ploughing brown fields, mobbed by seagulls. Winding down the window, the fresh country air flooded in, carrying along a faint tang of salt.

I was there to visit my parents. Not so long ago, they had followed their dream of living by the sea and had moved to the small town of Marske by the Sea. It was my first visit, but I felt like I knew the place from all the photos Dad sent. Wide open skies over a grey expanse of beach, lush green woods and a small, tidy town center made up the main body of his scenes. It looked idyllic and Mum and Dad had settled right in.

As I parked on their drive, I could see Dad stand up in the kitchen to greet me. A twinge of sadness swept over me as his hands massaged the stiffness in his back, and I took in the slow jerky movements as he straightened up. In my mind, he was still that strong, supple man, able to pick me up and throw me around. The sadness floated away when I saw his big, open smile and before I knew it, I was swaddled in his large arms and familiar aftershave.

After they had finished fussing over me, asking me how I was doing, if I was seeing anyone and all that, conversation drifted naturally to the town. It was a quiet place, with next to no crime, or anti-social behavior. No chavs loitered under lampposts; no drug dealers hung out behind shops. Dad boasted of how he could leave his door unlocked at night, and still feel safe. My skepticism must have been obvious.

The Snakes of Errington

"You don't believe me, right?" questioned Dad.

"It's not that I don't...no, I don't. And even if it was safe, that's a daft thing to do."

"Ha! Told you she wouldn't believe us."

"Dad, I'm from the city. I don't even know my neighbor's name."

"Trust us, sweet pea. This place is as safe as houses."

With the conversation lingering around how safe the town was, I knew I wasn't going to persuade them to start locking up. Catch ups done, small talk winding down, I decided to head out to stretch my legs and check out the town.

The sun had burned off the drizzle and clouds, leaving behind a beautiful warm day, smelling of flowers and cleanness. After the city, it made for a welcome change. As I walked out the house, the neighbor eyed me with barely disguised suspicion.

"Oh, I'm Anne, I'm visiting my parents," I said, even though he didn't ask.

"Ahhh, YOU'RE the daughter!" he said, his face instantly brightening up.

"Welcome to Marske! I'm Dave," said Dave thrusting his hand out. "Thank you. Mum and Dad certainly seem to like it," I replied, shaking his hand. I took an instant liking Dave. When he talked to me, he looked me in the eye, and only once did his eyes flicker to my chest.

"Oh yeah, it's a great little place to live," he said and launched into what was close to a sales pitch for the town. We chatted some more, and I enjoyed the easy manner of the conversation. The birds were singing and somewhere in the distance I could hear a lawn mower firing up.

Armed with some very specific directions from Dave, I wandered into town. The sun shone brightly but a gentle breeze coming off the sea kept the temperature comfortable. Maybe it was because I was on a mini vacation, or maybe slightly giddy after my conversation with Dave, but I don't think I'd ever seen a town so beautiful. People greeted each other on the street, others relaxed on benches and chatted. When people walked past me, they smiled and said Hello. Such a change from the grim city I was living in. Everywhere in the town, it felt calm and relaxed. Cars parked up with their windows down, dogs were left outside of shops unattended. Not once did I hear a distant siren or feel threatened by some drunk urinating down a back alley. Even the small group of kids hanging around the shop entrance moved out of the way with nothing to say but a genuine "sorry." I started toying with fantasies of moving location, fooling myself that it was just to keep an eye on my parents.

That evening I listened to Mum and Dad tell me how great the town was, and I had to admit, I was starting to agree. It was only when we started chatted about the surrounding countryside that a warning bell started to ring.

"Oh, we don't go up into the hills," said Dad, "the locals say there are snakes up there."

"What, slow worms?" I laughed. England was not exactly famous for its wide range of dangerous and exotic snakes.

"Listen to your dad," chimed in Mum, "it's true!"

"Rubbish. Tomorrow, I'll prove it."

"Ooooh, come on now sweet pea," but it was too late. My mind was made up.

And so, the next day, I set off for the woods. Even early on, the sun was up, and the day was shaping up to be as beautiful as the day before. Dave was out in the garden, sorting out his flowerbeds. He spotted my walking boots and a small frown formed.

"Going up the hills, eh?"

"Yeah, Mum and Dad said something daft about snakes, so I'm going to see for myself."

"Hmm, they're not wrong, you know."

"Really? But...this is England. We don't really have snakes."

"Hmm, maybe. Just be careful, okay?" and with that, he went back to his flower bed.

The Snakes of Errington

Feeling a little out of sorts, I continued with my walk. There was only one way towards the hills, and I strode out, determined not to be afraid of snakes or any other creature. The road led uphill, and I forged ahead, keen to get in the woods and prove to my parents and Dave that there was nothing to worry about. Mind pre-occupied, it wasn't long before I found myself at the edge of the woods. A path led into the trees, and I paused. I looked around, hoping no one was watching me hesitate, feeling annoyed with myself for feeling so apprehensive. It was just a small forest, for God's sake! Nothing to worry about. As I stepped into the woods, silence wrapped itself around me. The only noise was the sound of the wind in the trees, boughs creaking and groaning.

I followed the path, looking around, half expecting to see a snake slither its way in front of me. Further into the woods, I could hear the faint drip of rainwater where the sun hadn't dried the trees from the day before. As I walked on, I started to feel more at ease, and started to enjoy the quiet. My mind started to wander and my daydreams of the day before returned. Maybe I could re-locate to Marske. It made sense in a lot of ways. The commute to work would be longer, but it was still feasible. I made a mental note to check the housing market when I got back to Mum and Dads and started to draft out a list of things to do. Pre-occupied with this mental list making, a rustling in the undergrowth caught me off guard, and I stopped still for a moment. The rustling also stopped. I looked around but could see nothing apart from lush green foliage. Just as I was about to start walking, I heard the noise again. Not the erratic flutter of a bird, or mouse, but a steady, almost mocking sound.

I held my breath. Why, I don't know. Did I expect something to leap out at me? A creature from a B-movie? At the thought of some actor sweating away inside his rubber lizard suit, a bubble of laughter burst from my mouth and the noise stopped. I turned around and slowly started to walk back the way I came. Not because I was afraid, I lied to myself, but because I was getting hungry and lunch time was calling.

Dave was still gardening when I reached home. I was sweaty and out of breath. Putting one arm up to shade his eyes from the late morning sun, he frowned ever so slightly.

"You okay? You look a bit pale."

"No, I'm good. Just a bit out of shape," I lied.

"Hmm. Did you see anything up there then?"

"Nope, all quiet. Just…. well…. I might have heard something," I admitted.

He didn't say anything, just nodded, as he stood there looking at me. I was about to make my excuses when he said, "Have you got time for a cuppa?" and before I could answer he turned and disappeared through his front door.

I stood on the drive for a moment. I wanted to take a shower, get changed, and forget all about those noises in the woods. Instead, I followed Dave into his house. Similar in layout to my parents' house, it was clear Dave lived alone. There was no clutter, no piles of toys, no family photos. Just a plain, tastefully decorated house. I felt my stomach glow and forced myself to get a grip. He was good looking, sure, but I was here for my parents, not a holiday romance.

In the kitchen, he clicked on the kettle and busied himself with making tea. We made small talk about the weather, how I liked my tea, my parents. I decided to wait for him to tell me what it was he clearly wanted to say.

Tea made, we made ourselves comfortable in the kitchen. I looked around, and idly wondered if we shared the same tastes in food or wine and for the second time told myself to behave.

"So, how do you like the town?" he finally asked.

"Yeah, love it! It's so clean and friendly, isn't it?"

"Safe too, have you noticed?"

"Ha! Not if you include the snakes!"

The Snakes of Errington

"Ahh, yes. The snakes. So…" he started, and then paused. I waited for him to gather his thoughts, not wanting to rush him. He stirred his tea, blew the steam away and took a quick sip.

"The town itself wasn't always so safe."

"Oh?"

"No. It used to be quite rough in fact." Another pause. I felt a twinge of cynicism. I'd met loads of people who liked to think they came from a hard town. I hadn't pegged Dave as one of those, but here he was, telling me what a rough town it was and how you had to be a real man to grow up there.

"Have you heard about Specky Eggy?"

The sudden shift in conversation threw me. I was expecting Dave to tell me about being a man's man and growing up at the school of hard knocks. Who was this Specky Eggy? Why was he telling me about him? I sipped my tea and eventually Dave continued with his story.

The Legend of Specky Eggy

Well, if you want to understand the snakes, I guess I need to tell you about Specky Eggy. That wasn't his real name, obviously, but that was what everyone called him, on account of his really thick glasses. Kids can be mean, I guess. Anyway, where was I? Oh yeah. So, back in those days people used to say the town was rough, full of rowdy families who would rob you just as soon as look at you. One particular family, well known for being troublemakers, were the Stonehouse's.

The story goes that one of the Stonehouse lads, Carl, I think he was called, really had it in for Specky. I guess some kids like to pick on the weak looking ones, and so Specky and his glasses, easy target, eh? Anyway, this Carl would pick on Specky all the time, calling him names, tripping him up, stealing his lunch money, all that crap. No-one really thought anything of it, until Carl and Specky both went missing. There was a search party, but after a week or so Specky turned up as if nothing had happened. As for Carl, he was never seen again. According to the rumours, the Stonehouse's left town soon after, never to come back.

The Stonehouse's weren't the only family to leave. I can't remember many names, but over the years there's been quite a few disappearances. It didn't take long for rumours and gossip to spread that if you are a troublemaker, you'd soon disappear. The police never made a big deal about it. Maybe it made their life easier, so why worry? One missing scrote, one happier town.

Yeah, I can see you're a bit confused. What has this got to do with the snakes in the woods. Well, the story goes that Specky bred snakes. Back in those days, it wasn't exactly common to breed snakes. Most people had a dog or two, maybe a guinea pig, but that was about it. So, to breed snakes was a bit out there. The rumor was that Specky was behind the missing people. He would kill them, chop them up and feed his snakes with the bits. Fed on such a rich diet, the snakes grew bigger and bigger. When they got too big, he'd release them into the wild. Or so the story goes.

When we were growing up, our parents would threaten us with Specky and his snakes. "Behave or Specky will feed you to his snakes." It worked for us, and you'll still hear people say it even now. Looking back, I think we really did believe Specky chopped up wrong 'uns to feed to his snakes, daft as that sounds.

Anyway, there you go. That's why people believe there are snakes up in Errington Woods.

⌘ ⌘ ⌘

Dave stopped talking and we sat in silence for a minute or two. A clock ticked somewhere hidden in the house. Dave gave a half-hearted chuckle that sounded forced.

"So, do you believe this then?" I asked.

"Well...."

The Snakes of Errington

"Have you ever seen these snakes?"

"I've heard them many times, but never really seen them."

"But you still believe it?"

Dave paused. He looked down at his cup of tea before answering.

"You've got to remember; I've grown up in this town all my life. It's a small, peaceful town. There are no troublemakers. And the woods do have some strange noises."

"Even now?"

"We've not had any trouble in these parts for some time now. Even if the stories are true, and there are snakes up in the woods, they aren't eating humans. What's the worry?"

I left soon after, not really sure how to process the information Dave had unloaded on me. Snakes in the UK weren't common, but they still existed. To think the ones in Errington has been hand reared, and on the meat of dead criminals seemed far-fetched. But it was just a story. Maybe it was more like the stories of alligators in New York sewers. I put it out of my mind and got on with settling in.

Maybe a day or two later, Mum needed some groceries, so I headed to the local supermarket. It was there whilst waiting to be served that things took a turn for the weird. The two ladies in front of me were talking about general stuff – kids at school, overtime, what to have for tea, that kind of thing. All of a sudden, they both stopped talking and turned to stare at something or someone behind me.

"There's Specky," one whispered to the other. Not sure I heard properly, I turned to look at where they were staring. A tall man was walking slowly with the casual confidence of someone who knew they belonged. His tanned skin, healthy thatch of silvery grey hair and well-tailored clothes gave the impression of wealth. As he wandered through the supermarket, people greeted him warmly and he returned their words with a smile here, a handshake there. The giveaway that it was Specky were his thick black glasses, behind which his eyes twinkled with intelligence and humor.

Dave hadn't mentioned how long ago the stories of Specky Eggy were. In my mind, I thought he was talking about events from many years ago, but this guy couldn't have been that old. Late fifties at the most, surely no more than that.

When I got home, I popped over to Dave's.

"Guess who I saw in the supermarket?" I asked, after he invited me in.

"Erm…. not my future wife," he joked with a little grin. Was he flirting with me? I smiled back. Not for the first time, I noted he was well groomed and not exactly ugly.

"Silly. No, Specky."

"Ahh, really? He does get out and about."

"Oh? You knew he was still alive?"

"Oh yeah. He's well known in the village. Don't you remember the other day when I told you about the snakes?"

"Yeah but…I didn't think he was still alive You made him sound like he'd be ancient."

Dave paused at that, looking out the window.

"Hmm, you know, I've never thought about that. He's always been around. Most of us are still a bit scared of him. Daft, eh?" and he half chuckled that sounded forced. We both fell silent.

"So where does he live?" I asked, to break up the silence.

"In one of the big houses that back out onto the woods. I guess that's another reason why the stories get passed around."

We chatted the rest of the afternoon about other things, but I kept thinking back to that man I'd seen in the shops. I felt my mind drift as I imagined him cutting up criminals and thieves to feed to his snakes. Feeling a slight chill, I was surprised to see goosebumps on my arms. I laughed to myself, embarrassed I was scaring myself with old legends that were obviously made up to keep kids well behaved.

The Snakes of Errington

Dave asked me out a few days later and I thought, why not? We had a lovely lunch in one of the small cafes in town. Stepping outside, the sun was warm, and a fresh breeze blew in from the coast.

"Fancy a walk?" suggested Dave and I smiled, patting my stomach. A walk would be just the thing to burn off that slice of cheesecake I hadn't needed.

We walked up the main street of the town and were soon in a leafy suburb that I hadn't explored before. Large houses slept in the afternoon warm, discretely tucked away behind walls and trees. Dave pointed out one or two, and sure enough we passed what was Specky Eggy's house. It was tasteful and modest, but it was easy to see that it was an expensive property. A polished sports car sat in the long drive, speaking of money way beyond my means. We continued our walk, past Specky's house and into the woods behind.

"Are you scared of the snakes?" I teased, as Dave reached for my hand.

He didn't answer, and for a moment I wondered if my comment was a bit too close to the truth. He turned to me, and my heart fluttered like a silly teenager. Our eyes locked, and just as we both started leaning into each other, a loud rustling noise in the undergrowth made us freeze like statues.

After a second, we broke apart, the moment lost. The rustling continued, and for the second time that afternoon we locked eyes. Dave grinned, and before I knew it, he had plunged into the bushes in the direction of the noise. After a moment's hesitation, I followed him. Even now, I don't know why.

Head down to avoid scratches, I collided into Dave a few moments later. He was motionless, squatting and peering intently at something to our left. I crouched down next to him and looked at whatever was holding his attention so keenly.

Russell Smeaton

It was a large garden, neat and tidy, with large cages lined up on one side and chicken coops on the other. A few chickens scratched the floor near their coop, making faint clucking noises.

From our viewpoint, we could see things moving inside those cages. I parted some bushes to one side to see clearer. Goosebumps roughen my skin and scalp as I saw what was inside.

Snakes. Lots of them, all slithering around. But that wasn't what caused my skin to crawl. They all had tiny arms and legs, albeit useless but present all the same. There was something about their heads too, but without getting closer, I couldn't be sure. As I squinted to get a closer look, a noise from the house made me scuttle back, almost falling.

It was Specky Eggy, walking towards the cages, large knife in hand. Seeing him wasn't a massive shock, especially after seeing the snakes. But even so, for one insane moment I thought he was coming for us for trespassing on his land. Instead, he headed towards the chickens. In one swift movement, he plucked one up by the neck and carried it over to the snakes. The snakes started twisting and turning, more and more agitated as Specky got closer. I could hear him making soothing noises, as if talking to a baby.

Reaching the cages, he sliced the head off the chicken, nearly pouring the gushing blood into a bucket. Chicken drained, Specky sliced chunks off the bird, throwing them into the snake cage. The snakes writhed and slithered, fighting for the feathery meat. And that's when I realized what was wrong with them. It was hard to be sure from where we crouched, but I would swear their faces had human features. A small nose here, tiny eyes there, maybe even the hint of ears. I know it sounds impossible, but that's what I saw.

With the bird gone, Specky scattered what looked like pellets into the snake pen. Frenzy over, the snake creatures settled down to eating peacefully. I looked at Dave and from his wide eyes I knew he had seen the same as me. I opened my mouth to say something, but he shook his head quickly, pointing over to Specky. What happened next is something I keep coming back to, time and time again. Even now, I know what I saw, but can't quite accept it. Specky strode back over to the chicken coop and deftly scooped up another bird. We could hear a sickening snap as he twisted the neck, killing the bird instantly. From our vantage point, we both watched as he tilted his head back, dislocating his jaw, allowing him to swallow the bird. It took some time, and we watched, mouths open, as he gulped hard to get the meal down. I don't remember how long it took, but I remember my legs becoming numb from remaining motionless for so long.

Eventually, the feast was done. Absently wiping a stray feather off his clothes, Specky cast an eye around his garden. My heart froze as he looked in our direction, but he wandered back into the house and didn't come back out.

Dave tapped me on the shoulder, and I jumped, close to screaming. Pointing back into the woods, he crawled away from the garden, and I followed suite, happy to leave the insanity and snakes behind.

We didn't speak for some time, and instead focused on getting out of the woods, both of us trying to process what we had seen. Did those snakes really have faces? Had Specky really dislocated his jaw to swallow that bird? Upon reaching the path, we both start talking as one, the floodgates open. Words poured out, both of us babbling in an attempt to stop our brains breaking with the madness of it all. We both agreed that Specky had murdered those miscreants from yesteryear. What we couldn't decide or agree on was what had he done with the dead bodies. Had he fed them to his snakes, or worse? We debated if we should tell anyone, but then who could we tell? The police? They didn't seem to care, and who would believe that an old man, popular in the village, was a serial murderer. Oh, and by the way Officer, did we mention he might have swallowed his victims whole? Then there were those snakes, with their all too human features. What was that all about? Eventually our excited babble of words dried out, and the conversation dropped to a more normal tone.

We walked the rest of the way in what would normally be considered a comfortable silence. The day was still warm, and as we walked back through the town, everything seemed so utterly average, it made the events we'd just witnessed all the stranger. Cars trundled past, people waved at each other, and the world continued to spin even though three miles away there lived a creature who was half man, half snake.

I coughed to break the silence.

"So, I get the Specky bit," I started slowly, "but why the Eggy?"

Dave didn't reply for a moment, looking straightforward. When he turned to me, I couldn't read his expression.

"Don't know about you, but it looked to me like Specky was their dad."

I let that sink in. It made a kind of sense, as much as any of it could make sense.

"Ok, yeah, I can see that," I conceded, "but people talk to their pets all the time like that," even though I knew he was right. Those weird snake things and Specky were somehow connected.

"True, but you saw what he did to that chicken," he said I couldn't deny it anymore.

"Right. Ok. But even so, why the eggy?" I persisted.

"Where do snakes come from?" Dave answered with a question.

"Oh god – you mean...."

"Yep, Ol' Specky must have gotten laid...and, well, somehow laid the eggs that hatched those things."

I started laughing at the absurdity of it. Dave joined in, and I think we both laughed a little too long, a little too loud. When Dave reached out his hand, I took it without thinking, like a drowning person would for a life buoy.

⌘ ⌘ ⌘

That was a few years back now. My holiday romance turned into an actual romance, and it wasn't long before I had moved in with Dave. Besides, it's easier to keep an eye on my parents from next door. The

The Snakes of Errington

event at Specky's garden slowly faded into a hazy dream. It was only when I saw him in the supermarket did all the memories come flooding back with a rush so fast I almost stumbled.

He was easy to spot, that thick silver hair and those thick black glasses a dead giveaway. As far as I could tell, he looked exactly the same as he did before. Like before, he was immaculately dressed, and walking with that casual confidence and strength. I stood behind him, holding my breath. He stopped and turned, looking me straight in the eye, causing my skin to crawl and my cheeks to flush. A slight grin appeared and for a split second I think I saw a forked tongue flicker out, but then again, maybe not. What was certain was the fact that he knew who I was and where he had seen me. He raised his eyebrows and bringing his forefinger up to his mouth I could hear him make a faint "sssssh" sound. I ran home, drew the curtains, and waited in the darkness for Dave to come home.

Neither Dave nor I have been back to his house. Neither have we walked up in Errington Woods. We intend to keep it that way.

END

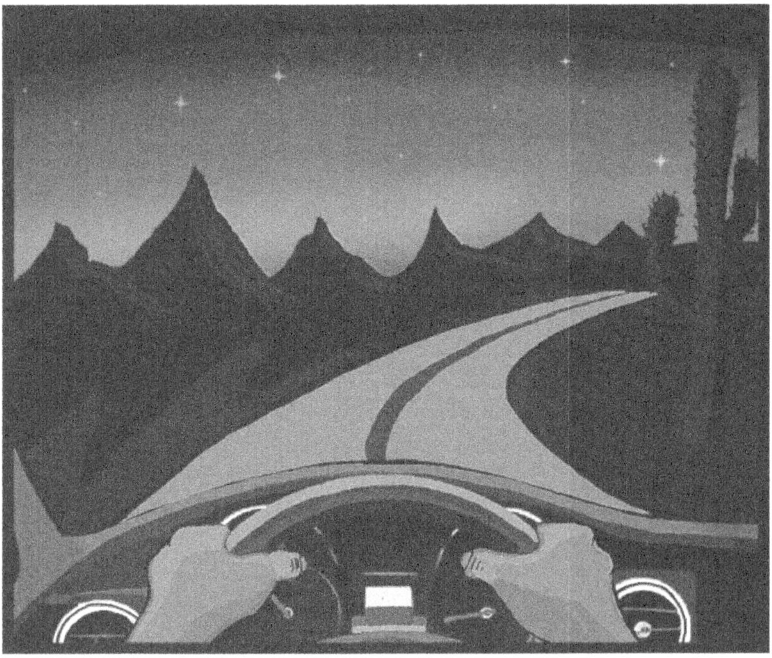

You Will Know Not the Hour
by Sean M. Thompson

The flashing red and blue lights are visible for miles on the desolate desert highway. There isn't a house in site, just blinding white sand. Further off the mountains, which are just barely visible in the dry September air. The crash is just outside of White Sands national park in New Mexico, and Detective Vargas is exhausted when she rolls up in her unmarked black SUV.

She exits the vehicle and takes a sip from the old coffee in her thermos, twists her face in disgust when she realizes she added cream and the thermos was in her car for a number of hours; the milk now long since curdled, coffee as destroyed as the tiny compact sedan on the highway before her. She ejects the spent coffee pod from the mug and flicks open the bottom of the silver thermos, taking out a fresh pod. She places the coffee pod into the side of the mug and says "brew, full strength." A British woman tells her, "Your coffee will be ready in 2 minutes," from the tiny speaker built into the handle.

"You left the cream in again, didn't you?" detective Harris says, with a smirk.

"Kiss my ass, Harris. Tell me what I'm looking at."

"A car all smashed to shit, Vargas."

"Well, no kidding, idiot, I meant why are you calling me to the middle of nowhere for a car crash? Shouldn't that be local PD stuff?"

"Well, I have a friend who works this jurisdiction, and he requested I stop by."

"And you wanted me again because…"

"The vics were wearing i-glasses."

Vargas sighs. The 'i-glasses' have been on the market now for about a year. They both make her job easier and make her feel like an amateur film maker, all at the same time. The glasses have such a massive data storage capacity and cloud backup to boot. She's literally had cases where she's reviewed over one hundred hours of footage waiting to find some vital clue.

"I assume they both died," Vargas says, as Harris hands her the evidence bag, two pairs of i-glasses inside. She has to admit whatever resin they coat the glass of the lenses with is strong. There's not a crack on either pair.

"Indeed. Based on the tire marks on the road the data analysis scanner indicates they were driving at about ninety mph."

"On this fucking road?"

The highway is small, not the best paved. This road is one that is irregularly used, except by tourists, and the occasional drunk local teenagers looking to do designer drugs around where they once dropped a nuke in 1945.

"We get a positive ID on either of them? Vargas asks.

"Yes. Both had wallets on them. Tammy Buckworth and Farid Salib. Young. Both twenty three years old. We haven't contacted the families yet."

"I swear to god if you make me call—"

"Relax. Local PD is on that. My friend wanted us to help with the investigation. Understand, middle of nowhere New Mexico police

departments aren't always filled with a crack squad."

"What kind of last name is Buckworth?" "A tragic one, for a tragic end."

Inside the small station Vargas can feel the overhead lights drilling into her brain. She's tired and annoyed, having reached that point where the caffeine is no longer any help, just leading to excitation in the body. Harris' smug face is making her damn near grind her teeth. And Barbara has been texting her non-stop asking when she's getting home and if everything is okay. Honestly, she doesn't even blame her wife, because Harris called her while they were eating dinner on a fucking Saturday night to drive an hour and a half away for what sounds like a favor to one of his god damn buddies!

"How you feeling Var—"

"Fuck you, Harris."

"Okay. I guess let's get started."

The first few hours of footage from Salib's i-glasses are uneventful, downright boring, really. He meets up with Tammy at a coffee shop in Santa Fe and they make plans to drive to white sands. They get a rental car because Farid's car is in the shop and Tammy's sedan is on its last legs. They go to a rental car agency and get the hybrid electric and gas sedan they will eventually die in. It isn't until they're on the road for a few hours and the sun goes down that things get interesting.

...

"How much farther is the hotel?" Farid asks, rubbing sleep from his eyes. They've been driving for four hours, and he's pretty beat.

"My glasses say about 2 miles."

Farid spots a rest stop off of the highway, a gas station, with a small store attached.

"You want some coffee?" Farid says.

"No, I'm good. Thanks."

Inside the store Farid orders from the machine, "Coffee, cream and two sugars." The cup is moved by the robotic arm, begins to pour as he watches the cream and sugar spill in from separate tubes. He uses the self-checkout, says aloud to the i-glasses beforehand "bank balance," and after it gets his eye recognition the glasses tell him. He knows he has enough in the account, but he likes to check, even for small purchases. He didn't always used to have money in the bank. He's able to afford random vacations like this now. Granted he's not exactly breaking the bank. The hotel they made reservations at is modest, though you'd be hard pressed to find anything very extravagant out in this part of New Mexico.

Back in the parking lot he can hear the music thumping from inside the car, some sort of rap. He'd prefer to drive in silence, he's always been a bit jumpy when it comes to sound. But it'll keep him conscious. The i-glasses display what song is playing based on a predictive app he's installed. He's also able to stream porn onto the i-glasses if he's really desperate but he wants to stay awake, not drive the car off the road. Come to that he'll probably delete most of this from the cloud once it's uploaded. Not exactly a thrill a minute watching some guy drive a car in the middle of nowhere desert. He has the record function set to record automatically as soon as he puts the glasses on, which is the only reason any of this footage exists. He's too lazy to shut off the auto-record.

"Ugh, where's my coffee?!" Tammy yells once he's back behind the driver seat.

"What, no you said—"

"I'm kidding, dummy."

"Jeez, can you drive this last leg? I'm dead on my feet."

"Sure, babe."

They drive for about twenty minutes, listening to loud top forty rap before he sees the thing in the road. A dark shape. At first Farid thinks his i-glasses are malfunctioning. He takes the glasses off though and the dark shape persists.

"You see that?" he asks Tammy.

You Will Know Not the Hour

"See what?"

He blinks and the dark shape is gone.

"Nothing. Just seeing things."

...

Vargas pauses the footage. She stares at the black amorphous shape on the screen. The shape appears to be about five feet across, by five feet tall. The shape seems to be about half a mile from the car when the i-glasses catch the footage.

"What the hell is that?" she asks Harris.

"Is it some sort of malfunction with the glasses?"

"I don't think so," Vargas says. "I got the i-glasses verified. No errors, or malfunctions in the footage."

"Trick of the light, maybe?"

"What light? It's just moonlight."

"Well shit, I don't know, Vargas. What does this have to do with how these two died anyway?"

"That's what we're trying to figure out," Vargas says.

She lets the footage play again.

...

Inside the hotel they make love in the shower. He has to convince Tammy to take off the glasses. She says it'll be hot, but he reminds her they do not need a sex tape on the cloud; they are far too easy to steal. When they finish he orders a pizza, delivered by drone of course. It always throws him when he answers the door and there's a flying robot. He pays the little buzzing black machine cash, and they sprawl out on the bed eating mushroom and extra cheese.

"Did you see that shape earlier?"

"What shape?" Tammy says through a mouthful of pizza.

"It was like this big black shape."

"No."

"No wise ass remark?"

"No. That's just... creepy."

"I was probably just seeing things." "Yeah," Tammy says, worry on her face.

"What?" Farid asks.

"You ever heard of La Mala Hora?"

...

"What is that? La Mala Hora?" Harris asks.

"Oh what, just because I'm Mexican I know every fucking Latin myth?"

"Fuck, Vargas, I'm just asking."

"Hold on," Vargas says, doing a quick search online, paraphrasing a few sites she reads.

"Descriptions vary. In Mexico it's a beautiful woman in a black dress, in New Mexico accounts say it's more like a black shape. The through line is it visits travelers at midnight to lead them to their deaths."

"Sounds fun," Harris says, taking a sip from his coffee.

...

He isn't sure what compels him to suggest the drive. It's 11:30 and he supposes it's a form of kitschy thing he can do with his girlfriend; look for the spooky urban legend woman and or black blob, then maybe they can fool around again. At the back of his mind is the shape he saw as well; perhaps a morbid curiosity, what one might call the death drive, which compels him to take this very much alive drive.

"Let's drive around white sands some more."

...

The rest of the footage is the couple driving to white sands, until a moment about 10 minutes before the couple's untimely death. The curious thing is the footage. If anything, the video does more to confuse Vargas than to explain anything. A black shape, off on the horizon, floating towards the couple. The two lovers park the car. Salib asks something like "what is that?" something innocuous enough, nothing to clarify what he, or indeed now Vargas, is seeing.

The rest, well, the rest is the couple driving off at high speed.

Vargas sighs and rubs the bridge of her nose.

"This doesn't tell us anything. I don't understand."

"Neither do I."

"God damn it," Vargas says, followed with "hey asshole coffee cup, brew full strength," as she pushes a new pod in. The coffee cup tells her in the British woman's voice "pod not inserted," to which Vargas says, "insert this," after tugging on the crotch of her pants.

"Let's call it a night, yeah?" Harris says.

Vargas looks out the window of the station. Daylight peaks over the horizon.

"Probably for the best, yeah."

You Will Know Not the Hour

"Come back tonight, I'll call you to confirm."

"All right, dumb ass."

"Hey, you're the one that's my partner."

"Blow me," Vargas says, sipping her coffee, gingerly, as it's still quite hot.

…

The next night Vargas has the idea they revisit the crash site.

"Maybe there was something at the scene we missed."

Yet, at the scene, there appears to be nothing. Vargas sighs again, sipping from her iced coffee (now a store-bought sugar bomb). She chews on the straw to alleviate her frustration at all she doesn't know.

"I can't crack this," Vargas says. "What are we missing?"

"Well, the accident happened around midnight."

"So, you're saying we should come back at midnight." "You got a better idea, Vargas?" Admittedly, she does not.

The sun set and darkness enveloped the stark white landscape; the moon shining as a prophet in the sky, come round at last. The heat continued unabated, an angry heat, which seemed hellbent on keeping Vargas soaked in sweat, cursing her very existence; at the very least her decision to wear jeans.

"You know anything about the bomb drop?" Harris asks.

"Sort of," Vargas replies, wiping sweat from her brow, shaking her hand off in disgust.

"July 16, 1945, during the Trinity test. They put the bomb on top of a 100-foot steel tower. The name for the bomb, 'Gadget.'"

"Real cutesy name for the deadliest weapon ever made."

"Tell me about it. Anyway, after the explosion, they surrounded the site with a mile of chain-link fencing—put up signs and shit. Only nuke dropped on U.S. soil."

"That's not true," Vargas says, her smart tablet open, at the ready. She points to an article. "It says here we accidentally dropped one out of a B-47 on South Carolina, in 1958."

"Holy shit, really?"

"Well, there was no nuclear core. I mean, it killed people, but it was more like, you know, a regular bomb. They stored the core somewhere else, thankfully. They were transporting the thing."

"Even still, colossal fuck up."

"Oh yeah."

"And we dropped some in Nevada for tests, too. Frankly, we tested a shit load of nukes here."

"Jesus fucking Christ, this ruins the drama entirely," Harris says. He lights a cigarette, the cherry a single red eye in the semi-darkness, save for the headlights of the unmarked. He coughs.

"You really should cut that shit out," Vargas says.

"You're probably right."

The two stand in the stillness, the semi-darkness. They hooked up a few times before Harris got married and it's a wonder they're still partners. Vargas and Harris work well together, though. Vargas has a hard enough time getting along with people, so she harbored the rough patches post boffing.

The rest of the night is positively dull. They never catch a glimpse of the black shape. And as the sun starts to rise and Vargas tells Harris they should get going, she's already mentally checked out of the case. On her ride back to her home, an hour or so away, she tells herself the mystery is likely that there is no mystery. A nice couple died when the husband decided to drive too fast. Case closed.

This is what she thinks until she hears about her partner's death the next night.

…

Tammy sees the shape before he does, as they are driving, approaching the car from behind, fast. She screams at Farid to go faster, to go faster! He darts a glance in the rear-view mirror to see the shape, so close to the bumper he imagines he can almost feel the weight.

And all at once, the world seems to slow for both of them, as the car hitches along the pavement, despite driving in a straight line; the vehicle flips end over end as the velocity smashes the two bodies against the now twisted metal of the rental car, blood pouring out of mouths, gushing out of lacerations from the broken glass that slices into their flesh with rapid aggression. If there is any blessing the two are essentially dead very shortly after impact—they can't feel the rest of the ways their now dead bodies smash, crack, lacerate, and bleed.

…

Vargas speeds the whole way to the site. She runs to the crime scene as the officers on site try to hold her back, telling her things she barely even hears. Her heart is thundering in her chest. She feels sick to her stomach. Everything seems to be moving way too fast.

You Will Know Not the Hour

Harris is sitting on the road. His skin is a mottled red. He looks like he's been severely burned. His eyelids are burnt off. His skin bubbles and blisters. His corpse is frozen in a strange position, hands outstretched, the body in rictus.

"What the fuck happened?"

"We don't know," an officer tells her.

"How did he…"

"We don't know," the same officer tells her.

"Well fuck you have to know something!"

A tech on site turns to her, from her place on the ground by the body. Her face is grimacing.

"He's irradiated," the tech says.

"What?"

"These are radiation burns."

"I don't understand."

"I don't either," the tech says. "These sorts of radiation burns normally only occur in areas with nuclear fallout."

"I don't…"

Yet, Vargas does. She really does know. Not the particulars, not exactly what happened but she has a sick feeling; a premonition that the black shape, the nuclear tests, and the stories locally of La Mala Hora may all be connected. And she's smart enough to know she has to grieve and let the case die. She has a wife who loves her. A decent enough life. She doesn't want to die from radiation burns. Vargas needs to do her best to block all of this out but right now it seems like that will be impossible.

She gets on the phone to call Harris' wife

Illustrations:

1. Dragon Illustration by Russell Smeaton Page 8
2. Already Weeds Are Writing Illustration by Sarah Walker Page 16
3. Accident at Black Spot Illustration by Sarah Walker Page 20
4. The Other End of the Line Illustration by Sarah Walker Page 24
5. Do Not Read This Illustration by Sarah Walker Page 42
6. Market Price Illustration by Sarah Walker Page 56
7. School's Out illustration by Sarah Walker Page 80
8. Case #7: The Babes in the Woods Illustration by Sarah Walker Page 100
9. Undercity Illustration by Sarah Walker Page 112
10. The Office on the Seventh Floor Illustration by Sarah Walker Page 118
11. The Bandage Man Illustration by Sarah Walker Page 130
12. Bloody, Meaty Ends Illustration by Alan Sessler Page 142
13. Satanic Panic Illustration by Alan Sessler Page 144
14. Bridge of Lies Illustration by Alan Sessler Page 146
15. Blucifer Illustration by Sarah Walker Page 150
16. Along a Rural Highway Illustration by Sarah Walker Page 160
17. Face the Music Illustration by Sarah Walker Page 164
18. Half-Sick of Shadows Illustration by Sarah Walker Page 168
19. Mother Will Be Displeased Illustration by Sarah Walker Page 186
20. Fish Story Illustration by Sarah Walker Page 198
21. Beware The Slenderman Illustration by Sarah Walker Page 216
22. Third Eye Delight Illustration by Sarah Walker Page 218
23. Mrs. Saltonstall's Dybbuk Illustration by Sarah Walker Page 232
24. Invoking a Playmate Illustration by Sarah Walker Page 246
25. Spring-heeled Jack Illustration by Sarah Walker Page 250

26. Midnight Train From Tokyo Illustration by Sarah Walker Page 252

27. The Yellow Man Illustration by Russell Smeaton Page 274

28. Coulrophilia Illustration by Sarah Walker Page 292

29. The Legend of Johnny Nepkin: A Home-Grown Boogeyman Illustration by Alan Sessler Page 296

30. Necker Illustration by Sarah Walker Page 310

31. Figures of Shadow Illustration by Alan Sessler Page 320

32. The Visitors Photograph by Sarah Walker Page 324

33. Danse De L'Amour Illustration by Alan Sessler Page 330

34. The Snakes of Errington or The Legend of Specky Eggy Illustration by Sarah Walker Page 338

35. You Will Not Know the Hour Illustration by Sarah Walker Page 354

Dedicated to the wonderful people who helped us to make this book a reality! Thank you!

Alien Sun Press would like to thank all of the wonderful people who helped to bring this project to fruition!

Sean Werner

Chris Kalley

Clegane76

Ryan McWilliams

Thomas "Poultrygeist" Richardson David Young

Justin G Kahn

Julia Morgan

Jason M

The Creative Fund by BackerKit

FredH

Stephen Ballentine

Bob Riordan

Mary Savelli

David Hallblade

StevieDee55

Balki

Edward Fitzpatrick

Joshua Cooper

Aref Dyer

Therese

Lars Backstrom

Chris Karr

Shawn Gore

Chaz Kemp

Scary Stuff Podcast

Matt Cuttle
Susan Jessen
Elise Feldman
John Howard
Jennifer C. Oshita Archer
Caroline Coriell
Mary Walker
J Sturner
Rachel Daugherty
Susanne McGirr
Scarlett Algee
Frank Lewis
Stephanie
Rachel E. Robinson
Jocelyne Desforges
Jeff
John Garrett deleted
Lars Sveen
Alice E. Walker
Stephanie Ouellette
Andrea
Frank Coffman
Angela Castille-O'Keefe
Heather
Nicholas Stephenson
Cathy Green
William Jones
Lee Wilcox
Giusy Rippa

Susan Rosen

Stewie

Cameron Jones

Nicki Mulhall

Jeff Cilione

michaeleldridge777@gmail.com

Tyler Hagenow

Jessica Enfante

Len Shaw

Kat Jansen

Dan Hinderliter

Chris Chastain

Rian

BuddyH

Robert Tkacz

JOHN HOLT

Skyler

Danielle

Anna

Aaron Moxcey

John Evans

GMark C

Adi Gurovich

Eric Hadley

Steven Parry

Ira M.

Paul

Giuseppe Lo Turco Brian

Meghan Thomas

And a Special Thanks to our biggest backers!

Stephanie Ouellette

Mary Walker

Lars Sveen

David Hallblade

Without you all,

we could not have made this happen!

Made in the USA
Las Vegas, NV
23 February 2023